Comely Grace

Alexine Crawford.

Comely Grace

Alexine Crawford

Wrayworks

Published 2011 by Wrayworks.

ISBN 978-0-9570992-0-3

Printed and bound by CPI Group (UK) Ltd, Croydon, CR0 4YY

Wrayworks
73 Lodge Hill Road, Farnham, Surrey, GU10 3RB

By the same author

The Challenge of Caring
(non-fiction)

Acknowledgements

In addition to the authors of the numerous books I have read about the Civil War and Farnham's part in it, I would like to thank Julian Bacon for prolonged loan of the Leather Technical Handbook by J H Sharphouse; Alan Turton of Old Basing for military information; Tim and Ruth Harrison for showing me over Spreakley Farm; Dr. Catriona McLeod for showing me round Tanyard House; and Jane Churcher, Gill Ellis, Susie Johnson, and Peta Sandars, for their individual encouragements.

My chief and patient encourager over many years, giving me space to write and skill to use the computer, is my husband Warren, who has my heartfelt thanks and love.

Chapters

Love me not for comely grace
For my pleasing eye or face
Nor for any outward part;
No, nor for my constant heart.
For those may fail, those may fail,
For those may fail or turn to ill
So thou and I shall sever.
Keep therefore a true woman's eye
And love me still but know not why
So hast thou the same reason
Still to dote upon me ever.

Madrigal by John Wilbye
1574 - 1638

Abigail

Abigail stood on the brambly ridge above the river Wey, her basket laden with blackberries, about to scramble down between the mean cottages huddled below her to reach the street and home.

Suddenly she heard crying. Not ordinary crying but desperate, fearful. From one of the houses. Basket in hand she slithered quickly down the bank. A bramble caught her skirt. She tugged to release it, snagged her finger. Would no one comfort the child? Oh quick, quick! Whatever could cause such terrible crying? She reached the road. Where to go? She listened, agonised.

The crying stopped. No one in sight.

One cottage had its door open. She walked towards it. Suddenly a skinny little boy catapulted out, running blindly. He almost collided with her. Wild-eyed, he checked and ran back inside. In a moment he was out again. Abigail lunged to catch him, grabbed an arm. There seemed nothing of him under his ragged tunic.

'What's the matter?' she demanded.

His breath came in gasps, strangled with crying. No words, but as she held him he pulled her through the doorway. She could see little at first. A bare squalid hut. Then in the dim light she saw a woman's shape on a rough bed, a bed soaked in blood.

'I'll fetch my mother,' she said, and fled.

The basket banged against her side as she ran, dripping red juice onto her apron where it turned to purple, like blood. Hardly noticing she hurtled on, dodging a hand cart, bursting through the street door into Tanyard house, shouting for her mother.

'Please come Mother!' she panted, 'Something dreadful!'

Phoebe was swilling the stone-flagged floor with a broom, wearing wooden pattens to protect her slippers from the water. Seeing Abigail's stricken face she propped the broom against the wall and came at once, running awkwardly because of the pattens.

'What is it?' she asked

'A woman....blood...Oh Mother, a little boy,' Abigail panted out as she ran. The child was hovering in the doorway, half watching for them coming, half drawn into the room behind him. He rushed out to her, clinging to her skirt. Phoebe went into the house and was quickly out again.

'She's dead,' she said. 'You had best take the child along to the Tanyard.'

At that he dived towards the doorway, trying to dodge Phoebe. She grabbed him, putting his dirty little hand into Abigail's.

'This is no place for the child. Take him, Abigail.'

Abigail pulled him away along the road, twisting her fingers around his wrist. There was surprising strength in his little body. She almost lost him when a wagon passed, the pair of horses dragging it dripping out of the ford. He doubled back after it. She seized him with her other hand.

'I'll find food for you!' she said desperately. 'Come on, it's only across the square!'

He quietened then and allowed her to take him into the tannery yard. The two bull mastiffs by the gate leapt and barked at them, straining their chains, then wagging their stumpy tails once they recognised Abigail.

She towed the child across the cobbled yard into the house.

'Is this your doing Abigail?' Her older sister Hannah met her brandishing the basket. 'These blackberries have dripped everywhere....' She broke off, staring at the child. 'What in heaven's name?'

'Mother told me to take him. His mother's dead. Get me some bread Hannah.' For once Hannah need not boss her. Abigail was doing what Phoebe had told her to do.

The boy seized the hunk of bread she gave him, gnawing at it like the starveling he clearly was. He crouched warily.

'It's the whore's brat,' Hannah said, 'and dirty too.'

'Mother told me to bring him here.'

'She can't intend to keep him here!' Arms akimbo, Hannah watched him eat. 'Not in this house!'

Abigail was crouching beside him, trying to reassure him. She looked up. 'He could be a little brother to us.'

'More like a servant!' Hannah retorted. 'What are you going to do with him?'

'Wash his face' Abigail said. She wrung out a cloth in the bucket outside the door and almost lost him again as he ducked her scrubbing. It was useless. He would have to stay dirty.

She took hold of his hand. What next? Towing him with her she wandered round the yard. The centre of it held rows of oak-lined tanning pits with poles across them suspending hides in the liquor below. Either side, bordering the house to the east and the tannery sheds to the west, iron-stone cobbles led down to the river.

Abigail stood looking over the river and across the water meadows to the square-towered church, the child at her side. Her brothers used to go to school behind the church and she thought wistfully of the hours she had sat beside Thomas, gleaning an education from the Latin and Mathematics he brought home. How she longed to learn more!

Alas, they were no longer children. Yet she was still the youngest. Tall and agile, fast becoming a woman, her light brown hair hung in a long plait down to her waist. Her dress of brown kersey wool over a linen shift, workaday attire, was protected by a coarse apron. She adjusted the kerchief which kept her hair tidy, still contemplating the view on the other side the river.

All around the town soon-ripe hops hung from long poles with hop kilns like russet cones peaking among them. And across the valley high up on the chalky escarpment, the red brick tower and wide stone palace of the Bishop of Winchester kept its eye on the town. Behind it rose the rugged castle keep.

The child! She must not be distracted from the child. He was fidgeting, and now he pulled her towards the gateway. The dogs started leaping about, tugging their chains.

'Have a care,' she said, 'they're fierce to those they don't know.'

Close to them he stood still, regarding them. The dogs hovered on their haunches, not quite sitting, tentatively wagging their stumpy tails. He held out the back of his hand and one of them licked it. And then they were licking his face and he had his arm round a neck. They almost knocked him over. Abigail had never seen them accept a stranger like this, and the dogs seemed to calm him.

It was very quiet in the yard. Where were the tannery workers, and her brothers James and Thomas? Then she heard her father's strong clear voice, haranguing the men in one of the sheds. Thomas hadn't taken to tanning. Maybe his reluctance came from the terror of being apprenticed to his father.

Her mother was a long time coming back. What was she doing, and why had the woman died? Why all the blood? Could a person bleed to death in her monthly courses? Or could it even have been a murder? She shivered at so much unknown.

'What's your name?' she asked the child.

'Hal' he whispered, more to the dogs than to her. A horse cart rattled along the lane and for a moment he looked up.

At last Phoebe returned, her plump face flushed from hurrying round the town arranging for the woman's burial. Seeing the child with Abigail she stood still as if in her business she had forgotten all about him.

'And what is to become of you?' she said.

'Oh Mother, could we keep him here? He's so hungry and frightened.'

Phoebe said nothing, but when later from the bake-room window she saw her husband crossing the yard, she called him quickly indoors.

'Take him in? You must be out of your mind, woman!' Jacob Mannory exploded. 'Bringing in every waif from Abbey Street!'

'Just one,' Phoebe said in her quiet way.

'Whose child did you say?'

'Judith – you know the woman?'

Jacob turned away. 'I have no reason to.'

'Her people were weavers, or maybe fullers, it matters not. Either way, there was no more work for them. She has dwelt in Abbey Street these eight years or so, in that house Abe Trussler rents out.'

'A house if ill repute.'

'But the child, Jacob. He has nobody.'

'The son of a whore. Put him on the parish.'

'You know the parish will not support bastards.'

'No more will we.' Jacob's mouth set hard.

'Jake.' Phoebe laid her hand on her husband's arm. 'Have mercy on the fatherless and orphans.'

Hal never did like washing, after Phoebe's onslaught on him that first evening. She wasted no time for the light was fading and soon the men would finish work and need their meal.

She sent Mary the serving girl to the river for water, and dragged a wooden tub round in front of the immense fireplace. Hannah she sent to fetch Jacob's long razor and soap and a linen towel and an outgrown shirt.

Faced with this authoritative bustle Hal stood mesmerised and apprehensive. Phoebe took down a copper dipper from its hook in the great beam above the hearth and scooped hot water out of an iron cauldron simmering at the side of the fire, to add to the water in the tub. Only then did she turn to the child.

'You're to live with us now,' she said, 'and so I must make you clean and give you fresh apparel. I'm going to shave your head. We can't have nits and fleas in this house.' She threw the hair into the fire followed by his tattered tunic. He fought the washing, wetting them both – 'Hold him, Abigail!' Phoebe ordered - and she persisted until every bit of him was clean. She dried him gently. Enveloped in the outsized shirt he stood small and lost and silent with elfin ears, his thin face more peaky than ever without hair around it.

Water was steaming on the flagstones in front of the hearth. Hannah and Mary carried the tub to empty it into the river. Hal looked about to run, but the men were coming in from the yard washing their hands in the bucket outside, and there was no way of escape.

The ground floor of Tanyard House was one long hall. A passage led either side of the wide fireplace through to a single storey bake room with a still room beyond. Either side too a door led outside, one into the yard, the other into the garden with a winding staircase beside it. At the opposite end of the hall, the door where Abigail had earlier burst in opened onto the lane.

'Take him, Abigail,' Phoebe said again. Abigail took his hand, her sleeves wet and clammy against her arm, and led him to the table. She longed to ask her mother what had happened, why's Hal's mother had died, but there seemed to be no opportunity. Indeed, no explanation at all was offered, to Hal or to the household. Jacob Mannory said a brief Latin grace, sure sign that he was displeased, and they ate their pottage in silence.

After the meal the elder son James brought the big Bible to Jacob for him to read a passage as he did every evening.

Later Phoebe said, 'Husband, I know the child will have to sleep in the loft with the men, but at first I would like him to have the trundle bed in our chamber. Do I have your agreement?'

Abigail, still at the table with Hal beside her on the bench, watched the silent deliberation. The fire light flickered on her father's lean handsome face, his working clothes loose around his tall figure, his feet now slippered for the evening. Beside him Phoebe stood looking into the fire, saying nothing more, her hands under her apron across her ample waist. Abigail longed to plead with her father to be kind to the child, if only she could be sure of his humour. Hal seemed unaware that he was being discussed.

At last Jacob took his pipe out of his mouth, holding it aside. 'Very well,' he said, 'if you consider it needful. But he must realise that the loft is his proper place.'

'Thank you,' Phoebe said, and went to prepare the low bed stored under her own plain four-poster. Jacob resumed his evening pipe. Abigail's brother Thomas winked at her, but James sniffed and went outside.

When Abigail was sent to rouse Hal at dawn, he did not wake at once. 'Come,' she said, kneeling beside the trundle bed, 'we need to take the geese to the meadow.'

He turned away from her, pulling the covers around his head.

'I'm to show you the tasks we have to do,' she said. He shut his eyes. 'You're to help me with them, and learn how to do them.'

If only he would speak.

'There'll be no breakfast until they're done,' a hint of threat in her voice. He shrugged a little under the blanket.

'Oh please do get up, or James or my father will come and force you to do so.'

Hal turned over and squinted at her. 'Why must I do tasks?' he said.

'We all have our tasks,' Abigail said. 'If you don't they will not care to clothe and feed you. Hal, you have no choice.'

The geese which they drove across the ford to Goose Meadow were almost as tall as Hal, their beaks on a level with his face. When they brought the two cows in for Hannah and Mary to milk, he could not handle the pitch fork to bring them hay from the sweet-smelling stack. The calves, separated from their mothers, lowed hungrily, eager to suckle. Hal rubbed their backs and they nuzzled his hand and sucked his fingers with their rough tongues. Milking done they were released with the cows into the meadow beyond the tannery buildings.

At least he could learn to split kindling. With years of practice Abigail could slice thin slivers swiftly and surely, yet she had no idea how she did it. The axe seemed big and dangerous in Hal's small hand.

She looked up as her brother Thomas pushed the hand cart towards the gateway. 'Having trouble?' he asked.

'Oh Tom, you taught me to cut kindling. How do I do it?'

Thomas laughed and squatted down beside them.

'It's all in the eye,' he said. 'Keep your eye fixed on where you want to cut. And let the axe do it for you. Swing it, don't swipe.'

Hal practised and suddenly the knack came to him.

Intent on the lesson they did not notice James until he was right beside them. 'That's not your work Tom,' he said sternly.

Tom looked up. 'Abigail needed my help.'

'You are not employed to help Abigail.'

'Not every moment has to be filled by work.'

'There's much work to be done, tannery work. That is what you are meant to be doing.'

'Brother.' Thomas stood up, taller than James. 'You may be my elder but my governor you are not. You've only just qualified as a journeyman, if you recall.'

James glared at him. 'Father's wrath will be on you for delay. He knows exactly how long it takes to fetch a load of pigeon dung from the Culver Hall dovecot.' He turned on his heel back towards the sheds.

'He's right of course, as ever.' Thomas shrugged, seizing the handles of the hand cart. 'Now if we had a horse....'

Hal looked up, eyes bright. 'Might you?' he asked.

'I'm working on it,' Thomas said, and pushed his way into the lane.

The brat can't remain sleeping in our bed chamber,' Jacob said only a few days later.

'Take him up to the loft would you?' Phoebe, elbow deep in bread dough, told Abigail.

The loft was a male preserve. Although empty of the apprentices and journeymen who slept there, all now outside at work, it was with some trepidation that Abigail led Hal up the narrow upper staircase. The loft, the same length as the hall, was low under the rafters, and cross-beams barred the way at regular intervals. She could see that the favoured bed position was around the chimney stack, which also warmed her parents' bedroom a floor below.

'It looks as if this bed's unused,' she said, pointing to a wooden frame laced with rope, 'You'll need a mattress of some sort.'

'A blanket,' Hal said, testing it.

'But look Hal,' she said, 'I won't be able to wake you up any more in the morning and coax you out of bed. James will be after you if you're not out when the men are.'

She was all too right. Day after day he tumbled out into the yard with eyes so full of sleep that she could see he had just been hoofed out of bed. Then came Thursday, market day, with the pressure to finish normal work, take tanned hides to be vetted and sold, and for Phoebe to purchase provisions, all before the market closed at noon.

That morning Abigail was anxiously watching for Hal when she heard a yelping cry. He emerged soon after, walking gingerly as his breeches rubbed on the welts James' beating had raised. She ran towards him to offer a comforting hug but he turned abruptly away and stalked round to the goose pen. She followed him, over the bridge while the geese waddled through the ford, and back again, but he did not speak. Nor did he all morning as the girls worked around the house, until hearing the church clock strike the three-quarter hour they hurried to put on clean aprons and cross the river to the church.

Jacob expected everyone, family and tannery workers alike, to attend the sermon which took place immediately after the market closed. Several years before, frustrated with poor preaching by the clergy who were often absent anyway, the burgesses had instituted a weekly sermon, given by an invited preacher whom they paid out of town funds.

Mr Duncomb the lecturer stood on a level with the people, not in the pulpit or behind the altar rails as the clergy did. They felt he was accessible, for all his learning and fine teaching and preaching.

Not that Abigail took much of it in that morning, her heart yearning for Hal. Wearing the little breeches Phoebe had hastily cut down for him, and a cap to cover the head she had shaved, he stood and sat when they did, fidgeting a little on his sore behind, remote.

But when they sang the final psalm, tears began oozing down his cheeks. He gazed into space, letting them ooze. The last verse rang out, the meeting was over. Hal sniffed once and left the tears to dry unaided. It would be years before he ever cried again.

The congregation broke into chattering groups. Abigail sought out her friend Joan Bicknell, the hop-grower's daughter.

'What's this I hear?' Joan said. 'The gossips are all agog!'

'Have they some real news then?' Abigail said.

'You must know, for it concerns you.'

'Me? I've done nothing to merit gossip.'

Before Joan could reply they reached the door and there John Harding, son of Phoebe's brother of Spreakley Farm, stood talking with a couple of men. In looks he was not unlike Phoebe, nor her daughter Hannah, round faced and inclined to be plump except that in him the plumpness was already tending towards coarseness. He laughed a lot, loudly, at what Abigail could never quite make out.

'So I had to sell,' one man said, 'at the King's price, in order for him to make for himself another Park. He has three parks already, can't see why he needed Richmond as well.'

'To them as has will more be given,' John laughed.

'Given! Grabbed more like. And all that Court, it takes some feeding.'

'All dressed in silks and finery too aren't they?' his companion asked.

'And fine paintings and frenchified furniture that Catholic Queen of his has to have. And now another park.'

''T'aint the park, 't'is the revenue,' his companion said.

'Are you agin' the King?' John laughed again. Then he caught sight of Abigail and Joan Bicknell.

'Hullo there cousin!' he boomed. 'And young Miss Bicknell too! A worthy sermon was it not.' Abigail and Joan bobbed little curtseys. 'What young women you are! Now with your sister Hannah,' he went on, 'you'd make a fine treble line for some glees, some madrigals.'

'That would be entertaining,' Joan said.

'I can't sing,' Abigail said.

'Ah! But now with the new curate we have an able tenor. Indeed we must arrange it. Yes indeed, I will arrange it.'

He walked away and they moved into the porch where Joan's mother was deep in conversation with a couple of women.

Abigail turned to her friend. 'No swains today?'

Joan tossed her head, fair curls escaping from under her cap. 'I was dodging some attentions. Never the ones I would like. Now, there's a horse dealer who comes to the house sometimes, I could favour him. But Abi, what's this about....'

'Why, Abigail!' Joan's mother, taking breath in her gossiping, noticed her. 'I hear the strangest news! Is it really true? Betty here tells me that the whore's brat is at the tannery, brought in there by you!'

'You mean Hal?' Abigail asked innocently. She turned to draw him forward but 'Oh Mistress Bicknell! Where's Hal? Oh my goodness, where has he gone?'

'Hal? Hal?'

'A little boy - I can't stop, I must find him, forgive me,' and gathering her skirts she ran down the cobbled path and round the curve of Church Lane and on towards home. By the time she neared the bridge she was out of breath and, slowing her pace, had time to think. Would Hal in fact have run back to the Tanyard? Would he not be more likely to have gone down Abbey Street, to the old haunts that she suspected were never far from his mind?

She walked steadily now, collecting her breath, crossing the bridge and turning left. A few children were out in the street but Hal was not among them. She peered at the cottages as she walked along, until she was level with the hovel that had been his home.

She stood in front of it, uncertain what to do. As dilapidated as ever, its door was closed. She could hear hammering round behind it in the space against the bank. Should she venture between the houses? Hesitating, she heard a sort of roaring shout, and the next moment Hal was propelled down the alleyway by an angry man. He had him by the collar and was aiming kicks at his heels.

'This ain't yorn no more!' the man shouted, 'And you can keep clear. Little bastard! Likes o' you aren't wanted.'

'Hal!' Abigail cried, and the man stopped short. He peered at her.

'If it isn't Miss Mannory,' he said, dropping Hal and half mockingly touching his cap. 'Abe Trussler at your service.'

'At my service indeed! Then you can lay off the child!'

'Oh oh! Snarling vixen are we!' Abe aimed another kick at Hal who lurched forward.

'Lay off him you beast!'

'I've every right to lay into him. I owns this house and I've a deal of work to set it to rights for the next tenant. The woman's dead who never did nothing to maintain it. The bastard can keep clear.'

'And you can keep clear of him,' Abigail said, still fierce.

'Spitting serpent aren't you, flashing a forked tongue,' Abe said. 'You're mighty bothered about the little runt.'

'He's...he's living with us now. I have to mind him.' Abigail reached for Hal's hand. Abe gaped.

'The bastard? At Mannory's the tanner? Can't be!'

'He is. It was I who found his mother... or Hal who found me...' her words tailed off. Perhaps she had said too much.

'Can't credit Jacob Mannory sheltering a ragged bastard...'

Abigail looked at Abe squarely, remembering the words she had overheard her mother say. 'Have mercy,' she said, 'on the fatherless and orphans.'

'Oh the high and mighty virtue of it!' Abe mocked. 'The good Christian Jacob Mannory!' A thought struck him. 'I'll wager he has another reason for taking in the brat. Ha! The hypocrite!' He looked speculatively at Abigail. 'A turnaround for that self-righteous tanner! We'll see about that!'

Back at the Tanyard Phoebe was unusually flustered. 'Where can Hannah have got to? Have you seen her? She always disappears on Market day.'

So Abigail said nothing about Hal.

Thomas

The need for a horse and cart kept growing in Thomas' mind and he wished he had the courage to suggest it to his father. Alone among the apprentices it was always he who had to fetch hides or dung or anything else in the ageing hand cart. Built on the same principle as a wheel-barrow it had two big wheels forward of centre and a pair of legs at the handle end to support it in repose. Empty, it slewed only slightly in the loose sandy road surface, but once loaded it easily got stuck. How much more efficient a horse drawn cart would be!

The shambles was the source of fresh killed cattle hides. In the opposite direction in West Street lay Culver Hall, a beautiful house whence came pigeon dung. Beyond it was Timber Hall, both houses recently inherited by Henry Vernon.

Hop-grower Robert Bicknell rented Timber Hall. Jacob Mannory, proud of his fine house in the Tanyard, never tired of quizzing Robert Bicknell on why he chose to rent a house when he already owned several dwellings in the town.

Robert would smile, saying 'I like the house and I like the landlord' and when Henry Vernon became his landlord he reported 'A fine man, Henry Vernon, a worthy heir to the old 'un.' Vernon gladly continued the pigeon dung arrangement which served both him and Jacob.

Sometimes Thomas would wander into the Culver Hall stables to make acquaintance with Vernon's horses and his groom.

''T'aint just a matter of harnessing and un-harnessing and putting them out to grass,' Sam told him. 'You has to know them. And groom them. 'T'aint for nothing I'm called a groom.'

'I'm not afraid of work,' Thomas said.

'I can see that, pushing that gurt cart.' Sam leaned a shoulder against the flank of a big horse with a quiet 'Give over now' and when it moved, scraped the floor clean beneath its hooves. He gave the flank a friendly slap and the horse eased back. Then he settled in the tack room to oil the harnesses.

The work seemed straightforward enough but Thomas wondered about this matter of getting to know the horses. With people you just did it. Either you had always known them or you went to school with them, and you talked and fooled around. You could hardly talk or fool around with a horse, and Sam would say no more than 'You has to know them.'

By May Henry Vernon's gardeners were too busy beautifying his garden to prepare pigeon dung. Jacob became annoyed that the errand was taking Thomas so long.

'Take the brat,' he said, 'and send him into the dovecot. He's little enough use here.'

Thomas threw some sacks on the cart, topped with a shovel.

As they pushed it together across the bridge and up the hill in total silence, he wondered again about knowing a horse, or a person even. Six months now Hal had lived in the Tanyard, washing in the same bucket, eating at the same table, working in the same yard, but who could say they knew him? Not even Abigail, his rescuer. Hal so seldom spoke. Who was he, anyway? His father could have been anyone – well, almost anyone. Thomas tried to imagine who might father a whore's brat, who would go to a whore. Perhaps that rogue Trussler had taken the whore in lieu of payment for that hovel he rented to her.

And what kept Hal in the Mannory household? Jacob had beaten him often enough as well as James, sometimes, it seemed to Thomas, quite arbitrarily. Perhaps food and raiment were enough to cause him to stay, seeing what he had come from.

They pushed on round the corner into West Street. Men were unloading a wagon, carrying bundles of long hop poles through between the houses to the hop fields behind. The wagon horses stood with drooped heads, chomping hay in their nose bags.

When they arrived at Culver Hall, Henry Vernon himself was mounting his horse. Sam the groom held its bridle while it danced its back legs from side to side. Once in the saddle Mr. Vernon looked down at the new arrivals.

'So this is young Mannory, is it , come to relieve us of the pigeon muck? And the lad, is he another Mannory?'

'No, sir, it's Hal.' Thomas said. 'He's going to shovel it out for me, to save your men the bother.'

'Very good of you I'm sure,' Vernon said. He gathered the reins and turned the horse towards the road. Sam tipped up his cap and rubbed his head, a satisfied look on his face.

'He's a beauty,' he said. 'Reared him ourselves, and I rode him all the way down here when we moved. Takes a bit of handling though.'

'Not a carriage horse then,' Thomas ventured.

'What are you thinking of!' Sam retorted. 'Carriage horse indeed! That's a gentleman's riding horse. Well bred hunter.'

Sam looked round abruptly. 'Hey, where's that young lad gone?'

He was quickly inside the stable, checking up and down the stalls. And there was Hal right in beside one of the carriage horses. He stood looking up at the great head above him, and the horse looked down at him. As Thomas followed Sam into the stable, for a moment he had the oddest feeling that Hal and the horse were conversing.

'Well, I'll be danged.' Sam said, tipping up his cap and rubbing his head. 'I'll be danged.'

Discomfited, Thomas said, 'Come Hal, we must to business.'

Across the yard the sturdy circular dovecot was festooned with pigeons perched in its little arched nest-holes. When Thomas opened the low door the pigeons inside waddled and peered down. Then as Hal bent through the doorway they, with banging and clattering wings, took flight in all directions. Thomas handed Hal the shovel and held sacks open for him to fill.

As he scraped the last bits together and wriggled out into the daylight Hal asked 'What is it for?'

'It goes into the mastering pits. Mixed with water and dog dung. For softening the fine hides.'

Hal looked at him sceptically. Thomas laughed.

'Truly, some sort of alchemy takes place.' He settled the shovel between the filled sacks. 'Open the gate, Hal.'

Outside he turned the cart in a series of rocking movements. Now that it was loaded, the loose sand of the roadway offered more resistance than ever to the wheels. So intent was he on the manoeuvre that he did not notice two men approaching until they were right beside them.

'Good day young Thomas,' the older man said. Sturdily built, of medium height, his smile was genial above a square-cut beard. 'You could do with a horse.'

Thomas looked up amazed. 'Oh, Mr Bicknell, good day!' He steadied the cart on its legs and straightened his back. 'That,' he said, 'is just what I keep saying.'

'You do, do you,' Mr. Bicknell grinned. 'And to whom do you say it?'

'Well, mostly to myself I reckon,' Thomas admitted.

'If it's a horse you're after,' Bicknell said, 'Ralph Attfield here is your man.' He gestured to his tall, well-tanned companion, perhaps not far off thirty in age. 'Come, we'll walk along with you.'

Thomas lifted the cart handles again, leant his knee against the edge between them and started it moving.

'You must be well into your apprenticeship,' Robert Bicknell said after a while. Thomas nodded. 'And do you take to tanning?'

Thomas considered. Not only was Mr. Bicknell the father of Abigail's close friend Joan, he was particular friend of Thomas' father Jacob. Fathers seemed to assume that sons would follow them in their trade. His brother James had done the expected thing. No one had asked him as far as Thomas knew what trade he would like to follow, whether he wanted to be a tanner. He had just been sent off to Southwark where so many tanneries were concentrated, to serve his seven years' apprenticeship.

Thomas had not even been sent away. Everyone seemed to know that Jacob Mannory was the best tanner for miles around. Probably Mr. Bicknell would think he should be honoured to be taught by Jacob Mannory. And he was waiting for an answer.

'I'd rather be a carter,' Thomas heard himself say.

He stopped then to pay the toll at the bridge. A carter? Not just a horse and cart for tannery business, but a trade of his own? He felt silenced by his own effrontery.

Phoebe had killed two old hens that morning, and Abigail's task was to pluck them. She set herself up in the far corner of the Hall, away from any draughts through the doors to the yard or garden that would scatter the feathers. Beside her stool she placed two leather buckets and in each an open sack. One was for the down and fine feathers from the under-side of the chickens. They would be gently baked to kill any insects lurking among them, and then kept to stuff pillows and even feather beds. The second sack received the rest of the feathers.

She sat with one of the birds between her knees and started with the fluffy down, easy to pull out. When all of that was plucked and stowed she folded over the mouth of the sack and started on the tougher feathers. It was as she was struggling with the firmly rooted pinions that she heard Tom trundle the cart into the yard and then her father's greeting and Robert Bicknell's reply.

They stood talking in the yard. She could not hear what they were saying, nor was she listening, for she was concentrating on extracting these resistant feathers. But then came a third voice, a voice that made her stop and prick up her ears for another sound of it.

It was a rich, brown voice, conker-coloured, deep with a curious break in it, almost a crackle in the tone. Abigail sat looking intently at the doorway as if looking would sharpen her hearing. She was not eavesdropping, she simply wanted to go on hearing this marvellous voice.

He spoke again, and this time she could hear a Hampshire burr that was more pronounced than their own, a lingering over the `R's', a wideness in the vowels. `Horse dealing, that's my trade' she heard him say. Could this be the horse dealer Joan Bicknell said she fancied?

Starting on the second hen, Abigail wondered what sort of a man would own such a voice. Did voices fit their owners? Was her father's handsome face reflected in his voice which was sometimes tense and angry? But that was the way he spoke, not the quality of the sound. She thought of cousin John Harding and his melodious singing voice, such a contrast to his coarse looks and manner.

She folded over the neck of the sack of down and addressed herself to the hen's back feathers. That brown voice could belong to a great big blundering man, or to a florid old lecher with a beer belly. Or it could be a mean-looking man with a straggling beard. It ought to belong to someone rich and deep, someone whose arms would be a glorious embrace.

Suddenly they were there, the three men, coming through the doorway, her father saying ‘Come indoors and sit for a while,’ benches scraping on the stone floor. She sat embarrassed, furiously plucking. But Robert Bicknell noticed her and called ‘Good day young Abigail!’

She stood up, clutching the chicken by its legs against her apron, and bobbed a curtsy. A long-limbed man was sitting at the table with Robert and Jacob, his broad back towards her. He half turned and she saw thick brown hair cut level with his collar, and a tanned cheek.

‘Ah, Abigail!’ her father said. ‘Be so good as to fetch some ale for my guests.’

She laid the half plucked carcass on her stool and almost ran past the chimney stack and through the bake house to the still room, scattering tiny feathers as she went. Holding tankards under the ale barrel tap her hands were shaking.

'This is foolishness!' she told herself, arranging the tankards on a tray. She stood still a moment, brushing hen fluff off her apron, collecting herself. 'To be shaking because of a dark brown voice!'

When she placed a tankard beside him he said 'Thank you' without looking at her. He turned to take it and she saw a generous mouth, the jaw full and rounded over strong teeth, lips firm.

'This is Ralph Attfield, Abigail' Robert said.

'Your servant Ma'am,' just glancing up. She stood for a moment unsure what to do. Then she bobbed again and fled back to her plucking.

'Attfield is stabling his horses with me overnight on his way from Andover to the Haslemere fair,' Robert said.

'You cover a wide area?' Jacob said.

'Oh aye, all around Andover, Winchester, and over to Guildford and Haslemere. Always in the saddle.'

That explained the long boots right up to the knee, Abigail thought, and the hint of firm thigh muscles above. She allowed herself a long look at him as the talk continued. That voice really did reflect the whole man, and what a man he seemed to be! His leathern jacket sat easily on his broad shoulders. Well-shaped hands rested relaxed on the table.

'You're not riding off to fight the Scots, then?' Robert asked.

'With that rabble?' Ralph Attfield said. 'Have you not heard how pathetic they are? No training and scarcely a musket between them, and generals who know nothing of war. They need men experienced in combat.'

'You seem to know much about it.' Jacob's tone was cool.

'My late father saw service in Germany,' Ralph Attfield said. 'He was of the party the King sent to defend his sister when she was forced to flee her home. They learnt in action, he used to tell me. Some fine young gentlemen they had as their officers, Sir William Waller and Sir Ralph Hopton. Good friends to each other, both Hampshire gentlemen. Those are the quality to lead men.'

'I doubt not they've hung up their armour now and settled into their estates,' Robert Bicknell said.

'A better place for them,' Jacob said, suddenly fierce. 'War is wrong, and no one truly wins. King Charles is the son of a Queen of Scotland and now he's fighting the Scots. And for what? I hear he wants them using his new prayer book, and Bishops. I can hardly blame them for refusing. Bishops try to force their papist ideas on us. But whatever our views, war is an inexcusable means of pursuing them.'

'I'll wager there's more to it than Bishops and the Prayer Book,' Bicknell said.

Jacob said, 'Haven't the Scots captured London's source of coal up there?'

'London won't love the King and his war with the Scots, if it's causing a shortage of fuel,' Bicknell said. 'London has a strong militia has it not?'

'You sound as if you're talking civil war,' Jacob said. 'Surely no one can want conflict between fellow countrymen.'

'Like the devastation you hear of in Germany,' Bicknell said.

'Precisely,' Jacob said. 'Twenty years of war in Germany, Protestant against Catholic, nothing resolved, thousands dead, countries destroyed. Pray God we'll be spared war in our own land.'

'There are those who say Englishmen have become soft and effeminate for lack of warfare,' Robert Bicknell said, a provocative twinkle in his eye.

'They'll work hard enough if disciplined,' Jacob said. 'They don't have to kill one another.'

'Well,' Ralph Attfield said, 'I must confess that if war were nearer at hand, and a man such as Sir William Waller were raising troops, I would be tempted to enlist. A great life for a horseman.'

He stood up, tall and erect, saying 'If you'll forgive me, I have some errands to do,' and he took his leave.

Abigail began tidying up the feather sacks while Jacob talked on with his friend.

'I hear you've bought another cottage.'

Robert chuckled. 'A bastion against disaster.'

Jacob raised a questioning eyebrow.

'You know the uncertainty of hops,' Robert said. 'Last year was good, prices high. So this year I'm planting more hops, and buying a house.'

'You'll have more houses than hops e'er long!'

'Whatever goes wrong with hops, folk go on needing houses.' Robert leant forward, warming to his subject. ''T'is a matter of not having all your eggs in one basket. Look at the weavers. When fashions changed, those failed whose whole business was cloth. Those who had something else to fall back on, survived. Diversity, that is the wise counsel.'

'I'll not be buying houses' Jacob said.

Robert considered his square hands. 'What about,' he said slowly, 'What about a horse and cart? A carting sideline?'

'Hah!' Jacob said mirthlessly. 'A horse! I know nothing of horses.'

'Didn't Phoebe help with horses as a girl at Spreakley?'

Jacob grunted.

Robert stretched himself. 'Can't see my Joan coping with a horse,' he chuckled. 'She copes with the men, though, fending them off!'

'I keep my eye on Abigail' Jacob said, as if she were not within earshot.

Robert rose to go. ''T'is not that one who needs an eye kept on her my friend. 'T'is the other one, Hannah.' He moved towards the door. 'And remember, diversity. Should you decide on a carting sideline, Attfield is your man.'

'Please yes,' Abigail breathed, 'so I can see him again.'

Glees

May was a wet month. John Harding came to market once or twice, calling in at the Tanyard on his way into town, talking with Phoebe and finding a private corner with Hannah when he got the chance.

'There's hoeing to do every day, the weeds grow so fast, and Father is unwell.'

'What ails him?' Phoebe asked, anxious for her brother.

'He's no energy, no appetite. And with grandfather's sight failing, there's little they can do on the farm.'

All the same, John remembered the glees he had proposed, and stayed one market day.

'Hullo there cousins!' he boomed as he came into the yard and the dogs barked. He was followed by the new curate, a slight young man too thin for his worn suit of clothes.

'Well, we've a merry evening ahead of us!'

'Ah yes, full of glee,' curate Shepheard said.

John slapped him on the back. 'A good one, Hermann, a good one! We'll enjoy your new glees.'

Boots clattered on the stone flags as journeymen, apprentices, family and guests settled onto the benches around the long table. Jacob said a blessing and then tackled the meat, a leg of mutton brought in from the farm and keeping warm on a huge pewter dish. He carved with the skill of one accustomed to using knives precisely in his trade. As each person's plate, paved with a round of bread, was handed up he lifted a slice of mutton on the tip of the knife and laid it, dripping with juice, on top.

There was cabbage as well, and apple pie. Mary the serving girl made sure the tankards were kept supplied with ale. Hermann Shepheard ate as if this were the last meal before judgment day.

'Now who's for singing?' John cried. 'Gather round now, let's have a good choir going. Here's my pretty treble,' putting his arm around Hannah's shoulders, 'and Hermann is well versed in the tenor part. Who will sing the bottom part? Uncle? James? Anyone else?' looking round the other men before anyone could excuse himself and go up the stairs.

'What about yourself?' Hermann Shepheard asked.

'If need be, yes, if need be,' John said, 'but I prefer the counter-tenor part. Abigail, will you sing?'

'You know I cannot sing,' Abigail said.

'What nonsense, you have a sweet voice,' her mother objected.

'I cannot hold a line of music,' Abigail said. 'I would spoil it.'

Hermann Shepheard patted the bench beside him. 'Come, sing the part with your sister and that way you will learn.' Abigail shook her head.

'Who is to be the bass?' John insisted and at last prevailed upon James.

Singing the second part in the high falsetto that belied his heavy frame he sat close to Hannah, keeping one arm around her waist while his other hand strayed to her breast.

Abigail picked up her spindle and settled on a stool near her father, whose whole attention seemed to be on keeping his pipe alight. He did not appear to notice what was happening to Hannah. Abigail span mechanically as she watched and listened.

They sang a few songs that they all knew well and then John said 'Hermann has another – it isn't new, but 't'is well tried.'

Hermann Shepheard laid a sheet of music on his knee and they gathered round him. The music was printed in four directions, one along each side, so that the four singers could sit round and each see their own part.

They sang it several times, learning it as they went, and gradually Abigail made out the words.

Love me not for comely grace
For my pleasing eye or face
Nor for any outward part;
No, nor for my constant heart;
For those may fail, those may fail,
Those may fail or turn to ill
So thou and I shall sever.

She looked at Hannah, lost in singing and nestling close to John. She looked at John. He could have chosen this song specially for her, for he had no comely grace whatsoever. And Hermann Shepheard, singing his tenor line in that confident reedy voice he used for church services, had no grace to commend him that she could discern. She looked at her father, both comely and graceful, but to be feared.

Keep therefore a true woman's eye
And love me still but know not why
So hast thou the same reason still
To dote upon me ever.

Abigail could imagine doting on that Ralph Attfield, he looked and sounded so comely. But John Harding….

In the final glow of sunset she and Hannah prepared for bed without the aid of a rush light. They braided their hair, took off their garments and got into the bed they shared. It was all they shared, on the whole. There was little intimacy between them, Hannah always behaving as the elder sister. But now Abigail wanted to cross the boundaries, to know what Hannah was feeling, understand how she could let John fondle her as he had been doing.

'Hannah?… Hannah, while you were singing….'

A murmur indicated that she was still awake. She lay on her side, away from Abigail, hugging herself. She said nothing.

'I couldn't help seeing….none of us could….John had his hands all over you.'

Hannah flung herself onto her back. 'How dare you Abigail?'

'But he was, squeezing you, feeling you.'

'That's none of your business. If you won't sing, keep your eyes on your spinning.'

'I don't need my eyes to spin, you know that.' Abigail didn't want to quarrel, or to have Hannah rebuking her. She wished her sister could be more of a friend, like Joan Bicknell. But did those men Joan said she was always fending off do this to her?

'But John, Hannah. Do you like what he was doing?'

'I wouldn't let him if I didn't,' Hannah snapped. Then suddenly she softened. 'Oh Abigail, it stirs me up something terrible. I don't know how long I can endure like this. I love him so much. And every market day….'

'John? Cousin John Harding? How can you? I can't bear him near me. He's so loud and coarse.'

'And loving, and musical don't forget.' Hannah turned over, her back shutting Abigail out

Hay

The days turned warmer as May turned to June and suddenly there was hay to be made. On a misty morning that held the certainty of clear heat before long, Abigail was carrying a pail of frothing milk across the yard when a bare-foot lad vaulted the gate and came running towards the house door. She recognised him as one of the labourer's children from Searle's farm.

`Morning!' she said.

He pulled his forelock. 'Morning, Miss. Master sends word he's starting the hay.'

'I'll fetch my father.' She found Jacob in one of the sheds tending the delicate calf hides fermenting in an infusion of pigeon dung. If the leather was to be soft and stretchy for the glove-makers across the river, this 'bating' had to be halted at precisely the right moment. He leant on the side of the oak bin, his hand in the liquor, feeling the hides to assess their progress, a skill perfected from years of practice. He looked up as Abigail came in.

'Where is James?' he said.

'James? I don't know. I came to tell you they are starting the hay.'

'Very well. Ah, James,' as his elder son came into the building, 'feel this. What say you?'

James knelt down and felt a hide as his father had been doing. After a while he said, 'I would say it is not ready.'

'Correct.' Jacob straightened up. 'With the heat that this day promises it should be right by midday. The journeymen can transfer it to the bran pit then. Now to hay-making.'

'Hay-making?' James sounded incredulous.

'Have you been so long from home you forget our neighbouring with the farm? Hay in exchange for hay-making.'

'But Sir,' James said, 'three men already have leave to make their own hay...'

'The apprentices can move the hides from pit to pit. Everything in its season, James. Don't argue with me. Fetch the tools.'

Silenced, James stalked away to the tool shed.

'Thomas!' he shouted.

The mist was now no more than a wisp across the meadow, the sky clearing to hard hot blue. In deep barn shadow, Thomas was stirring some curing hides to ensure their even exposure to the mixture of tannin, leached from shredded oak bark, and water.

'Thomas!' James stood in the barn entrance. 'Didn't you hear me? We're to go to the hay fields up top.'

'Oh aye,' Tom said. 'When I have finished this. Have you told Hal?'

'Hal! He's probably run off to Vernon's stable. Anyway, what use is he?'

'He has to learn,' Tom said. 'And Daniel, (the hewer of wood and drawer of water) have you found him?'

Tom stretched, easing his shoulders and flexing his arms. He leant the pole up beside the bins and ambled into the yard. Phoebe came out with the straw hats she had made last winter and had kept for the heat of summer.

'We'll follow later,' she said. 'Will you take the pitchforks?'

She watched as her husband and sons loaded themselves with sickles, reaping hooks and pitchforks. 'Daniel, take the honing stones and a rake,' she said, 'and where is Hal?'

'We'll not trouble with him,' Jacob said. 'He can follow with you.'

Indoors Phoebe assigned tasks. 'Mary,' to the servant girl, 'slice the loaves and wrap them in the cloth in this basket. Abigail, gather up the tankards and bestow them in this other basket.'

Hannah fetched a whole cheese from the still room, like a down-sized millstone deeply golden. She took a long sharp knife and see-sawed it down through the rind gradually halving the cheese. Then quartering and quartering she reduced it to modest wedges which Phoebe arranged deftly in a wide cloth-lined basket.

'I am woefully unprepared,' she said. 'No lemons for barley water and no time to make it with this sudden change in the weather.' She lifted the lid of the wooden flour bin. 'And no way near enough flour to last through hay-making. And where is Hal? He can carry something.'

Abigail saw him, crouched beside the dogs. Scarcely pausing to wonder why hay-making should provoke him to seek their comfort, she placed two jugs of ale on the ground and called him to take them. Then they set out in a string, carrying jugs and baskets between them.

Walking steeply up the gully to Searle's farm atop the hanger, Phoebe asked 'Who was the lad who brought the message about hay-making?'

'One of the labourer's children,' Abigail replied. 'I don't know his name.'

'How odd it is,' Phoebe said. 'Along our lane we know every family and the names of all the children, but up here it's like another world. Scarcely more than a furlong and how little we know them.'

'They look down on the Abbey Street folk,' Mary said, panting, 'won't never mix with them.'

At the top the land levelled out into a gradual rise to the south. The hay field was already a quarter cut. Men and women were moving forward spread roughly in line across the field, each cutting a swathe of the tall feathered grass which fell in lines between them, to the steady swish swish of their blades. From time to time one would stop to hone his reaping hook, so that the line became temporarily staggered. Notwithstanding uneven progress, the scene was rhythmic and purposeful.

The bearers of refreshment settled in the shelter of the hedge where the food could keep cool.

The arrival of Mistress Searle the farmer's wife with her provisions signalled a break from work. She greeted Phoebe and set her baskets a little further along the hedge. Men and women gathered from all over the field to the sources of food. Sweating, they swallowed tankard after tankard of ale before falling to on the bread and cheese.

'Time you did some work,' Jacob said to Hal. 'Yes, you. Take a hook and cut whatever has been missed.' He got to his feet, picked up his reaping hook and moved back to the cutting line, followed by the others, all except Hal who stood holding a sickle, hesitating.

'Go along then,' Phoebe said. 'You can see where grass is still standing.' She turned away to talk with Mistress Searle.

Abigail watched Hal's attempts with the sickle while Hannah began to gather together the remains of the meal.

'Wake up!' Hannah said. 'Those tankards need to go in this basket!'

Abigail reached for the tankards, still watching. Some ale tipped onto her skirt as she handed them to Hannah.

'I'll just help Hal a little,' she said.

It was like teaching him how to cut kindling, thinking just how she handled a sickle and then trying to show him without insulting him.

'I thought I'd do some too,' she said coming beside him, and gradually he began to acquire the flick of the wrist and the levelling of the blade that cut through the stubborn tufts of grass.

She became aware out of the corner of her vision that someone was parallel to them, someone who was not working. He had a stick and was flicking the cut hay, watching them. Looking up she saw it was the young messenger of that morning.

'Hullo again,' she said. 'What's your name?'

'Willy. What's yours?'

'Abigail, and this is Hal.' The boy went on flicking hay.

Provoked, Abigail said 'That won't do the hay any good you know.'

Willy made a scornful noise. 'What do you know about hay, you down there?' gesturing over the edge of the hill.

'More it seems than you do' said Abigail, nettled. Willy flicked again at the hay.

'Abigail and Hal, Abigail and Hal, Stinky old tanners, Abigail and Hal...' he chanted, and continued in a crowing sing-song, 'Tanners making hay, Abigail and Hal!'

Abigail did her best to ignore him, carrying on raking, but suddenly Hal dropped his rake and gathering up an armful of hay threw it all over him. Willy, taller by a head and shoulders, was taken by surprise. He reeled back momentarily, then threw a bigger bundle over Hal. Back and forth they threw, and the throw was sometimes a punch, until they were wrestling, rolling in the hay, stuffing it down each others' shirts, kicking their feet through piled stalks, hay in their hair, their mouths, their clothes.

'Willy!' a shrill voice came across the field. A woman, red faced and untidy from the field work, strode over and cuffed him over the ear. 'Idle clotpole! Look at that hay! Master will thrash you for that! As for you, you varmint' she reached for Hal's breeches and hauled him upright, 'Who do you think you are?'

She shook him and took a closer look. 'Lordy! It's the whore's brat from down below! Keeping proper company now are you.'

She turned to her son and gave him another cuff over the ear. 'You're not to go playing with the likes of him, d'ye hear Willy? No good never comes out of that Abbey Street lot, and you,' turning back to Hal, 'you can keep clear of 'ere. Bastard!' She spat the word out at him.

'It isn't his fault what his mother was,' Abigail snapped back at her.

'The sins of the fathers...' the woman flashed.

'That's not fair.'

'It's the word of the Lord,' the woman said. 'The sins of the fathers are visited on the children...'

'I don't care what you say.' Abigail stamped her foot. Picking up her rake and Hal's sickle she grabbed his sleeve and left the field.

As they cleared the supper late that evening Phoebe carrying a dish in the same direction as Abigail asked quietly 'What was all the shouting about?'

'That boy Willy,' Abigail said. 'He was taunting us, especially Hal.'

'Was there a fight?'

'I thought it was a game at first, but it turned into a fight, and then his mother came, and Oh Mother! they won't let it rest that Hal's mother was a whore. Was she really?'

'So it is said,' Phoebe answered.

'This wretched woman quoted the Bible about the sins of the fathers being visited on the children.'

'"To the third and fourth generation",' Phoebe capped the quotation. 'But that is a statement of cause and effect. It does not instruct us, us people, to do the visiting.' She adjusted the lid on a crock. 'Besides, the verse that follows says that God shows mercy on thousands who love him and keep his commandments.'

Abigail stood twisting the corner of her apron. 'Please, does Hal have to go back up to the hay field tomorrow?'

Phoebe considered, folding her arms. 'I have only enough flour for the next bread-making. Tom had better take the cart to the Corn Exchange and then to the Mill, and I will arrange for Hal to go with him.'

The cart

The sun was high and fiercely scorching in the way that presages thunder as Tom set out with Hal the next morning.

`You're pushing skew,' Tom said.

`No,' Hal said, `I'm pushing like I always do.'

`Empty it should be easier than this,' Tom said. `That left wheel seems to twist.'

Uphill and they met the ironstone cobbles curving round from Church Lane towards the Borough. There the cart ran more easily. Few people were about in the broiling heat, with the threat of thunder hastening hay-making.

They swung the cart into Castle Street and pushed it up to the Corn Exchange where the corn chandler loaded up two sacks of wheat.

The cart shuddered and reeled its way back down Castle Street.

`Mother said to go to Bourne Mill,' Tom said.

Bourne Mill was a full mile away along the Guildford road, with a downhill slope at the end. While they waited their turn for the milling they cooled their feet in the mill pond, and the miller's wife brought them out a hunk of bread each and some small beer.

`Better than hay making,' Tom said and Hal grinned. But perhaps hay making would have been better than the return trip. The whole valley seemed saturated with heat, the road deep in dust and grit which slid about under the wheels. By the time they reached the Borough they were soaked in sweat, coated with dust, weary and dejected. The left wheel wobbled alarmingly over the cobbles.

`Once we're in Snow Hill we'll let it rip,' Tom said.

Jolting over the cobbles they started to run. At the very moment that the weight of the handcart took charge, a horse and hay-laden cart came round from Church Lane. The two hurtled together. Tom scraped the handcart's legs along the stones, vainly braking. The cart driver pulled on the reins, shouting furiously. Wheel hit wheel in loud impact.

It threw Tom off balance. Something slid and hit his shoulder. Hay was showering off the cart, the horse rearing and neighing, the driver shouting. People appeared instantly.

Tom picked himself up and saw that he was covered in flour. Flour was all over the cobbles. He caught the second bag as it too began to slide. Someone propped it at the roadside.

Hal, where was Hal? Please God not under the wreckage. He peered around, floury eyelashes blurring his vision.

Suddenly he realised that the hay cart had stopped junketing about. The horse was standing still, flanks heaving, mouth frothing. At its head stood Hal, apparently doing nothing.

The moment of quiet was broken by the carter. He leapt down and attacked Tom with fists and feet and fury, until a bystander stepped forward and pulled him off.

`Hold hard Abe,' he said sternly. `It ain't your cart that's ruined. Lay off the lad.'

`Them perishing Mannorys with their perishing nipper!' Abe spluttered.

`Perishing nipper?' Tom's rescuer asked. `Look at your horse.'

Abe Trussler, almost as floury now as Tom, turned to look. Hal had his hand on the horse's neck yet the touch seemed hardly needed such was the understanding between them. Abe was momentarily silenced. Then he re-opened his attack.

`Get that hand cart out of the way. I ain't got all night. Blocking the bloody road. I've got hay to move.'

One wheel, the one that had been causing trouble, had sheered off at the axle while the other was scarred and broken where it had collided with the cart-wheel. The hand cart lay on its side, skewed across the road. Tom took hold of its handles and gave a weary tug. It seemed stuck fast.

Bystanders combined to lift and pull the wreckage clear of the road. Tom, so weary and battered that he could scarcely think, half sat against it rubbing his grimy hands over his filthy floury face. Abe was back up on his cart, shouting to Hal to get out of the way, beating the horse forward again. The cart gave a shudder and started to roll up the hill. Hal came and stood by Tom.

`He could have thanked you,' Tom said.

`He hates me,' Hal said matter-of-factly.

A few fat drops of rain alerted Tom, who bent to heave the remaining flour sack onto his back. A woman's voice stopped him.

`You'll never get that to the Tanyard before the rain comes,' she said. `Put it in my shed till the storm passes.'

Tom obeyed, and thanked, and set off for home under darkening clouds which poured rain on them well before they reached the bridge. `Lord knows what my father will say about the cart,' he said.

Jacob was right. The journeymen had transferred the calf hides from the mastering pit into a bran solution which neutralised residual lime. Now as thunder reverberated across the valley Jacob gathered his apprentices to learn how such delicate hides should be scudded free of the last traces of hair, ready for the currier.

Nathan Armstrong was shaping up well as a beamsman. He stood behind the beam, a steeply sloping working table, convex in section like the blunt two-handled scudding knife he held. With it he scraped the hide draped over the beam with long firm strokes. These fine skins of bull calves born that summer could easily be damaged, and he needed care as well as strength.

`See the pressure of his strokes' Jacob told the boys. `Watch carefully.'

James, a little put out that it was not he who was demonstrating, looked up at the sound of rain pounding like a sudden waterfall. `Thomas is a long time coming back,' he said.

`What's he fetching?' one of the men asked.

`Flour! It'll be gruel if he's bringing it through this downpour!'

`It is to be hoped he found shelter on the way,' Jacob said.

But the dogs' barking announced Tom's arrival through the rain. They heard him tell Hal to go into the house, and then he was standing hesitant in the shed doorway.

Thomas wished that he had found his father alone. He walked over to him, leaving a damp foot mark on the floor with each step.

`Father,' he said, `We've… I had a... Sir, the cart is broken.'

`Broken? What do you mean, broken? Where is it? Where have you left it?'

`It's in Snow Hill near the top. People helped me pull it out of the way.'

`Show me.' Jacob untied his leather apron and slung it over his shoulders although already the rainstorm was easing, the clouds rolling off eastwards. Tom thought longingly of a dry shirt but dared not disobey. As they walked he tried to explain.

`Sir, I know I took the corner too fast. But we had been troubled all day with the near wheel.'

`That is no excuse. What broke it?'

`A loaded cart coming out of Church Lane. Truly we could do nothing to stop the collision.'

Jacob made no comment. At the turn of the road he went, not on up Snow Hill but into the great wagon yard dotted about with sheds and workshops. A small man with a long nose and big hands was working in a shed stacked with wheels and timber.

`Evening, Moth,' Jacob said. `My cart has been damaged. I would be obliged if you would take a look at it.'

Without a word Moth came with them. He went as if towards the Tanyard but Jacob jerked his head up Snow Hill.

`Ah, t'was your cart then. I did hear shouting. Folks said it was Abe Trussler again. Never know what he'll be at next – second rate tanning in Mead Lane, letting mean houses, carting.....'

Jacob grunted.

`He keeps me in work with his damaged carts,' Moth chuckled.

`But it was our cart he damaged,' Thomas said.

They could see it now, tipped against the grassy verge, the broken wheel propped beside it, sodden flour all around it. Moth inspected it minutely.

`That wheel sheered off at the axle.' He turned to Tom. `Had trouble with it?'

`Mightily,' Tom said. He shivered in the damp breeze blowing round the corner from West Street.

`Was Trussler's cart damaged?'

`Not that I noticed,' Tom said. `He was in a main hurry to get his hay out of the rain.'

As Moth continued his inspection the woman who had taken in the second sack of flour came out of her house.

`What a to-do, Master Mannory,' she said. `Your hand cart was fair thrown across the road. I've your sack of flour indoors keeping dry.'

`I'm much obliged to you Mistress Gary,' Jacob said.

Moth stood still now, scratching his head. `I can't mend it overnight,' he said, `nor yet in several weeks. You'd be better advised to buy a new one.'

`And from whom can I buy one on the instant?' Jacob asked. `Not from you surely?'

`Not from me.' Moth chuckled again. `All taken up at hay time. Though...' he paused and looked sideways at Jacob. `I do know as how old Jackson's executors are wanting to sell his horse cart. Quite a small one. Done good service mind but sound, certainly sound.'

`What would I want with a horse cart?' Jacob said.

`Is there a horse to go with it?' Thomas could not hold back the eager question.

`I wouldn't know about that,' Moth said, and to Jacob, `It could meet your needs for the present at least.'

`Do you require your flour now the rain is passed?' Mistress Gary asked.

`Father...' Thomas began, his mind on a horse.

`Take the flour to the yard,' Jacob said. `You can go now.' He heaved it onto Tom's back and he, holding the ears of the sack over his shoulders, wove his way down the street propelled by its weight. By the time he had carried it home and lowered it beside the flour bin in the bake room his shoulders and arms had no strength left in them, and there was water in his shoes.

`Mercy, what a sight you are!' Phoebe exclaimed, and all the household gathered round, his sisters and the servants, and Hal looking clean and neat with his hair slicked down and a dry shirt, wanting to know what had happened.

`Abe Trussler went for him.' Hal's hands were clenched as he broke in. `He kicks, Abe does.'

Tom paused and smiled at him. `You should have seen how Hal calmed the horse.'

`Whatever did Father say?' Abigail asked.

`He said little. When he comes home I suppose I shall be for a beating.'

He did not return until after dark, until both Thomas and Hal had long been asleep. Phoebe looked up from the big Bible that she was reading by the light of a single tallow candle clamped to the table. Her eyes spoke a silent question, a whole cluster of questions. Jacob stood for a moment, his thin shoulders stooped, looking silently at her hands laid on the book. Then he reached his long clay pipe from the beam above the fireplace and sitting in his high backed chair, started to pack it with tobacco.

Phoebe closed the book and turned towards him. `There's scarce a spark left in the fire,' she said. `Have you eaten Jake?'

Jacob nodded. `At Bicknells.'

Phoebe nodded too, and rose to replace the Bible on its shelf, sensing the anger in Jacob that somehow his friend had eased. She asked no questions, but was not surprised when next morning Robert Bicknell walked into the Tanyard. He did not come alone.

Walking to the Tanyard, Robert Bicknell told Ralph Attfield, 'Mannory was in a bate over the damage to his hand cart, but he's coming round to the idea of a horse drawn cart. That's where you come in.'

Attfield chuckled. 'You're doing my selling for me!' he said.

'If a man wants a horse...' Bicknell pushed open the gate and shushed the dogs. 'I'll see if I can find Mannory and pave the way.' He crossed to the outside stair leading up to Jacob's office.

Ralph Attfield looked about him. A prosperous place, he thought. Substantial buildings, a good house, well arranged tanning pits and the river close by. He peered into the open sheds where men were at work. A man's world. His kind of world.

He walked up and down below the stair and turning, caught sight of someone spinning outside the house door. It was the girl who had served ale that other time he had been here. Her spinning slowed and she looked up at him, at which he switched direction in his walking, pausing as if to make a close examination of the lime pit.

He was happy enough with male company, but maidens.... With his good looks and physique he was an obvious target for their flirting, which often seemed hollow. Suppose this Mannory girl was like Joan Bicknell, pretty and knowing it, fluttering near whenever he visited the Bicknell home. Perhaps avoidance was the best policy. Yet that other time she hadn't seemed like the Bicknell girl. She had been plucking a chicken, and then silently served them ale.

'Attfield! Come along indoors!' Jacob and Robert were crossing the yard, ushering him through the house door. Jacob paused. 'Ah, Abigail. Fetch Thomas would you and send him to me.'

Tom was dusty from milling oak bark. He brushed his clothes roughly with his hands while he followed Abigail into the house.

`Ah, Thomas,' Jacob said. `This is Mr. Attfield. I believe you've met.'

They shook hands and Abigail went as before to fetch ale. Once she had served it she returned to her spinning.

Jacob addressed Mr. Attfield.

`My son is the one who would drive the cart.'

Robert Bicknell, seeing Tom's bewildered look, smiled at him.

`Your father is well nigh persuaded to buy a horse and cart,' he said. `Ralph Attfield here may be able to supply the horse.'

`Indeed I can,' Attfield said. `I have a string of horses stabled at Bicknells overnight. You may take your pick.'

`Mannory claims he knows nothing of horses,' Robert said. `Would it not be best for you to select the one most suitable?'

`You're very trusting of a horse dealer!' Ralph Attfield laughed.

`From good experience,' Robert replied.

Tom found his tongue. `I to drive a cart?' he gasped. `I know nothing of horses either!'

Ralph Attfield laughed again. `Your father is expecting you to be the carter.'

`Only as occasion demands,' Jacob said. `Your first call is the tannery, and I cannot have a horse put to shafts for every errand.'

`But how can I learn?' Tom stuttered.

`Your mother had a care for horses in her girlhood at Spreakley,' Jacob said.

`Nay, but your young lad, Hal isn't it, I hear he has a way with horses,' Attfield said. He went on, extolling the horse he had in mind, a good-natured cob with plenty of pull. And it seemed that harness went with the cart, which Jacob had all but agreed to buy. Tom recovered a little from his initial shock.

`There's much I could collect for you, sir,' he said to his father. `Oak bark when you want it instead of having to wait on the woodmen...'

`As I said, this is not to interfere with your ordinary work.'

Ralph stood up. `So Bicknell will stable the cob until you are ready to take her. I must away. I've the horses to take over the wasteland ready for Haslemere market tomorrow.' He waved a general goodbye and went outside. The girl Abigail was still sitting there spinning, and it was easy enough to walk straight past her and out of the gate.

Tom's expression was dazed when he emerged into the yard. He stopped by the spinning wheel. Abigail looked up from her work.

'I'm to drive a horse and cart' he said. 'A reliable little cob Attfield says. For tannery business.'

'Oh Tom!' Abigail stood up and hugged him.

Goodwife Martin

A pungent smell filled the Hall as Phoebe ladled boiling water into a jug full of Feverfew leaves, pushing them down with a wooden spoon to release their potency. She looked up at her daughters.

'Old tanner Martin's grandchild is sick of a fever, and the father has no work. When the tisane has infused we will take some along to relieve the fever.'

'They must be hungry if the father has no work,' Abigail said.

'The poor are generally hungry. More so this winter with bad harvest and high prices,' Phoebe said. 'We'll take some food along.'

She set two clean jugs before the fire and holding back the feverfew leaves with a whisk of twigs, poured the tisane into each. Then she put a loaf, a basin of butter and some hard boiled eggs in a basket and set off with Abigail carrying one of the jugs.

The Martin home was a one room cot beside Snow Hill, little more than a garden hut among hops. Although the earth floor was cleanly swept there was scarcely any furniture. A box bed built into one corner had an old quilt neatly folded on it. There were a couple of stools but no table. The rudimentary hearth was empty.

As her eyes became accustomed to the dim light Abigail saw a pile of heather on the floor where a little child lay among rumpled cloths.

'I'm at my wit's end to know how to tend him.' His young mother bent over him, anxiety in every line of her thin body. 'He's my only child living,' she added, putting her hand on his hot forehead. 'I'm so afeared to lose him.'

Phoebe sent Abigail to fetch water from the conduit at the foot of Castle Street, and coaxed tisane into the little boy's mouth. 'He needs to drink,' she said, 'though I can see he is reluctant. Feverfew is not a pleasant taste.' She wrung out a rag to cool the boy's brow.

'Shall we pray for him?' she asked.

'Oh Ma'am, I've prayed and prayed, please God spare him.'

'Then together we'll commit him into the hands of God, trusting him for whatever is best.' The mother's eyes were full of tears as she murmured her Amen.

Abigail was so troubled by the suffering there that she felt jarred, back out in the rutted street, to hear a cheerful call. Her friend Joan Bicknell waved from where her mother Elizabeth was chatting to Mistress Gary, standing at the Garys' front door, shawl wrapped around her shoulders against the autumn chill.

Joan put her arm through Abigail's whispering 'The gossips are at it again.'

'I see you've been into Martin's cot,' Betty Gary said. 'Always something amiss in that cottage, and the man never at home.'

'He does casual work when he can,' Phoebe said. 'The child is very sick. Will you keep an eye on them Betty? You are so much nearer than I.'

'Indeed, indeed,' Betty Gary said, bridling.

They prattled on, about the fever and the weather and the high water in the river, until Elizabeth Bicknell suddenly asked 'Betty, why did you move here from the shop?'

'The rooms above the shop were needed for storing cloth, and this house is much more commodious,' and she invited them in.

Dark panelling around the walls made the room almost as dark as the Martin cot. A heavy table stood against one wall, with good greenware pots on it. Soft cushions bore witness to Michael Gary's trade as a woollen draper.

Yet that poor woman next door, Abigail thought, has scarcely a bench let alone cushions for it. She felt quite indignant at the contrast, and then she wondered if they themselves were any different from the Garys because, for all her mother's benevolence to the poor, they never lacked for essentials.

'Come upstairs,' Betty said. When they followed her up the narrow stair she flung open a door to reveal an enormous bed almost filling the room.

'Our kinswoman has bequeathed her great bed to our son Christopher, ready for his marriage.' She paused, with a meaning look at Elizabeth and Joan.

Christopher. Joan. Christopher, that lanky youth, had always seemed sweet on Joan, though she gave him scant encouragement. Joan caught Abigail's eye and made a face, shrugging at the mothers' plotting.

'You'll have heard that the King is expected for hunting in the Park? ' Elizabeth said. They were back downstairs, sitting on the softly cushioned seats. 'Such a to-do some folk make of it, and I suppose the Bishop will come too, and the Rector – we haven't seen much of him for a good while, leaving the parish to that ill-fed curate of his. He's one who could do with a kindly patron – or a wealthy wife – Lord know how he survives. His housekeeper must be an ill manager, or the man just takes no interest in food.'

Abigail laughed. 'He had plenty of interest in the food Mother provided when he dined with us.'

'Dined with you has he, at the Tanyard?' Betty said, gathering fuel for gossip. Abigail almost stamped her food, wishing she had held her tongue.

'Speaking of bequests,' Elizabeth began again, 'did you know that my late brother-in-law has left a bequest for the education of six poor men's children?'

Walking home with her mother Abigail asked 'Will Hal go to school?'

Phoebe shook her head, watching her footing among the ruts.

'Mistress Bicknell said "Six poor men's children",' Abigail insisted. 'He's a poor man's child.'

'A poor woman's child.'

'Oh, but that's so unfair!'

'Unfair or not, that is how it is. But daughter, you could teach him to read. You could teach him his letters before the winter is out.'

'Oh Mother!' Abigail saw at once an opening for spending time with Hal. 'If he could be persuaded to want to read, there is nothing I would like better.'

For the moment her dismay at poverty alongside prosperity was overlaid by the possibility of nurturing Hal. But the contrast arose again as they sat round the last of the fire after the evening meal.

'Mistress Bicknell said that the King is expected for hunting,' Phoebe said.

James turned to Thomas, 'You'll find,' he said, 'Your cart commandeered to move his goods, and no payment for it either.'

'Are you sure they don't pay?' Thomas said.

'Maybe the Bishop does,' Phoebe said. 'The Bishop of Winchester is a wealthy man by all accounts.'

'Why,' Abigail said, 'if the Bishop is so wealthy is the curate so poor?'

Jacob took the pipe out of his mouth. 'It's not the Bishop who pays the Rector, who pays the curate. It's Master Vernon.'

'It is all so wrong,' James exclaimed. 'I've been looking into it. Master Vernon has the interest of the Parsonage, the tithes and everything. Part of his inheritance. No properly qualified preacher would work for what he pays.'

'Master Vernon?' Thomas asked, surprised.

'Master Vernon,' James said. 'So he can afford his coach and his fine horses and garden and house and servants and all.'

'When King Henry shut the monasteries,' Jacob said. 'he gave their property and the right to appoint the clergy to whomever he liked. But to be fair, Master Vernon has other properties.'

'Very well,' James said. 'If that is so he does not need the church revenue to go to him, a layman, and for his own purposes. And the Bishop, what does he need with a whole series of palaces?'

'The diocese is very large' Phoebe said.

'But so much wealth!' James became vehement. 'It should be levelled out. The rich are too rich and the poor are too poor. Church revenue should be levelled out, and then we could afford to pay for clergy who can preach.'

'You always say Mr. Duncomb preaches well,' Tom said.

'Paid by the Burgesses for a weekly lecture! He should be the Rector. The Rector is forever away, fawning on the Bishop, and we're left with Shepheard. On Sundays he dresses up and bows and bobs and issues instructions – stand, sit, kneel – and on Thursdays he's at the lecture. What is he playing at?'

'Run with the hare and hunt with the hounds?' Thomas murmured.

'The worst of it is,' James went on, 'that with the system as it is, be he never so feeble he could find preferment if he had a wealthy patron or a well-dowried wife.'

Hannah giggled. 'Would that be why he was making up to Abigail when we had that glee evening?'

The King did not come, for in November 1640, desperate for funds, he recalled Parliament. The Bishop did come, accompanied by the Rector, but stayed only briefly before they both went to London. There they found that Parliament, grasping the opportunity to curb the King's autocratic rule, had confined his chief adviser the Earl of Strafford to the Tower.

Perhaps their brief visit strengthened Hermann Shepheard's resolve to practise all the church rituals that Archbishop Laud had so arbitrarily decreed. Offended that, despite Archbishop Laud's attempt to suppress lecturers, Duncomb was still in place, he tackled him after a lecture.

'You're in open disobedience to their Lordships' authority,' he said, anxiety putting a squeak into his voice.

'I am employed to preach by the Burgesses,' Duncomb said quietly, 'not by the Bishop.'

'The Bishop has authority over the church,' Shepheard insisted, 'and you are commanded to read the Prayer Book service before you preach.'

Duncomb smiled. 'The people come to hear the preaching, as it seems you do too.' He patted the curate's arm and walked away. James who had heard the exchange followed him, full of indignation.

'The man's a toady! Putting on all this show because of the Bishop. How dare he tell you what you must do!'

'A small man, a weak man,' Duncomb said. 'A man who longs to be somebody, but can achieve it only by climbing onto the backs of those who are. I pray he may arrive at some real and personal convictions.'

The following month Archbishop Laud was also imprisoned in the Tower.

Since Moth had repaired the axle and replaced the broken wheel, Jacob was more likely to send the hand cart out than to tell Tom to put the horse to shafts. Tom knew better than to argue with his father. He did attempt occasionally to suggest that using the horse might save time, without effect. Then at last on a dull overcast day in December Jacob said 'Take the cart to the forest and load up with oak bark.'

Tom called Hal. 'Fetch the horse,' he said, as casually as he could, for he hated to admit that he could not catch the beast. Steady little horse as she was once harnessed, she was skittish and provocative in the meadow.

Tom had come storming in one day early on, all his normal good humour used up in the frustration of stalking the horse he had so much wanted.

'Good natured cob!' he exploded. 'That rogue Attfield, he's not fit to sell horses. The cart's no use if the horse won't be caught!'

He had stood fuming in the doorway. Phoebe, his mentor up to then, smiled at him. 'See what Hal can do,' she said, and the lad was outside in an instant. He had come back astride the cob.

'Fetch the horse,' Tom now told Hal, 'while I get the cart ready.'

Hal did not succeed at once, for the cob was becoming at ease in the meadow. By the time he led her into the yard Tom was impatient to be off. He lifted the head collar over the horse's neck, eased on the bridle, and then backed her between the shafts of the cart. He climbed up and took the reins while Hal opened the gate. Hal went to jump up beside him, but as ever Jacob's eye was on them.

'No need for you to go, boy,' he commanded, emerging from the fleshing shed. Hal turned back, his whole body speaking disappointment.

Abigail was watching from the house window, glad to be warm indoors on such a chill and dreary day. She saw Hall turn back, and saw too that her father had nothing particular for him to do. She went to the door and called him.

'Come inside.' He dragged himself over. 'Mother has told me to teach you to read and write.'

'Read? Whatever for?'

'Well, so you can read books, and the Bible, for yourself. And letters, and write letters.'

He screwed up his face and said with utter disbelief, 'Write letters? Whoever to?'

Abigail decided to be firm. 'It may seem pointless to you now, like some of your other tasks. But it is time you learnt to read.'

She found her old slate and they sat down next to a window to take advantage of the wintry light.

'First,' she said, 'we'll learn some letters.'

After a while she guided his hand as he tried to copy them. When he began to flag she said 'Just one more thing. We have only learnt a few letters so we can't make many words yet. But we can make one.' Pointing to them she got him to make the sounds. 'B – a – d' again and again till they ran together.

'Bad!' he exclaimed, and then he drooped. 'Bad. Like me.'

'Bad!' Abigail was horrified. 'You're not bad Hal!'

'Bastard, son of a whore,' Hal muttered.

'That doesn't make you bad!'

She could hardly hear him as he said 'Then why do they beat me?'

'Oh Hal!' Abigail would have liked to cuddle him. 'You've been so good this afternoon You have been a good pupil. You've learnt fast. We'll find some other times to do more.'

With the coming of spring, Abigail and Joan went about together in the town and for the first time in their long friendship Abigail noticed how Joan flirted with all the men. Many fell victim, not least the curate Hermann Shepheard.

'Good day to you!' he called as they walked up Snow Hill together. Joan waved her hand and smiled.

'You'd think he'd been on the look-out for us to come by, he's always doing this' Abigail muttered.

'Just on a pastoral visit,' he said, catching up with them.

'How kind you are!' Joan said.

'Is someone sick?' Abigail asked.

'No no.' He fell into step beside them.

'I like Spring,' Joan said. 'Everyone comes out of their houses and chats and moves about after being shut in all winter.'

Children were playing tag in the road and around the bushes alongside it. Beyond the bushes a young woman looked up from her digging. 'Get off you varmints!' she shouted as they strayed onto her newly turned earth.

'It's Goodwife Martin!' Abigail exclaimed. 'Good day to you!' calling across the bushes. 'How is your little boy?'

The woman stood her spade up in the soil and picked her way across to them. 'My boy Charlie? That's him there,' pointing to a grinning imp skilfully eluding capture by his playmates.

'Oh, that's wonderful!' Abigail turned to her companions. 'He was very sick with a fever in the winter. And look at him now!'

'The fever turned that same day that you came with your mother. I'll not forget that day, I was so afeared I'd lose him. And we had food after that because his pa found work for a while. I was that grateful to your mother.' She wiped her nose on the back of her earthy hand. 'Draper Gary's let me have a corner of the hop garden – and my Goodman bought me a spade (looking proudly at it). Please God I can grow a bit of food this year.'

'Have you seeds?' Abigail asked, but before the woman could reply a posse of small boys cannonaded into Joan almost knocking her off her balance. Hermann Shepheard made a sort of lunge at them, his voice squeaking as he said 'Have a care! That's enough!' The children backed off, surprised.

'Come on Abi,' Joan said, moving away with the curate in tow.

'Just a moment.' Abigail turned back to Mrs. Martin. 'I'll ask my mother if we have any bean seeds that you could have.'

The woman bobbed a curtsy and Abigail hurried after the others.

'Ah, the poor are always with us,' the curate said. 'Are you intending to visit Mistress Gary?' as they drew level with her house.

‘Oh no!’ Joan did not give Abigail time even to think of a reply.

He stood uncertainly by the Garys’ street door, weighing perhaps the choice between Betty Gary’s good cakes and prolonging Joan’s company. Joan simply bowed a ‘Good day’ and saying again ‘Come on Abi!’ walked on up the street.

It was certainly preferable, Abigail thought, for the curate’s attentions to be on Joan rather than any hint that they might be on herself. However, some weeks later Joan said ‘Ralph Attfield was lodging at our house last night – have you met him? Tall and dashing and upstanding, quite a man.’

‘Lodging at Bicknell’s?’

‘Yes, he’s a horse dealer and stables his horses in Father’s barn on his way to the horse fair. I could really favour him, though he’s hard to engage in conversation.’

Abigail caught her breath. Then quickly, hoping that Joan had not noticed, said ‘You never mention Christopher Gary.’

‘Oh Christopher!’ Joan laughed. ‘He’s such a boy, and no one could call him handsome. He’s like a floppy puppy.’

‘Your mother and his mother looked as if you were intended for one another.’

Joan tossed her head. ‘I am not an heiress, to be sold to the highest bidder. I shall marry whom I will. There is plenty of time, and plenty of real men, like your brother James, and this Ralph.’

Duncomb

In the autumn of 1641 a letter came from James' former master in Southwark, requesting him to do a spell in the tannery there where they were sore pressed and short of skilled workers.

`Moreover,' James said quietly to Hannah later, `the trained band there is preparing in case of conflict. I was with them while I was apprenticed, but don't ever tell Father. You know how he considers that differences should never be resolved by force of arms.'

Hannah snorted. `Just by force of the rod - but I suppose he'd say that's different. Discipline and proper chastisement.'

`Has he beaten you?' James was suddenly the protective older brother.

`Not since I was a child. But he's ready enough with the rod for anyone else, men and boys.' She adjusted her apron. `So you're going away again. What did Father say?'

`He's none too pleased, because now I'm useful to him.' He shrugged. 'But Hannah,' looking at her earnestly, `don't ever let a man beat you.'

`How do you think a woman could prevent it?' Hannah said. `And who knows what man may one day beat his wife?'

`Not John Harding, please God,' James said. Hannah looked down, twisting her fingers. `How is it between you? Is he serious?'

There was a long pause while Hannah avoided his searching eyes. `Hannah?' he said at last.

`I believe he truly is,' she answered, scarcely above a whisper, `but I think he's afraid of Father. He's young you see, the same as you, and I think Father believes a man should be nearer thirty before he's ready to wed.' She sighed and said even more quietly, `Waiting is hard.'

Despite the brevity of Jacob's supper grace that evening, denoting his evident displeasure, James had soon packed up his belongings and taken the mail coach to London.

`So you see,' Abigail said to Hal a few days later, trying to re-activate his reading, `how important it is to be able to read. Off James goes to London and all because of a letter.'

But Hal was not listening to her. Horse's hooves in the yard had him poised to run, even before the shout of `Boy!' He was outside in a jiffy, beside the shaggy farm horse as John Harding swung his leg over the saddle booming `Hold my horse, boy!' and then `Where's my aunt?'

He did not wait for reply. Hal gestured towards the house but John was already through the door. He glanced left and right, saw Abigail, `Where's your mother?' then saw Phoebe on a stool by a window, fallen asleep over her sewing. She jerked awake at his voice.

`Aunt,' he said, `Aunt!'

`John!' She looked up surprised as he launched towards her. `Whatever is the matter?'

`It's my father,' he said, blundering forward and kneeling down beside her. `I think he's dying.'

Phoebe blinked sleep out of her eyes and put her hand on his shoulder.

`Oh Aunt! You know he's not been himself all this twelvemonth. He's got weaker all the time. I didn't really notice at first, but now...'

`Is he much worse?'

John nodded. `He can't eat, he hardly drinks, he is thin as thin, and any physic he's given he can't keep down. Oh Aunt, could you come?'

`My poor brother.' Phoebe folded her sewing and put it into a bag. `I was disquieted when I saw him a while back - why, it must have been before hay-making. Is he very weak?'

`He has not left his bed for days. You will come, won't you? You must take the horse. I can follow on foot, I won't be far behind. It's you we need, and I fear that time is short.'

Phoebe patted his arm absently, her mind already on arrangements to be urgently made. `Tell Hal not to water the horse since we will set out straightway. Abigail, find Hannah, and gather my second shift and my shawl. And Abigail, tell Mary to put some of the cold broth into a bottle. I will speak to the Master,' and she went out into the yard, gathering her skirts and running up the steep stair to Jacob.

The scurrying lasted barely twenty minutes, then John hoisted her onto the horse, she settled her skirt over the saddle and her bundle of clothes behind her, and she was away.

Hannah turned to John. `You'll take some ale before you go too?' she asked. He was still gazing after his aunt and took a moment to turn his attention to her. `Have some ale before you go,' she repeated. He followed her meekly into the house. She signalled with her eyes to Abigail to fetch the ale, and led him to her father's seat beside the fire, standing close by him. After a while he put his arm around her waist and pulled her closer.

`My dear,' she said, touching his hair. At that he buried his face in her side, and wept.

Coming in with a brimming tankard Abigail saw, put the tankard quietly on the table and retreated, at first to the bake room and then out into the garden. Seeing big loud John suddenly vulnerable overturned her suppositions, leaving her too feeling vulnerable. She dawdled around the garden where the tops of turnips were drooping from an early autumn frost, and only the leeks stood up growing and firm among the last remains of summer. She hardly knew her uncle, and yet a great sadness came over her, a sadness really for John. She stood by the hedgerow, absently dismembering a fluffy seed-head of Old Man's Beard, and then another, the down-light pieces floating around her feet.

After a while Hannah came out. 'Abi,' she said, 'Cousin John would like me to send him on his way, just to the edge of the heath. Could you and Mary see to the meal?'

For answer Abigail put her arms round Hannah's neck and laid her cheek against hers, where she felt the dampness of tears. Then she said 'Shall you tell Father?'

Hannah shook her head. `No, I should be back before they come in to eat. It's best that way.' .

The evening drew in and end-of-work sounds came across the yard, and still Hannah was not back. Abigail went out to the gate and peered towards the hollowed lane that ran south and up to Searle's farm and the heath. Whatever would Father say if Hannah were not present at supper? What might he do, and Mother absent to smooth things? He was at the bucket now, washing his hands.

Turning to go in she heard running footsteps and panting breath. She did not wait, for Jacob was indoors now and Oh mercy! he was standing by the fire informing the men of some change, all attention on him, while Hannah slipped in by the street door and shimmied in the shadows by the back wall through to the bake room.

`Hannah! Thank God you are back! What have you been doing? Your cap is all awry, and look at your dress and your pinny!'

`I ran all the way,' Hannah panted. `I'll help Mary, and straighten myself out at the same time. You go through and pour the beer.'

Jacob prayed a long blessing that evening, praying for those who travel and those who are sick and those who anxiously wait, until he almost forgot, or his listeners thought he would forget, to bless and give thanks for the food. Abigail added her own silent thanks for the delay, and prayed that Hannah would have had time to appear her normal self.

She was not entirely tidy as she ladled out the broth, with flushed face and dishevelled hair. She sat down as far as possible from her father. Abigail stole a look at her from time to time, sensing something about her that she could not quantify. She did not dare to ask her about it, even after they were in bed side by side.

They began to settle into a routine without their mother, much busier than before with a multitude of things they had hardly realised that she normally did. One way and another Abigail did not see Joan for nigh on two weeks, until she came one afternoon to seek her out.

`Abi! Have you a minute to spare for your old friend?' Joan asked, letting herself into the Hall. Abigail hugged her. `Every time I catch sight of you, you're running.'

Abigail laughed. `We're not as ordered as we'd like to be. But we're improving, and no one has complained that they have gone hungry.'

`Why don't you employ someone to cook? Surely there is no need for your mother to do it all?'

`I don't know.' Abigail was aware than many of the tradesmen's wives had servants to cook as well as those to do the other household tasks. `She always has done. Perhaps it's because she comes of yeoman farmer stock.' They sat down.

`When will she come back?' Joan asked.

`It's hard to know what to want' Abigail said. 'When she comes back it will mean that her brother has died, and I ought not to want that.'

They were silent for a while, and then Abigail gave herself a mental shake and asked what news Joan had.

`Oh, I've been longing to tell you,' Joan said at once. `Young Master Vernon has returned from the University at Oxford. He has finished his studies and will be at home now, living the life of a gentleman. His father Master Vernon brought him to present him to all of us - can you imagine how kind and friendly? He's so handsome and elegant Abi, young Harry Vernon that is.'

`Did he take notice of you?' Abigail could not resist asking.

`Oh, we've met since then. And Abi he is charming, and wondrously well informed. He told me about the dons at Oxford and how they support what the King does and how right they are to do so. He is a little worried about Lecturer Duncomb and his opinions, though he does not attend the lectures.'

`This is a new turn of thoughts for you!' Abigail laughed. `You were never interested in politics before!'

`Is this politics? I'm just telling you what Harry has said, he's quite in earnest, those are the kinds of things he talks about.'

`Who else have you been talking with?' Abigail asked.

`Oh lots of people of course! The curate keeps on turning up. He's started talking politics too, something to do with a petition to abolish the bishops. I don't see anything wrong with bishops and the Castle is lovely - have you ever been inside the Bishop's palace? The Great Hall is amazing, though it must be draughty in the winter.'

`James says it should all be more equal, that the Bishop is too rich and the clergy are badly paid.'

`You would think the curate would like to be better paid. Anyway, he is worried with talk of changes, and abolishing bishops, and he says that judging by the way Mr. Duncomb talks in his lectures he is against having bishops. He gets quite heated about Mr Duncomb.'

`Why can't people just accept one another's opinions?' Abigail said.

`And you know Abe Trussler?' Joan went on.

`I certainly know Abe Trussler.'

`He has become quite a crony with the curate, at least they talk together after the lecture, and people are remarking on it.'

`Abe Trussler at the lecture? I'm not surprised people remark on it!'

`Why? Doesn't he work for the Bishop?'

`Whoever he works for, he is a godless man.'

`Abi! You sound quite stern, more like your brother James! How is he, have you had word from him? He went so suddenly! I saw him just before he left.'

`Another of your admirers,' Abigail said a trifle ruefully.

`He's rather splendid though isn't he,' Joan said. `But I think I prefer a man who is more able to chat. I like that in Harry Vernon, he has plenty to say though sometimes it is rather a lecture. That's the drawback of that handsome Ralph Attfield, he isn't chatty.'

Abigail watched her as she chattered on, thinking that she would have to guard against seeing people through Joan's eyes, seeing them with preconceived notions.

The next day was Thursday and she decided to make an effort to listen properly to Duncomb so as to come to her own conclusions about what he was saying.

The atmosphere of expectation in the church suggested that others too were attending with the same intention.

`Today,' Duncomb said, `I begin with a word, a word familiar to those of you who have Greek, and that word is episcopé. You will recognise that from this word episcopé we derive our words episcopacy, episcopal, meaning to do with Bishops. But the word has far wider connotations than this, wider and yet simpler.

`It is the root of the word which those godly men who translated the scriptures rendered in some places as "visit". You may think of a visit as of someone just calling round for a chat. However, episcopé implies a visit with a purpose. '

He spoke of Moses visiting the Hebrew slaves to see how they fared, of the apostle Paul visiting scattered congregations to encourage them, of the greatest of all such visits when God visited mankind in the person of Jesus.

`You will see that all these visits had a purpose. They are not just social calls; they are to nurture, to encourage, to save.

`And so we come to the word `episkopos', the Bishop or overseer or superintendent. You will no doubt have heard that a petition was brought to the Houses of Parliament, a petition asking that Bishops be abolished. We need to think carefully about this matter. Do we sense the care, the spiritual welfare, that we might expect of a Bishop? Does the wealth and power and worldly position that now accompany the office of Bishop, do these accord with what the scriptures prescribe? Would such leadership really be better undertaken by elders, appointed by the local church?'

`Presbyterian!' someone shouted.

`Calvinist!' came another voice. `Go back to Geneva!'

Duncomb raised his hand. `Allow me to continue. I am simply asking you to consider. We want the best for our church, for our people. Should we not work towards that best? We read that bishops, elders, should tend the flock of God "not for shameful gain but eagerly, and, (mark this) not as domineering over those in their charge but being examples to the flock."

`Not as domineering. Recall the last episcopal visitation and the ceremonial imposed upon you. Is this a right use of authority?'

`Shame!' a shout interrupted him. `Shame on you!' and Hermann Shepheard stepped out into the aisle.

Duncomb continued, ignoring him. `How do you view the worldly wealth that is the privilege of Bishops? Yes, my Lord Bishop has repaired churches out of his own pocket, but that pocket is deep. Many of you are the Bishop's tenants. We may ask, should a Bishop be also a landlord? Should he indeed be concerned too in matters of state?'

`You'll destroy the lot of us!' Another voice, a rough voice from the south aisle. `You and your lousy petitions!'

`Nay friend, it is not my petition, but it is a matter we need to consider. It may be argued that clerics in the seat of government render that government righteous. But on the other hand you have read that no man can serve two masters.'

`How dare you!' Shepheard was scurrying up the aisle. `How dare you!' his voice beginning to squeak. `How dare you imply misconduct?' He shook his fist under Duncomb's face.

Suddenly Abe Trussler erupted from the side aisle, shouting again `You'll destroy the lot of us,' his voice rougher than ever. `Presbyterian rubbish!'

He grabbed Duncomb's arm. Shepheard seized the notes out of his hand and threw them aside. Pushing and shoving the two of them tried to drag him away. All over the church people called out, shouted for one or the other.

In an instant Jacob was on his feet, almost leaping out in front of the men. Abigail looked for her mother's restraining hand but then, no Phoebe.

`"Dare" did you say? Dare?' he said, not shouting but in a ringing voice that everyone could hear. `How do you dare to disrupt a properly authorised meeting?'

`Out of my way!' Shepheard squealed.

`Hypocrite! Whoremonger!' Trussler shouted.

Jacob reeled back, his face white and fierce. Then he cried `Where's the constable?' scanning the noisy audience. `The constable, where's the constable?' people echoed. From somewhere, Will Chuter came forward.

`The Bailiffs' clerk!' Jacob sounded ill-pleased. `You can arrest as well as any I suppose.'

`Come with me Sir or I'll never restrain them.'

At that others came forward to take hold of Abe and the curate, crowding out of the door with Will and Jacob and off to the magistrate. Argument sounded all over the church as people milled about.

Duncomb shook out his coat and ran a hand two or three times over his head. He walked back towards the choir steps, searching the floor for his notes but they were hopelessly scattered. He turned to face the people, and one by one their attention returned to him and the noise subsided. After a while he spoke.

`Forgive me,' he said, and then paused a long time, smoothing his hand over his head again and again. At last he said, `We live in a time when many questions are being asked. You have every right to conclude that you prefer things to stay as they are. Just because the status quo is being questioned does not mean that it has to be changed. If you feel that society as it is now is right and just, so be it. But let me leave you with two thoughts.

`First, every citizen ought to know what is being said and debated if he is to make right judgments. And secondly, a society that calls itself Christian ought to be aware of what Christ and his earliest followers taught us as of God.

`And now, let us pray.'

The hush was tangible as he prayed, slowly and hesitantly yet restoring calm. Such was the sense of peace after the storm that Abigail stayed quite still, afraid lest it be broken. And broken it was. The sound of talk began to rise steadily all around her. Then the few who held strongly to one opinion or another raised their voices, gathering the like-minded around them, arguments going hammer and tongs.

Her feelings were in turmoil as she walked home. That people should get so angry about questions of religion....and what did Abe Trussler mean by calling her father a whoremonger? She began to feel angry herself.

The whole day became angry. Returning late after dealing with the curate, Abe Trussler and the law, Jacob ate a hunk of bread and a chunk of cheese standing up in the bakeroom, his eyes watching the yard while his free hand tapped his thigh impatiently. Swallowing the last mouthful he seized one of the jugs always kept full from the well, sloshed some water into a tankard and gulped it down. He was already out through the door as he wiped his mouth on the back of his hand.

`Thomas!' his ringing voice commanded.

Tom looked up from the pit he had been told to fill and mix. `Sir?'

Jacob peered into the pit. `Waste of time stirring that any more. Can't you see it's already mixed enough?'

Tom looked down at the pungent liquid, not answering.

`Well?'

`Yes.'

`What do you mean, "Yes"? Is it or isn't it properly mixed?'

`I guess it is.'

`Guess!' Jacob snorted. He turned towards the fleshing shed. `Time I saw you rounding a hide. Othen's dissatisfied,' and he strode off.

Tom propped up the mixing pole, heavy hearted, though the term `rounding' always amused him since it referred to making a hide rectangular, not round. He followed his father. However much he dreaded demonstrating his ham-fisted efforts to him he dared not dawdle.

`Which knife?' was Jacob's first question.

As an apprentice Tom did not have any knives of his own but a set of communal knives was laid out on a shelf. No problem there. He reached without hesitation for the strong blade. He was taking it over to the bench when he remembered `edge' just as Jacob barked out `Edge?' He ran his finger along the blade. `I think it's sharp' he said.

Jacob took it and felt it. `Should have been sharpened before it was put back. (Another beating for someone, Tom thought.) Go on now, razor sharp.'

An oil stone sat permanently on the shelf. Tom approached it gingerly. To him getting an edge on a knife was a matter of luck. Sometimes suddenly it was there, but other times all his efforts only blunted the blade. This was one of those other times. Jacob stood by, tapping his hand on his leg, while Tom rubbed and tested, rubbed and tested.

`Give it to me!' Jacob ordered. `Lord! What a mess! I'd not have believed it possible. Now watch!'

It's no use me watching, Tom thought, I've watched and watched. It doesn't work for me. All the same he watched, his attitude attentive, his mind still not understanding how to do it, why it went wrong; thoughts wandering towards the next task to be demanded of him, the dreaded rounding.

Satisfied at last with the blade Jacob held the knife out to him.

The big damp hide lay on a wide table. He had to fold it in half exactly down the line of the backbone, and at this he succeeded. Then with his fingers he tried to feel along the sides where the beast's belly had been and the hide was thinner. There should be a definite place where the substance reduced. He felt, and he hoped, but he knew that again he had guessed. He picked up the knife and held his breath.

`Breathe, boy!' Jacob ordered. `You've no control if you don't breathe! Your hand is tense.'

Tom took a breath, but concentration had hold of all his muscles.

He reached forward to make the required single cut the length of the hide. It went wildly wrong. Only one layer severed, not both. The knife slewed. The cut wobbled. He panicked and dropped the knife.

Jacob picked it up. `Small wonder Othen despairs of you. How long have you been apprenticed? Will you never learn?'

Tom looked across the bench at him, not feeling brave. He muttered `I don't think I will.'

Jacob ignored him.

`Two years at my expense and you've learnt nothing. Can't tell when brine is mixed, can't scud a hide without damage, can't round one either. You're useless. You'll never make a tanner.'

Something stirred in Tom and he almost shouted `I don't want to be a tanner!'

A moment's total silence. Then Jacob through clenched jaws; `What did you say?'

`I said (did he really dare?) I don't want to be a tanner.'

`You'll honour your father and do as you're told. There's many would be grateful for training in an honourable trade. Not that I want gratitude. I want effort, and attention, and proper work.'

`I'm no use at it,' Tom said.

`Don't argue with me.' Jacob was brandishing the knife. `Nothing but argument all day.'

`Father, I'm only saying...'

`I will not have you answering back! Get out!'

`Father...'

`Get out I say! Before I give you a beating!'

Tom edged round the table, watching the knife. Did Jacob realise it was not a cane he was holding? To be beaten with a knife! Eyes never leaving its blade he reached the door, and ran for it.

Only the bakeroom seemed safe. He burst in on the girls who were sitting on stools around two barrels, sorting walnuts.

`We heard shouting,' Abigail said.

Tom stared at them, short of breath.

`Seems like it's been shouting all day,' said Hannah, throwing some bad nuts into a bucket

`Mercy on us!' Mary exclaimed. `You looks as if you'd seen a ghost!'

Tom's knees felt weak and he was shaking. It was a relief to laugh.

'Substantial ghost! Father's in a terrible temper.'

'With you?'

He nodded, and suddenly he had to sit down.

`What's he angry about?' Abigail said.

`I'm too ham fisted. I messed up a hide.'

`And he shouted for that?'

`I said,' Tom lowered his voice, `I don't want to be a tanner.'

`Oh Tom!' Hannah rubbed some nuts between her hands to shake off bits of husk. `That's almost sacrilege to Father.'

`What do you suppose he'll do?' Abigail said.

`I wish Mother were here' Hannah sighed. `She's been too long away.'

Tom scratched his ear thoughtfully. `I could go out to Spreakley and be back before dark if I went straight away, and discover what's the news.'

`Would Father let you?' Abigail was wide eyed.

`Perhaps if you asked him, or Hannah did.'

The sisters looked at each other.

`Do you dare, Abi?'

Abigail looked from brother to sister and then said, `Yes, I'll try. Where is he?'

`In the fleshing shed, at least he was.'

She gathered her apron corners to collect the bits of nuts scattered in her lap and went round the chimney stack to tip them into the Hall hearth.

The yard seemed oddly still as if everyone and everything was holding its breath. She looked cautiously round the open shed door. Jacob was sitting on a block of wood, his head held in one hand and the rounding knife in the other. He did not move as she tiptoed in. `Father....'

He looked up. `Mmm?' hardly seeming to see her.

`Father, we all miss Mother... we've had no news... would you allow Tom to walk over to Spreakley and find out? '

`Tom!' Jacob interrupted her. `Tom! Let him see what his mother can make of him. But no tomfoolery with that horse. He can go on his own two feet.'

Suddenly daring Abigail asked `Might I go too?'

Jacob looked at her as if seeing her for the first time. `You? You're not accustomed to walking any distance.'

`Oh but I can! And perhaps I can aid Mother.'

Jacob shrugged, as if losing interest. His eye caught the knife still in his hand and he blinked at it. `Go then!' standing up and replacing the knife on its shelf. `Just go, the pair of you.'

Grandfather

Tom walked so fast that Abigail had hardly breath to keep up. Clasping her shawl around her with one hand she hastened after him, then finding she needed to swing both arms she stopped and knotted the shawl corners on her chest, and had to run to catch up with him. The water-worn track wound up, up, up, the hedges sparsely leafed above steep banks. Past Searles' farm, past fields winter-brown or tired green until beyond the brow of the hill the sandy road plunged steeply down.

Three ridges, two streams, through heath land with makeshift hovels and attempts at cultivation amid scattered scrub oaks and bracken flattened by rain; cows and sheep grazing among sparse clumps of grass, wild ponies which wheeled and stampeded away, until at last they swung round above the green river valley overlooked by Spreakley Farm.

The oak framed walls of the farmhouse in-filled with brick had an ancient warmth to them. One bay window reaching up into the gable added a touch of grandeur. Beyond the house Abigail glimpsed a great barn and ironstone farm buildings from which came sounds of cows and pigs.

Tom knocked on the heavy oak door calling `Anyone at home?' It was opened in a flurry by Madge the housekeeper.

`Lordy! If it isn't young Mannory and his sister!' Then calling back into the house `Mistress Mannory! 'T'is your son and daughter!'

Phoebe bustled round the chimney breast, wide-eyed.

`Tom! Abigail! Dear ones! Come inside out of the cold. But what has brought you? Have you heard?'

`We've heard nothing, nothing at all. That's why we've come,' Tom said.

`Master Harding,' Madge said. `He died this morning.'

Mother and children stared at each other for a long moment.

`Uncle John?' Tom asked.

Phoebe nodded. `My brother John.' She put an arm around each of them and steered them into the kitchen living room. `I am astonished that you should choose to come today.'

`We're at sixes and sevens at home,' Abigail said. `Father..' but Tom caught her eye and shook his head.

`How was it with Uncle John?' he asked.

Phoebe stood between them in front of the low fire. `He just faded away. He was so thin and weak, it was a wonder he lived as long as he did.'

A slight noise from the dim corner beside the fireplace made them all turn. `Father!' Phoebe said, `Forgive me. I am so astonished to see them. Here are Thomas and Abigail, come from Farnham this very afternoon.'

Tom shook the hand of a very old man sitting in a deep wooden chair. Abigail dropped a little curtsy but he did not look at her.

`Take his hand, Abi,' her mother prompted. `He has not seen you.'

The hand was sinewy with knobbled joints, and looking in his face she saw that his eyes were palely veiled, almost opaque. `Grandfather,' she murmured, awed.

They sat down then and re-worked the manner of John senior's death, though there was little enough to the story. Madge brought ale and some cake.

'To have reached an age,' the old man said at one point, `when only my grandson is left.'

`How is Cousin John?' Abigail asked.

`Distraught. Strangely so, since we have all had weeks to prepare for this death. I will seek him in a little while. It may help him to see you.'

Suddenly Tom started up. `Mother! Father is expecting us back before dark, and it's almost dusk now! We'll have to set out at once.'

Phoebe looked at him, considering. `I think I shall write a note to your father, and you can take it later once the moon is well up. It's a clear night and the moon not far off full. Abigail, you had best stay here tonight at least. If the coffin is ready we will bury him tomorrow, and then you and I can go back together in a day or so.'

She stood up, smoothing her apron. `I will write in the farm office, and send John to you.'

They heard her call for John and heard her say `Your cousins are here.' He came quickly looking eager, but on seeing them his faced dropped. `Is Hannah not with you?'

`We came on an impulse,' Abigail told him, `because we had had no news. Mother has been here several weeks now, and we wondered....'

`He lived longer than anyone expected. My aunt's care...' John broke off. He sat down heavily, leaning his elbows on his wide knees and staring into the fire. After a while he looked up, first at one and then at the other though it was Abigail he addressed

`Could you speak for me?'

`Speak for you?'

`With your father.'

`What should we speak to him about?'

`About? About my marrying Hannah.'

`Ask Father if you can marry Hannah?' Abigail repeated stupidly.

`Yes.'

`What, now?'

`When you're back home.'

`But your father has only just died. Everyone is mourning him.'

`Don't you think I know?' John's tone was anguished. `I need her all the more because of that.'

`Have you spoken to Mother?' Tom asked.

`Not while... how could I?... No, I haven't.'

`We can't speak for you,' Tom said. `You'll need to talk with my father.'

`But I can't leave the farm now! There'll be the probate to see to, besides minding the farm and everyone.'

`I suppose,' Abigail said gently, `you could write him a letter.'

John looked at her as if she were the vehicle of a revelation.

`Why! Yes! I could do that!'

`Mother's in the office now writing to our father.'

`I'll dip into her ink well.'

John stirred his heavy limbs and lumbered out of the room.

`He's full of worries,' the old man said. `Mind, he's been running the place for months back, but now it's all his own.'

`I expect you advise him,' Abigail asked.

`O aye, but you can't tell the state of a crop if you can't see it. I'm useless now.' Then he turned towards her. `Can you read, child?'

`Yes, Sir. Mother taught me.'

`Then pray fetch the Bible from that shelf yonder, and read me a psalm. Light a rush from the fire if you can't see - they are in a tray by the hearth.'

Several books stood beside the big Bible. She raised the rush light close to inspect the titles. Lily's Grammar! Tom used that, they had a copy of it at the Grammar School.

`Grandfather,' settling herself down beside him, `the Latin books there...?'

`They belonged to my brother. You'll have heard of him.'

`Not to my knowledge,' Abigail said.

`He was a John Harding too, much older than I. A right scholar, a school man. He was one of those translated the Bible you're holding there.'

`Translated it from Latin?'

`From Latin and Greek and Hebrew. Those scholars converse in Latin.'

`Did he translate all this?' turning the great volume in her hands.

`Nay, just the Prophets and Lamentations.' He chuckled a little. `Mind you, there's plenty of those.'

`What, all by himself?'

`It was a group of them, Oxford men, called themselves a class, did it together. Now what about my psalm?'

`I just wondered,' Abigail said, `If I might look in those books. I learnt a little Latin looking over my brother's school work.'

Tom laughed. `More than I ever did.'

`You certainly may when there's light enough. But now, Psalm ninety two if you please.'

The print was very black on the mottled paper, and the flame of the rush light flickered as Abigail turned the pages, searching first for the book of Psalms and then for number XCII.

Oddly enough, it was a song of praise and thanks. When she had finished Grandfather reached out a hand towards her. `Read the last verse again, the last bit.'

`"To show that the Lord is upright; he is my rock, and there is no unrighteousness in him."'

`"The Lord gives and the Lord takes away. Blessed be the name of the Lord." Job said that, child, though I don't recall where. Well, he's taken my son.'

They fell silent.

At last Phoebe returned, carrying a sealed letter. `The moon's well up,' she said to Tom. `You'll be able to see your way home, and your father may be anxious.' (Tom and Abigail exchanged a glance.) `Just go up and pay your last respects to your Uncle. Abigail too. I'll show you where.' She took them upstairs and left them in the bed chamber.

Abigail quailed at having to look at this dead relative. She stood hesitating just inside the door. Then Tom stepped forward to the bedside and she had to follow.

There he lay, her uncle, in the great bed in which he had slept all his married life, the thin pale vestige of a man, no more than a shell. Her memory of the only other death that she had glimpsed, the death of Hal's mother, was full of horror and blood, but here was a still emptiness. She felt oddly reassured by this sense of an empty shell, the person gone. So this was death, a vanishing.

They went downstairs silently, met by John who caught Tom's arm. `Here's my note' he said gruffly.

Tom left, bearing the two letters.

Tanyard House was silent when Tom reached it after his moonlit walk. Although he crept upstairs Jacob heard him and emerged from his room and took the letters. In the morning Jacob spoke to no one, not to Tom, not to Hannah, and to the men only when he had to. Tom tried to make himself inconspicuous, doing exactly what he was told, saying little.

`It's all my fault,' Tom said to Hannah, `For answering him back.'

`It wasn't just you.' Hannah said. `He was angry with the curate.'

`Come to think of it, he's been getting angrier ever since Mother went to Spreakley.'

`Is she coming back soon? How are they there?'

`I guess they need her as much as we do, or more. John...'

`Yes, John. How is he?'

`I brought two letters for Father.'

`Why two?'

`One from her and...one from John.'

Hannah looked down. `I'd give a lot to know what those letters say.'

A second silent day began, silent except that Jacob started sorting out a corner where rubbish and discarded objects had accumulated, the men scurrying round him rescuing treasures and disposing of trash. A litter of stuff lay all around the floor while he barked commands.

The onslaught was such that the dogs' barking went un-heeded until Robert Bicknell walked quietly into the shed. He stood in the entrance watching for a few moments, then with a smile he said a general `Good morning'.

Jacob turned towards him, and stopped.

`Whatever you're doing,' Bicknell said, `can the men finish it off while you and I have a word together?'

Jacob straightened his back and brushed his hands on his leather apron. `Othen, see to it,' he said, and led the way up to his office. They sat down, facing each other, every line of Jacob's body taut.

`I thought perhaps I'd see you after the business at the lecture,' Bicknell said.

`Other things happened here.'

`Other things have happened with that business too. It begins to look like a hornet's nest.'

Jacob said nothing.

'After you arrested Shepheard, opinions were flying all over the church, people taking sides, getting vehement. It seemed to polarise opinion. Half of it I'd say is to do with personalities, not principles; there are many who mislike the curate. All the same, whatever the cause, I'd hate to see the town split as a result between popish and protestant.'

‘Are you saying I shouldn't have pulled Shepheard in?'

`Maybe it was unwise.'

`He behaved unpardonably. Manhandling the lecturer...'

`I admit it did go beyond normal heckling.'

`Heckling! The man was violent. And that rogue Trussler too.'

`Shepheard has had a day in gaol now, and - well, I have to tell you he's been to Master Vernon in great distress.'

`Hm.'

`For him to conduct worship this Sunday after what's happened...'

`Whose side are you taking? You've always had a high regard for Duncomb.'

`I still have. I just wanted you to know...'

`Do you imagine I can do anything about it now?'

`Jacob.' Robert's tone was conciliatory. `I didn't come here to argue. Are you still angry with him, or have you other matters troubling you?'

A long silence. Eventually Jacob reached into a pocket and pulled out a crumpled letter. `Read this.'

Robert read and looked up with the hint of a twinkle in his eye. `It's no more than I'd have expected.' He re-read the letter. `I told you months ago that Hannah needed an eye kept on her. It's common knowledge that she and John are sweethearts.'

Jacob made an explosive sound. `They're children!'

`Not any more, my friend.'

`And he hasn't the courtesy to come in person, nor the delicacy to see his father into his grave first.'

`Have you replied to his letter?'

`Indeed I have not.'

Robert got to his feet and wandered around the little office, pausing to gaze out of the window before he sat down again.

`I remember being in an agony of anxiety when I was courting Elizabeth. There are so few certainties at that stage. I feel for young John.'

There was a long pause, Robert not pressing his point. Then Jacob said `I need to write to Phoebe, but I lack a messenger.'

`Why, I believe I have the answer to that!' Robert said. `You remember Ralph Attfield?'

`I'd hardly forget him. Sold me the cob that only Hal can catch.'

`The very man. He's on his way to effect some deal yonder in Sussex and stables his horses with me over the Sabbath. He could surely carry a letter to Spreakley on his way."

Jacob assembled paper and ink on his table and Robert stood up to go.

`Be merciful,' he said.

All Frensham mourned John's father, following the coffin down to the church and back to the farmhouse.

Grandfather Harding, too old to make the walk, had stationed himself near the door and greeted everyone as they came in. Aware of his blindness most of the guests identified themselves to him, and Abigail standing by saw how he had a gracious word for each, greetings fleshed out with up-to-date awareness of their families and circumstances.

When the last had crowded into the kitchen for food, he reached for Abigail's hand. `I am weary, child. Take me to my chair if you would. I will eat a little there.'

She fetched a plate of victuals for him and one for herself, and pulled a stool up beside him. `There's ham on a round of bread,' she said, `and a slice of pie, and an apple.'

`Go on with you, I can't eat an apple. I've hardly teeth enough for the meat.'

He felt for the bread and took a bite.

`Phoebe always was a good cook. And you, child, you're a good lass, looking to your old grandpa.' He ate a little more. `When this is all over, we'll do some Latin together.'

`But the books...' Abigail hesitated to say that he couldn't see to read them.

`You'll read the books. I'll check how you go.'

`You know Latin then?'

`I can remember enough to start you going. "Amo, amas, I love a lass...".' He chuckled. `Whatever else is decrepit, the memory is still intact.'

And so it was while she was sitting on the same stool on the Monday morning writing Latin exercises on a slate with Grandfather Harding snoozing beside her that she heard a deep brown voice with a crackle in it out in the yard. Her heart leapt. Surely only one man had such a distinctive voice. But could it truly be he out here at Spreakley?

She strained her ears, hearing John's hearty greeting, hearing snatches of voices among horses' hooves and evident movement. The sounds receded. She told herself to re-apply herself to her Latin but all she could think of was the voice, and the man who owned it. Then suddenly the house door opened and John and Ralph Attfield were coming into the great kitchen.

`Bicknell told me of your father's death,' Ralph was saying. `I'm right sorry to hear of it.'

`Thank 'e, thank 'e,' John said. `I confess I am more knocked by it than I ever expected. We realised weeks ago that he was dying.'

`It's a shock whenever it comes' Ralph said. `Like you, I've lost both my parents, in fact I'm all the family I have.'

`Well in that case I'm more fortunate than you. Come over and greet my grandfather, if he's awake.'

Abigail stood up to allow them room, clutching the slate as she had the chicken carcass that first time she had seen Ralph. Grandfather was sound asleep and John stood uncertain what to do.

`Why!' Ralph exclaimed, `If it isn't the chicken plucking maiden!'

Abigail bobbed a curtsy, blushing.

Ralph turned to John. `I have a letter to give to Mistress Mannory, and I believe there is one for you as well.' He took them out of his leather pouch. `Shall I give them both to you? I would like to reach Midhurst before dark. Or is Mistress Mannory about?'

`You could give them to me... but I'd best seek her - or will you take some refreshment?' John looked ready to grab the letters.

`I drank some water in the yard, thank'e. If it is not impolite I would prefer to make no more delay.' He handed the letters to John and took his leave.

As soon as he had gone John, oblivious of everything but his letter, broke the seal and read it quickly. Then he collapsed onto a stool and read it again. He looked across the hearth at Abigail.

`This is no more than formal condolences - and a reprimand,' he said.

Harry

Phoebe's lips twitched a smile as she read her own letter later on. She glanced through it a second time. `Your father is urgent that we should return home,' she said to Abigail. 'We'll go on Thursday, with those who are going in to market.'

`In that case,' John boomed, his disheartened slump suddenly changing, `I shall send our cart. It is high time we sent to market, and I'll put in some provisions for you.'

`That's good of you, nephew.'

`A small thank offering for all that you have done for us. I will go and arrange it.'

Phoebe too had things to arrange, which left Abigail beside her grandfather. The Latin grammar on her lap mocked her with disappointment that her studies should be so abruptly ended.

`Are you still there, child?' the old man asked.

`Yes, grandfather, I'm still here.'

`Such a flurry of persons. I am a little confused.'

`Mother and I have to return home on Thursday.'

`And we were planning a long period of study,' he chuckled, `scholard that you are.'

`Do you think,' Abigail hesitated, `I could manage on my own?'

`You're welcome to take the book with you, my dear. And look on the shelf. There used to be an old Latin missal. You could practise translating the Psalms.'

Her mother woke her on Thursday before dawn. Just a thin strip of pale grey showed between the horizon and a blanket of cloud. Down in the yard a horse stood hitched to the farm cart. Half a dozen young pigs were squealing under a net in the back of it while men loaded sacks towards the front. Ricky, the little farm carter, held a lantern for them. Its light caught the smallpox craters on his face and swung as he moved anxiously about ordering the balance of weight in the cart.

Phoebe embraced John, Abigail submitted to a dutiful embrace from him, and they climbed into the cart.

Once they had left the cluster of cottages around Spreakley an eerie quietness enveloped them. Ricky was jumpy, peering left and right.

`It's them vagrants,' he said. `Got no work, just wander the roads. You never knows...'

`Lord, protect us,' Phoebe said cheerfully. `I just hope the rain holds off.'

The way began to rise. `Would you be good enough to walk this last steep bit?' Ricky asked as the horse struggled, the wheels slipping in the sandy ruts. He talked as he too walked, leading the horse. `It'll be Papists next. There's many a secret Papist, and any time they could break out.'

`Break out from where?' Phoebe asked.

`Why, like in Ireland. You must have heard - all rose up and killed the Protestants, hung whole families from trees. Slit open pregnant women they do, and roast babies on their spears - ah! 't'is terrible, terrible.'

`Where do you hear all this horror?' Phoebe sounded reluctant to believe him.

`The pamphlets are full of it.'

`No pamphlets have come our way.'

`Oh, they're the new thing. Farm carpenter gets them and reads them out to us all. 'T'is dangerous times we live in,' and he started peering left and right again. They topped the ridge and he applied the brakes as they began the long descent. `I'd be glad if you'd keep walking,' he said.

Abigail kept a hand on the cart which seemed like an ark of safety in this wild heathland. Somewhere deep behind the clouds the sun must be up, for just enough light was penetrating to reveal shapes and lumps among the heather and gorse.

A grey shape, like a man crouching. Abigail stared, stumbling behind the cart. There was another in that clump of trees! She held her breath - it moved! It could be an ambush. Any minute now!

She stopped, terrified.

The shape lifted a heavy head. She heard the steady chomp chomp of a cow chewing the cud.

Still shaking with fear and feeling foolish with it, she ran to catch up the cart.

`Never sure of The Bourne,' Ricky muttered, urging the horse up the next, gentler, incline. `Bad lot what squats hereabouts.'

Now it was the scattered cots that threatened to erupt with malefactors. Occasional windows glimmered where a fire was being kindled. Somehow she knew that people were moving about, invisibly. More cows? Robbers?

Suddenly she held her breath, and listened. A steady pounding, muffled by sand and distance. Something was coming down the hill behind them, fast.

`There's a horse coming!' she gasped.

`Whoa!' Ricky called. They stopped, straining their ears.

`Someone in a hurry,' Phoebe said.

The sound came nearer, cantering. A skilled rider on a sure-footed horse. Ricky was trembling. `There'd not be a highwayman on this track,' Phoebe said, but he was transfixed with fear. Then the rider was beside them, reining in and sweeping off his hat.

`Good morning to you!' he said. `I'm glad I've caught up with you!'

`Mr Attfield!' Phoebe cried.

`My apologies if I alarmed you. I had no means of warning you.'

`How is it you're here,' Phoebe asked, `descending like an angel from heaven?'

`An apocalyptic horseman!' Ralph gave a deep laugh. `I called at Spreakley in case you had letters that I could deliver, and learnt that you had already set out.'

`You had us all scared.'

`Allow me to escort you. Protect you from the ruffians of the Bourne.'

As they started to move off Abigail said, `Tom never mentioned ruffians when we walked this way last week.'

Ralph looked at her thoughtfully. What a child she seemed! A plucker of chickens and a spinner of yarn. 'Ah!' he said.

They were descending steeply now, walking beside the cart, Ralph high above them on his beautiful great horse. Only one more valley bottom and they were up the last steep climb.

`The road is easier from here,' Phoebe said to Ricky at the top, `and I am weary. I'll perch beside the pigs the rest of the way.' Ricky halted the cart for her to climb in and Ralph stopped beside her. It was light now, all mystery banished. Abigail went ahead down the sunken track. Rounding a corner she heard a shout from below.

`Tom!' She lifted her skirt and started to run. `Hal!'

Thomas caught her and swung her round like he used to do when they were children. `Father sent us out to look for you.' Hal stood watching.

Last week with all its anger came flooding back to her. `Tom, how is it with Father?'

`It's about the first time he's spoken to me. He seemed anxious about your arrival - he's been up for hours.'

`Here's Tom!' she called as the cart came into view.

`Attfield!' Tom exclaimed. `How do you come to be of the party?'

`Just an escort,' Ralph said, reaching down to shake his hand. `I was on my way from a deal in Midhurst... yes, I made an early start, and my horse is fast. Where's your horse then?'

`More like Hal's horse if you ask me. She doesn't let herself to be caught by anyone but him.'

Ralph looked at Hal who was inspecting his horse, a bay stallion with dark points, very handsome.

`What do you think of him?' he asked as if Hal were a fellow horseman and not a little boy.

`Is he a good goer?'

`There's a lad!' Ralph laughed. `Don't go on looks alone - and you'll admit he's handsome. Yes, he's a stalwart.'

He turned to Phoebe. `Well, you're in good hands now. I'll take my leave,' and he eased his horse into a trot.

They had no sooner pulled into the Tanyard than the yard filled with people, tanners pausing in their work, Hannah and Mary rushing out of the house, Jacob leaping down his outside stair. He went straight to Phoebe, helping her down as if she were the only person there, just nodding a brief `Good morning' to Ricky. She reached for her bundle out of the cart, but he quickly took it from her. Then with his other hand at her waist he steered her into the house.

Hannah stood a moment holding a big round cheese in its cloth wrapping. `Is there anything from John?' she asked.

`Just the victuals,' Abigail said.

`You know what I mean, Abi. No note or anything?'

Abigail shook her head. `Sorry.' She wandered into the house behind her sister, wondering what she should be doing, out of step. She went upstairs to find a clean shift. Then she sat on the side of the bed and tried to make out some of the words in the Latin missal.

`Abi!' Hannah called up the stairs. "We're off to market. See you at the lecture.'

There the atmosphere was subdued. Mr Duncomb preached on the need for good works, Hermann Shepheard was not in evidence, nor Abe Trussler, and Abigail felt she did not have to pay much attention. As soon as it was over Joan came and caught her hand. `Come back with me and tell me all the news!'

For once it was she who had news to tell. They sat together in the main room of Timber Hall with the children in and out and sometimes interrupting. Elizabeth Bicknell sat with them, nursing the latest baby.

Abigail told of her Uncle's death and funeral.. She told of her grandfather, and discovering the Latin books. 'So I have the means to study Latin,' she said, pleasure in her voice, and only then asked `What has been happening here?'

`All the talk is of the curate, the Reverend Shepheard,' Elizabeth said. `Who'd have thought he'd have it in him to go for the lecturer like he did? Quite a to-do it was, and my good man sees the whole matter rumbling on through the town.'

`He conducted worship on Sunday,' Joan said.

`We reckon all sorts of folk were there who normally risk fines for non-attendance, there just out of curiosity,' Elizabeth said.

`I wonder how he felt,' Abigail said.

`Joan can tell you that better than anyone, for it seems she is his confidante, isn't that so daughter?'

Joan ignored her question saying to Abigail, `Did you know he was arrested along with Abe Trussler? A night in gaol for both of them!'

Elizabeth lifted the baby to her shoulder to rub its back. `Trussler is often in trouble of one sort or another, or should I say making trouble, but the curate is a gentleman whatever your opinion of him, and prominent in the town. He was humiliated. He was that distressed, Joan had to comfort him didn't you Joan?'

Abigail looked at Joan who made a face in return. Elizabeth put the baby to her other breast.

`Mother!' a young Bicknell called from the doorway. `Young Mr Vernon is here.'

`Oh Joan, you and Abigail entertain him while the babe finishes feeding.' She hurried out another way. `Ask him to come in Billie.'

Joan presented Abigail to him, a slight young man with a mop of dark hair, elegantly dressed in a well cut velvet jerkin set off by a broad lace collar. She bobbed a curtsy.

`Pray take a chair and tell us all the latest news,' Joan said. `Is there any news yet other than Hermann Shepheard?'

`You cannot dismiss him as not newsworthy,' Harry Vernon said gravely. `Indeed I fear it is but a symptom of a growing conflict. I wish there were some way for King and Parliament to agree instead of this threat of war.'

`War?' Joan exclaimed. `But the King and all that are a long way from here, up in London.'

`We're scarcely a day's ride from London,' Harry said.

`Oh well.' Joan shrugged. `Abigail has just returned from Spreakley.'

Harry Vernon looked baffled. `Spreakley?'

`The farm at Frensham where my mother's family lives, all the Harding cousins.'

`Ah yes, the Hardings. Harding was an Oxford man I believe.'

`Oh, the scholar, yes. My grandfather says Dr Harding translated some of the Bible out of Latin,' Abigail said.

`So that's where you get it from!' There was an edge to Joan's voice. She turned to Harry. `Would you believe it, Abigail is trying to learn Latin.'

Harry did not reply at once. Then he said `And why not?'

Seeing Joan silenced Abigail rushed to the rescue. `Cousin John's carter who brought us home told us of terrible things in Ireland, he's read of them in some pamphlet, whole families being slaughtered by the Papists, and he was frightened the same might happen in England, he was ever so jumpy as we came through the heathland....' She ran out of breath.

`Where's Ireland?' Joan asked.

`An island to the west,' Harry looked surprised at her ignorance. `Our people colonised it. One can only hope that the reports are exaggerated.'

`They sounded horrible, horrible,' Abigail said.

`An Army is being raised to deal with it,' Harry began complacently, but then his tone changed. `It's not that easy though. The question of funding, and who is going to lead the Army. Some want to wrest control from the King. It could easily lead to war here in England. Farnham Castle may have to be garrisoned.'

Abigail looked at him aghast. `What, here in Farnham?'

`Garrisoned?' Joan said.

`A small group of militia probably, to keep an eye on things.'

`So there is some danger here? I mean, from Papists or rebels?' Abigail said.

`Each side would want to secure Farnham against the other. Important roads converge here.'

`Militia, that could be fun,' Joan said. Abruptly she changed the subject to one nearer herself. `Tell me, Mr Vernon, have you been writing any more poetry?'

`I've.. no.'

`You have yet to read some to me.'

`I did read some poetry to you and your parents.'

`But that was not your own. It was about a garden.'

`So you remembered! Andrew Marvell. Your father admires the garden that my father is creating.'

`Love poems are the best.' Joan gave her shoulders a little toss.

Elizabeth bustled in. `Forgive me for deserting you. May I offer you some refreshment? My husband will soon be home.'

Harry declined refreshment, declined waiting for Mr. Bicknell, and took his leave.

`Such a gentleman!' Elizabeth exclaimed. `I wonder why he called? Maybe he finds time heavy on his hands after his student days in Oxford. A young gentleman must be quite stuck for occupation, his father busy with his properties, and no particular part to play in local affairs. How glad I am that our boys will have a trade! Yet Mr Bicknell is becoming such a man of property that maybe they will fancy themselves as gentlemen and never dirty their hands. Father loves his hops though, and the business of the town. Now your father Abigail keeps aloof from town affairs does he not?'

Aloof, Abigail thought, does that describe my father? I don't really know about what concerns him. Tanning, and godly living, and to be in control? Perhaps he is aloof and that is why I'm uncertain how to reply.

Elizabeth however was not waiting for a reply. `Now Joan dear, if your chat with Abigail has come to an end, be so good as to help in the kitchen with stoning raisins and dried plums for tomorrow's pudding, and I expect Abigail you will be wanting to get along home.'

`Back to her Latin,' Joan said.

Newsbooks

The second week in January 1642 Jacob sent Thomas to the shambles with the horse and cart. Although Thomas kept the thought to himself, he had noticed that lately his father directed him to use the horse more than before. He had also noticed that he was becoming on better terms with the horse. She did not so often humiliate him by playing hard to catch, and with practice he harnessed her more quickly which perhaps ameliorated Jacob's habitual im-patience. Hal seldom accompanied him for nowadays he was expected to spend his time endlessly shredding oak bark and feeding it into the mill which showered him with dust, to make the tanning liquor. Any spare moment he was round at Vernon's with Sam in the stables.

'On your way back,' Jacob had added, 'Call at the Bush for any mail.'

An east wind whipped chill across the meadows as Tom left the shelter of the shambles. He rounded the corner to the Bush Inn, his hand holding the reins already stiff with cold. By contrast the Bush exuded warmth and the nose-tingling smell of mulled ale. Oh! how welcome a swig of that would be, but as an apprentice he was forbidden to drink in an ale house. Moreover he had only the money from Jacob to pay for the package, addressed to Jacob Mannory, which the publican now handed him.

After the evening meal and the Bible reading Jacob spread the contents of the packet on his end of the table, and stood up.

`I have a letter from my son James, which I shall read to you all.' He lifted a sheet of paper from the pile of what looked like wide very thin books, and held it under the candle.

'Such momentous happenings have occurred in Westminster,' he read, *'that I am sending you some of the newsbooks which are now appearing all over London. The King himself went to the House of Parliament accompanied by a large guard, to the alarm and indignation of the members. Trained Bands of the London Militia will now to be in attendance whenever Parliament is sitting. The Militia is in excellent order, with drilling each Sunday afternoon and firing practice in the Artillery Fields.*

I trust that you are all in good health. Our business here prospers.

Much leather for saddlery and boots will be needed if posturing becomes war.

I am, your devoted son, James'.

Jacob looked round his household. `We abhor armed conflict, none more than I. But the Irish rebellion has put a new complexion on things, and as Mister Duncomb said we should know and understand what is occurring in our nation. So I will lay out these news sheets for you all to inform yourselves.'

Journeyman Nathan Armstrong turned a newsbook around into his view and began to scan it silently. Apprentice Peter Knight read another.

`Hey!' someone objected. `Read it out for all to hear!'

`No bishops, no bishops!' Nathan was relishing the drama in the *Diurnall*'s story of a virtual riot outside Parliament. Peter Knight read of the King's dramatic entry into the House of Commons.

By the time they finished Abigail had grasped much of the contents, but she was still eager to handle the pages herself. The men dispersed, discussing, carrying their debate with them up to the loft. She picked up one of the news sheets and moved towards the light of the fire, where her father was sitting in his habitual chair smoking his pipe.

He looked up. `Are you wanting to read these too?'

`Oh yes,' Abigail said, `though I heard most of what was read aloud.'

`What do you know of these things?'

`A little.'

Jacob returned his gaze to the fire, where armies of sparks were suddenly moving up the iron fire-back pursued by a spurt of flame. She read through the pamphlet silently, standing across from him. Then she said `Young Mr. Vernon would be interested in this.'

Jacob looked at her sharply. `What do you know of young Mr. Vernon?'

`He was at Bicknells when I was with Joan, Oh, weeks and weeks ago when I first came back from Spreakley. He explained things to us, and he was worried about the conflicts, like it says in here.'

`No doubt as an educated gentleman Mr. Vernon has his own copy, and there's no call for you to go running after the likes of him.'

Abigail opened her mouth to protest, but there was a finality about Jacob's expression which cut her off.

Try as she might, she could make neither head nor tail of some of the Latin. Such a puzzle, with cases and genders, and sentences in an order different from English with the verb at the end - and to think that people actually spoke it to one another! If only someone could unlock it for her!

`What are all these books which are keeping you at the table?' Phoebe asked one afternoon.

`Grandfather lent them to me.'

Phoebe picked up one lying open and flipped the pages over to inspect the title. `Latin! You studying Latin?'

`I tried to learn a bit when Tom was at school.'

`You'd be better teaching Hal his letters. When did you last hear him read?'

Abigail had to admit that lessons with Hal had lapsed. `I don't know where he is.'

`Then make it your business to know.' Phoebe spoke sharply, not for the first time in recent weeks, as if she were distracted by her own concerns.

Wrapping her shawl around her shoulders Abigail went out into the yard to look for Hal. Tom and journeyman Nathan were standing beside a pile of hides, threading leather thongs along an edge of each one, then looping the thongs over thin poles which would rest across the curing pit, submerging the hides in the liquor below. The hides were damp from their washing, and the men's hands were red chapped in the wind blowing up from the river.

`Have you seen Hal?' she asked.

`Nay my pretty one, and what would you want with him anyway?' Nathan said.

`I'm not your pretty one, and I've been sent to find him.'

`If he's not in the shed,' Tom said, `he'll have slipped out to Vernon's stables.'

She set out almost running in the chill wind the half mile to Culver Hall, arriving quite short of breath. She stopped at the gate. There were people in the yard. Sam was holding a horse, Hal hovering close behind him, and young Harry Vernon was dismounting. Harry had a word with Sam, who handed the reins to Hal to lead the horse towards the stable. Intending to follow Hal. Abigail pushed open the gate but Harry saw her and came forward to greet her.

`I've thought often of your Latin studies,' he said. `Do you not find them hard with no tutor to help you?'

`Very hard indeed Sir,' she said. `I am frequently baffled.'

`Do you come often to visit the Bicknells?'

`Whenever I can.'

`Next time you call there, bring your primer and your work, and I will see if I can set you on the right road. One of the children can come to the Hall and tell me when you are there.'

`That is exceedingly kind, Sir.' Abigail felt constrained to bob a curtsey.

`I shall look forward to a little study.' He went into the house.

Hal was rubbing down the horse with a switch of straw, straining to reach high up its hind quarters.

`Mother sent me to find you, she wants you to do some more reading.'

Hal kept on rubbing. `Do I have to?'

`It's a long while since you last had a lesson.'

`Why do I have to?'

Abigail sighed. `Why do we have to do so many things. We have been told to do it, so we must. Besides, it is profitable to be able to read and write.'

Hal went round to the other side of the horse, leaning against its side and easing it over to make space for himself.

Abigail was suddenly firm. `Profit or not, we have to do it. Finish off and come, if you please.'

He obeyed in the end, once the horse's flanks were dry and gleaming and the rug thrown over its back, and the whisps of straw collected and disposed of, and a last check made.

Sam came through from the tack room. `He's a good worker, is young Hal.'

They scampered back to the Tanyard, the chill air refreshing and invigorating. Hal even laughed. They burst into the house which wafted warmth at their burning cheeks.

`You get the slate and chalk and I'll find the primer. Let's waste no time.'

After the first few hesitant sentences his reading began to flow. It seemed that the interval since they last studied had brought improvement rather than him slipping back.

`And writing, how is that?' Abigail reached for the slate. `Write something about a horse.'

He sat in silence, staring at the slate, sometimes sucking the chalk and then spitting at the unpleasant taste. In the end he said `I can't write the words.'

`You can write "horse".'

`But not wither, and fetlock, and croup, and pastern, and hock.'

`Is that what Sam teaches you? Tell me them again, and I'll try to write them for you to copy.'

`Fetlock.'

`Where's that then?'

`It's above the hoof.'

The slate got fuller and fuller as Hal explained and Abigail wrote and he copied. When they finished he surveyed their handiwork. `Can we leave them on the slate?' he said.

She watched him carry it carefully to the far end of the room, mouthing the words as he went, laying it on the shelf where it was kept. Then Mary shouted for him to prepare the rush lights, and the moment passed. He was again the silent serving waif.

The day was drawing in. Outside, men were clearing up at the end of work. Others were calling goodnight and filing home down the lane. High up in the corner of the yard a square of light showed that Jacob was still at work in his office.

Abigail stood by the window watching. This orderliness, this order in the working of the tannery, with each man and boy seemingly knowing exactly what he had to do, was so familiar that she had never pondered it. Though her father seemed apart from it all, up there at his desk, they must feel that he saw everything, expecting obedience, and they were obedient to him.

We're reared to obey, she thought, and often obedience has a good outcome. But suppose the order were mistaken, even ungodly, should one obey then?

Phoebe's sharp remarks had not actually forbidden her to study Latin. So if she did, she would not be disobeying her mother so long as she balanced her own study with teaching Hal.

Jacob's objections to Harry Vernon stung. How her father did like everything, everyone, to be in its proper place! The social hierarchy was natural law to him. Tradesmen did not consort with gentry. But the Bicknells did - or maybe it was the other way around, the Vernons choosing to consort with them.

I'm not `going after' him, she thought, her father's phrase repeating itself in her head as it had done often since his dismissive attack on her. I'm simply accepting a kind offer of tuition.

Hearing her own statement she knew that she had already decided. She already knew that, at the first opportunity, she would visit Joan, Latin books in hand.

Nathan and Peter and Tom were clattering in along with the other living-in tanners, standing around the fire to warm themselves and chaffing each other. She had better see what needed to be done.

`There's cabbage to chop' Mary said. `I've washed it.'

Abigail shredded the cabbages, posting the pieces into a string net. Once filled, she carried it to the big pot which was simmering over the fire. A wonderful smell of salt bacon, carrots and herbs wafted out as she lifted the pot lid. She lowered the net of cabbage into the water, securing its mouth under the lid. Not long now before the whole mixture would be perfectly cooked.

When she went back to the bakeroom Phoebe was slicing bread. `Where is Hannah?' she asked.

Abigail shrugged. Hannah was so withdrawn lately that she might have been inhabiting another planet.

`Kindly draw some ale then,' Phoebe said.

Abigail carried through the heavy pottery jugs topped with froth and at last Jacob came and they could eat, first the salty broth and then slices of boiled bacon with the carrots and cabbage, and more and more bread. Hannah was there, and after the meal and Bible reading and the clearing, she drew Phoebe away into a far corner of the long room, leaving Mary and Abigail to wash the dishes.

Daniel stood around in the bakeroom making sure they had enough water.

`If it weren't for the Master we could play dice,' he said.

`That's gaming,' Mary said. `You know it's not permitted.'

`'T'is good sport. What the eye doesn't see...'

`Now Daniel,' Mary warned.

`Something to do these dark evenings,' Daniel muttered.

`There's always story telling.' Mary stacked the bowls on the shelf and dried her hands. `Or you could spin.'

`Spin! That's woman's work,' Daniel said. `Best go to bed.'

Abigail followed his advice. She did not want to spin, sewing needed light, and there was nothing else to do. Except, she realised as she carried her rush light upstairs, that while the flame lasted she could study a little.

The rush had burnt down to its holder and extinguished itself and she was lying awake in the dark when Hannah came upstairs carrying a lighted candle stub. She watched sleepily as her sister took off her kirtle and stood shaking out her hair. The candle flame flickered on her silhouette, plumper than ever. She blew it out, pulled off her shift and climbed into bed.

`Are you awake Abi?'

`Mm.'

`Give me some warmth. I've got chilled when the fire burnt out.'

Abigail wrapped her arms around her back as she moved closer, and shivered. `You're like ice! What were you doing all that time?'

`Talking with Mother.'

`But you were ages!'

Hannah rubbed her feet up and down against the rough linen sheets, trying to thaw them. `I should have heated a brick for the bed. You're nice and warm.'

`I shan't be much longer if you don't keep still.' Abigail yelped as a foot met her own. `Just keep your feet still and I'll try and warm them.' Sisterly love, she thought, is losing your own warmth to an icy cold body.

`You didn't have to get so cold,' she said.

`I had to talk to Mother.'

`It took you long enough.'

`Don't be cross Abi. I'll tell you what it was about if you promise not to tell anyone else.'

`Is it so terrible?' Abigail was still resenting her heat loss.

`Not terrible at all, good in some ways, but I don't want you telling anyone, not for now.'

`What, then.'

`Promise?'

`Oh, very well.'

`I am with child, Abi.'

`With child?' Abigail almost leapt. `What child?'

`John's baby.'

Ranging thoughts closed in. All she could say was `When?'

`When will it be born? In the summer I suppose.'

`No, I mean when did you....?'

`Oh. Well. You remember when he came to fetch Mother, and I went some of the way back with him?'

`You mean... in the open?'

`There is shelter up there on the heath. Abi, he was so distressed. So in need of comfort.'

`So you lay there together in the heather.' Abigail tried to picture it, imagining clothing rumpled and the prickliness of the ling. `No wonder you were dishevelled when you ran in home.'

`I ran most of the way back down the hill.'

`Did it give you pleasure?'

`Pain and pleasure both.'

The sensation which the thought started in Abigail's innards was pleasurable and made her think of Ralph, and then even of elegant Harry Vernon. It might be worth a little pain. She brought her mind back to Hannah.

`Whatever did Mother say?'

`Her chief concern seemed to be Father. He will be so angry, that I have done this and not waited and married with his approval. But then Abi, the funniest thing. Mother smiled that little half smile of hers and said that perhaps she too is with child.'

That was almost an image too much for Abigail, her parents in their great bed....yet it must happen else how would they children exist. But no children had come after herself, so had not passion been spent? Except, when they were unloading the Spreakley cart, and Jacob had gathered Phoebe into the house as if there were only she....

`When we were at Spreakley,' she said, thoughts converging, `John asked Tom and me to speak for him to Father, about his marrying you.'

Hannah turned right round to face Abigail in the dark. `You never told me.'

`We said we couldn't act for him. He wrote Father a letter.'

`Oh Abi, I'm so glad to hear that. I've heard nothing, and I dread Father's anger. But if he knows John's intentions he may be more merciful about my condition.'

`At the time John said that Father's letter in reply was a reprimand.'

`I can only trust to Mother. She has a way with Father.' Hannah pulled the covers around her shoulders. `She has to deal so carefully with him, I sometimes wonder why she married him.'

`He's a fine looking man,' Abigail said.

Latin

Abigail had always looked on Joan as her confidante, but now she was less sure. She longed to tell someone about Hannah before she burst with the private knowledge. The bulge under Hannah's apron would soon raise suspicions, so then what loss was there if Joan already knew the reason?

Then she thought of Joan's mother Elizabeth, that innocent prattler quite incapable of keeping anything to herself. If Joan knew, she might hand on the news to her mother and it would be all round the town in no time.

She was thinking it over yet again as she walked up towards Bicknells', clutching her Latin books in a bag under her shawl. Going up Snow Hill, she noticed Mrs. Martin out in her little vegetable patch digging up some sizeable leeks. She waved in response to Abigail's greeting, leek in hand, the earth falling off the cluster of rootlets.

`Those look a good size' Abigail said.

`Aye, they've done well.' Mrs. Martin came over to the roadside. `They make capital soup.'

`How do you get them to grow so fat?'

`Muck, down at the roots when you plants them.' Mrs. Martin's voice held the pride of knowledge newly won and newly proved. `I nips out whenever a horse obliges in the street and scoops up the droppings. My good man laughs at me - but he likes the leeks.'

`And how is he? Does he have work this winter?'

`Why bless you he's up at the Castle, volunteered as a substitute for the garrison.'

‘ A substitute?’ Abigail asked.

`Some man with money to spare paid him to take his place. So he went to the muster yesterday and got took on, along with militia-men from other bands roundabout.` She laughed. `I don't know what they do all day, but they're paid to do it, up there at the Castle, so that's a blessing isn't it, and work scarce in winter.'

`So you'll not go hungry through the cold weather,' Abigail smiled.

She moved on. Local men was it, not strange uniformed men with flags flying. But would they somehow become real soldiers and turn into an army? Would they become different, un-familiar, and would they do some of the dreadful deeds that rumour reported of armies?

She passed Culver Hall and knocked at Bicknells' door where young Billie let her in. Joan came running.

`Have your heard, Abi? There is actually a garrison at the Castle!'

`Yes I have, I heard just now.'

`Did you hear the muskets? They were firing them this morning and Billie ran up the hill to see, but by the time he got there they were doing some other drill.'

`Pikes,' said Billie, `and shouting.'

`We'll know where to find you from now on,' his sister said, `off with the army.'

`But Joan, it's just the militia. It's digger Martin and volunteers from the band that meets every month. People we know.'

`Who told you that?'

`Martin's wife. She said they're volunteers, from the Farnham trained band and others roundabout. Ordinary people.'

`Well, I suppose soldiers are ordinary people aren't they?' Joan led the way towards the fire. `What have you got in that bundle?'

`Oh, Latin books. Master Vernon offered to look over some of the exercises I've done. He said perhaps one of the children could call him over when I was next here.'

`When did he say that?'

'He happened to see me when I was looking for Hal in the Culver Hall stable yard. He just offered.'

`Well!' Joan was silent for a moment. Then she turned to Billie. `You might as well see if Master Vernon is at home - and if he really wants to come and study.'

Billie scampered off and they settled themselves beside the fire.

`I wonder what the garrison does all day,' Joan mused. `They can't be forever firing muskets.'

`That's what Mrs. Martin said. She doesn't care so long as they are paid.'

`You can't imagine it, all those men together, and I suppose some of them cook for the rest, and who does their washing and things?'

`Can't they come into the town? I mean, they can't just stay in the Castle all the time.'

Billie pushed the door, beaming at having found his quarry so quickly and followed by Harry Vernon. Greetings made, Harry asked about the books and Abigail handed him the grammar and the slate with her attempt to translate one short psalm. He studied it carefully, Abigail holding her breath for fear that anything so elementary and poorly executed would be beneath him.

`This psalm is quite familiar, isn't it,' he said, `which helped you to work it out. Suppose now you take a few verses from the English version of another psalm and render them into Latin.'

Abigail rubbed her previous work off the slate and bent to this more difficult task. Harry sat at ease in a cushioned chair and at first Joan sat erect and silent on a stool.

After a while Abigail said `There are too many words I don't know.'

`Let me write down some of the vocabulary you will need. Draw your stool up beside me.'

They concentrated together, heads down, while Joan sat and watched. Then she went to the kitchen where her mother was talking to the cook, the baby clasped upon her hip. She turned to Joan.

`It all seems very quiet in there.'

`Master Vernon and Abigail are studying,' Joan said. `I thought I'd find some refreshment.'

`Your father might be glad of some. I'll call him. Put several tankards on the tray, and cut some slices of our good plum cake.'

So then a procession proceeded into the hall, Joan with the tray, her mother with the baby, and Robert Bicknell bringing up the rear.

`Here's refreshment!' Elizabeth cried. `Have you completed what you are doing? My! it all looks very clever.'

Abigail shook her head and went on with her work, Vernon beside her occasionally glancing at the slate on her knee..

`We were talking about the garrison, Father,' Joan said as she handed round the tray.

`Ah yes.' Robert sipped his ale. `Quite a surprise.'

`I think not, Sir,' Harry said, looking up. `The new Deputy Lieutenant, Sir Richard Onslow, is one of Parliament's creatures. He's taken control of the militia, and now the Castle, a logical step to guard the approaches to London in their own interests.'

'And the militia, where do their loyalties lie?' Robert shook his head as if unable to answer his own question.

`I wonder if they mind about loyalties,' Abigail looked up to say. `Food and money are what matter.'

`However;' Harry sounded formal and distant. `There are important principles of sovereignty at stake.'

With scarcely a knock the door burst open and Hermann Shepheard precipitated in. He went straight to Harry Vernon.

`I called at Culver Hall but no one was in and they told me you were here...' he broke off and looked round. `Forgive me, Bicknell, Mistress Bicknell, young ladies.'

`Would you care for some refreshment?' Elizabeth asked.

`Yes yes, thank 'e, but this garrison, shocking! An act of rebellion!'

`Anyone would think that war had been declared!' Harry exclaimed.

`Rebels! How dare they? My Lord Bishop put his palace at the King's disposal, and the dissidents take possession of it! To foist a garrison on Farnham, a town loyal to the King! And the lecturer - perhaps he has a hand in this. He'd be glad to see an end to Bishops, I'll wager.'

`Come come,' Robert said.

`What an insult!' Shepheard went on, ignoring him and walking back and forth in agitation. `How can I be expected to carry out my Lord Bishop's dictats when I'm surrounded by dissident rebels?'

`But I thought you said Farnham supported you, and the dissidents and rebels have been foist upon us.' Robert suppressed a smile.

`Oh it's impossible, impossible!' Shepheard gulped some ale and scattered cake crumbs on the floor.'

`There are some in Parliament who have the bit between their teeth,' Harry said. `They're in danger of stampeding.'

`They are stampeding!' Shepheard squeaked, `and it's our duty to stand firm against them.'

`So how will you treat Parliament's garrison here, which includes some of your own parishioners?' Robert asked.

The curate spluttered, and must have been glad of yet another knock at the door. Billie ran to open it saying `Someone else to join the fun.' But on the doorstep stood Jacob Mannory, tense-faced. He looked round the assembled company, now suddenly silenced; at Shepheard standing tankard in hand, at Joan and Elizabeth playing with the baby, at Robert, and at Abigail with her stool still close to Harry Vernon's chair.

At sight of her he almost exploded.

`Abigail! How dare you!'

Everyone looked at him open-mouthed. He ignored all but Abigail.

`How dare you! Go home at once!'

Abigail stood up, blushing as she had never blushed before, and pulled her shawl round her shoulders.

`At once!' her father repeated.

Too embarrassed even to look her thanks at Harry and her hosts she picked up her book bag and rushed past him and out. She was shocked and shaking, incredulous too. To be shamed in front of dear friends for taking it on herself to accept help with study! Gradually she slowed her pace. Whatever might come next from her father, at least she had not told Hannah's secret.

The Bicknell baby started crying, louder and louder. Harry stood up and, ignoring Jacob, said to the curate `Come over to Culver Hall where we may continue to talk.'

`In peace,' Shepheard said, looking gratified.

They bowed to Mistress Bicknell though all her attention was on trying to calm the baby, and to Joan, and left. Joan gathered the empty tankards and the remains of the cake, her mother excused them both over the infant's howling and they too left the room.

Jacob stood glaring at Robert, and for once Robert glared back.

`What do you mean by humiliating your daughter - and insulting mine too - and my family and my guests!'

Jacob stared and glared.

`You spoke to her as if she were a stray dog!'

`Disobedient wench!' Jacob exploded.

`Disobedient? She is constantly in and out of here, always has been.'

`She disobeyed me.'

`You had no call to reprimand her in public, shaming her.'

`Strumpet!'

`What, Abigail?'

`I told her not to go after young Master Vernon.'

`What nonsense! She's not going after anyone.'

`She couldn't have sat closer to him.'

`I understand he is helping her with some study.'

`Hah! Study! A new excuse I must say.'

Robert blinked, and swallowed once or twice, regaining composure.

`Jacob.' He put a hand on his arm. `Come and sit down. You didn't come here in pursuit of Abigail - you didn't even know she was here. What's behind all this?'

Jacob followed him to the fireside and sat clenching and unclenching his fists, his jaw working silently.

`God! You warned me!' he burst out at last. `Strumpets! I've bred a couple of strumpets! Furtive, deceitful strumpets!'

Robert sat silently watching him, waiting for the anger to subside. Eventually he said quietly `So?' and Jacob looked up and caught his breath.

`Hannah is with child by her cousin John.'

Robert smiled, which re-ignited Jacob's rage. `Oh, you may well smile, the gossip's husband who knows it all. Fornication! My daughter committing fornication! And not even in a bed, but out in the open field like any slut!'

`She told you all this?' Robert asked, aghast.

`I made her. She came with her mother to inform me, and I made her tell me the truth. And John Harding, how dare he force my hand in this way!"

`Wait a moment,' Robert said. `Let me understand the sequence of events. When was the child conceived?'

`The day Phoebe went to her late brother at Spreakley.'

`And when did John Harding write to you to ask for her hand'

`I suppose three or four weeks later.'

`So he had no idea then that she was with child?'

`No doubt he feared it was so.'

Robert tried another tack. `Does Hannah care for him?'

Jacob turned away from Robert and gazed into space. Eventually he managed to speak. `She wept, Robert. She wept, and begged me to let her go to him.'

`Once women experience the delights of the marriage bed there's no holding them,' Robert said lightly.

`Little considering the consequences.'

`They will breed sooner or later whether you like it or not.' Robert, whose offspring popped out with minimum trouble, poked the fire.

`Who will see her through child-bed away at Spreakley? Child-bearing is a fearful thing.' Jacob was clenching his fists again, and Robert considered him thoughtfully until he said very quietly `Phoebe?'

Jacob looked at him sharply, his face stricken. `Phoebe said - as if to justify Hannah - that she may also be with child.' Robert said nothing, and Jacob went on `Every delivery has been worse for Phoebe. We lost a babe after Abigail, and all but lost Phoebe too. She was feeble for months and months. You must remember how ill and frail she was.'

`I did not realise,' Robert said.

`I vowed she should not have to endure this again. And I have broken the vow. If I lose her...' His voice choked as he battled with tears.

Robert sat quietly beside him, a silent support as he shuddered with emotion, his face in his hands. After a while Robert fetched a tankard of water and a kerchief and offered them to him, sitting silently again until Jacob had collected himself.

At last he said `Let us separate these matters. If Phoebe is with child, all we can do is to pray for her safety. As for Abigail I am certain that your suspicions are without foundation. Can you bring yourself to apologise to her?'

Jacob opened his mouth to speak but no words came.

Robert went on, `You showed me a letter from John several months ago asking for Hannah's hand. Surely the sooner they are married the better.'

There was a pause. Then Jacob let out his breath with a great sigh that sounded as if it came from the depths of his being. He sat silently for a long time, gazing at nothing. When he looked up at last the tension was gone from his face leaving a weary sadness.

`Yes,' he said, `I have to let her go.'

Hannah's wedding day was one of those bright winter days that raises the hope of spring yet is still sharply cool.

The last time Abigail had been in Frensham churchyard was for her uncle's funeral. She looked towards his grave where winter had not yet allowed grass to clad the turned earth, and felt again a little pang of the sadness she had known then. But, she told herself, this was not a day for sadness, with family and friends all around her, waiting for the bride and groom to arrive at the church door. Maybe the sadness was because she felt alone.

It had been a rushed and confusing couple of weeks. First Jacob had sent Tom riding the horse out to Spreakley with a letter for John, who had returned with him in a state of astonished excitement. That was the first Hannah knew of her father's change of heart, as John swept her to him to ask his blessing. Then Phoebe pointed out that Lent began very soon and in those forty days before Easter no weddings were permitted. So off rushed John all the way to Winchester to the Bishop's office for a special license. He had ridden to the Tanyard in such haste that he had brought little money with him and again Phoebe came to the rescue, arranging with Jacob for an advance on Hannah's dowry to pay the license fee.

Hannah's excitement was tempered by distress that she would have no time to sew for either herself or her groom - so little time to prepare herself to leave her home. Moreover her parents decided that the marriage would best be celebrated at Frensham rather than Farnham, and John was eager for a feast and a party to bring cheerfulness back into Spreakley.

Back he came with the license, and he and Hannah bore it off to the Rectory to arrange for the curate to read their banns just the once.

`First cousins?' Shepheard had said, leafing through the prayer book list of consanguinity, `Ah yes, that is permitted, and a good thing too' glancing at Hannah's figure.

And all those days Jacob had uttered not a word to Abigail. She sensed a total wall between them which she interpreted as hostility. For her, surrounded by and caught up in the scurry of activity, those days had been lonely. Phoebe had gone to Spreakley as soon as John had completed the arrangements, riding pillion behind him on his stout farm horse. Her absence accentuated Abigail's alone-ness.

And now John had stepped out from among his friends to stand before the Vicar in the church porch, and Hannah was coming up the path on Jacob's arm, her long hair flowing loose over her shoulders as the custom was, the new russet kirtle, which they had all sewed so hastily for her, stiff with newness over her fresh white shift. Her only adornment was her bride veil, a length of blue ribbon into which she and Abigail had laboriously knotted sprigs of rosemary and which hung around her neck and looped over her arms. Jacob was in his Sunday best, tall, slim and grave.

The vicar read the introduction to the marriage service, about marriage being an honourable estate with spiritual overtones.

`Who giveth this woman to be married to this man?'

When Jacob took his daughter's right hand and gave it to John, his face gave nothing away. He was doing what was expected of him, with dignity and some grace, whatever his private feelings.

The pair exchanged vows, (could anyone truly keep them, Abigail wondered) John placed a ring on Hannah's finger, and then they all trooped into the church for a sermon. Abigail knew few of the congregation, though the Bicknells were there with Joan alone of their children. Nathan Armstrong the journeyman for some reason had come along too.

The sermon was finished by noon. Led by the bridal pair they all poured out of the church and set off briskly in the frosty sunshine along the road and up the hill to Spreakley. Near the rear of the column a pipe and drum started a cheerful foot-tapping marching tune and some began to sing, while young men darted forward and back trying to nick a sprig of rosemary from Hannah's bride lace to stick in their hat bands. Hannah laughed at them and pretended to resist, crying out for fair play, while John feigned to protect her from these assaults. Abigail had seldom seen her sister so playful.

Amused by watching these antics she had not much noticed who was taking part until, as they crossed the mill bridge, Nathan fell into step beside her.

`Hey, my pretty one,' (did he always address a girl thus? Did he know no other greeting?) `will you accept a favour?'

`A favour?'

He pulled rosemary out of his hat and held it out to her.

`Wear it on your breast for me,' he said and without waiting for reply put a hand on her shoulder, slowing her step and diverting her alongside the column of walkers, and with the other hand tucked the sprig into the lacing of her bodice.

`You have it now, favoured one,' and with that Nathan ran off with the lads. The rosemary stem scratched the skin between her breasts through the fabric of her shift and she adjusted it, gratified enough to want to keep it though not without misgiving.

Inside the great barn next to the farm, the floor had been cleared of stray beet tumbled from the piled store, trestle tables set up, and the feast was the most lavish that could be prepared at short notice in mid-winter. The meal extended through the afternoon, enlivened by the cask of claret which Mr Henry Vernon had sent as a mark of respect for the Mannory family.

When the light faded the servants, their numbers augmented from the village, placed lanterns around the walls and dismantled the emptied tables. The piper took up position with the tabor player beside him.

`Everyone on the floor!' he cried.

All Ralph Attfield wanted was a secure place for the night. He had sold all but one of his string of horses at Haslemere fair. A few miles on his way with the heavy bag of coins, the unsold horse he was riding had gone lame, forcing him to lodge it at a farm under the lea of the Hindhead down, and to continue up and over the down on foot.

Just before he descended the water-worn track he passed a group of wild ponies. He went on down, the banks high on either side. Then from the whin bushes high above him he heard a whistle. Another answered it. He swore to himself. Thieves must have watched him at the fair, and now he with his bag of money was at their mercy.

Suddenly he heard the ponies behind him. Disturbed by the whistles, they were stampeding down the track. They surged around him. He grabbed a mane, held on hard, almost of his feet, swung himself onto the pony's back. On they hurtled, until the track opened out into a clearing and he knew they had outpaced the thieves.

No time to waste though, it would soon be dark, and he determined to seek a bed for the night at Spreakley.

Arriving there, his hoped-for refuge, the last thing he expected was the sound of pipe and tabor. Not a house of mourning as he had thought, but a wedding feast. Aware of his travel-worn clothes and the soil on his boots he approached the barn door cautiously. The old blind grandfather was sitting just inside the door beside a glowing brazier, tapping his foot to the rhythm, with John Harding and the older Mannory girl beside him.

'Ralph!' John caught sight of him and bounded forward. 'Come and join the festivities! I am married this very day to fair Hannah,' drawing her towards him. 'But what brings you?'

Ralph explained and John readily stowed the sale money safely and then insisted he return with him to the barn. The Bicknell family were refreshing themselves nearby, Joan flushed from dancing.

'Why, Attfield, what a pleasant surprise!' Robert Bicknell exclaimed. 'You must partner Joan in the next dance.'

'In my boots?' Ralph said.

'Oh yes!' Joan cried. 'Come, I'm sure you will not tread on my toes,' and she whisked him into the nearest set.

Abigail saw him from where she had agreed to dance with Nathan, not a happy dance for he took it upon himself to ensure everyone followed the sequence correctly, if need be pushing people into place.

Glad when it was over she bobbed a modest curtsey to him and went over to her Grandfather.

`It's me Grandfather, Abigail,' she said, touching his hands.

`Ah bless me! My granddaughter-in-law as well as my grand-daughter! What a happy day!'

`The dance has left me breathless.' She pulled a stool over beside him.

`Tell me,' he asked. `How do your studies fare?'

`Oh.' Abigail was silent for a moment. `I'm not sure that my father approves of my studying. At least... I don't know, Grandfather. I wish you could come and live with us and help me with it.'

`Dear child.' Grandfather reached out for her hand and held it. `Your mother suggested that very thing, but I declined. I am at ease in my corner by the kitchen fire. I am under no-one's feet, and I know my way about the house without having to see. I'm old and blind dear child, too old to move. But I will think about your studies.'

She sat on, holding his hand and looking at him with a depth of love which she did not understand. Then a deep voice behind her said `Chicken plucking maiden, will you favour me with this dance?'

Grandfather patted her hand as if in dismissal and she stood up and turned to look at Ralph. His generous mouth was smiling and there was a smile in his brown eyes. It had taken all his courage to approach her. He had watched her dancing with Nathan, and now attending to the old man. He thought she looked serenely beautiful, a young woman not a child. Here was a chance which might never recur to try being with her without the need for talk. Then he noticed the rosemary in her bodice.

`But I see you wear another man's favour.'

Abigail glanced down at it, and shrugged. `Weren't they all vying to snatch them out of the bride lace?'

He took her hand to lead her out into the circle. Grandfather's bent and sinewy hand had just aroused deep feelings in her, but this was new and different, a hand reassuringly padded which she wanted to hold and hold. They took their place in the circle and he released it. She saw her parents on the far side.

The music began and he took her hand again to circle left, then linked arms to turn her and she thrilled at the feel of the firm muscle under his shirt sleeve. Back round again and a swing with the other arm. After that they were detached, men circling together followed by the women, then men and women in turn into the middle and back.

Waiting the women's turn she looked about her, and suddenly saw Phoebe rush out of the barn clutching her skirt. Jacob followed instantly. The piper was scarcely through the next sequence when he was back. He looked wildly round the dancers, then caught Abigail's shoulder from behind.

`Go to your mother at once. She is unwell.'

She just caught Ralph's surprised look as she rushed out of the barn.

Where had her mother been sleeping? She ran up the twisting stairs and from room to room. No sign of her. Then she thought, how stupid I am! She must be in the privy. Perhaps she had needed to vomit. She hurried out into the darkness and called through the privy door.

`Oh Abigail, thank goodness. I'm bleeding Abi. Could you find some cloths and bring them here. I dare not move.'

Cloths, cloths, where would she find cloths. Quick - or would Phoebe die as Hal's mother had done, in a welter of blood? She stumbled into the scullery, and there was housekeeper Madge at the sink.

`Madge, quick, my mother is bleeding, she needs some cloths, lots of cloths, quickly!'

Madge lost no time. From some store cupboard she produced a bundle of rags and stuffing them into a basket thrust it into Abigail`s hands.

`I'll carry some water up to her bed chamber,' she said. `She'll want to cleanse herself.'

`It's better now,' Phoebe said as Abigail passed the basket in to her round the privy door. After a while she emerged, clutching her groin.

`Madge is taking water up to your chamber.'

`Ever thoughtful Madge.' Phoebe waddled up the stairs and stopped as she saw Madge hovering at the top. `Thank you,' she said, `and please would you go tell Master Mannory that all is well,' dismissing her. She sat down on a hard stool and looked up at Abigail's stricken face.

`What happened Mother?'

`I'm uncertain. I thought a little while ago that I might be with child. If that were so then it was a babe that aborted itself before it had even received its soul.. But at my age the courses come and go and that could be all it was. Either way, it was certainly violent and unexpected.'

`A baby!' Abigail exclaimed.

`I'm thankful not to be with child. I do not give birth easily. I shall be glad to be past the age of child-bearing.'

`I thought you might die like Hal's mother.'

`Poor Judith. No my darling, not like that.'

So busy was Abigail helping her mother clean herself up and putting her stained shift to soak in cold water that she hardly noticed the clatter and ribaldry on the stairs as the young people took the bride and bridegroom up to their bridal chamber and put them to bed.

`Do you not wish to join them?' Phoebe asked.

Abigail shook her head. `I'll stay with you for a while.'

`They'll be off home soon, and then you must go and reassure your father.' She lay down on the bed, pale and tired. Abigail pulled the covers over her and sat down on a stool. She waited a long time, leaning against the bed post and grieving for the lost dance with Ralph, until there seemed to be little noise downstairs, and she went down. Perhaps her mother's trouble might open a chink in the wall between her and her father.

He was standing restlessly where grandfather still sat, back in his corner in the kitchen beside the dying fire.

`Mother wants you to know that all is well with her. She is in bed.' Abigail glanced between the two men. `It was a mighty flux, but it has lessened now.'

Jacob looked hard at her. `Good girl' he said, and went to his wife.

Grandfather eased himself upright, slowly unbending his stiff joints. 'Time for us all to be abed,' he said.

1642

Soon after their return home Phoebe and Abigail sat together sewing.

`It is time for some re-arrangements,' Phoebe said. `Your father wishes to use Tom's bedroom. Now that Hannah is married I would prefer you not to sleep alone. I thought that Mary could share your bed.'

`Oh Mother, does she have to?'

`You get along well enough with her don't you?'

`But not as a bedfellow!'

Phoebe laughed. `I don't know how else to arrange it, unless Tom sleeps in the loft with the men. With so many men in the house it might be wiser for you not to sleep alone.'

`Can I not lock the door? I would so much rather.'

When the following week Phoebe hired Carey as a second maidservant Abigail was the more glad that she had prevailed, for surely she would have had to share the bed with her as well. Twelve years old, Carey was a bony girl, and Abigail could imagine what those elbows would feel like in her ribs in the night. Since the death of her parents Carey had lived with her old great aunt who seemed to have done everything for her. Now the aunt herself needed help and the relative who had moved in with her could not do with the girl as well. Carey had much to learn.

The mastiffs had scarcely barked one day in February when the door latch clicked and Joan's voice called `Anyone at home?'

`In the bake room!' Abigail called, from beside the wooden trough where she and Mary were kneading dough. Joan looked so neat and fresh in her hooded cloak of green worsted that Abigail was suddenly aware of her own workaday state and wished she could tuck dishevelled wisps of hair back under her cap, but her hands were sticky with dough up to the wrists. Carey stood by watching, learning, they hoped, the household arts. Joan simply addressed Abigail.

`I decided I had to come over, I haven't seen you for weeks and weeks, well not since the wedding and not to speak to then. Wasn't it cheerful, no hint of mourning for the old man - well, not the very old man of course, he seems to be the ancient of days there in his ingle nook. I thought the sermon would never end, but the walk to the farm was so much fun - did anyone give you a favour? - and the dancing! I saw you dance with Ralph Attfield, (he's not much of a dancer is he!) but then you disappeared.'

`I had to attend to Mother - a sudden malaise.'

`So you missed all the fun of undressing John and Ann and putting them to bed, though the young men were bawdy enough the things they were saying. I'm not sure I'd care for that aspect of the proceedings, but Hannah took it in good part. And the bed, is that the bed your uncle died in?'

`Why yes,' Abigail said, the kneading stiffer now.

`I wouldn't fancy sleeping in a dead man's bed.'

`Dying and birthing and conceiving, a bed sees them all,' Mary said. `You'd not buy a new one for each.'

`Oh well, once the bed curtains were drawn I don't suppose they worried. You could see that John could hardly wait.'

`The dough's turned now,' Mary said. `Look Carey - feel it. See the stringiness of it.' Carey poked a cautious couple of fingers into it.

'You'll not feel it that way. Lean your knuckles into it.'

Carey made a fist and pushed, cautious still.

`What ails the child?' Mary said to Abigail, sprinkling flour on their hands so that they could rub the dough sticking to them off into the kneading trough. They washed the rest away in a bowl of water and Mary went and emptied it onto the garden, `Not that the garden needs it,' she said as she returned, `after all this rain.'

`So how's the garrison?' Abigail asked.

`They go on firing muskets' Joan said.

`But have you met any of them?'

`They wander round the town sometimes, but Curate Shepheard seems to have appointed himself as my protector. I only have to walk into the Borough and he appears, I can hardly shake him off.'

Abigail laughed.

`You may well laugh, but he is an inconvenience.'

`They're no more than local lads,' Mary broke in. `No more nor no less.'

`Do you come across them Mary?'

`I have done.'

`Come on Mary, I can see you have,' Abigail said. `Tell us all!'

`They must get bored up there day after day,' Joan said.

`It's not just firing muskets you know,' Mary said. `They do drill all the morning. Some carry on their trades. Then there's meat to kill and prepare, and carrot and salad, cabbage, you know, all the cooking that's needed for forty men. But I reckon some must have gone home by now - why, it's time for harrowing and sowing, they can't go on just laying around at the Castle. Francis says...'

`Who's Francis?' Joan pounced.

`Oh...'

`Come on Mary, tell us,' Abigail said.

`He's a young man from Godalming I sees sometimes.'

`Is he handsome?' Abigail again.

`Not so you'd call handsome.' Mary was cautious. `Well set up like, big hands, big beard...'

`Not much comely grace.'

Mary bridled. `That's not everything you know. A hard-working man with a good heart, that's what a woman needs.' She spread a cloth over the kneading trough. `Now if you want to talk, be so good as to go into the Hall so's I can sweep up in here and put Carey to her tasks.'

Once they were alone Joan asked `Why haven't you been to see me? Is it because of last time and your father?'

`What must you all have thought? I was so confused and ashamed.'

`Father made it right with Harry Vernon. I think he explained that Master Mannory gets angry sometimes and says things he regrets.'

`If he regrets them he never says so or admits it.' Abigail heard a note of bitterness in her own voice.

`Whenever I meet Harry he asks when you'll next be at our house. He seems quite taken with you and your Latin I must say. Why have you not been? Do you not want to come?'

`Father accused me of being disobedient, though he had given me no definite command. I think I should have to ask his permission.'

But it was Tom who bearded their father first. His rash outburst before the turn of the year about not wanting to be a tanner had changed nothing that he could see. He was still going through the motions of tanning, still trying Othen's patience, still operating the horse and cart to an extent which did not, in his opinion, earn its keep.

On one of his quick illicit visits to the Bush Inn between going to the Shambles and returning to the Tanyard, he fell into conversation with one of the militiamen and learnt that the garrison was in need of gunpowder. There was gunpowder in plenty at Chilworth where it was manufactured but someone needed to go and collect it.

`A hazardous load,' the militiaman said. `A spark from any iron could set it alight. But,' he added, `you'd be paid to collect it.'

Tom considered this for a day or two, waiting for the right moment to approach his father. A couple of evenings later the meal had been cheerful and Jacob, having succeeded in lighting his pipe unusually quickly, seemed to be mellow in his chair. Tom squatted on a stool opposite him.

`Father,' he began, `I want to... may I ask you...I've found a way for the horse and cart to earn some money.'

Jacob took the pipe out of his mouth and looked a question.

`You know the community is supposed to provide the militia with carts for moving ammunition and such?'

Jacob grunted, still a question.

`Would you allow me to offer our horse and cart to bring gunpowder from Chilworth? I could drive it and we would be paid.'

`Gunpowder,' Jacob said. `The means of waging war.'

`They're only practising. They need it for that at least.'

Jacob considered in silence, drawing deeply on his pipe. Then he said `I suppose it would be in barrels. The cart is scarcely big enough.'

Tom muttered `It could take four or six,' but Jacob went on as if he had not spoken.

`Twelve to fourteen miles to Chilworth - you could do it there and back in a day now the days are lengthening.' Tom hardly dared to breath.

`I doubt there would be much in the way of payment,' Jacob went on, 'And the cart of course is mine. Any payment would come to me.'

Another long tantalising silence.

Then `You may offer.'

Tom's surprised delight made him nearly leap out of his seat. He just had to tell someone and the first person he met was Hal.

`Can I come with you?' was Hal's immediate response.

`That might be too much to ask' Tom said

He told Abigail too, and she decided that a request from just one of his children might be enough for Jacob for the time being. So she found occasions to do a little more Latin study, and to hear Hal read and to help him write, and bided her time.

Joan however was less patient. After the lecture one Thursday she way-laid Abigail, took her arm and steered her towards Jacob.

`Master Mannory,' she said, her head engagingly on one side. `May I ask your permission for Abigail to visit me?'

`Does she need my permission to visit Bicknells'?'

`It seems she thinks she does.'

Jacob looked at Abigail and Joan did too.

Hesitantly, because something was evidently expected of her, Abigail asked `Were you not displeased with me Father, when I was last at Bicknells'?'

Phoebe was beside her husband. As he stood silently appraising his daughter she slipped her arm through his. `Let her go, Jacob.'

He released a long sigh.

`Let them all go,' he said wearily. `Very well.'

`Come now!' Joan said. She sent Billie across to Culver House almost as soon as they were inside Timber Hall.

`But I haven't my books with me,' Abigail protested.

`I'm sure he'll think of something,' Joan said, busying herself preparing ale and some walnuts, and she was right.

Harry simply said `Then we will work orally,' and for the next half hour he threw out phrases, some in Latin, some in English, for her attention.

Eventually Joan could wait no longer and carried in the tray she had prepared, which brought translation to an end.

As they sat, Joan asked `What news do you have today? Any news?' It was the standard opening to every conversation among townspeople.

`News?' Harry said. `There is altogether too much of it.' He selected a couple of walnuts and chewed them thoughtfully. `One scarcely knows what to expect next. Who would have imagined that the Bishops would be expelled from the House of Lords.'

Bishops again, Abigail thought.

`Not only that,' Harry went on, `but a dozen of them have been arraigned for "haughty ambition and abrogating power and authority to themselves". For heaven's sake, they head the church, they have every right to power and authority.'

`My brother says they have too much wealth, and that it's not fair.'

`I have deep respect for our Lord Bishop. Our friend Hermann Shepheard speaks very highly of him.'

The following weeks Abigail tried to have some work to show him and each time she went to Timber Hall Joan eagerly sent for him and plied him with refreshment. While they studied she would sit nearby, mending the children's clothes or sewing away at the latest garment she was making. Her stitches were small, neat and exact, and the clothes she made were always elegant. Invariably as they finished with Latin she would ask for news, though the news was rarely of the local gossip kind.

`Do you buy newsbooks?' Abigail asked Harry.

`I do indeed. But what do you know of them?'

`My brother sent us some at the turn of the year, and sometimes the men buy them. They are interesting.'

`I didn't realise women interested themselves in such things.'

`Why shouldn't we?' Abigail asked.

Harry laughed, more to himself than at her. `Did you hear about the crowd of women who presented a petition at the House of Lords?'

`Oh yes! A petition about the decay of trade! I did admire them for doing that.'

`But they laid hold of a noble Lord when he tried to dismiss them! A rabble of women started a fight!'

`He should have listened to them. They had more courage than their menfolk.'

`The Lords actually called a group of them right into the House. Women will be wanting to sit in Parliament next.'

'There are lots of women who have their own business,' Abigail said. 'Why shouldn't they take part in politics?'

Joan looked up. `I couldn't be bothered with all that talk and disagreement.'

At their next meeting Abigail asked Harry why he thought the King and his court had gone far away to York.

`I suppose he expects to find more support in the north,' Harry said. `Disaffection is rife in the south, support here and rebellion there, neighbours taking opposing sides....'

`Nathan says the king's mad to go so far away from London, leaving Parliament a free hand.'

`Your Nathan seems very well informed and opinionated,' Harry said.

`He's not my Nathan. He's just a journeyman in the house who buys newsbooks and reads them out,' Abigail said.

`Well I have some news for you,' Joan said brightly. `Mistress Gary is with child yet again, and completely confined to her bed. Mother took them some pies, and found things quite upside-down.'

Harry smiled abstractedly at her and her domestic interests and turned to Abigail's Latin. He was a good teacher and she, a willing pupil, made rapid progress.

`Why are you wanting to learn Latin?' he asked her one day.

`It fascinated me when I used to look over Tom's school work,' she said. 'I like puzzling it out, the logic of it and how it all fits together. I just enjoy it. And when I've rendered a passage, I have such a feeling of satisfaction.'

`The female scholar,' Harry said. `Well, you have distinguished precedents. Queen Elizabeth for one.'

The days lengthened into April, and calves were born. Beesting pies made from the first milk gave a taste of spring, and butter churning began.

Harry announced `His Majesty has commanded the gentry to appear before him in their equipage.'

`What's equipage?' Joan asked

`Horse and armour and weapons, and groom and servant besides.'

`That must be quite an expense,' Abigail said.

`It is expected of a gentleman.`

Joan was wide eyed. `Will you go?'

Harry shrugged. `I have followed the way of a scholar. I would be of little use to him.'

Towards the end of the month Joan came to the Tanyard, forestalling Abigail. She found her in the garden planting onions.

`He's gone away,' she said without preamble.

Abigail looked up, still bending over the onion setts. `Who has?'

`Why, Harry Vernon.'

`What, with his equipage?'

`No. He and the curate have ridden off to Oxford. It's their old University. They are becoming very thick, the two of them.'

`Oh well.' Abigail straightened her back and brushed earth off her hands. `There's plenty to do here now. I'll give Latin a break for a while.'

`Don't you want to see him?'

`There'll be time enough when he comes back.'

`I thought...' Joan began, and then turned away and picked a sprig of lavender, pinching it and putting it to her nose. `Do you still have any lavender water from last year?'

`We may do. I've some onions over. Should I start another row do you think?'

`I've no idea.' Joan looked about her. `There's plenty of empty soil.'

"I think I'll put them in even if they don't make a full row.' Abigail bent again, making shallow holes with a dibber and tucking the little onions in.

`Harry said there's a petition begging the King not to make war.'

`Isn't he making war already? I mean we read that he's still besieging the city of Hull and the governor won't give it up to him. It doesn't make sense, fighting and sueing for peace at the same time.'

`Do you think there will be war?' Joan asked, fidgeting with the lavender.

`What does Harry say?' Abigail said.

`It's you he talks to.' Joan threw down the tattered lavender. `Don't you realise what a hit you have made with Master Vernon?'

Abigail, still planting, looked at her out of the corner of her eye. `Do you mind?' She stood up again, laughing. `You've always had a string of admirers. Perhaps if what you say is true it's my turn for a change.'

Joan was not laughing. She pulled another stem of lavender and stood there shredding off its leaves. Abigail picked up the now empty basket preparing to move away, but Joan just stood, and suddenly Abigail said seriously `You do mind, don't you.'

Joan shook her head, not to deny but because there were tears in her eyes. Abigail put a grubby arm round her shoulders. `My poor Joan, are you losing your heart to him?'

She nodded, sniffing. `He doesn't notice me at all.'

`He must do. You're always there, and you bring things to eat and drink.'

`A servant could do as much. And I can't do Latin even if I wanted to, and I don't really care about politics except that I don't want there to be a war and everyone be killed.'

Abigail said more lightly `How perverse of you, falling for the unattainable...' at which Joan looked at her sharply.

`Unattainable?'

`Harry Vernon is a gentleman..."

`And there's many a gentleman who has bolstered his family fortunes by marrying trade.'

`And tradesmen who have become gentlemen - or bishops,' Abigail had to agree. `I'd have thought Harry too solemn for you.'

`It doesn't matter.'

They began to walk about the garden.

`I don't know what we can do about it,' Abigail said.

`It seems hopeless,' Joan said. 'All that romantic stuff about unrequited love – it's not very romantic in real life. Do you truly not return his affections?'

Abigail did not answer at once. He was so utterly different from Ralph who thrilled her each time she saw him. Was that just because of Ralph's robust looks and rich voice? Harry was good looking in a totally different way, delicate looking, and after a study session with him she felt satisfied, her mind met and stimulated. But that is not love, she thought.

`No,' she said at last. `Perhaps I had better leave off my Latin studies.'

`Then I shall have no pretext to invite him in.'

He did not return until early June. By then the tanners started work at five in the morning and everyone broke off for their main meal soon after mid-day. So with Phoebe away at Spreakley to stand by for the birth of Hannah's baby, Abigail and the servant girls were kept busy from early morning, leaving little time for studying.

The evenings brought debate. Nathan and the other men read the newsbooks when they could get them, and many were the discussions with no one clear about the rights and wrongs and whether they would, if need be, support one side or the other.

Harry however - and Joan was urgent for Abigail to visit - had no such doubts. King Charles was right and he was staunchly behind him, a conviction reinforced by many conversations in Oxford. Shepheard was often with him now. They would walk around the town together, talking earnestly. Relieved from the isolation of his position and stimulated by Harry's company, the curate's confidence was growing.

He was as protective as ever of Joan.

`Not troubled by the garrison I trust?' he asked when they happened to meet together outside Michael Gary's drapery shop.

`No, no, not at all. They've mostly gone home now anyway.'

`Have the King's Commissioners of Array not been here raising troops?'

Joan shrugged. `Not to our knowledge,' she said.

`Surrey is reluctant to obey the ordinance,' Harry said.

`The ordinance demanded the loan of money and men and horses,' Shepheard explained.

`For the King?' Abigail asked.

`Why of course for the King! What else!'

It was mid-July when Abigail went to Bicknells with a basket of late strawberries and a request for Mistress Bicknell's receipt for Lombardy Pie. Harry was already there, holding forth to Joan and Billie and some of the younger children too though they were taking little notice.

`King Charles is right. He must take possession of Hull in his own interests.

He nodded to Abigail as she came in, and continued in full flow.

`How can he defend himself without armaments? He needs Hull with its arsenal, and it is most irksome that the city is holding out against him. He cannot allow the armaments to fall into rebel hands.'

`Rebel?' Abigail asked. `From what I read, Parliament is raising forces to defend His Majesty and his Kingdom against his evil advisers. If they're defending the King they can't be rebels.'

`Defend indeed! They are traitors! Don't tell me they propose to fight under the King's command!'

He was carrying on in the same vein when Abigail suddenly stopped listening to him and pricked up her ears in another direction. That dark brown voice alerted her just before Ralph Attfield came into the room talking earnestly with Robert Bicknell.

`I was in Winchester,' Ralph was saying, `and I ran into my old friend Jim Hosier. He's one of Sir William Waller's coachmen, at least he used to be. Now Sir William has lent him along with his other coachman, to fight for Parliament. He told me Sir William is raising a regiment of horse, and I can tell you, I didn't take much persuading to join them. A great life for a horseman!'

`But your trade,' Robert objected. `What about your horses and your customers?'

`The horses are only mine in transit. I have sold most that I held, which is why I need your help, to be my banker.' He and Robert went out of the room together.

Harry could hardly contain himself for astonishment. `He's for Parliament!'

Back again, Ralph addressed Abigail. `Would your brother like another horse? That little cob ought to be got in foal - we're going to need plenty of horses.'

`You had better ask my father,' Abigail said, and he was off, moving with an excited urgency.

`Master Bicknell,' Harry said, `Sir, I have to ask you, are you in favour, I mean do you join yourself to the rebel cause as Horseman Attfield has done?'

Robert smiled. `Ralph Attfield is my friend. Friendship is stronger than politics and I value his friendship.'

`And you?' Harry looked at Joan, standing surrounded by her siblings.

She opened her mouth as if surprised, then closed it smiling, and said nothing.

Portsmouth

From where he was scraping lime-soaked hides over the scudding beam Tom saw Ralph stride between the pits in the yard and up to Jacob's office, a purposeful stride which Tom envied, for he himself felt adrift. Several times now he had been permitted to fetch gunpowder from Chilworth, even, after that first trip, to take Hal with him. Hal was invaluable in urging the horse through poor stretches of road, helping to keep the cart moving. Tom's confidence was growing. He was even beginning to `know' the horse as Sam had said he needed to do, and he had a better understanding of how best to handle the cart. Once or twice Jacob had told him to keep a shilling or two out of what his carting had earned.

Yet here he was, dispiritedly carrying on with the routines of tanning, with the prospect of four more years' apprenticeship and then presumably a lifetime as a tanner. Perhaps he should volunteer as a soldier. How that would horrify his father! He grinned to himself at the thought.

Ralph was a long time up there with Jacob, strange when Ralph seemed to be someone who was quickly in and out, always eager for the next thing he had to do, wasting no time on words.

Othen moved him and Peter to the regular job of moving hides. Holding either end of the suspending pole they raised each heavy dripping hide and lowered it into the next pit of more concentrated tanning solution. Hard work and repetitive, it yet required care to ensure the hides did not touch one another. Tom wished that unlike Peter he did not find it all so boring.

At last Ralph and Jacob came down the stair from the office and paused in the yard.

`Evening young Tom!' Ralph called, and as he came over to him, `I hear your mare has been putting in some useful work. I've been persuading your father to get her in foal.'

`Will she be able to work then?'

`Well, no, not for a while. I've really come to say farewell. I'm about to join Sir William Waller's troop of cavalry.'

`I wish you well then. When do you go?' (Or even `where?' Tom thought, knowing little about cavalry or troops beyond the playground of the militia.)

`I'm off to London very shortly.' Ralph shook his hand and turned to Jacob. `May I bid farewell to your good wife?' They moved into the house and soon he was gone.

The mare in foal, Tom thought. An end to carting. Back to pushing the hand cart. Lord! I'd almost rather trail a pike

Jacob offered no further information either that evening or in the days following, and soon attention was diverted by the news that Hannah was safely delivered of a son, another John, and they were bidden over to Frensham for his christening. All Spreakley claimed him as their own, John incredulous at this miraculous fruit of his body, Grandfather reassured that here was another Harding to redress the death of his son, Phoebe proud of her part in the safe delivery, the servants relieved and joining in the joy, whilst Hannah sat quietly, struggling with sore breasts, not sure of her feelings about this baby but content to be cosseted and looked after for the time being at least.

When Jacob called Tom up into his office one day in early August, Tom climbed the stair with a sinking heart, stomach churning with dread of what might be to come. He stood just inside the door, not daring to look his father in the eye, while Jacob took his time to say why he had summoned him.

At last he spoke. `I have bought two horses from Attfield. You may have noticed them in the meadow.'

Tom looked up, startled. So sunk had he been in melancholia that he had not in fact noticed any new horses among the cattle and horses that grazed the meadow all summer. He made an indistinct, non-committal sound which Jacob ignored.

`I have decided to release you from your indentures here.' Tom opened and shut his mouth, but this time no sound came at all.

`Moth is constructing a new cart and from today you may assist him in finishing it, as well as using the present cart for any carrying work you may obtain. The cob is to go to the stallion and you will use the new horses in turn.'

`Two horses? Two?'

`The new cart is considerably larger and will need two. I have agreed a contract with Piggott the corn chandler for you to carry corn as he requires. I shall of course continue to need some carrying done for the tannery from time to time.'

`Father!' Tom's eyes were wide.

`I haven't finished. The horses and the cart will remain my property until you have paid for them out of what you earn by their use. After that they will be yours.'

`Father!' Tom gasped again. `How can I ever thank you!'

`I don't want gratitude. I want to see that you can put spirit and energy into this enterprise and make a success of it. I only hope that you have some business sense.'

Now that Tom looked, out in the meadow, he saw that there were indeed two strange horses, noticeable because they were grazing side by side, moving in unison. They were a sturdy pair, much the same size and build as the general run of working horses with no trace of Arab refinement. He put a handful of grain in his pocket and walked towards them across the water meadow, watching them intently.

They lifted their heads and began to move away yet always with an eye upon him, keeping a constant distance between him and them. When he stopped walking they stood still, but as soon as he moved forward again they retreated. Further and further over the meadows they went, advance and retire almost like a dance. Tom sighed. It would be the cob all over again, with only Hal able to catch them. They made a little trotting spurt and he turned away, dispirited, and began walking back again.

Suddenly he became aware that they were following him. Should he look back? Would that discourage them? He walked steadily on, wondering. And then he stopped and very slowly turned round to face them.

They danced back a little, flank to flank, and then as he stood, stock still and watching them, they edged nearer.

They were rough-coated bays with whiskery muzzles, their eyes big and their ears alert in this venture of investigation. One had a long white mark down its nose, the other a splodge, and Tom smiled to think that they should obviously be given the time-honoured names of Blaze and Star. He slowly held out his hand with a little corn in the palm, and cautiously Blaze approached and nuzzled it.

Not to be outdone Star followed, pushing Blaze aside with his head. Tom felt the soft tickle of their beards, thrilling at their kindness to himself. The cob had been a challenge, and to many men a horse was simply a means of trans-port, but he knew then that these two were to be his companions and friends. He felt a rush of gratitude to whoever had reared them to such trust of man. Going into the barn he tipped corn and bran into a wooden dish to reward them for allowing him this closeness, and patted their necks as they ate it.

Then he went to the wagon yard to seek out Moth. The little man grinned broadly at him. `Well young man, so you're taking to carting after all.' He put down the tools he was holding and led Tom round to the side of his workshop where the shell of a large cart sat on the ground.

`Not much more to be done to the bodywork,' he said. `Just the wheels now.'

`Is that it? My cart?'

`That it is. Your gov'nor don't do things by halves.'

Over the following weeks Tom took every opportunity to watch and if possible help Moth with constructing the wheels and fitting their iron tyres. At last it was ready.

'Keep an eye on your wheels and axles, and never let them reach the state that hand cart o' yourn was in,' Moth said. 'Grease them here and here, and never miss the chance to go over a ford. The wet swells the wood and secures the joints.'

It was a beautiful cart. When he and Hal took the pair of horses to the yard and harnessed them in tandem (though they hardly needed the two of them to go empty through the long bridge ford to the Tanyard) Tom felt he would burst with pride. What cared he for the ribbing the tannery apprentices were giving him or the scorn of journeymen such as Nathan Armstrong who had stayed the course of his apprenticeship and not left half way? His father had wondrously given him the desire of his heart, and the wonder was not only the gift itself but his father's acknowledgement of that desire.

Piggott's first assignment for him was to collect a load of barley from Horsham way. Where on earth was Horsham and how did you get there? Tom stood in the corn merchant's office reading the chitty he had given him, with the name of the Horsham farm and a few scant directions for finding it. But how to find Horsham? He tried to conceal his ignorance as he enquired of Piggott.

`Well,' Piggott answered slowly, `There's several ways you could go. Depends if you like hills or longer valley ways.'

Tom stood twisting the paper in his hands. Piggott was not deceived. `Go seek advice from the carters in the Goat.'

The little Goat's Head Inn opposite the foot of Castle Street was crowded with men, a fraternity which Tom supposed would one day be his. Now it alarmed him and he did not feel like thanking Piggott for plunging him into it. There was an air of initiation.

With half a pint of ale inside him, Tom turned to a man standing near him and muttered `Which road would you take to Horsham?'

Had he really muttered that indistinctly? The man said loudly `Horsell? Into Windsor Great Park, no distance at all, back in a day.'

`Horley's miles away,' another said, `past Oxford, past Banbury, a couple of miles beyond Cropredy.'

Cropredy, Thomas thought, a strange and memorable name, and he wondered if it meant as it sounded. Cropredy. Not time to wonder though, for directions were coming from all sides.

`Wrong Horley, mate. Take the road along under the North Downs and when you get to Reigate turn right.'

`More likely to be Hawley up the Blackwater valley, and a right mess you'll get into with them marshes. Mind you don't lose a wheel.'

`But,' Tom ventured to speak, `It's not Horley, it's Horsham.'

`What's to choose,' declared another, 'between one whore and another?' and they roared with laughter.

As the laughter subsided an older man spoke quietly to him. `See here. Go along under Guild Down, Seale and Compton way, and over the river at Shalford.'

`That's the way to Chilworth, I know that.' Tom felt relieved.

`Aye, but you go south before Tillingbourne, don't go on to Chilworth. What takes you there?'

`Collecting gunpowder for the Castle garrison.'

`Ah.' The old man looked at him keenly. `Word's got about that you were doing that run. There's some as takes exception to you butting into the carting business.' He jerked his head towards a corner of the Inn parlour. Tom followed the jerk with his eyes. There sat Abe Trussler, staring at him.

The stare lasted only a moment, but that moment conveyed such hostility that Tom was shaken. Almost at once Abe turned his attention back to his tankard.

The old man gave Tom time to absorb the warning and then went on, `You done that run much?'

`On and off' he muttered. `And after Shalford?'

`Ask as you go. Anyone will tell you.'

And so he went, alone, on a bright August day with an empty cart and Attfield's horses working harmoniously together. Just as the old carter had predicted there were plenty of people to point the way for him, glad to pause in their harvesting, even to offer him and his horses a drink of water. He spent the night lying under the cart with the horses tethered alongside, a warm mellow night. Waking at dawn with a light mist lifting from the fields around him he stretched, full of contentment with this new life.

On the return, slower, trip laden with sacks of corn, at the turning to Chilworth he saw the man he dealt with at the powder mills, and hailed him to show off his new outfit.

`I'll be glad to carry any quantity of gunpowder now,' Tom told him.

The opportunity came sooner than he could have imagined. Word came to him that the Parliamentary troops besieging Portsmouth had need of new supplies. Emboldened, he asked Piggott if he wished any grain collected from the Portsmouth direction, and all at once he had his first major job, and some good pay too, sixpence a mile all the way to Portsmouth.

The older carter - Ted they called him - gave some advice on the route. `Keep to the valleys,' he said, `and travel with others for safety. You'll be liable if anything is stolen from your load.' He thought for a while. `Tell you what. My son Dick does London to Portsmouth most weeks. If you can be at Godalming by mid-day on a Tuesday, you could go on with him.'

Tom started calculating how long this journey was likely to take. `The corn has to be picked up near Hambledon,' he said.

`Ah, then that's the best way back, over to Alton and then home. You'll need the best part of a week.'

He told Phoebe whose prompt reaction was `I'll put up some victuals for you.' Mary showed unexpected interest.

`Might I have a few days off Mistress?' she asked. `I'd be glad to go to Godalming.' She was blithe about the return journey. `Someone will give me a ride, or I could walk.'

Phoebe looked at her with that little half smile of hers. `Are we going to lose you Mary? Carey still has much to learn.'

`I wouldn't like to say.' Mary closed her lips.

`Is it Francis?' Abigail teased.

`I'd just be glad to go to Godalming.'

`It's a pleasant enough place, wedged between its hills,' Phoebe said. `Very well. Just one night away, and be prudent.'

Hal was close by, watching each as they spoke, eyes wide and anxious.

`You'll come with me,' Thomas said, `So long as the Master agrees.'

Despite having started out before dawn, when the gunpowder barrels were loaded and secured the sun was already well up.

Back across the ford to the main road they joined other wagons going south, and Tom sent Hal running between them to enquire for Old Ted's son Dick. He was well known, and the general answer was `Dick? He'll be at Godalming by now.'

What if he had gone on before they got there? Tom felt near to panic, fearful of losing his way, fearful of being alone and unprotected. Other carters all seemed to know each other. He felt very young and green. They trundled on along the valley until Godalming came into view.

`What should we do?' he asked Mary. The bridge into the town lay ahead of them, the other carts rumbling across it into and through the streets. He called `Whoa!' to Blaze and Star, pulling the cart to the side of the roadway to let others pass.

`I need to find the forge,' Mary said.

`I can't take gunpowder near a forge,' Tom said. `Suppose we set it alight and it exploded! Hal, you stay here and keep watch and I'll go with Mary.' At least he would be active, however much the worries assailed him.

`Better the other way around,' Mary said. `You've a valuable load here.'

She set off with Hal while Tom settled to wait. He filled up the horses' nosebags, and the time dragged. How he hated waiting!

The wait felt much longer than it was. Hal came running back, calling as he came `We found the forge! And Master Dick is there - his horse cast a shoe.'

`Can I bring the wagon?'

`They said it could stand in the High Street.'

Tom pulled into the street within sight of the forge leaving Hal to mind the cart and horses. Clear of fire and anvil, Mary stood watching as the blacksmith, burly with a wide beard, hammered out the shoe. Nearby a man held a horse.

`Are you Ted's son Dick?' Tom asked.

`Nay, Dick's gone to buy bread, but he'll be back.'

Tom breathed a sigh of relief, and began to watch too.

The blacksmith tested the shoe for fit, filling the air with the smell of singeing hair and hoof. Another small adjustment, his assistant gently moving the bellows to give just the right degree of heat to the fire. He plunged the finished shoe into water and then he nailed it on, twisting off the ends of the nails as they emerged through the hoof, filing a clean finish. `There we are,' he said, and smiled at Mary.

`Francis, this is Tom, who brought me here,' she said, and Tom found his own hand grasped in an enormous warm handshake.

`From Farnham eh?' Francis said. `You've brought me a surprise,' smiling again at Mary. `I was in Farnham, garrisoning the Castle.' He laughed. `Funny old business.'

`Why was that?' Tom asked.

`Well, the ironmaster Captain Quennell called out our trained band for the King, and we drilled a bit, but then the Lord Lieutenant disarmed us. He wanted the arms for the Parliamentary side.' Francis laughed again. `So no more fighting, nothing to fight with.'

`Hang up your armour...' Mary began.

`And make love.' Francis put a huge arm around Mary's waist. He planted a kiss on her nose, and laughed again.

`Who's a-bundling then?' called an approaching man who proved to be Dick, weighed down with provisions, happy to share them with everyone. He seemed to be in no hurry. `We'll go on our way and see how far we get,' he said. `Summer days are long and we can sleep anywhere.'

In the event they rested just short of Haslemere. Dick made numerous detours to deliver and collect goods at different farmsteads and hamlets, and Tom took his time from him. Next day Dick picked up passengers who were glad of a ride through the wildness of Liss Forest. Beyond the forest the roads were less dusty, though the ruts were harder in the chalk and the way often no easier. Petersfield did not welcome a load of gunpowder, and at Buriton where Dick and his man often slept, the Five Bells refused it too.

`You can take yon cart down to the pond where it can do no harm,' the innkeeper's wife shrilled. `I'll have no explosives here.'

That was no hardship, with grazing for the horses and shelter under the cart, and they were off early in the morning, over the knee of the downs and through a long valley. From there Tom and Hal went on alone, climbing steeply up onto Portsdown on the old Roman road.

Every now and then they heard thuds, crackle and thud, sounds dulled by the hill.

Nothing could have prepared them for their first sight of the sea.

They breasted the hill and there it was, a wide wide expanse so wide it stretched from extreme left to farthest west, horizoned by the Isle of Wight. Both of them gasped, wordless, and stood gazing as the horses recovered from the climb.

Nearer, steeply below the cliff edge of the Down and across the inlet, Portsea Island spread out towards the sea flanked by its two harbours. Fields were ripe with corn around the town which stood far down the island at the narrow entrance to the western harbour.

`That's where the thuds come from,' Tom said. `Look, you can see flashes either side of the channel. See? There! and an answer the other side. They must be firing cannon.'

`There are tents too,' Hal said, pointing towards the centre of the island.

`We've been told to go to Colonel Norton's house up here somewhere.' Tom consulted his instructions and they plodded on.

`More tents,' Hal said. Indeed there were, clustered in the home fields of Colonel Norton's farm, with people moving between and around them. Soon they were challenged by a couple of men armed with muskets.

`I've a load of gunpowder,' Tom said, and was directed to a barn Here another sentry challenged them and Tom repeated, `I've a load of gunpowder ordered from Chilworth.' The sentry shouted to another man, `Hey! Find the Commissary for us!'

`He doesn't look any different from any man,' Hal murmured to Tom.

`You mean no uniform? Militia doesn't get uniform, you wear your own clothes.' He took advantage of the wait to give the horses their nosebags.

The Commissary of Munitions, a short fat man with a bright cockade in his hat, was out of breath when he reached them followed by a straggle of men. He inspected the consignment note Tom handed him, nodded, and counted the barrels against the list.

`Some here,' he said, `and the rest down at Portsea - I'll send a man to guide you.'

The man led them down the steep way to narrow Portsbridge, then on past fields already over-ripe to where the Parliamentary forces were encamped. Here also a barn had been allocated for the powder barrels.

`Do the cannon never stop?' Tom asked their guide.

`That's right. The dogs bark all day and night.'

`What do they hit?'

`Fortifications I suppose. Men too if they're unlucky. We had to dig in over Gosport way, the shots were coming so close, one after another.'

`Frightening,' Tom said, though it hardly seemed real.

Their guide arranged for them to spend the night in a barn where soldiers had established beds on piles of old straw. A makeshift kitchen stood in one corner of the farmyard with wood fires keeping enormous cauldrons bubbling, watched over by some women. `You can eat with us,' the man said, `and the horses go on the lines.'

`Can I take them?' Hal asked. He led them towards where numerous horses stood side by side, tethered to lines of posts. Tom squatted in the barn doorway in the fading light and cleaned the harness of its road dust and dirt, keeping an eye out for Hal's return.

When he came, he was running and so excited he was almost inarticulate. `Tom! Tom! You'll never guess!' He gulped some breath. `Mr. Attfield! At the horse lines! He's coming over here to see you.'

Tom stacked the harness neatly and stood up just as Ralph Attfield strode into view, resplendent in his new buffalo leather cavalry coat and bucket-topped boots. Almost simultaneously they said `Well! what a surprise!' and laughed.

`Gunpowder eh?' Ralph said. `That's a valuable load.'

`I'm glad to be relieved of it I can tell you,' Tom said. `We weren't too popular with villages along the road.'

`You'll be popular here. Plenty gets used in this siege.'

`Those horses you sold my father - what a pair!'

`Work together well do they? They're out of a good stable.'

They settled themselves on a stone bench to dip bread into the pottage they had been issued as men poured into the yard to collect their rations.

'All well at home?' Ralph asked. 'Bicknells? The tannery? And that sister of yours, how is she?'

`Tell us about the cavalry?' Hal begged.

Ralph considered, chewing his meat. At last he said, `Did you ever play at "Tom Tiddler's Ground"?'

`I'm on Tom Tiddler's Ground, picking up gold and silver,' Tom said. `Of course we did. Daring to cross the line and darting back when Tom Tiddler tried to catch us.'

`It's like that,' Ralph said, `only much more exciting.' He pulled another mouthful of bread off the hunk in his hand. `Early on, when only the two troops of horse were here, twenty of us volunteered and we galloped over the passage at Portsbridge and caught the enemy's rearguard. Full gallop we went, with the two Colonels leading us.'

'Was anyone hurt?' Tom asked.

'No. They were so surprised, we took a couple of prisoners and the rest ran away.

'Right onto Tom Tiddler's Ground!' Hal said, his eyes wide.

Later on Sir William chose a larger group of us and we rode right up to the walls of Portsmouth to show them our colours. They fired cannon at us, and their horse sallied out, didn't do much, it seemed like just a gesture. That was good sport.'

'Does no one get hurt?' Tom asked.

`A few have been killed. One mad Scotsman,' Ralph chuckled at the memory, `went right into the town, without his helmet, thought he could take it single-handed and got three great gashes in his head. He couldn't see for blood. They patched him up and sent him back in exchange for some prisoners we were holding.'

`A game of chess.' Tom's tone was abstracted.

`A lot more fun than chess. No fun to be in the town though. Deserters come over every night when it's dark. They say they're running out of corn and salt and everything else too – everything bar gunpowder and they've plenty of that. . No use having gunpowder if there's no food.'

'So the deserters come to where there's food?' Tom asked.

'Aye, I suppose they do. But our troops need bringing up to strength. so I reckon we're glad to have them add to our numbers.'

One of the women came round with a jug of ale, and they drank silently for a while, listening to the bark and thud of the cannon.

Then Ralph said `You'll have heard that the King has raised his standard. So it really is war now. Once we've secured Portsmouth there'll be more to do in earnest'

`Those boys,' Hal said, `at the horse lines. What are they doing?'

`They're called Paddy Boys. Help look after the horses.' Ralph smiled at the look on Hal's face. `Would you fancy being a Paddy?'

`Would I' Hal breathed.

`Hey, I need you!' Tom said, and they laughed.

Hearing the rain in the night they were glad to be sleeping in the barn rather than under the cart, though the barn was full of men and snores. Tom woke up eager to be on the road and away. He fetched Blaze and Star himself and saw some of the raggedy boys, hardly older than Hal, who were busying themselves at the horse lines. Surely Hal would be better off carting than with them.

The climb up Portsdown with an empty cart was easy, and they made good time through the rain to Hambledon and the farm to which Piggott had directed them. The farmer was clearly surprised to see them.

`Corn? You're too late. It was collected two days ago.'

`But...but Mr. Piggott contracted me to cart it.'

`Can't help that. I needed it carted, 't'was all threshed and I needed room for the new harvest. Besides, I wanted it sold before the military collared it. So I was glad to see him.'

`See who?' Tom asked, hardly expecting an answer.

`Old what's his name,' the farmer said, `From Farnham way. You know. Does general carting.'

A horrible thought struck Tom. He recalled his talk with old Ted in the inn full of carters, Ted giving directions that many could have overheard. `Not,' he said, `not Abe Trussler?'

`Abe, yes that's the name, the old rogue.'

`You may well say that,' Tom muttered.

`Never sure of his carts,' the farmer went on, unaware of the impact on Tom. `So I didn't fill it right up. In fact some sacks are still waiting - you could take them.'

They were not many. Abe must have come direct by Alton, a couple of days' travelling at the most, while Tom was meandering down with Dick. He had taken all but a few of the sacks, and Tom thought bitterly of the money he had expected to earn, now almost halved. If Abe was set on continuing these tactics, what hope would there be of his ever owning the horses and cart, of ever paying back his father, of ever being a carter in his own right.

Nathan

Abigail felt herself to be alone in the house when the shooting began. Tom was out as he so often was these days, sampling the inns. Her parents were dining at Bicknells' to mark Joan's eighteenth birthday. The men and boys had helped themselves to what Mary had laid out on the table, and dispersed. Maybe they were in the attic, maybe they too had gone out. She did not know and she did not much care.

She was full of cold, rheumy and shivery and sorry for herself. She should have been at Bicknells' too, but all she wanted was to wrap herself in shawls and curl up by the fire.

The last of the late September day was rapidly fading. Faggots against the fire back flickered erratic light, all that she wanted or needed. In the embers at the side of the hearth a small pan of spiced ale simmered, near enough for her to reach and ladle out a drink whenever she wanted to be warmed inside. It soothed her throat as well.

Mary came down the stairs with Carey. `Love-a-duck!' she exclaimed, `You're well wrapped up! It's a warm evening.'

`I'm cold right through.'

Mary placed another faggot on the fire. `Should I fetch you a blanket?'

`Thank you, but the fire's enough.'

`Well,' Mary said. `If you've all you need Carey and I are just going round to see her aunt. We've heard she's poorly too.' She opened the yard door. `The stars are out, we'll easily see our way.'

Abigail sipped her drink, thinking. When Tom told them about his encounter with Ralph Attfield she had tried not to sound too eager for details. How dashing Ralph must look in his new uniform! Tom told of bucket top boots, the wide top allowing his knees to bend when in the saddle while protecting his thighs. He had a sword and pistols, and an orange scarf. She wondered, though, about what Tom recounted of his attitude to the fighting, like a boyish game.

She shivered, not only because of her cold. Spreading her fingers, she counted off what she knew about Ralph. A trustworthy horse dealer; often in a hurry; no parents living; vigorous.... She arrived at her little finger and all she could think of were his looks and his voice. And now a side of him that her father must surely disapprove, opposed as Jacob was to war, a side that dismayed her. She wondered, if and when she ever saw Ralph again, whether he would still stir her as someone special.

She ladled some more spicy ale into the tankard and wrapped her hands around it, warming them. Perhaps it would be simpler to believe what Joan said about Harry's regard for herself, though to follow it through would spoil their friendship. Yet his attention to her was so unlike what she had seen of John Harding's for Ann, that she doubted it could signify affection. John was lusty, and where did lust overtake desire, and where did desire relate to affection, or were they all woven through together, inseparable. Was it desire that stirred in her whenever she saw Ralph, lust even, seeing there were so few grounds for affection beyond how he looked and sounded?

`Love me not for comely grace, for my pleasing eye or face,' went round in her head.

She drained the tankard, closed her eyes, and dozed.

In her dream the strange landscape stretched limitless all around her, and into its distance Ralph and Hal were riding, surrounded by horses, riding further and further away. Then someone was shooting at them - and no! More! Shots were coming from all sides, and there was a clatter of footsteps on wood and she opened her eyes to see Nathan rushing after Hal towards the door.

Hal opened it, and the sound of gunfire was louder. Nathan peered over his shoulder. Then he pulled him back inside and closed the door.

`They've started fighting here!' Hal's eyes were wide with excitement. He ran off into the bake room for a better view across the river. Nathan stopped by Abigail.

`I feared you might be attacked!'

`Me?' Abigail lifted bleary eyes and burrowed in her shawl for a handkerchief.

`Haven't you heard the shots? Listen. There they go again.'

`Not close by,' Abigail said, blowing her nose. She listened. `Sounds like militia practice.'

`After dark? They're attacking the castle more like.'

`Well they're not attacking me whoever they are.'

Suddenly Nathan was kneeling beside her putting a protective arm around the bulk of her shawl-wrapped shoulders. `I couldn't bear it if they did.'

Abigail squinted at him. `Who are "they" anyway?'

`It doesn't matter - you're safe.' More shots sounded from across the town.

`Get up, please, Nathan. Don't be so dramatic. I don't need protecting.'

Nathan tipped back on his heels and regarded her. `I want to protect you.'

Seeing him squatting there it occurred to Abigail that in all the years he had lived in Tanyard House she had never really looked at him. Apprentice and journeyman he must have been part of the household for nearly ten years, growing from boy to man. And now here he was beside her and she was noticing the way his lower jaw jutted forward and his dun-coloured hair stood away from his head, noticing the stubbly beard and the sturdy hands such as someone surnamed Armstrong ought to have, all as if for the first time.

`Nathan, please. Do stand up.'

Hal came running in. `I saw flashes up in the park, by the Castle.'

`Perhaps the garrison is being attacked,' Abigail yawned.

`What's left of it,' Nathan said, his eagerness stemmed.

Abigail addressed Hal. `You'll see it better from the window in the loft. And,' turning to Nathan, `I am perfectly at peace down here alone.'

He looked at her then in such a manner that she turned her eyes quickly away, and he followed Hal up the stairs.

The gunfire had ceased and she was dozing again when she heard running outside, running and loud voices. The next moment a posse of young men burst through the doorway, led by Tom. They were laughing, slapping each other on the back, breathless from running, and they were drunk.

She stood up, shedding shawls around her. `Tom!'

Tom lurched towards her. `Oh Abi, such a lark!'

`There'll be some feasting, that's for sure,' said one of the lads.

`Venison feast!'

`Gentry food!"

Nathan rushed down the stairs again, all prepared for defence against invasion. Seeing Tom he stopped short. `What in heaven's name?'

Some had been in the spree from the start and pieced together the story, which had begun with tavern talk. An absent Bishop. A poor harvest. Apprehension of what might be ahead. Resentment over loss of Castle work. `Why don't we...' growing to a crowd with one mind. Men poured out of the inns, gathering numbers as they went, with the lads tagging along for the fun of it. Some had spent the day shooting in the forest and still had their guns with them. Others picked up weapons as they passed their homes, muskets, bows and arrows, catapults.

Up to the deer park. Someone unlocked the gate, others broke down the fences. As the deer bounded away the shots rang out and even in the dusk a few were hit. Mostly the musket fire achieved nothing except to provoke answering salvos from the Castle.

These had cooled their spirits. Leaving a few to drag down the carcasses to wherever they could conceal them, the rest ran pel mel back into the town and scattered before anyone could be arrested and blamed.

`So we came here, and escaped,' Tom said jubilantly.

`If you're here when the Master comes home you'll have hell to pay' Nathan said.

`Oh glory!' Tom rubbed his tousled head.

Nathan took command. `Go on, Tom, go upstairs. And the rest of you, out!'

They straggled out, still giggling and pushing each other, herded by Nathan. Abigail could not but thank him, but when he came back towards her making as if to speak to her again she held up her hand.

`Goodnight Nathan,' she said, clasped her shawls in a bundle and went up to her bedroom. Above in the loft she could hear Tom blundering about to the annoyance of his fellows already abed, and sometimes Hal's voice too, and Nathan telling him to shut his gob and lie down. She snuggled under her blanket and settled to a disturbed sleep. Perhaps to share with Mary and Carey would be wise, if only she could have her own separate bed.

Whether it was because of the riot, or because news came from the Midlands of encounters between the two armies, a couple of weeks later a new garrison of nearly a hundred men arrived at the Castle under the command of their part time Captain, George Wither.

Wither was not unknown to the local gentry for he lived but four miles from Farnham towards Guildford. He however was eager to know everyone and everything. Ardent and nervous he hastened from person to person and place to place, anxious over possible attack from the King's forces and impatient to improve and defend the Castle. Digger Martin volunteered his services again and quickly confirmed his nickname, employed as a pioneer digging defensive trenches.

Wither was the talk of the town. He made people laugh with his satirical and sometimes scurrilous attacks on the King's supporters. As a pamphleteer he kept in close touch with events, taking particular note of Royalist reverses, which did not endear him to some of his fellow gentry.

`I hardly have time for writing with my military duties,' he said to Harry, as yet unaware of the latter's loyalties. 'My inclination is to wield a pen - the pen is mightier than the sword - but by God we need the sword at this present time.'

Hermann Shepheard could not resist taking a close look at the happenings in the Castle - just checking on ecclesiastical property. He reported to anyone who would listen that he had been like the prophet Samuel confronting King Saul with `What then is this bleating of sheep in my ears, and the lowing of the oxen which I hear?' as he saw the livestock driven in from Wither's own farm.

`Be sure,' Shepheard said to Harry, `the man is being paid for this procurement. He is not giving it for love, lawyer that he is.'

Robert Bicknell was so even-handed about political allegiance that Wither visited him more than he did most others, intrigued to dig out his views and if necessary provoke him into support. Besides, he was one of the two newly elected Bailiffs who ran the town.

The autumn had encouraged Abigail to revive her Latin studies, a move not unwelcome to Joan. Shepheard told his little joke to them both as Harry corrected the Latin.

Harry looked up. `Were he not for the traitors' cause,' he said, `he would be amusing company.'

`He is drawing away tradesmen for his military schemes,' the curate said. `I need the Rectory roof looked at, and all the carpenters are repairing the stables up at the Castle, I cannot obtain the services of one.'

`He writes poetry,' Joan said. `He gave me this verse;
"I loved a lass, a fair one
As fair as e're was seen;
She was indeed a rare one,
Another Sheba queen".'

`Would that I had penned that myself for one so fair,' the curate said. `Now you, Harry, could do as well.'

Harry turned firmly to the Latin text and Abigail applied herself to it too, but as soon as they finished she moved away, fearful lest that satisfied feeling of a translation well completed might be interpreted otherwise by him. She crossed the room to where she had left her bag. It was to this tableau, Harry gazing intently at her as she turned her back and busied herself packing books and slate into the bag, that Wither himself entered. He paused, his mental antennae alerted.

Only a momentary pause before he enquired for Hopgrower and Mistress Bicknell. When they came he spoke of his alarm at enemies on every side.

`It all seems quite peaceful to me,' Elizabeth said, `except for your companies for ever drilling and firing off muskets and the like.'

`Ah, they need to, they need to. The newsbooks and pamphlets would alert you to these necessities.'

`Miss Mannory is a great pamphlet reader,' Harry said. Abigail pretended not to hear. She picked some tangled threads out of Joan's sewing basket and began to unravel them.

Later, as if unconnected with anything that had gone before, Wither asked the company in general `Do you know my poem `The Manly Heart'? I'll not recite it all, it is too long, but one verse will give you the flavour of it.

"Shall my foolish heart be pined
Cause I see a woman kind;
Or a well disposéd nature
Joinéd with a lovely feature?
Be she meeker, kinder than
Turtle dove or pelican,
If she be not so to me,
What care I how kind she be?"'

`Oh you cruel man!' Elizabeth exclaimed. `Have you never heard of maidens acting coyly when indeed they love?'

`Affection should be reciprocated. What use expending time and devotion if it is never returned?' Wither said. He laughed ruefully. `Perhaps I should regret how little is reciprocated between Surrey's Lord Lieutenant and myself.'

`Did he not appoint you to the garrison?' Robert Bicknell asked.

`He did indeed, no doubt because he needed someone with military experience - you know of course that I fought against the Scots in '39. But I can't say there is any love lost between us.'

`"If Satan is divided against himself..."' Shepheard began, and the smile on Harry's face was not lost on Wither. He left soon after, muttering to Robert about his malignant neighbours.

Within the month he was gone, in a state of near panic. The first set battle of the war, at Edgehill, had resolved nothing, and the Royalists were approaching ever nearer. They occupied first Oxford, then Reading, and Wither was in London begging for guns when the cavalry under Prince Rupert reached Windsor. Far from obtaining what he asked for he was commanded to abandon Farnham Castle in order to release resources for the capital. Twenty four hours later he and the garrison were gone.

Once more the Castle was empty, and some in the town again cast covetous eyes at the deer park. Not for long however. Only two days after Wither withdrew, Royalist Sir John Denham took over with a hundred members of the Posse Comitatus, gentlemen who enjoyed a little soldiering while not bothering much with regular musters. Sir John, another poet but half Wither's age, made the most of the Bishop's spacious house and the supplies his predecessor had left behind, entertaining the local gentry in a pleasing manner.

It could have been reports of this ready hospitality which prompted the Rector to leave his other benefice for a visit to Farnham. Curiosity was such that even those who risked being fined as recusant for their ill attendance at church made the effort to be at morning service the Sunday after his arrival, a service taken with every observance of Laudian practice.

After Mattins Elizabeth Bicknell and Betty Gary with her new baby inevitably drew around them those eager for gossip.

`Reverend Shepheard must have called him in to give him support against the lecturer,' someone said.

`He's taken his time if that is so,' said another.

`Nay, my husband,' Elizabeth sounded confident, `My husband thinks he's checking up on behalf of the Bishop, checking up on whether the Market dues are being paid.'

`Well I suppose he should know, being Bailiff.'

`You're all mistaken,' Betty Gary said with a secretive, knowing look. `There's a woman in the case.'

All eyes turned to her. `What woman?' `He a married man!' `How do you know?' `What is he at?'

`I have my informations,' Betty refused to say more, satisfied with her present power.

`Well! A gentleman of the cloth!' Elizabeth said. `But then of course they're only human, but as a minister he should be above reproach....' and she rattled on.

Joan, standing on the edge of the group, raised her eyebrows at Abigail and shrugged. `If Mistress Gary says so, everyone will soon believe it.'

The curate was hastening over to the girls. `My dear Joan,' he said, `You must do me the honour of allowing me to present you to Sir John Denham,' and he steered her, ignoring Abigail, to where Sir John was speaking with Harry Vernon.

Nettled by his rudeness to herself Abigail followed and to her surprise realised that Nathan was following too, a large presence just behind her right shoulder.

`Forgive me Sir John,' Shepheard squeaked, `for butting into your converse. I would so much like to present my dear friend Joan Bicknell to you.'

Joan, who was looking her prettiest, bobbed a curtsy. Denham contemplated her as if he too would very much like to call her his dear friend. He took her hand.

`Bailiff Bicknell's daughter, yes? Charming, charming! Such charm demands a poem. Poor rhymester that I am, I must yet find a moment to contrive a few verses.'

Joan blushed and avoided his gaze, but Shepheard exclaimed `Another poet!'

`You must be referring to my old rival Sir George Wither. I don't know which of the two of us is the worse poet - I rather think it is he.'

`Master Vernon writes poetry.' Although Joan spoke to Denham her focus was on Harry.

`Really Vernon?' Denham exclaimed, but Harry was not paying attention. He was looking past him at Abigail, yet not at Abigail. Beyond her, at Nathan, fixedly. As Abigail watched, his expression became a challenge, one side of a facial duel which held for long seconds. Then Nathan, as if taking possession, put his arm round her.

She stiffened, startled. Still watching Harry she saw the challenge on his face turn into a look of disdain, a disdain which encompassed both herself and Nathan. Almost in defiance she relaxed and lent against Nathan. It was not unpleasant, this strong arm, this firm body.

Denham was saying, `You should put your talents to support our cause Vernon. We shall be needing scribblers to counter all the news sheets the rebels put about.'

Harry turned vacantly to him. Abigail felt Nathan's fingers move against her arm, exploring.

`News sheets, yes, we could use your rhyming, though the rebels will soon be defeated. We must talk more of this.'

`Yes. Indeed, yes.' Harry's returned his attention emphatically to Sir John.

Nathan squeezed Abigail's shoulders. She felt his face come near, that jutting bristly face, as if he were about to kiss her and suddenly she woke up to the message she must be giving him. She broke sharply away from him and without looking back, sped off to where Tom was chatting to some of his friends and stamping his feet.

`This church is freezing,' he said.

`It's hardly winter yet,' said one of his companions.

`My feet are cold all the same. That's one disadvantage of carting, cold feet.'

Relieved now to be in this atmosphere of humdrum practicalities Abigail said `I'd better try and knit you some stockings.'

`Would you Abi? Would you really? I'd bless you for that.'

The lads received her awkwardly. Though feeling unwelcome she stayed by them watching out of the corner of her eye as Sir John and Harry left the church with Joan, talking earnestly. Nathan hovered uncertainly for a while, then suddenly followed them through the north door.

She ought to go, but suppose Nathan were waiting outside. She could not bear to face him, not now, not yet.

Talk among Tom's friends dwindled, embarrassed. She dithered, between Nathan outside the north door and perhaps the Rector and Shepheard going home outside the south door. She would rather face the curate if need be.

The lads started to move, and she bolted through the south door. The churchyard was empty. She stood for a moment and then ran, ran down past the Rectory to the meadow path below Vernons' gardens.

No one was about this cold November Sunday, and she slowed her pace. The water meadows, their dank grasses colourless, were submerging under the damp chill of winter and she felt likewise, as if everything was coming to an end and she was to blame. She stood on the mill bridge, watching the water swirling under it, as out of control as her life seemed to have become.

Her eagerness for Latin had entangled her and caused her friend to become her rival. Maybe Mistress Bicknell was right and she had been coy, but she had only meant to help Joan by detaching Harry.

Now he was well and truly detached, and by the most unwelcome means. She shuddered, recalling the disdain on his face, he who had sparred with her on politics and commended her studies.

Shivering now, she hurried from the mill bridge and into their lane. Despite the sort of pleasure she had just experienced leaning into Nathan's side, she could no more relish the idea of bedding with him than she could have done with John Harding. That leaning, though, must have encouraged him, for he had almost kissed her.

Sooner or later she must try to explain herself to him. For the present she only wanted to avoid him. She would start knitting Tom's stockings.

Her parents were sitting either side of the fire, Phoebe reading, Jacob sucking on an empty pipe as he dozed. She found some skeins of wool and brought them to her mother.

`No,' Phoebe said, feeling the weight of them in her hands, `that's too little for stockings. You'll need to spin some more.'

Spinning, however, was out of the question on a Sunday, the day of rest. She went to the window and looked out at the tannery works, drearily familiar and drab. The swollen river was lapping up into the bottom part of the yard below the tanning pits. November seemed like the low point of the year.

Phoebe looked up from the book on her lap and said `Do stop wandering about Abigail.' So she sat at the table, wondering what to do through the afternoon, on edge for fear of facing Nathan.

Then he came down the stairs. She stood up hastily and went to the shelf at the far end of the Hall where their few books were kept. He hovered uncertainly by the table. She stole a few glances in his direction, needing to keep an eye on him yet fearful lest she catch his eye. Then to her relief Hal came in with Peter full of the latest news.

'There's been a battle outside London!'

`The King won.' Hal sounded disgusted.

`Are you for Parliament then?' Nathan asked, half mocking.

`Judging from all the bulletins you read,' Peter said, `Parliament is what you favour isn't it?'

`Not if they're going to be defeated.'

`That's just time serving.'

Nathan raised his voice. `Haven't you read what they've been doing, raiding houses and carrying off loot?'

`Who's "they"? Which side?'

`Both. They're as bad as each other. And that battle at Edgehill, a stalemate.'

`Miles away' Peter said.

`London's not miles away.'

`No, and they sacked Brentford.'

`There you are then. You need to stay on the winning side.'

`You'd be a deserter!' Hal exclaimed.

`I don't intend being a soldier so that doesn't arise.'

`It's common knowledge you're not in the militia,' Peter said.

`There's plenty of fools willing to become substitutes. Digger Martin jumped at the chance.'

From her seat by the fire Phoebe said `Would you two stop disputing and allow us some peace?'

`Let's go out and see what more we can discover,' Peter said, and Nathan went with him.

Hal came up beside Abigail. In a small voice he asked, `Do you think Mr. Attfield was in that battle, that one outside London?'

Seeing Hal's anxious face Abigail said nothing for a moment, then quietly, `Brentford? Would that be bad?'

`Peter said they were driven into the river and drowned.'

`Oh Hal, I hope not.'

At supper around the table Nathan kept his eyes so constantly upon her that it was all she could do to avoid meeting them with her own. She concentrated her attention firmly on her plate, and afterwards hurried to help Mary and Carey clear away and wash the dishes.

`All finished,' Mary said. `I'll dowse the light,' and they had no option but to return to the dim light of the Hall. Nathan was waiting just beyond the chimney stack.

`Abigail' he said, touching her arm, `Come where we can talk.'

Stomach tense and trembling she followed him to the further end of the room where light from the rush lights scarcely reached, and stood there dumbly. For what seemed an age they stood, not facing each other, neither able to begin.

At last he blurted out her name. Just `Abigail!', putting his hand on her shoulder. She shook it off.

`You let me this morning!' in an injured tone.

`You gave me no choice!'

`Oh come on now! You liked it! You fairly nestled into my arms. You nearly let me kiss you.'

`I did not!'

`You seemed to be expecting it.'

`I? Expect it? I didn't invite you to come near me. And as for kissing you! I didn't stay to try it, did I.'

`Shimmied off like a silly chicken.'

`Better than being kissed against my will.'

Nathan thrust his hands into his pockets in a determined gesture.

`Look Abigail. Quieten down. You must know that I've cared for you for a long time. I haven't the airs and graces of some, (a meaning pause) but surely you realised...'

Abigail shook her head.

`Well I'm telling you straight. I can offer you as good a life as you've had in your father's house. I'm an able tanner with a fine trade and a head for business, and you'll not get better than that.'

Now she did look at him, squarely. `I am not a business proposition,' she said.

`Good Lord, girl, I'm asking you to marry me!'

Her look did not waver. `And I am refusing you.'

His jutting lower jaw jutted even further as he swallowed this. `Take your time. I know you'll come round to it in the end.'

`But I don't care for you in that way, not in the least.'

'Kind of you to say so, whatever "that way" may be.'

`You've just always been here, I mean for years, one of the boys, one of the men, like the rest of them.'

`Part of the furniture you might say,' he said grimly. `Well I intend to change all that. You're a spirited lass I know, with your interest in the affairs of state, and such spirit is worth having so long as it is tamed and moulded.' Abigail stood her ground, silent.

`I want to protect you too.' His tone softened and he tried again to touch her. `You know I want to protect you in these troublous times.'

She shook her head.

`At least allow me,' he pleaded, `to court you.'

`I would prefer,' she said, `to have no obligation to you. Please do not press me.'

Monday took the men back to work outside and at every opportunity Abigail span, and then started knitting, plain and purl ribbing on four needles. November was nearly over, colder by the day, and Tom needed his stockings. He was full of news he picked up on his travels.

`Sir John Denham is full of Royalist victories,' Tom said after delivering provisions to the Castle, for whether the current garrison's loyalties lay with King or Parliament, they still needed carters. `Reckons they'll all be home by Christmas.'

The constable came with warnings of billeting, assessing and noting where troops could be accommodated.

`Hm. Plenty of room here. That long loft, and the out-buildings....'

`Isn't there space enough in the Castle?' Phoebe said.

Right at the end of November Hal rushed into the Tanyard hot from an errand. `The soldiers are coming! Up at the Castle and in the town! Horses! Cavalry!'

Siege

What a long way to go for some kegs of claret, Tom thought as the small cart slithered down the chalky clay off Guild Down. He slithered too, walking at Blaze's head, helping him avoid the worst of the pot holes which gleamed with water. He was in constant danger of a bootful from those or from the deep cart ruts.

Sir John Denham must think he was in for a long stay at the Castle to need all this claret. Tom grinned as he remembered how he had just outbid Abe Trussler to fetch it from Sir John's seat at Epsom. For all the struggle along the wintry roads it did mean money in his pocket at this slack time of year. And Sir John's housekeeper had allocated him a comfortable bed for the night and fed him well. Evidently the servants were making the most of being left to their own devices.

Now at last he reached the foot of the down, he and Blaze and the cart without mishap, and set off at a better pace across the valley towards the rise into Farnham Park. He had decided to approach the Castle this way from the north, so avoiding the steeper climb up from the town.

It was already late morning. Here and there men were digging out ditches and repairing hedges, the ongoing winter jobs. Then suddenly as he emerged from a narrow lane his way was blocked by horsemen, streams of horsemen.

Trotting in a sort of order, strung out along the road from Bagshot, they came and still they came until Tom stopped trying to count them. There was cavalry uniformed like Ralph, in buff coats and helmets and wide boots all looking dirtier and more worn than they had before Portsmouth. A smaller group followed, perhaps the commander. Then more and more horsemen, these carrying muskets, some taking the road south towards the town. So many horses.

And then he thought Park; Castle; Cavalry. Which side were they on? Denham was sitting pretty up there. This army couldn't be reinforcements for him. They must be from the other, the Parliamentary, side intent on attack. He started to follow up through the park, not knowing what else to do. Whether he went this way or through the town, by the time he reached the Castle they would surely have surrounded it. Whoever was going to drink these kegs of claret, he needed to be paid for carrying them.

The nearer he came the less he could imagine how a body of horsemen alone could possibly take the castle, perched as it was on the edge of the steep drop into the town and surrounded by its high curtain walls. He had seen no cannon for breaching the thick stonework.

Arrived in sight of the Castle he saw that the cavalry was grouped around the north, uphill, wall just out of reach of musket fire. There must have been two or three hundred of them, still mounted. Tom made a wide detour around them, clear of any pot shots from the Castle walls, moving down towards the gatehouse which was the only way into the outer court.

But he could not get near. Several hundred held horses were grazing in every direction while their dismounted riders assembled in front of the gatehouse, helmeted and armed.

A loud trumpet call startled Blaze. Someone appeared on the wall and had a shouted exchange with a man from the surrounding army, evidently the commander. Clearly the Royalist garrison was refusing to surrender, not surprising seeing the lack of Parliamentary artillery. The soldiers began to spread out.

They heard the trumpet at the Tanyard too.

Othen had been hard put to it keeping the men at their work. Hal had been unusually vocal.

`Cavalry!' he insisted. `Pouring up Castle Street!'

Nathan said laconically `More soldiers?'

`Hundreds of them! Come and see!'

Othen, anticipating a stampede, said `Get on with your work.'

The young men obeyed half-heartedly. Hal was hopping from foot to foot with excitement. `Can I go Sir, can I go?'

`You've work to do. And stop jumping about.'

Hal trailed into the bark room. Shredding oak bark, his tedious task, while armies were assembling, there might be a battle, anything could happen, real action, as the apprentices kept saying. And they couldn't even hear.

Until the trumpet sounded loud and clear across the town. Hal darted outside. He almost collided with Jacob standing in the yard, sensing unrest, gauging the mood of his workers.

`Oh Sir. May I go and see?'

Jacob looked down at him, as if from afar, speculatively. `A taste of war?'

`It's cavalry Sir, horses, hundreds of them.....'

'Ha!' Jacob's voice came out more like a bark than a laugh. `Horses, horses, always horses.'

`Sir....' Hal wheedled.

Jacob considered him for a long moment.

He turned to Othen.

The dismounted dragoons spread themselves out around the walls wherever there was foothold. They began firing their muskets, and the garrison returned the fire. It all seemed somewhat desultory. Tom wondered if he should go past or through them down into the town, where he and the claret might be safer. On the other hand he would like to see the outcome - and be paid.

He was not alone in wanting to see the outcome. A few townsfolk at first, and then more and more, mostly young men, appeared up the hill. Keeping well clear of the musket fire they milled about, watching and speculating.

The soldier nearest to him broke off from firing and leant on his musket. He nodded to Tom. `Bit of action for a change,' he said.

`Are you cavalry?' Tom asked.

`Nay, we're dragoons, what do the real fighting. Ride there quick and then fight on foot. Colonel Browne's dragoons we are.' With one hand he pulled a cartridge from his bandoleer, opened the top with his teeth and tipped gunpowder from it into the flash pan on his musket. In the other hand he held a lighted length of match which he used now to set off the musket. Blaze shied again.

Tom had been there for over an hour, Blaze chomping on his nosebag, when he spotted Hal with Peter and some of the other apprentices.

`How ever did you get time away?'

`Hal asked the Master!' Peter said. `Never known Hal ask anything of him before.'

`All those horses,' Hal said.

`He thought a bit,' Peter said, `And then he said we'd learn by tasting war and anyone who wanted to, could go.'

`No Nathan?' Tom asked.

`He's got some idea about protecting the women.' Peter sounded scornful. `Real reason I reckon is he's scudding some fine hide and doesn't trust anyone else to do it properly.' He looked about him. `Not much happening here.'

Down at the gatehouse however dragoons were concentrating in a semi-circle around the door, taking pot shots over the walls.

`Hey, let's stand on the cart and get a better view,' Peter said.

`Good idea. Here Hal, stand on the wine casks,' Tom said, 'you're light enough.'

From his perch Hal peered over the heads of the dragoons.

Then he scrambled down. 'It looks as if a man is screwing a sort of pot to the door,' he said. `An iron pot.'

The soldier, Tom's informant, turned round to them. `It's a petard,' he said. `You'll see. You'd better hold your horse.'

Now the encircling dragoons drew well back and they could see clearly. With a length of glowing match dangling from his fingers the petardier went forward alone to where a short fuse hung from the iron pot. Breathless moments passed before the fuse caught alight. Immediately the petardier ran back, clear just before the pot exploded.

Blinding flash, deafening blast, Blaze leaping, tugging at the rein, rocking the cart. The dragoons rushed through the shattered door, shouting and firing muskets. Confused noise, shouts, shots, clash of swords, a cry of `Into the castle!' and then voices cried for quarter, others for surrender. The noise subsided. Suddenly it was all over.

`Reckon that's it then,' Peter said. `Best get back to the Tanyard. Come on young Hal.'

`I need to deliver this claret to someone,' Tom said. `Go on Hal. You go, or the Master might regret letting you out.'

He led Blaze down to the gatehouse where guards were already in place.

`I've a load to deliver to Sir John Denham,' he answered their challenge. They laughed.

`He's a prisoner along with his fancy garrison.'

`I need him to pay me for it.'

They laughed again. `Something we can make use of?'

A slight man with wispy hair and beard came towards them, enquiring why this cart was blocking the entrance.

`Sir,' the guard said, `he says it's a load for the prisoner.'

`For Sir John Denham,' Tom said, and feeling that he could trust this man added `casks of claret.'

`A timely consignment,' the man laughed, `to celebrate our success. Bring it in.'

`But Sir,' Tom said, `he needs to pay me for cartage.'

`Indeed he shall.' The man took a notebook from his pouch, tore out a page and scribbled a note which he gave to the guard commander.

`Take this to the Keep and tell the guard that Sir William Waller requires it to be handed to Sir John Denham.'

He smiled at Tom and gestured him through the archway. Logs and debris, the failed barricade, lay higgledy piggledy on all sides. Some of it Tom had to shift to make a way for the cart, then up to the familiar door into the kitchen. He had no sooner unloaded the casks than the messenger returned and handed him a bag of money with a chit to be signed.

As far as he was concerned, the day's work was over.

Not so at the Tanyard. Even before the trumpet had sounded the quartermaster had appeared at the tannery, list in hand. He met Jacob in the yard. `You're down here for sixty men and their horses.'

`Sixty!' Jacob turned towards the house shouting `Phoebe!'

`Sixty,' the quartermaster repeated, `and ten paddy boys.'

`I've nowhere to put sixty horses.'

`Those barns?'

`They're not barns. Look, they're full of tanning pits.'

The quartermaster glanced in and shrugged. `Hobble them in the meadow' he said. `You have hay? We pay sixpence a day for hay and corn.'

`We have hay. And you pay for the men.'

`Three shillings and sixpence a week, if we're here for that long. And mind you feed them well.'

Phoebe came and heard the news. `Your big loft ma'am, and a bedroom for the three corporals of horse.'

She looked at Jacob. `It seems we have no choice.'

Indoors she made quick arrangements. `Mary and Carey, you must share Abigail's bedroom, and be sure to lock the door. The trundle bed from under my bed can go in your room Mary, for I doubt three corporals would fit in your bed. The men in the loft will just have to squash together. Mary, you go and re-arrange the beds. Abi, we'd better prepare the biggest stew our pans will hold if we are forced to feed this crowd. And make some bread too.'

They lifted a side of bacon off its ceiling hook in the still room and put it in the big tub to soak. Abigail dug leeks from the garden and fetched carrots from the straw clamp, onions from their string. She washed and scraped and chopped while Phoebe kneaded a trough-full of dough.

`I wonder how long they will stay,' Phoebe said. She sent Carey to stoke the fire.

They were so used to the sound of musket practice that they scarcely noticed the gunfire from across the town, though it was more and louder.

In the afternoon they lifted the bacon out of the tub and scraped it clean. Taking a big cleaver Phoebe smote it in two so that each half occupied its own cauldron. Together they carried the cauldrons to the fire, hooked them above the heat and poured in jugs of water. `Now some bay leaves and cloves,' Phoebe said, `and Carey, be sure the fire keeps to a good steady heat.'

For the time being they had done all they could do so Abigail took up her knitting. Strange, she thought later, how on a day of momentous happenings my chief concern was correctly turning the heel of a sock. Then she looked up, listening. The musket firing had ceased.

Suddenly an explosion echoed across the town. Carey leapt up from the hearth-side poker in hand. `Whatever was that!' A moment later the firing began again.

`Daniel!' Phoebe called. `Fetch me some gorse from the store.' He did it with irritating slowness, a task he disliked because of the fierce gorse thorns. He would have dropped it all in a pile on the floor had not Phoebe made him push half of it into the bread oven. Once alight it burnt up fast at great heat. After a few minutes Phoebe opened the oven door and quickly shovelled loaves in on top of the white hot ash. They would rise in the intense heat and cook through as the oven cooled. She put a cloth over the remaining loaves to wait their turn

When Tom returned with the cart Peter and Hal were already back at work, regaling their fellows with what they had missed. So he sought an audience indoors.

`They've taken the Castle! We saw it! Sir John and his garrison are prisoners!'

`Did he pay for the claret?' Mary asked.

`He did. The commander saw to that.'

`It won't be Sir John who drinks it, I'll wager.'

`Don't be too sure,' Tom said. `Sir William seems a fair gentleman.'

Phoebe looked up, her face red from shovelling the last loaves out of the bread oven. `Tom, make sure you secure your horses. Perhaps you and Daniel should sleep in the stable. They're quartering sixty troopers here with all their horses, and they could well covet yours. And Mary, put the vegetable nets into the cauldrons.'

At dusk the troops clattered into the yard, their horses side-stepping around the tanning pits, crowded together, a melée. Jacob leapt part way up his office stair and called for the corporals of horse.

`Turn your horses out in the meadow. It's wet, but the best there is. Hay in the loft yonder. Pile your saddles where you can - some of our benches may serve.'

He watched while order gradually emerged, the horses hobbled in the meadow, the paddy boys shown the hay loft where they were to sleep. Only then did he direct the troopers round the river end of the house to the garden door close to the staircase. Some paused by the river to splash their faces and even to drink before filing upstairs with their snapsacks.

They were soon down again carrying their wooden bowls and horn beakers to join the household on benches the length of the table. The smell of unwashed bodies concentrated. Abigail poured them jug after jug of water. `We're parched,' one said.

Then she stopped. The next man, his thick hair brushing his collar, was Ralph Attfield. Waiting to be served he looked up at her with a glimmer of recognition and said `Thank you.'

How they ate! Loaf after loaf and ladleful after ladleful of the stews with the boiled bacon cut up into chunks. Once their initial thirst was quenched Phoebe served them ale. In the dim illumination from the rush lights some were falling asleep where they sat, toppling against one another on their benches.

The order came to wash their bowls and faces in the river and go to bed. Soon the hall was cleared. Nathan could be heard organising the apprentices in the loft, reserving space for themselves, before the house settled into silence.

Phoebe mopped her forehead with the corner of her apron. `It will be pea broth tomorrow,' she said, `else we'll have nothing left. Mary, put the dried peas to soak.'

In the morning the men called for bread and ale before mustering for church, a service they interrupted with hectoring and whistles. The Rector and Curate staggered on through the liturgy but did not attempt to preach.

When they had finished, someone called for the lecturer and the cry was taken up until Duncomb came forward and mounted the pulpit.

Preaching extempore he took as text `If God be for us who can be against us?' He warned them that not all victories would be as easy as taking the Castle, at which some shouted out `Who do you think you're telling?'. He laughed and parried, and went on to exhort them to godly living such as would bring the Almighty's favour on their endeavours.

A night's rest and a good meal seemed to have restored the soldiers. They did not take kindly however to peas pottage in the evening. `Give us meat!' they said in no uncertain tones. `Slaughter some cattle!'

While the troops mustered and drilled in the Park on the Monday morning the paddy boys squatted on the river bank washing the shirts and stockings of the half-dozen troopers they each served. Hal stood near them, watching. Then Daniel made him help carry water from the well to rinse the clothes.

`Hey! clean water!' one paddy cried, and they started splashing each other as well as the clothes. Clean streaks appeared on their dirty faces. Soon they were shivering.

`Towels, boy!' the biggest of them commanded Hal.

`Towels yourself!' Hal said. There was a tense pause.

`You heard what I said. You live here don't you?'

`They're not my towels.'

`God almighty! We soldiers take what we need! Come on lads!'

They surged towards the doorway, to find it barred by Daniel. He held his favourite tool, an axe. `You dare!' he growled.

As the boys hesitated Hal slipped beside him.

`I'll show you where to hang your linen.'

His adversary raised his fist against his face, and then stopped, eyeing Daniel's axe. For a moment no one moved. Then he turned to his pile of sodden shirts. `Go on then,' surlily, and the others followed, dripping their way into the bake room. Hal showed them the ropes stretched high up at the far end. They wrung out the garments onto the stone floor and draped them up, jostling each other for space.

Then, reluctant to leave the warmth of the room, they poked around, commenting on pans and dishes. A boy with a long rip in his breeches opened the door into the still room.

`Hey! Look at this!'

The others crowded after him to gaze at the cheeses on the high shelves, the casks and the hanging hops. They would have barged in had not the opening door concealed Phoebe and Mary who were busy preparing balm for the next brew of ale. Phoebe grasped the door handle and faced them.

`What are you wanting?' she asked with calm authority.

`We was just looking,' torn trousers said.

`Bread and cheese,' a bolder voice said.

`You've had bread already this morning.'

`Just a mouthful ma'am.' The bully was suddenly polite.

`Just a mouthful!' Phoebe laughed. `Out of here, no one but women come in the still room.' She picked up a cloth-wrapped quarter cheese from the shelf and followed them out. They crowded round her as she cut chunks of bread and slivers of cheese and distributed them.

Then Abigail opened the oven door to shovel out fresh loaves and hot yeasty air flooded into the room.

`Stand clear!' she said, for the boys were drawn towards the warmth so that she scarcely had turning space to transfer the loaves with their delicious smell from shovel to table.

Phoebe watched the paddies consuming the snack she had given them, noticing. `If you give me your breeches I'll mend that rent,' she said.

The boy, who was slightly built like Hal but malnourished and small, looked horrified. The others giggled.

`He'd have to go bare,' one said.

Phoebe turned to Hal. `Those breeches you've just outgrown – fetch them for me Hal and lend them while I do the repair.'

He obeyed. The boy, Alan they called him, found a private corner in which to change breeches and Phoebe started to herd the rest of them outside.

Hal wandered after them. They hadn't finished with him.

`Good little mother's boy.'

'Hal, Hal, Mama's gal!'

'Needs a big bully to protect him.'

At that Daniel, standing still wielding his axe, suddenly remembered his duties and ambled off to guard the stable. The taunts went on until one said, `Try him with the horses, Norman.' Hal's expression gave nothing away as he followed them towards the meadow. Abigail, mopping up water behind them, smiled to herself, knowing Hal's skills. But he turned aside into the bark shed before they left the yard. The boys laughed and shrugged.

The beef that the troopers had demanded took all afternoon to stew, Carey minding the fire until she hollered for Hal to take a turn. Then she went outside and hung about the paddy boys.

The beef went down well, and the cabbage and bread that went with it. This third meal had a different atmosphere, as if the troopers were almost at home. They talked and laughed and teased Mary and Carey and sometimes Abigail too, and when the meal was over they hung around, chatting in groups, playing dice and chequers, calling for more ale. Phoebe responded slowly, attempting to ration their intake.

The crowd in the hall was thinning when Ralph came in from checking the horses. He stood in the doorway letting them pass. Beyond them he saw Abigail, dishevelled from the kitchen work, standing by the fireplace. Yesterday, when he had dined with the Bicknell family, the daughter Joan had been lively, flirtatious with engaging looks and chatter, like girls often were with him. The way that Abigail this evening had gone about quietly serving the men, responding to their teasing with a smile, intrigued him by its contrast. He would like to talk with her, if only he could muster the courage. That time when he had found himself at John Harding's wedding his courage had had scant reward, for no sooner had they started to dance than she had rushed out of the barn with her father and did not return.

As the last bunch of men left with Tom, heading for the taverns, Abigail turned towards the doorway and seeing him, smiled. He came across to her. 'That was a good meal,' he said.

'They demanded meat after yesterday's pease pottage,' Abigail said.

'Pease pottage eh?' he said. 'I missed that, dining at Bicknells'. He chuckled. 'Young Vernon is an outspoken Royalist if ever there was one!'

'I believe he always was. He was there too was he?'

'For a while. Quite a catch for the Bicknell daughter.'

Abigail caught her breath. Could that really be how it was? Had Harry's disgust at her apparent attachment to Nathan, a mere journeyman, turned his affections to Joan? All she could think of to say was 'She's very pretty.'

Ralph looked down at her, his brown eyes warm. Dishevelled or not, she had a certain beauty which he could not quantify. Then he became embarrassed and turned away, kicking a log further into the fire.

'The Colonel of the Surrey Dragoons was wounded when we took the Castle,' he said. 'He is mortally sick – a musket ball through both cheeks.'

Abigail made a small sound of horrified sympathy.

`Bad for the Dragoons, losing their commander,' Ralph said.

`For the Dragoons! But his wife, and his family, his mother....'

`That's war, the risk of losing your life.'

`Leaving a widow and fatherless children.'

`The women send off their men with their blessing.'

`Surely hoping they'll not be killed.'

`Our business is fighting,' Ralph said, almost harshly, `and if we die, we die.'

He was silent then, his hand on the beam above the hearth, his head resting on his arm. `No,' he said at last, more gently, `I suppose families do suffer. For myself, I have neither wife nor family nor mother. No one need trouble themselves about me.'

Abigail did not know what to say. Already, whenever news of conflict reached the household, anxiety for his safety troubled her. She was not alone in this, either.

'Hal,' she said. 'Hal was consumed with anxiety for you when we heard about the sacking of Brentford.'

'Hal?' Ralph said, surprised.

'We heard the soldiers were driven into the river, and drowned. It sounded a terrible way to die, and Hal was afraid....'

'That was a bad business,' Ralph said. 'But we were not there.'

For a moment he looked into her eyes, and she looked into his, those deep brown pools, and for a moment something stirred, but only for a moment.

He shook his head then, and turned away.

`Nay, it's best that you should not trouble yourselves about us, about me. We're birds of passage – who knows whither we shall be ordered next. More men die of disease than battle, tramping over the country. We're here today, and gone, even dead, tomorrow. Forget about me.'

Abigail too turned away, concealing the tears that suddenly came into her eyes, as men came back into the Hall on their way to the staircase and bed. Ralph went with them, puzzling in his mind. For so long he had avoided the maidens who tried to engage his affections, and now here was a lass who did not pursue him. Despite what he had just said, he would rather she did not forget him.

In the morning the wagon master came, a tall well-set-up man whose curious lisp belied his rugged appearance. He stood at the gate looking about him while the mastiffs barked and made sallies the length of their chains. The big paddy boy Norman was leaning idly against a door post.

`You, boy!' the wagon master called.

Norman strolled over.

`Where'th the carter?'

`Hal!' Norman shouted, `Where's the carter?'

Boys erupted from all sides. Hal came more slowly out of the bark shed and led the way to the stable. Daniel, stationed in the doorway, seized his axe ready to attack the intruder.

`Put it away man,' the wagon master said. `I'm theeking the carter.'

Tom came over from grooming the horses.

`The prisonerth are to be moved to London, and we require your cart tomorrow at dawn. There will be an ethcort.'

Later Tom said `So we're off to London, Hal.'

Hal said nothing at first. Then he blurted out `I'll stay here.'

`I was sure you'd want to come.'

Hal shook his head. `There's the cob. And the paddy boys.'

Tom thought he understood. `Help me get ready anyway.'

Hal checked the harness, rubbing the brasses. After a while he said `Tom. Those horses, the troopers', they're spoiling the meadow something terrible. And it's bad for their hooves, all that wet.'

“There's nowhere else here for them.'

`Searles have a barn.'

`It'll be full of hay in winter.'

`You could ask.'

`I could not. No more than you could. It's the quartermaster's job.'

Tom went out in the steady rain to try to find if any tradesman needed goods brought from London so as to make the most of the empty return journey. Wherever he went some other carter had preceded him. Hunched against the wet he came to Michael Gary's drapery shop just as Abe Trussler left it. Another missed chance he thought, but went in all the same because the rain had worsened.

Christopher, tall lanky lad with mousy hair still as tousled as it had been at school, was rolling up a bolt of cloth on the counter. Despite his little beard he seemed much as he had been in class with Tom. They exchanged casual greetings.

`I suppose you know why I'm here,' Tom said, `and I suppose Abe Trussler's bringing your order from London."

`Well you suppose wrongly. Father won't trust Abe with consignments of cloth.'

Tom perked up. `So do you have any to come?'

Christopher called to his father in the back of the shop and when Michael, a middle-aged version of himself, came through he had indeed a commission for Tom to fulfil.

Pleased, Tom took the short cut home over Goose Meadow. Yet he had slight misgivings at being preferred to Abe, just enough to take the shine off his pleasant anticipation of tomorrow's journey. Troopers were in the yard, Ralph talking with one of the Corporals of Horse, a weather-beaten man somewhat older than himself.

`Are you carting prisoners tomorrow?' he asked Tom. `Jim Hosier here will be in command,' and they shook hands.

`Let's go indoors and dry out.' Tom said. Hal was turning the spit, Abigail knitting yet again. Jim Hosier and Ralph sat down at the table while Tom went close to the fire, his clothes steaming in the warmth.

`Tom' Hal said, leaning on the handle of the spit while he watched him, `about those horses in the water meadow . Couldn't you ask Searles or someone?'

Tom thought for a while, turning himself in front of the fire as if he too were on the spit. It was true about the water meadow. No one would ordinarily put horses or cattle there in November, and this year it was particularly wet. He went over to the table.

`Hal's pointed out that the water meadow's suffering from having all your horses on it, and the wet is bad for them.'

`Don't I know it,' Jim said. `We were given no choice.'

`There's Searles' farm above us. They might have space.'

Jim considered. `We didn't expect to be in Farnham more than a day or two.'

`The land's dry up there,' Ralph said, 'And they've good barns.'

`You know it then?'

Ralph nodded.

`I'd better find the quartermaster to make an order.'

`Good work, Hal,' Jim said as he left. `You should join us.'

`He would too,' Tom said.

Hal looked towards Ralph who caught the look and drew a stool up near him.

`Let me tell you what it's like. The boys are servants. While we're out scouting, or harrying the enemy, they're with the baggage train, catching up behind the infantry, on foot.'

`A lot more walking than you've ever done,' Tom said.

`We lodge wherever the quartermaster arranges. The boys are usually with the horses. They serve us and care for the horses.' Ralph surveyed the Tanyard Hall. `Here you've seen them in comfort. It's not always thus.'

Hal nodded, listening eagerly.

`At Kineton the enemy looted the baggage train, a couple of miles behind the battle lines. That's where the boys were.'

`Hardship and danger,' Tom said.

`A soldier's life is hard and dangerous.'

`And battles?' Hal asked.

Ralph paused. `Only one actual battle.'

`We heard it was a stalemate,' Tom said.

For a moment Ralph looked taken aback. Then much more quietly he said, `For us it was chaos.'

`Tell us,' Hal said.

Ralph looked down, clasping his hands. How could he tell them the full horror of that day? A month trekking over the countryside, foraging for food, supposedly manoeuvring for position, the enemy doing the same, just scouting and skirmishing. Rain, rain and more rain, the infantry up to their ankles in mud, the horses floundering. And then October with clear, cloudless, even hot days. And we came to Kineton, to Edgehill. The agony of waiting. Waiting. Closing ranks, and waiting for the command to move, to put our training into practice.

Ralph looked up 'Here,' he said, trying to describe it with his hands, 'was a wide hill, quite steep, Edgehill it's called. The enemy was drawn up all along the top, and we were drawn up across the valley, facing them. We were in place soon after dawn, and we just stood, waiting. The horses were restive.'

He smiled suddenly. 'There was one incident in all that time that made us laugh. Who should come trotting along the valley but the local squire with his hunt, sounding the hunting horn. At first we just stared. Then someone went and told him there was going to be a battle. He looked around, as if he hadn't noticed all the troops above him. How we laughed!'

'What did he do?' Tom asked.

'He sent the huntsman home with the hounds, and he went and joined the enemy!'

'But the battle?' Hal was not to be diverted.

Ralph's smile faded. 'As I said, the enemy was all along the top of the hill opposite. They had the advantage of the hill, but when we didn't budge they started to come down it. We watched them approaching us for well nigh three hours.' He paused. 'It was one of those really hot October days.'

'And what happened?'

'Their cavalry started trotting towards us. And suddenly, though we'd heard no command, one of our troops spurred forward. It looked like a charge. And then they fired their pistols into the ground and pulled off their orange scarves and deserted to the enemy, the lot of them.'

'Deserted?'

'Some men do, under pressure.'

'It sounds pre-meditated,' Tom said.

'But what happened then?' Hal demanded.

'The enemy's trumpeters sounded the gallop and their cavalry came straight for us where we stood, shooting as they came. To our shame we couldn't take the impact. Our horses wheeled in panic, bolted out of control. We leapt hedges and ditches, friend and foe all mixed up together. We were out of the battle. The enemy went on to loot our baggage.'

He turned to Hal. 'The boys were there with the baggage train. We could do little to protect them or the baggage.'

'And the battle itself?' Tom asked.

Again Ralph fell silent. That dreadful night! The field littered with bodies, the wounded crying, screaming with pain, cries that became groans and moans with the chill of darkness, and death. Both sides numbed with the shock of their first experience of battle. Even the memory of it sucked at his innards, remembering the stark horror, remembering how both sides were too battered in spirit to move, to tend the wounded, to bury the bodies, to move away. The memory betrayed all eagerness for war and its skills.

Hal would make an exemplary horse boy, but could so young a lad, nurtured in this household, bear these things? Hal and Tom were watching him intently, waiting to hear the outcome. He spoke slowly, feeling for his words.

'The night was very cold. Many died.'

His tone changed. `We learnt our lesson though. Sir William keeps insisting, never receive a charge standing still. Always at the trot.'

Hal started turning the spit again and fat sizzled from the meat into the dripping pan below.

`Take me with you,' he said.

Ralph looked at him kindly. `Perhaps.'

No one spoke for a while. Then Abigail broke off her yarn and shook out the stockings she had just completed. `Here you are at last Tom, in time for your journey to London.'

Tom pushed his hand into the stockings feeling their quality and warmth. `Wonderful!'

`You wouldn't make some for me would you?' Ralph asked.

`Not before you move on.'

`No, no, the Captain's sutler would bring them to me.' He laid his foot beside Tom's. `Much the same size. What do you think?'

Jim Hosier came in then, with everything arranged, evidently to the Searles' discomfort. `There's just enough light left to move the horses tonight.'

Hal shot into the bake room. `Here Carey, take hold of the spit.'

Carey protested and questioned before she obliged, and Hal hurtled off outdoors. Ralph and Jim followed less hastily.

When, well after dark, troopers and household assembled for the meal, Jim said to Tom `Your young brother sure has a way with horses.'

Tom frowned. `My brother? My brother's a tanner in London.'

`No no, the lad. Hal isn't it?'

Tom laughed. `He's not my brother. Just an orphan bastard my mother took in.'

`Well,' Jim said, `I just thought he resembled you. At all events, he's a wonder with horses.'

London

A considerable body set out at first light. The gentlemen of the garrison were permitted to ride their horses, closely guarded by cavalrymen. A string of carts carried their piles of baggage, while the servants and common men walked, all guarded side and rear by a party of troopers. Carrying a bag of Michael Gary's money as he was, Tom was glad of the protection.

At last the carts, long left behind by the mounted prisoners, came to the end of the muddy journey and crossed London bridge into the City. The great bulk of the White Tower loomed up ahead of them in the dark as they waited to be admitted across the drawbridge. A crowd of urchins attracted by the convoy reminded Tom that he needed a messenger to go to Michael Gary's woollen merchant. Scanning the boys he selected one a little bigger, a little less ragged than the rest.

`Do you know Blackwell Hall?'

`Aye' said the boy. Tom gave him a coin and the folded paper with Gary's message. `Bring word back and I'll pay you more. We're lodging here overnight.'

`Blackwell Hall's shut - it's late.'

`Take it first thing in the morning then - and mind you bring word back.'

The convoy moved on, across the drawbridge over the malodorous moat and into the courtyard. The troopers bundled the prisoners away, the carters were shown to stables and left to tend to their horses. Tom had expected to see Abe among them, though straggled out and struggling on the road he had not seen him.

`What's become of Abe?' he asked Matthew Woolgar, a curly-haired young carter he had sometimes spoken with in Farnham, who was rubbing down his horses alongside Blaze and Star.

`Abe Trussler? Think he lost a wheel way back.'

`He doesn't have much luck with his cart.'

`Strange character,' Matthew said. `Seems to be agin the world.'

`Specially the Mannorys,' Tom said. Then following his own train of thought he said `I've a brother in London.'

`Big place.' Matthew twisted up a fresh handful of straw to rub down his second horse.

`He's in one of the trained bands. I could ask around.'

They ate some of the victuals they had brought with them, and a serving man brought ale and showed them the bare room where they might sleep, a patch of hard bare floor among the other men lodging there.

As soon as Tom woke he went to the gatehouse and waited for the messenger to come. The Warder there was stamping his feet in the chill dawn mist.

Tom grinned at him. `I recommend my sister's stockings.'

The Warder stared at him. `You wear your sister's stockings?'

Tom laughed. `Stockings my sister knitted. She just finished them. Made all the difference.' They chatted idly for a while.

`You wouldn't know, would you, how I could trace my brother? He's in one of the trained bands.'

`There are a lot of them. What's his name?'

`James Mannory.'

`Oh Mannory! Sergeant in the Infantry. Comes here from time to time for ordnance.'

`Do you have any idea where he lives?'

The guard shook his head and turned to challenge Tom's messenger.

`Says you've to pick it up,' the lad said, handing Tom a note.

`Can you guide me there, the quickest way?'

He went to harness the horses.

`Oh there you are!' Matthew exclaimed. `I was looking for you. Care to travel together? I've a load to pick up at Kingston.'

`I'm to pick up in the City. No idea how long it'll take.'

`Meet me by the bridge at Kingston. I know a place to lodge. Take the road over London Bridge and enquire from there.'

Carters might complain about traffic in Farnham and the congestion of wagons parking illegally in West Street, but it was nothing compared to London. Closed in by the jetted upper storeys of the houses, the thronged streets swilled with refuse under the horses' slipping hooves. His cart felt large and ungainly, hard to manoeuvre round sharp corners among other wagons. Everyone shouted.

Arrived at Blackwell Hall he gave his guide a farthing and promised another if he guarded the cart. Inside, trestle tables piled with cloth stretched from end to end of the vast Hall, each trader at his own pitch. Tom's courage almost failed him, standing in the entrance open-mouthed. The doorman rescued him, directing to Tranter, a stout man with a balding head.

`Porter!' Tranter shouted, and they were there, half a dozen of them in varying degrees of dress. They carried the bolts of cloth, each wrapped in sacking, out to the cart. With a start Tom realised he should be checking them against Gary's order, and ran out to count them. Then back again to pay for it all.

`You new to this?' Tranter asked.

Tom nodded. `New to London too.'

`Keep a close eye on that cloth. The King's troops have a taste for stealing it.'

Tom asked the boy the way to the bridge and paid him off. At last he was leaving the threatening crowds of the city and heading for home. Near the river he spotted a ship's chandler. He would have liked to take a look inside, perhaps buy a tarpaulin to keep loads dry on the cart, but he dared not stop. Too many carts, too many ragged folk, too many people altogether.

So much for this great city of London. The bridge was ahead and soon he would be out in the country.

It all looked different by day. What had been dim shapes the night before he saw now to be houses crowded along either side of the bridge. He slowed for the narrow entry.

A man was standing there, peering at carts as they came by. Suddenly the man threw back his head and shouted `Tom!'

He was beside the cart in a moment. Tom looked more closely.

`James! Good God! How on earth?'

James, more thickset than Tom remembered him, clasped his hand. `I heard of prisoners being brought from Farnham so I went to the Tower in hope of news.'

`Jump up on the cart,' Tom said. `We can't stop here.'

`What are you doing, driving a cart?'

`I'm a carter,' with some pride.

`That's a bit of a come-down. Father was set on you following into tanning. A good trade.'

`I was ham-fisted, and I hated it. I was amazed I can tell you when Father relented. The cart and horses are his but they will be mine.'

`How did you happen to be at the bridge?' Tom asked.

`I was at the Tower, and one of the warders mentioned you were seeking me. He said you were heading for London Bridge with another carter, so I ran here, but no sign of you. I feared I'd missed you. I'd almost given up when you appeared."

He directed Tom to an inn in Southwark. There, with the wagon clear of the thoroughfare and the horses dipping into their nosebags, the brothers sat on a bench outside with tankards of ale. Tom sensed an equality, a brotherliness, that he had never known before with James.

`The warder said you're a sergeant in the Infantry.'

`Yes, in a London trained band. A great band. We stood against the King's troops at Turnham Green and they had to turn away, praise God. We saved the town from being sacked like Brentford was. We're a force to be reckoned with.'

`I watched the siege of Farnham Castle.'

James seemed impressed.

`It didn't take long,' Tom admitted.

`And what news of home?'

`Just now we're over-run with cavalry, a whole troop billeted in the Tanyard! Father takes command of them. The Corporals do as he says.'

`I can imagine. And Hannah, how is she?'

`She has a son. You know she married John?'

`I did hear that. She's wasted no time. And Abi?'

`Much the same. She knitted me these marvellous stockings, a carter's joy!'

James laughed. `Major news of my child sister!'

`Not a child any more. I suspect that Nathan's sweet on her.'

`He'll make a reliable tanner, no doubt a good husband.'

`If she'll have him. Any lady loves yourself?'

`No time. The militia's my family.'

`You were sweet on Joan Bicknell.'

`So was everyone else,' James said a trifle bitterly.

'Greet them all at home for me,' he said, heading back to work. 'You never know, this war might bring me that way before long.'

With all the delays Tom feared that Matthew would not have waited for him at Kingston, but he was there by the bridge, his horses long stabled and his loaded cart locked in a barn, the decision to stop the night already made.

`I've booked a bed,' Matt said. They ordered food and warmed themselves beside the fire.

`You don't live in Farnham do you?' Tom said.

`Nay, out Bentley way. My old man had this carting business. Woolgar. I dare say you've heard of him.''

`Can't say I have.'

`He's dead anyway, and I had to take on.'

`So it's your business?' envy in Tom's tone.

`My mother's the governor.' Matthew raised his hand against possible protest. `No, not governess. You should meet my mother. She rules the business. Rules our lives.'

The food arrived and they tucked in hungrily.

`I've watched you in the Goat's Head,' Matthew said. `What would you say to a partnership? I reckon we'd get on well together.'

Tom could not see the advantage of a partnership, unless they always travelled together which was hardly practical. Matthew's idea seemed to stem more from a liking for Tom than for motives of profit. They talked until the fire dwindled, their ale ran out and they both yawned.

Sharing a bed was so commonplace that Tom thought nothing of it. He stripped and flopped under the covers and was almost immediately asleep. He slept soundly for several hours.

Long before dawn he was disturbed by Matthew moving about in the bed. His last turn brought him right up against Tom, too close for comfort.

`Move over would you?' Tom said.

Matthew did not move.

`Matt...'

He wriggled closer.

Tom tried to dig an elbow into him. `Move over Matt.'

Then he felt a hairy arm across his stomach. `I really like you' Matthew muttered.

What sort of partnership is this! Tom thought. He could feel movement in other parts of Matt's body. Panic paralysed his limbs for what seemed a long long moment, his mind racing. If he pushed Matt away, that would mean more bodily contact. Besides, it might not succeed. It might turn into unsavoury wrestling.

With a sudden squirm he flung off Matthew's arm and twisted out of the bed. He stood panting beside it.

Matthew groaned. The room was pitch dark. Tom was grateful for that, he did not wish to be seen. He pondered going to the other side of the bed and getting back in. No, too great a risk. He groped to where he had dropped his shirt and breeches and put them on, wrapped himself in his rough cape and lay down on the floor. What did a second night on a hard floor signify.

In the dawn light Matt behaved as if nothing had happened, so that Tom wondered if it had just been a nightmare. But if so, why was he fully dressed, and stiff from a night on bare floorboards?

Matthew pulled on his breeches and went out to the pump returning shivering. `It's cold' he said. `I've told them to mull some ale.'

They ate almost in silence, paid and went out to the stables. `As you're new to this route,' Matthew said, `I'll lead and you can follow.'

At least it was not raining, and the roads were quite well compacted in places, neither mud nor shifting sand. Beyond Kingston they fell in with a string of pack mules, well laden. These could have moved faster than the carts but their drovers were glad of company. `You never know when these wild soldiers will appear, no matter which side they're on.'

`I hear the Royalists have moved off towards Oxford,' Matthew said, `well out the way.'

`There's still t'other side,' the drover said.

In the event they travelled safely, both from marauders and from mishaps of the road. Their ways parted at the foot of Guild down.

The town was in mid-winter darkness, Gary's shop shuttered. Tom tethered the horses in the street outside it and went down to the Garys' house in Snow Hill. Michael opened the door to his knock, wiping food from his mouth with a bright linen kerchief.

`Oh, it's you. I expected you yesterday.'

`I'm sorry Sir. The cart's outside your shop and here are the dockets.'

Michael Gary took them, shouting `Christopher!' into the house. It was Betty who came.

`He's still eating his meat,' she said.

`And so was I. Tell him to come.'

They waited while evidently Christopher finished his own meat before ambling to the door. Together in silence they returned to Castle Street and Gary opened up the shop. Together in silence they shouldered the cloth up to the store room above, with its indefinable scent of wool. Michael Gary checked each roll against the docket until, when the last one was in he said `Correct' and Tom relaxed in relief. He hovered, wondering about payment.

Gary shut the door with a bang and turned the heavy key. `What are you waiting for? I'll pay the cartage in a day or two,' and he strode off.

`Your Pa's choleric tonight,' Tom commented to Christopher as they watched him go.

`Fond hopes dashed,' Christopher said. `You'll hear soon enough.' He strolled home while Tom drove his tired horses to the Tanyard, to water, hay and rest, and himself to some food rustled up by Phoebe. Two days away seemed like a month. He was reticent about his own news, but curious to know what had occurred in his absence.

After the prisoners' escort set out, Phoebe watched the remaining troopers out of the gate and up to Searles' for their horses with unmixed relief. Their weariness the first night and subsequent growing friendliness had now become irksome familiarity. They were everywhere, nosing about, teasing the dogs - and Daniel - and she feared for her winter stores. Although she was glad that the paddy boys no longer taunted Hal, she was uneasy about his becoming one of them. She was anxious too about Carey whose enticing ways would surely soon lead her into disgrace.

She set Carey to sweeping up, and Mary to kneading yet more bread, while she and Abigail saw to the hens and the wintering geese.

`At least we have some peace during the day,' she said.

It was instantly shattered. Hermann Shepheard burst into the yard, explosively angry.

`Those confounded troopers! Where are they? I'll have them hanged. Where are they I say? Just let me get my hands on them. Where have they gone? Where are they?'

`Gone to fetch their horses for their morning exercises,' Phoebe said.

`No respect for the cloth, mocking divine worship, and now this! It's trouble wherever I turn. Trouble! Trouble! I'll give them trouble!'

Phoebe and Abigail stood in the chilly yard, waiting for him to explain. He looked from one to the other, wringing his hands.

`My feather beds!' he wailed. `All gone!'

`Did you have so many?' Abigail knew her question was neither tactful nor sympathetic nor did it have the desired effect of reducing the drama.

Shepheard looked daggers at her. `I and the Rector. And mine,' wailing again in distress, `one from my mother's German family. And I had bought others. My only luxury!'

He looked wildly round the yard as if they might be stuffed in among the tanning equipment. `Where are the bastards sleeping? I'll have them, if I have to fight for them.'

`No need to fight,' Phoebe said. `Abigail, show the curate up to the loft.'

Abigail seldom went to the top of the house, the preserve of the men who were themselves meant to keep it clean and orderly. It was neither. The tanners had pushed their beds together at the chimney end and the rest of the floor was littered with odd blankets and a few straw-filled hessian palliasses. The soldiers' snapsacks leant at odd angles against every section of wall. Of feather mattresses there was not one.

Abigail saw Shepheard's defeated disappointment and, sorry for her earlier tone, said `We've only one of the troops here you know. Others are billeted round about the town.'

`I had so hoped...' Shepheard began. `To go searching round the town...I could not. And what will the Rector say. And my housekeeper, she is irate. They took a whole ham. Every day brings fresh humiliation.'

He seemed so desperate that Abigail put her hand on his shoulder. The next moment his arms were round her, his head on her shoulder, a prolonged embrace.

`Oh Abigail I need you and your good sense,' he said into her neck. She suppressed a giggle and tried to extricate herself. His hold tightened.

He moved his arm down to her waist and pulled her to him, close. He kissed her neck, once, twice, again with open mouth.

At that she reached for his wrists and gripping them with her work-strengthened hands forced them away from her body. `Hermann!' She had never before used his Christian name. `Hermann, this will not find your feather beds.'

With a pathetic expression he said `Is there no hope for me with you?'

`With me! I've never given you the least encouragement.'

`Don't think I didn't notice you, alongside your friend.'

`She was most evidently the object of your affections.'

`Alas! that cannot be. I can say no more. Another humiliation.'

`Come. You came to find your feather beds.' Abigail turned firmly and set off down the stairs.

`That adventurer Attfield is in the troop that is lodging here,' he said, following her down. `I wouldn't trust him, nor any others of their rebellious army. Robbing those they're pleased to call malignants. He told me as much, arrogant man.'

`Did you find them?' Phoebe asked.

`I did not. I'll go to the Quartermaster himself, that's what I'll do. Damned rogue I'll be bound, but at least he has authority.'

He went out of the door in time to see Robert Bicknell walking towards the stair to Jacob's office. `Friend of Attfield, friend of whoever is in power. And he a Bailiff. This whole town is becoming a hot-bed of rebellion.'

Jacob looked up from his ledger. `'T'is early in the day for the pleasure of a visit' he said, `Or are you the bearer of ill news?'

`Ill or good, depending on who views it,' Robert said. `I wanted to be the first to tell you, before the gossips get hold of it. Joan is to be married to Harry Vernon.'

`Well!' Jacob put down his quill and gave full attention to his friend. 'That sounds to be good news. Is that your view of it?'

Robert sat down on a stool, spreading his square hands on his knees in characteristic fashion. `I've seen it coming for a while, though I confess I began to wonder if Vernon would ever wake up to it. Joan was eating her heart out for him. Now he gives every appearance of eating his heart out for her.'

`It's certainly a good match. But didn't you have some understanding with the Garys?'

`Ha! To hear Betty Gary talk you would think it had been signed and sealed. But nothing had ever been settled. At any rate, Joan took that out of our hands, went and told Christopher to his face that she's marrying Vernon and that is that.'

`So it will be all round the town in no time at all.'

`Exactly. And there's the rub. They want to be married at once with a clandestine wedding, just their parents and that foolish curate. Oh, and Abigail, she wants Abigail to be there.'

`She's not with child is she, to be in such haste?'

`Oh no!'

Jacob smiled to himself at this vigorous denial. Robert went on, `I've talked to her, and I can understand her distaste for the usual bedding, but Elizabeth is distraught. It seems so hole and corner.'

`I suppose you could insist. You could even forbid.'

For the first time Robert smiled. `That from you Jacob, who wooed Phoebe against all odds, wooed her into town. What if her father, or my Elizabeth's for that matter, had forbidden our marriage? No, I can stomach the wedding, and Elizabeth will be won over. I can accept Vernon as son-in-law, a good match as you say, son of a landed gentleman. I suppose we should be jubilant.'

`So?' Jacob asked.

`He wants to take her away to Oxford. Yes, I know your Hannah went away, but 't'was only to Spreakley. Oxford is not the next parish. Besides, the King has his headquarters there. Sooner or later he'll be besieged. We would prefer her not to be there.'

`Does she want to go?'

`She'll go anywhere he asks her. She will listen to no argument. He is perfection. All she wants is to be with him.'

`Will Vernon listen to you?'

`I would not even try to persuade him. You must have heard his political views Parliament is in rebellion, right is with the King, and the last straw is having Waller's troops all over the town. No, his mind is made up, and Sir John Denham wants him contributing to some new newsbook being put together in Oxford.'

`So you are saying you have no choice but to bless them on their way.'

`And talking with you confirms it to me.' He shook Jacob's hand, a strong `Amen'. `I wanted you to be the first to know. And now if I may I'll take Abigail along to Timber Hall with me. Joan wants to see her.'

Walking there he told Abigail the simple news in a flat neutral tone. He got no further, for she clapped her hands and gave a little skip there in the road, all the answer he needed.

`What a good friend you are Abigail,' he said.

She greeted Joan with warm congratulations. `But how did it come about?'

Joan drew her into a corner of the room. `I have asked him and he scarcely seems to know. Something to do with Sir John Denham. He wants him in Oxford to work on a new newsbook, and Harry says that made him realise he didn't want to go without me.' Joan hugged herself, smiling.

`And you thought he had a low opinion of you!' Abigail laughed.

`I've taxed him with that, and that I'm not clever or bookish or anything, but he doesn't care. He says he loves me as I am. And Abigail we're to be married very soon and very quietly, in one of the side chapels with only our parents and please will you come and be a witness? My mother would like a wedding like Hannah's but there is no time for banns and things.'

`Why such haste?'

`Because of the *Mercurius Aulicus*, the newsbook, and because Harry wants to be where everyone is loyal to the King, and anyway he is fond of Oxford where he studied. And Abi, why wait? There's no reason to wait. He has an allowance from his father, we can afford to live. We want to be together

If confirmation were needed, it was obvious when shortly afterwards Harry called in. His expression when he looked at Joan was hungrily tender.

And then for the second time that day the curate burst in.

`Oh there you are Vernon! I could have guessed. I've just received terrible news. About the Reverend Clapham my Rector.' He had his audience's attention.

`He has been accused of scandalous behaviour in both his parishes - adultery no less! They've deprived him of his livings. What a terrible position this puts me in! He has fled to Oxford. And to make matters worse, that heretic Duncomb, lecturer Duncomb if you please, has been preferred to the pulpit and is to live in the Rectory!'

Harry looked him up and down. `You had better come to Oxford with us,' he said.

Without, Abigail thought, his feather bed.

Winter

My sweete Friend,

Sam is returning my father-in-law's coach to Farnham and I hasten to send you word with him. The journey here is best forgotten. I was jolted and buffeted in the coach, a trunk at my feet and all sorts of inconveniences. The men rode alongside. My mother wished a servant girl to travel with me but Harry insisted that I would be well looked after once we reached Oxford and so it has proved.

We are in the sweetest house right among the colleges. Rev. Shepheard being unmarried is able to lodge in the college. We have two little rooms above the landlord's quarters. His wife cooks and cleans for us. They seem to have a tribe of children.

That is all I have time to tell you, except to express my joy at signing myself, Mistress Joan Vernon.

Abigail read the letter twice, folded it carefully and placed it in the pocket hanging from her waist. Her fingers felt a smaller note which had rested there now for several weeks. No need to re-read that one, she knew it by heart. All it said was,

We are suddenly moving and I cannot find you to give you this money to buy wool for the stockings I hope you are knitting for me. Your faithful servant R Attfield.

Sudden their move had certainly been. Barely a week after taking the Castle, Waller organised a small garrison and took his Army off again. They were indeed birds of passage, here today and gone (please God not dead) tomorrow. Despite relief that the Tanyard was no longer a billet, it seemed almost lonely without them. But it was Joan's marriage to Harry Vernon, a few weeks further into December, which left Abigail feeling most bereft, missing even the irritation of Hermann Shepheard, gone with them to Oxford.

The day felt cold, empty and silent. Sounds of work outside only emphasised the quiet. So many extra head of cattle had been slaughtered to feed the billeted troops that the tannery had received an influx of hides to process, every available man being employed to scrape and round off and prepare the lime pits. They worked steadily, mostly without words, the sounds being physical noises with just occasional voices, remote.

Tom was away fetching Sussex grain. When he had asked to take Hal with him she knew that his reasons were as much the boy's sadness at losing the company of the paddies and the horses as it was Tom's need for help through wintry roads.

Abigail sat down by the spinning wheel, but after a while she decided to try some Latin. The last month had allowed no time for study. Now she welcomed it, becoming absorbed in the puzzles of translation. Daniel came in to stoke the fire and in the spurt of flame she realised that daylight had almost ended. She carried her slate and the text book over to the hearth, slanting them on her lap towards the light, frustrated at her failure to render these last phrases.

She was unaware than anyone had come in until she heard Nathan behind her say, `*Meae* agrees with *puellae*, not with *deliciae*. "My girlfriend, my darling," and *deliciae* refers to *Passer*, the pet sparrow.' She stared at the poem and at her slate, understanding slowly dawning.

`And *teneo* is the verb *tenere* to hold. "Oh sparrow, my darling's pet, whom she is accustomed *(solet)* to hold in her lap". He goes on to say he wishes he were in the sparrow's place.'

`Don't do the whole thing for me!' Abigail protested.

`If you don't want help...' Nathan said.

Abigail relented a little. `I didn't know you had Latin.'

`Of course I do. I went to school. It's a well-known poem by Catullus. I'm a little rusty but I can guide you through.'

`Mostly I can work it out,' Abigail said. Well, she thought as she gathered her books, at least he could be useful.

Mary came through with platters for the table. `My, it's dark in here!' she exclaimed with a look at both Nathan and Abigail. She picked a couple of rushes from their tray by the hearth and lit them at the fire.

'You look pleased with yourself.' Nathan said defensively.

Startled, Mary said `So I should be,' and went back round the chimney.

Abigail followed her. `What's the news then Mary?' Is it to do with the new garrison? They're the local Militia aren't they? Nathan ought to be joining that.'

`He gets digger Martin to go as his substitute.'

'And Goodwife Martin is right pleased. Come on, is it Francis?' watching intently. `It is! It is!'

'Just take the ale through for me.'

'Where is my mother then?'

Mary shrugged. `She left the cooking to me.'

When Phoebe did come in it was with a sulky-looking Carey. After the meal Phoebe said `Go up to the bedroom now Carey, and ponder.'

Having washed the dishes and wiped the last tankard Mary stood awkwardly and blurted out `Mistress, may I speak with you?'

Phoebe looked surprised. `Of course Mary. Alone, or...?'

`No, I'd be glad for Abigail to hear. Ma'am, my sweetheart Francis. He wants us to marry.'

`The blacksmith from Godalming?'

`Yes, but Mistress, he has volunteered as a substitute for someone in the Farnham Trained Band so he'll be in the garrison, and he's joining himself to the blacksmith in the Borough.'

`It seems he has it all settled,' Phoebe said. `Where do you propose to live?'

`There's a couple of rooms beside the forge that we can hire. And Mistress, if you'll have me I'd be glad to continue working here.'

`That is a relief,' Phoebe said. `I took Carey to see her Great Aunt who is frail and sick. Carey seems to have no feeling for her, and the aunt told me she never would settle to anything. Now Carey's mind seems to be only on boys. I need you Mary if we are to train her up in the way she should go.'

Over the following weeks at Phoebe's request, Abigail tried to teach Carey to spin, for every woman should have that skill, and there could be no knitting without first spinning the yarn. Carey did not take to it readily, and when it went wrong she would exclaim, `I'll not be doing this', folding her arms. Gradually Abigail learnt ways of coaxing her back to work.

Outside, it snowed.

Mary was wedded and bedded with minimum fuss, and Abigail now sharing her bedroom with Carey, discovered that she snored.

To Ralph, being in winter quarters was an unwelcome break in activity. Despite bitter weather throughout December, Waller's troops had marched and fought and marched again, until in early January they had sought winter quarters in the neighbourhood of Arundel and Chichester. Such had been their successes that when Sir William Waller went to London he was acclaimed as 'William the Conqueror'.

Billeted on a harness maker, Ralph had all too much leisure once he had exercised his horse with occasional skirmishes, and joined in the required training. His host stitched bridles and harness by the light of the little cottage's single window.

Seeing Ralph watching, he asked one day. 'Want to try your hand at it?' and Ralph had started to learn to ply a chisel-tipped needle, pushing it through the leather with the thick leather 'palm' strapped onto the palm of his own hand. As they worked they talked of the campaigning.

'I've heard,' the saddler said, 'you soldiers do more damage sacking and looting than in fighting.'

'I've lost the taste for it now,' Ralph said. 'At the beginning, we looted a swathe of vicarages, and gained some good food thereby. Then after we took Winchester, the soldiers clamoured to be allowed to loot. I joined in at first, but they went wild. And when they sacked Sir William's house....'

'Sir William Waller? Your commander?'

'Aye. I guess they didn't know it was his house, nor care. Such a waste. I had no heart for sacking after that.'

'But in Chichester cathedral you left a trail of destruction, I've heard.'

Ralph shook his head sadly. 'Not all of us. Some folk believe that any picture or statue is idolatry, and they hacked them all to pieces. And some were after treasure.'

'Church treasure?'

'Cached behind panelling in the Chapter House. One of the Colonels actually led that assault. Sir Arthur Hazelrigg, a choleric man.'

'So you've enriched yourself?' the saddler said, neatly cutting a thread from his work.

'We were paid well as part of Chichester's surrender. But no, I'm little richer than I've ever been. You've always to sell the loot you can't carry, so it's not as valuable as many looters imagine.'

The cottage was cold, even after the snow cleared, and Ralph wondered if Abigail would indeed be knitting him some stockings. His need was genuine enough, and he had hoped perhaps he might hear from her.

His hopes were the pretext for a letter.

Mary was out when Francis called at the Tanyard. Hefty he certainly was, yet warmer and more personable than Abigail had imagined from Mary's description, big and reassuring.

Phoebe greeted him, and asked him whether he found the smithy congenial.

`Aye,' he said,` and I've set up a forge in the Castle too. The horsemen there had need of a farrier.' He turned to Abigail. 'I was there today, and the sutler brought this letter addressed to you, delivered it to the garrison, and I've brought it down for you.'

The letter was very short.

To Abigail Mannory, it began. *We are in winter quarters, I in Arundel, with little to do except harassing malignants. Before Christmas our two troops easily re-took Arundel, and Chichester surrendered to us after a few days' siege. It is cold and wet and I long for the stockings I hope you are knitting for me. Your servant, R Attfield.*

If the sutler could bring letters, surely she could send a reply with Francis' help. The stockings were nearly complete, and she began to wonder what she would write.

In the event there was no need. In February, the weather suddenly turned mild and with it came troops, emerging out of their winter quarters like hedgehogs from their leaf burrows. Some men looked better fed than formerly, though others coughed and wheezed and many complained of the skimpy cut of their issue coats. Cobblers were kept busy repairing worn shoes. `Sir William is building up his troops again, based in Farnham,' Francis reported. `He's Major General of the West now.'

For the time being the quartermaster secured billets where the horses could be stabled, with some of the cavalry in outlying villages, and for the time being the Tanyard was spared, with little likelihood of seeing Ralph Attfield.

He came however, walking over the bridge with his easy stride, when Abigail and Phoebe were working in the vegetable plot. He hailed them and they went to meet him in the yard.

There Jacob joined them and they went indoors. `Does this mean we're to have troopers here again?' he asked at once.

`Nay, I know not,' Ralph said. `My errand is quite other. I've been sent out to commandeer horses. Sir William wants all his foot soldiers mounted as dragoons for speed of movement, and we lack mounts. The Sergeant reckoned that in view of my horse-dealing past, I'd be the one most likely to find them.'

`Do you buy them or borrow them?' Jacob asked.

`Or take them?' Ralph laughed. `We hear that Prince Rupert is having every horse he sees rounded up, to keep them from us. Where's Tom?'

`On a local errand today,' Abigail said. She went over to the spinning wheel where she had only yesterday put the newly completed stockings rolled together. Returning to the table she stood still, holding them against her apron, while the talk continued.

She approached timidly. `Here are your stockings,' she said.

He took them from her, opened them out, felt them, laid them beside his foot and looked up at her, smiling.

`How can I thank you! The stockings I have been wearing are well nigh worn to rags.' He hesitated, wishing he could hug her in thanks. But then he heard Tom's cart enter the yard and he bounded towards the window and stood watching the men unload faggots into the fuel shed. Very soon Hal appeared and took the cob's rein and led her off to be un-hitched, and Tom came in with a surprised greeting.

`Not on a horse Mister Attfield?'

`Not today.' Ralph grasped his hand. `Today I'm seeking horses. I see you're still working the cob.'

`I try to ring the changes so that she doesn't get idle. We had hoped she'd be in foal but your suggestion came too late in the summer.'

`You're saying then that she's scarcely needed any more, or do you drive both carts? Have you a partner?'

`No,' Tom said, more emphatically than might have been expected. 'Are you wanting the loan of her'

'I have to collect as many mounts as I can.'

`What do you say Father?'

Jacob did not reply at once, and in the pause they each became aware that his answer would be significant. The pause felt long. Then he said `Let Tom decide. He has earned that horse and cart for himself.'

He would not meet the grateful look in Tom's eyes, did not look at anyone as Tom absorbed this information and slowly made up his mind.

`I have the pair, and I can put one of them to the small cart when it is all I need.' He paused. Then he took a decisive breath. `You may as well have her. She works well, though after a spell at grass it still takes Hal to catch her.'

`Shall I take Hal too?' Ralph was half laughing.

Jacob looked surprised. `Hal? I hardly think so.'

Ralph turned to Tom, `If you need work, you could offer as a waggoneer for the army.' He stood up. `Well, I must continue my search. Someone will come for the cob.' He went outside, Jacob with him.

Abigail watched them through the window where he had stood not long before. She watched an extended conversation between him and Hal. At one point surely the question of Hal going with the horse must have arisen, for she saw Hal look at the ground and Ralph's arm go reassuringly round his still skinny shoulders. It's horses and Hal Ralph cares about, she thought.

But abruptly he turned and strode back into the Hall.

Abigail!' he said, `You are a kind, industrious girl! These are excellent stockings.' He opened his mouth again as if to say something else, and then shut it.

`I can knit you some more if you wish,' she said.

`I was about to ask if you would, except that it seemed ungrateful. Would you truly? I know not where we shall be, but dispatches do get through.' Then like a second thought he added, `You could write too. It's good to be reminded that life is not all war.'

`I will,' she said. `Yes, I will.'

The afternoon was well advanced next day when a young trooper came to collect the horse.

`There's that degree of coming and going,' he told Tom. `First light, guns and ammunition wagons set out. Then off go a couple of troops, scouting I suppose. Then off go gallopers after them, or maybe after the guns.' The man shrugged. `They don't tell us where or why, just order us to go.'

Hal fetched the cob and handed her over, and Tom pocketed the receipt, `Loan of one bay horse property of Thomas Mannory.' He liked that. Now he could work to earn ownership of Blaze and Star and the big cart

To Abigail Mannory. My dearest Friend. I am with child and sick day and night. Harry spends much time away in the town, and when he is home Hermann is often with him. I wish you were here. The landlady is kind but has neither time nor means to meet my needs. Though in truth I scarcely know what those needs may be, I feel so unwell. Pray do not tell my mother. She could do nothing here in our cramped quarters. Harry asks me to send you the latest issue of the Mercurius Aulicus. *I so miss your company and send you my warmest affection, your life-long friend Joan.*

Hearing that a newsbook had arrived from Oxford, the Royalist headquarters, most of the journeymen and apprentices lingered after the evening meal in the hope of learning of its contents. Abigail handed the sheets to Hal. `You could read it for us.'

Hal took it reluctantly.

`*Mer-cur-ius Aul-ic-us*,' he spelt out slowly. `Whatever's that?'

`Mercury is the heavenly messenger,' Nathan said, `and *Aulicus* is a courtyard or the Court. It's messages from the King's Court.'

`Oh.' Hal looked it over. `*Mercurius Aulicus*, The eleventh Week, 12, -18 March 1643.'

`Skip that!' Peter said, peering over Hal's shoulder `It's about the Lord Brooke's death before Lichfield. Go on.'

Hal began hesitantly, but Peter quickly summarised it for the listeners. 'Lord Brookes was commander besieging Lichfield for Parliament. And he prayed that if their cause was not just and right they would all be cut off. Which in the event he was, a bullet going right through his eye into his throat.

'"And this," the writer says, "May serve sufficiently to convince the conscience of those, who have been hitherto seduced unto a good opinion of so foul a cause, that it is neither justifiable in itself, nor acceptable unto God".

`Foul a cause?' Hal said.

`They must mean Parliament,' Peter said, 'as Lord Brookes was one of Parliament's commanders.' It says about Lord Brookes' so-called Accomplices, "Who being as deep as he in this Rebellion against God and the King, have little reason to expect any better ends, if they have not worse".'

`Where did this come from?' Nathan asked.

`Joan sent it . Harry asked her to,' Abigail said.

`That Harry Vernon always was blinded by royalty.'

To Thomas Mannory. Our scouting enables us to lead the regiments by sure routes. Winchester, Romsey, Salisbury, Shaftesbury, Sherborne, Bristol, success attends us. We are renowned for our night marches, stealthy and fast. God is surely with us. We are constantly on the move, in lodgings fair and foul. To carry our booty, our wounded and our ammunition, we need more carts. What say you? I remain, your friend, Ralph Attfield. Gloucester, 28 March 1643.

Easter

`Of course we celebrate Easter.' About to leave the church porch some weeks earlier, Rev Duncomb had encountered a debate becoming heated. `We hold a service with the appropriate canticles and readings,' he said in his quiet way.

`That's barely half a celebration. There should be sports and dancing, a proper celebration,' the young Captains now in charge at the Castle asserted.

'It was done in the past,' Bicknell said. `Mannory was champion of leaping.'

`See what you can organise,' Duncomb said, `and I'll support you. It soon may not be allowed.'

By Easter Saturday preparations were well advanced, all over the meadow between the river and the Borough. Straw butts for archery, a circle of stakes roped off as a wrestling ring, and Jacob erected his high jump with a willowy cross bar supported on pegs in firm uprights.

Walking home with Thomas, Jacob asked, `Have you a team for leap-frog? The apprentices are forming one.'

`Nay, I'll gather one tomorrow,' Tom said. Hal should be good at leaping though perhaps weak to be leapt over, and he could surely find four others.

On Easter Sunday anyone who had new clothes paraded them, noticing and being noticed as they attended the service. Rev Duncomb was as good as his word, starting off the day with his sermon.

`Easter celebrates the greatest event in history when Jesus who had died a terrible death was wonderfully raised to life. He opened the way to life for us all and surely we should celebrate this gift with bodies, minds and spirits. Here in this service we are praising with our spirits and considering with our minds. Let us go on to praise with our bodies.

`If the Independents in Parliament have their way, there will soon be no more sports and dancing on a Sunday afternoon. Make the most of them.'

Elizabeth Bicknell had been cajoling all her friends into making extra ale for her to sell and make a little money as a gift to Rev Duncomb now that he was properly set up as incumbent of the Parish. Betty Gary came through from Snow Hill trailing her children, her younger sons carrying a cask between them.

'Set it down on the ground for the moment,' Elizabeth said, `whilst I determine where to place the table. Billie, move that trestle round. No, it still wobbles. Boys, hold the table top and Billie see if you can find a better position. Shoo! girls, out of the way - Betty for mercy's sake, keep the girls by you."

'You need Christopher,' Betty said, `only he's busy with the leaping.'

'Oh that's much better! Thank you boys. Now the benches, and the casks go on them. Isn't that clever? Now where are jugs? Betty, where are we to put the money? And will folk bring their own tankards and drinking horns? Dearie me, there's so much to think about.'

Archery had already begun with small boys rushing forward to collect arrows which missed the targets. Jacob supervised the high jump, moving the cross-bar up and down and recording the contenders' efforts in a tiny notebook.

`Abigail.' It was Phoebe, come to stand by her as she watched. `Keep an eye on Carey if you can.'

`She won't be pleased to have me dogging her footsteps.'

`No, no. I'm just anxious for her in this crowd.'

`I haven't seen her since church.'

Phoebe flicked her head in the direction of the long jump. Carey was standing near Hal who appeared to be oblivious of everything but the jumping. His gaze followed each move of the boys competing, the walk back, the muscle flexing, the run up, the leap. Abigail moved nearer, wondering if he would take part.

Slowly and deliberately he stepped forward and booked a turn, and when it came he jumped efficiently, a good length.

`Go on Willie, beat that,' said a voice Abigail recognised, the mother of the lad who had tormented Hal summers ago and who had forbidden their associating together.

It was close, these two leggy lads striving to exceed each other's length. In the event Willie did better. He stuck his tongue out at Hal as he swaggered back to his friends. Carey sprang forward and flung her arms round Hal. He pushed her away.

`You did so well!' Carey squealed, `and that Willie...'

`Leave me be won't you.' Hal walked off briskly.

Abigail turned casually to Carey. `They may need help at the beer table. Come up there with me.'

`Back again,' Elizabeth was saying to men holding out their drinking horns. `You'll make our fortune.'

`Make a drunken brawl more likely,' Betty said.

`Oh Betty, it's not strong ale, just the ordinary.'

`Depends how much they drink,' Betty muttered.

Loud support and comment was coming from the nearby wrestling ring. Abigail followed Carey to watch with her. The wrestlers stood facing each other, alert for the slightest opening in the opponent's stance. Once they made contact they slowly moved about until suddenly one was on the ground, and it seemed that he had lost, for he was leaving the ring. Why, it was Nathan, stripped to the waist, his body gleaming with sweat as he pulled on his shirt.

He went across to Abigail. `Do you understand what they're doing?'

Abigail shook her head.

`Each tries to upset the other's balance,' Nathan said, `and throw him to the ground'

Not content with instructing her, Nathan began calling out instructions to the wrestlers. Losing interest Abigail returned to the women.

Phoebe joined them. `Did you see Hal?' she asked. `I'd no idea he could leap so far.'

`I'm not sure he had either,' Abigail said.

Little Eliza Bicknell stopped her careful ferrying of ale jugs. `Why is it all boys and men? I could leap. I can leap ever so high.'

`Indeed you could not,' Betty said, `in your skirts.'

`I could dress like a boy.'

`Your turn will come,' Elizabeth soothed, `when the dancing begins.'

`Do the men not dance then?'

`Of course they dance.'

`Then that is unfair. They sport and they dance, while we may only dance.'

`Look,' Elizabeth said, `Here comes another customer. Eliza, pray fill a jug from the cask there. I reckon,' she continued to her friends, `the high jump will be between your Christopher, Betty, and Thomas Mannory. You should have seen your father years back Abigail. He just sailed over the bar. Look now, who is in the wrestling ring? Isn't that the new blacksmith?'

Abigail stood on tiptoes to peer over the on-lookers. `Oh yes it is, Mary's husband Francis.'

` He looks as if he might be a match even for Abe Trussler,' Elizabeth said.

`For all his faults,' Betty pronounced, `you can't deny that Abe Trussler is a champion wrestler.'

Francis had worsted several opponents when Abe went in to face him. So well matched were they that their wrestling was long drawn-out. Each time Abe seemed to have got Francis off balance his sheer strength enabled him to right himself. Then suddenly Abe swung violently left and right and Francis was on the ground. Winded, he did not get up at once and they glimpsed triumph on Abe's face for all there were four bouts still to go.

The second was shorter. Francis twisted Abe's arm behind him and flipped him to the ground. He attempted the same move in the third bout, and then there was a long struggle, evenly matched. Suddenly the umpire shouted `foul!' and Francis was clutching his shin.

`No kicking allowed,' Elizabeth said. `You can see Abe's losing his temper.'

`So that's your servant girl's husband is it?' Betty said to Phoebe, adding with her knowing little laugh, `Doubtless Abe wishes it were the master he's wrestling rather than the servant's mate.'

`The master? My father? Why should he?' Abigail asked.

`Surely you know of the feud he has with Mannorys,' Betty said. `It's handed down like, the feud, father to son.'

`A feud needs two sides,' Phoebe said, `and Jacob has never taken part in it.'

`What about the lecture when he had Abe arrested? That added fuel to the feud.'

`Why is there a feud?' Abigail asked.

`We don't talk about it,' Phoebe said with a finality that for the moment silenced even Betty. Cries of encouragement and dismay were coming from the wrestling ring as Abe redoubled his efforts. Francis threw him once more but the last two bouts he lost.

Jumping had finished and the cry went up for leap-frog teams. Tom had done nothing about raising a team. He grabbed Hal - `Come, we'll have to make do with some carters' and they ran towards the Goat's Head. Many in there were too drunk to be capable of leap-frog.

Just as he despaired of finding anyone Tom heard his name and there was Matthew, sober and ready to go. `My mates here will make up numbers' he said and quickly raised the further three Tom needed.

`I didn't see you at the sports,' Tom said going back to the field.

`I've not been here long. That tyrant my mother disapproves. If my friends hadn't arrived and insisted, we'd have been virtual prisoners at the house. What's your sport? Wrestling?'

`I did as a boy, so I know the moves. Reckon I'm too light-weight now.'

Chaos of milling teams gradually took shape into heats, the men spaced out along the pitch, the first ready for the pistol blast to send them away leap-frogging and bending over ready for the next until all reached the finish. Everyone gravitated there to watch and cheer them on.

Abigail noticed a dark curly-haired girl standing somewhat apart. As Tom's team ran by having finished their heat the girl grabbed the arm of one of them saying 'Matt!' He turned, looking displeased.

`Matthew, you said you'd take care of me,' she said, `and you just abandoned me. Where have you been?'

`Oh.' The boy tried to shake her off. `Here, I'm sure this girl will companion you,' gesturing at Abigail.

`Matt!' Tom shouted, `we're needed for the next heat.'

`Are you all alone?' Abigail asked the girl.

`I'm with my brother, but he's just left me on my own. I thought it would be so merry, and it isn't at all. I don't know anyone.'

`Well, I'm Abigail, and it's very merry once the dancing begins. Do you know any dances?'

`No,' the girl said, `not one.'

`Come, let's try if we can work some out.'

They found a quiet corner of the field and were soon in helpless giggles as Abigail tried to be three people in order to demonstrate the figures of the dances.

`At least you know now what some of the instructions mean. With a good partner you'll soon pick them up.' She took the girl's hand to go to where a little band was preparing to play. `I still don't know your name,' she said.

`Susan. Susan Woolgar. And Oh! I do hope we can be friends.'

Using the back of a barn as sounding board to augment their volume, the players started tuning up. Elizabeth and Betty were totting up their takings.

`We had none too much ale,' Elizabeth said. `Now how many coins did I put in that pile?'

Bent over their task they did not notice the newcomers until little Eliza said, `Good day Mistress Vernon, Good day Master Vernon.' The Vernons had come through from the street, Henry Vernon holding his wife's arm. Failing eyesight meant that he seemed no longer the confident squire whom Thomas had encountered when, year's back, he had collected pigeon dung from Culver Hall. The Vernon children clustered around them.

`Forgive me!' Elizabeth said, turning and bobbing a curtsy in one movement. `Good day to you! We were so busy counting up that I didn't see you. So much ale we've sold, it will make a goodly offering to the Lecturer though I know we should call him the Rector now, and the children have been helping, such a busy day we've had!'

Mistress Vernon turned to her husband. `Mistress Bicknell and Goodwife Gary have been selling ale, and are just now clearing the table away.'

`Yes yes, I can sense that there is much activity,' Henry Vernon said. `Hard working women.'

Elizabeth ordered the boys to dismantle the tables and settled in hope of a good gossip with her young neighbour.

However it was Henry Vernon who said `We thought we would come along for the dancing. The children enjoy it. So, of course, do we, but my sight is so poor I fear I would be a hazard to the dancers.'

`There's always them as is a hazard from a bellyful of ale,' Betty said.

`Then we're to blame for selling it,' Elizabeth said cheerfully. `Have you any news from Oxford?' turning back to Mistress Vernon.

`You will have heard I'm sure, that we are to be grand-parents.'

`Grandparents... and you so young...' and then suddenly light dawned. `You mean, our Joan and young Master Vernon? Mercy on us, I'd no idea!'

`Is it so surprising?' Henry Vernon smiled.

`No no! But somehow our Joan... and she never told me!'

`I have to confess, we have only just heard. Harry is most remiss as a letter writer.'

`Step-Mother.' One of the older Vernon children, a plain brindled girl, pulled at Mistress Vernon's sleeve. `They are making up sets to dance. I would so much like to...'

Leap-frog finished, Tom had brought Matthew to where Abigail stood with Susan saying `Let's dance with our sisters.' No sooner was this settled than Nathan came over to ask Abigail to partner him.

She shook her head. `I'm dancing with Tom. Then she caught sight of the Vernon girl, watching with longing eyes.

`Excuse me ma'am.' She bobbed a curtsy to Mistress Vernon. `Would your daughter care to join our set for this dance?'

`There now Matilda.' Mistress Vernon gave her a little push. `A set ready made for you. Who is her partner?'

Abigail gestured to Nathan who still had his eyes on her. `Nathan Armstrong,' she said. `He works for my father and he knows the dances well.'

`That will be a kindness,' Mistress Vernon said to Nathan who slowly stepped forward. `What Matilda doesn't know she picks up quickly.'

`Picking up sticks', Tom said. `Come on Nathan, you can be first couple.'

Rapidly Nathan explained the patterns to Matilda who nodded and nodded. More quietly Abigail did the same for Susan. `We'll call out as we go' she said. She hoped that standing between the two girls she might help them along.

However, the dance required repeated changing of places. Nathan changed places with her and then with Matthew, so it was with Matilda that she doubled up the set and back. Tom followed with Matthew, though he refused to hold his hand.

`Now you go' Abigail whispered to Matilda who changed neatly with Tom and Susan, and was back with her partner at the bottom of the set.

Tom was poised to move next. `Not you!' Nathan shouted. 'Second woman!'`

'Whoops!' Abigail said as she skipped off.

Despite Nathan's called instructions they muddled the next formation and got behind the music. Nathan pushed and shoved until they all stood still in confusion.

Finally he led the men weaving in and out of the standing women, but Matthew coming last just skipped blithely about, colliding with the others as they passed. The dance ended lamely, none of the men swinging their partners.

Matilda smiled a shy `Thank you' to Nathan who evidently expected Abigail to return her to her parents.

`That looked a little complex,' her step-mother said, `but you managed well. So you are Abigail? Thank you for arranging it.'

`Abigail,' her husband said. `Were you not studying Latin with my son?'

`Yes Sir, he greatly helped me.'

`And do you continue with your studies now that he is gone?'

`I try to when I have time,' and then she added, she knew not why, `My mother prefers me to teach Hal his letters.'

`Hal - the horse-boy Sam speaks of? And are you successful?'

`He can read now, and write a little.'

`Henry.' Mistress Vernon turned suddenly to her husband. `Might this not be the answer to our dilemma?'

Without waiting for reply she addressed Abigail again. `What would you say to teaching my little girls? Their half-sisters are not suited to teaching them, and they are growing up ignorant. What do you think Henry?'

`It might well do,' Master Vernon said. `Would your father permit it, young woman?'

`I would pay you of course, and you would come to Culver Hall.'

Abigail smiled at the apparent certainty in her tone. `May I think about it?' she said.

A new dance was forming up and both she and Susan were quickly partnered. It was a simple circle dance, and joining hands with the women to skip into the centre Susan said to Abigail, `This is so much fun.'

`Even with Nathan taking it all so seriously?'

`He was marvellous, putting us right!' and they were back in their places.

Dusk was falling and dew dampening the grass when the last dance was called and this time Abigail could not refuse to partner Nathan.

`Must you always avoid me?' he said.

`Others asked me before you did,' she said, `and thank you for dancing with Matilda.'

`You just make use of me.'

Abigail turned to face him. `Do you want to dance with me, or quarrel?'

He took her hand then and they were away, a satisfying dance because properly executed. At the end he swung her well and would have drawn her close in conclusion as was often the custom but despite giddiness she resisted.

Suddenly she clapped her hand over her mouth. `Oh my goodness! Carey! I was meant to keep an eye on Carey!'

`That hussy' Nathan said.

`You don't have to condemn her.'

`You condemn her yourself by keeping an eye on her.'

`My mother asked me to,' still searching with her eyes.

`Your mother has a weakness for orphans.'

`You are insufferable!' all her attention now on him. `Everyone but you is always wrong.'

`Nonsense.'

`You think you're always right. And you swither between side and side in this war, just to protect yourself.'

`Pray what have you done in this war, other than ogle that scoundrel Attfield?'

'How dare you!'

'Knitting him stockings and writing him notes.'

'That's no business of yours."

'It wouldn't be if I didn't care for you.'

'Nathan I've told you...' she stamped her foot for emphasis. `Look, it's almost dark and I can't see Carey anywhere."

'Damn Carey, I want you for myself.' He grasped her upper arms in his powerful hands.

'Nathan, please!' She squirmed left and right trying vainly to free herself. `You know my feelings. Let me go.'

'Tell me one reason why I should.'

The meadow seemed deserted, just the two of them in the middle of a wide field and he impossibly powerful.

'Because I've told you I don't care for you. Because it's unmanly to force a woman. Because...'

'All those skills of argument...'

'Oh Nathan, you're hurting me. Please, please...'

'Ah, a little weakness for a change.' Suddenly he relaxed his hold. She lurched backwards, losing her balance. He caught her as she fell and pulled her to him. Now she was fighting an embrace.

`Uh uh!' A voice came out of the dusk. `We're off home, come to say farewell. Sorry to intrude on your love-making.' It was Matt with Susan.

Released, Abigail shook herself like a dog out of water, catching her breath and straightening her dress with automatic fingers.

`I'm glad you did,' she said pointedly. Then, `You've a dark walk home. Maybe we'll meet on market day Susan. I'll keep an eye out for you.'

`A better eye than you've had for Carey' Nathan said, watching their departure.

`Even if she was here you've spoilt any chance I had of seeing her.'

`She was probably romping in some hay loft.'

`I'm going home, while I can still see the way.'

`Allow me to escort you.' Nathan's tone was bitterly sarcastic. `So long as I walk two yards behind you.'

They processed down towards the bridge, almost the last to leave the field. Abigail plunged through the street door into Tanyard house. At the far end of the Hall Phoebe was banking up the last of the fire.

`Mother I'm sorry,' Abigail said. `I forgot all about Carey. I lost sight of her hours ago, before the dancing. I've no idea where she is.'

`I have,' Phoebe said. `She's gone to bed in a sulk.'

Rose and Lettice

`Rose would you please sit down and attend.'

Rose Vernon stood by the window looking over the stable yard. `Sam is leading out Mother's horse, I thought I heard him. So Mother must be going out. I wonder where she's going.'

Abigail sighed. `I expect she will tell you when she comes back. And she'll want to see that you've completed your tasks.'

Little Lettice looked up from the slate where she was laboriously copying lines of letters. `Come on Rose, we can't go and play till you do.'

`Sam's escorting Mother. Oh! and here comes the pigeon muck boy. He's always around Sam.'

From where she sat Abigail could just see the dovecot with the doves flapping out of all its windows when Hal opened the little door at its base. Too tall now to get easily through it he preferred to pull out the dung with a hoe, filling the sacks outside.

Abigail allowed Rose to watch a little longer before summoning her back to her slate. Rose picked up the chalk and attacked the letters with abandoned speed producing a scrawl.

Lettice put the tail on her final `g' with a flourish and looked up.

`Why does he collect pigeon dung?' she asked.

`It's used in tanning,' Abigail said.

`Simon the Tanner, that was in the Bible story we read. Do you know about tanning?'

`I should do. My father is a tanner.'

`Is his name Simon?'

`No, his name is Jacob.'

`Then he ought to be a shepherd with spotty sheep.'

`Well he isn't, he's a tanner. Now Rose if you've finished - this is a mess. Rub those letters off the slate and do them again, carefully.'

This is a game of bluff she thought, surprised that Rose was now actually doing as she was told, and anxious not to upset the change. Already Lettice's letters were better formed, but at least for the moment Rose was trying.

`What do they do with the pigeon dung?' Lettice asked.

`They mix it with water and other things for curing fine leather. To make gloves. The glove makers along by the river use it, once it's been finished by the currier.'

`I'd like to see them making gloves. And the tannery, could we see .that?'

`Sometimes it's very smelly.'

`I don't mind. Pigeon dung smells quite good.'

`Ugh' said Rose. `How can you say that Letty?'

`And horse dung too when they spread it on the garden.'

`You have extraordinary tastes' Rose said with all the superiority of eight years old. A kitten woke from its snooze on a cushion and jumped onto her lap. `Oh kitty, now you've jogged my arm.' She held out her slate to Abigail. `You see what he did. That wasn't me.'

She fondled the kitten but it was more inclined for play so she stood up and wandered about with it, flowing its acrobatic movements through her hands.

`Look kitty, they've loaded the hand cart now.'

Lettice scrambled over to the window. `Let's see! Does the boy push it all by himself?'

Abigail joined them and looked out. `Daniel will help him, the man over there.'

`Do you know them?' Lettice turned wide eyes to her.

`Why yes, they come from the tannery where I live.'

`Oh will you take us there?'

`Perhaps one day if you learn your lessons well. Now Lettice you copy these words while I hear Rose read, and then you can take turn about.'

For all Hal's reluctance, teaching him had been easy compared with these two little Vernons. A couple of hours three mornings a week, and market day offered a welcome change.

Susan came to every market, setting off from her home at first light. Mother Woolgar refused to let rest her son and daughter's defiance on Easter day, and continued to make life hard for them. What she did not know was that going to market enabled Susan to see her new friend. Together they would do the rounds of the peddlers, chatting as they went.

`Fine knacks for Ladies,' Abigail said. `There's a song about that they used to sing, my sister and her husband that is.'

`I wish I had a sister.'

`I don't see her at all now, not since she had the baby and we all went to its christening.'

Abigail told Susan about the Vernon sisters. 'Rivals they seem to be rather than friends,' she said, ' and I just hope I can keep patience with them teaching them their lessons.'

'You amaze me,' Susan said. 'I wouldn't know where to begin. Besides, I can barely read and write myself.'

They walked along to the lecture together. Susan deposited her basket in the church porch and they went inside.

`Oh look,' she said as they settled themselves, `there's Nathan.'

`Well of course,' Abigail said. `They're all expected to come. Tom would be here if he weren't away carting, and there's Peter and the other apprentices, and the servants and my parents.'

`Yes. Yes of course,' Susan said.

Mr Attfield.

I am hoping that these stockings will reach you. If they don't, Abigail thought, you won't know my hope, and what else can I tell him. *You may have given up hope of receiving them. Now that summer is here I have less time for knitting, also Mistress Vernon is employing me to teach her two little girls. It all began on Easter Day when there was dancing on the big meadow, and sport too.* Oh dear, this is very muddled, and perhaps he will not be at all interested. *Otherwise everything is much as before.*

Inadequate though she felt the letter to be, she signed it and dispatched it. An answer came surprisingly soon.

To Abigail Mannory, The Tanyard.

The stockings you sent reached me and are welcome.

We made a rapid night march to the city of Worcester but they resisted us. We lost nigh on three score men killed or prisoners, and others were wounded. They have been carried in barges down the great river Severn to join us here in Gloucester. A slow journey though not for us who scout. We cover many miles to find the best routes and discover the enemy.

Now we are quartered with little food and no pay. Sir William is gone south leaving our several troops of horse to await our pay while the collectors gather malignants' fines and ransoms.

Your servant R Attfield. Gloucester 2 June 1643.

Carey looked up from her spinning which in spite of herself had improved in both speed and quality. Abigail was sitting by the window where the evening sunlight poured in onto her sewing. She had strapped a leather-worker's palm to her right hand to push the needle through the heavy linen destined to be a carter's smock for Tom. At the next window Phoebe was embroidering distinctive stitches onto the still separate collar.

Carey looked up and said `Would you teach me to knit?'

Abigail was so surprised that she almost snagged her finger. She sucked the skin bruised by the needle.

`Why, certainly, if you'd like to.'

`I've watched you and it looks more interesting than spinning.'

`There's no knitting without spinning. But at the end of your work you do have a garment to show for it.'

'It would make a change too.'

Abigail secured her needle and went to the shelf where, since she had completed the last pair of stockings, the wooden needles had lain idle.

`Carey could just knit a straight piece to join up like a tube' Phoebe said. 'Many stockings are like that.'

So Abigail cast on and sat by Carey as her fingers began to learn the new skill. Despite the occasional `I'm not doing this' she persisted and over the following days Abigail and her mother hardly dared comment to each other for fear her interest would wane. She alternated with spinning and they began to have to call her to her other household duties. The finished lengths were uneven and flawed but complete and she cobbled them together proudly.

Phoebe said, `You may keep that pair for yourself to remind you of your progress.'

The days were so hot and dry that stockings were scarcely needed but she wore them day in day out, sweeping, weeding, hay-making, milking and of course, knitting. Whether or not the enthusiasm might wane, for the time being she was employed of her own free will.

To Tanner Jacob Mannory.

Sir. I would deem it a great favour if you would send the boy Hal to me for the care of my horse and a few others in the troop. I have a high regard for his skill with horses, and I will take all the care of him that I can amid the hazards of war.

I am your humble servant Ralph Attfield. Gloucester 14 June 1643.

Bath

Coming back from the powder mills on a warm evening in June, Thomas caught sight of the glint of new armour ahead of him. With a potentially explosive load he always approached the Castle through the Park rather than the town, and now he seemed to be catching up with several hundred men mounted on sizeable horses. Their armour was such as he had never seen, gleaming in the slanting sunlight. A cart trundled along in the midst of them, evidently setting their pace.

He arrived at the Castle gate as they did, and followed them into the bailey. Servants were unloading heavy chests and carrying them indoors, while a florid man wearing a General's sash berated the carter. Tom passed them on his way up to the keep to hand over his barrels, and when he returned the altercation was still going on.

'Your orders were to make speed to Bath. All you've attained is Farnham.' The General spat out the word 'Farnham' as if the town were beneath contempt.

'The chests are heavy Sir,' the carter said with the desperation of much repetition.

The General spotted Tom.

'Even this lad could do better.'

'What, with that little cart and one horse?' the carter ventured.

At this the General exploded, his face red and his words almost incoherent. How dared he answer him thus, insolent wretch, and on and on.

Tom could not get past them to leave so he decided to take a risk. Stepping forward he said, 'Sir, I have a large new cart and two excellent horses.'

For a moment there was an alarmed silence. Then the General turned to a lieutenant. 'Pay off that good-for-nothing, and use this man and his cart.' And to Tom, 'Mind you make speed.' He was up on his horse and away, his escort scampering after him.

'That's Sir Arthur Haselrig for you. Can't wait, gallops up from Bath, diverts us from Bagshot for protection here.' the lieutenant said. 'You'd better be up to expectation. Where's the cart? Fetch it and report back here. We leave before dawn.'

Driving the cart through the town as fast as he could, Tom rapidly assessed what he needed to do. Hal first, to prepare, then Phoebe for some food, and then of course his father.

Hal lost no time fetching Star from the meadow to hitch with Blaze to the big cart. 'And put some hay in a couple of sacks,' Tom said.

'Bath.' Phoebe said. 'I wonder where that is.'

'To the west, I think, some distance. I don't know when I'll be back. I've to be at the Castle tonight ready to leave early in the morning.'

Phoebe smiled at him. 'Dear Tom, this really is what you wanted isn't it. I'll see what I can do.'

Then he went to find his father, owner still of both horses and cart.

All Jacob said was 'You'll take Hal.'

'Thank you Sir, I'll be glad to.'

'And leave him there. Attfield requires his services.'

Thomas gasped. Then quickly to tell Hal, and Phoebe for another loaf of bread and a water bottle for him, and then up to the attic to bundle up a spare shirt or two for each of them. Their excitement was such that Tom almost expected everyone to come out into the yard to see them off, but in the event there was just a hug from Phoebe and a pat on the head for Hal.

The convoy set out before dawn, the cart loaded with the heavy chests stuffed round with the hay and some of the escort's belongings.

'Our baggage train is following,' a troop servant told Tom.

These soldiers were of a different order from those who had lodged in the Tanyard, well fed and well horsed with expensive armour covering the major part of their bodies. Tom asked the servant about them.

'They're cuirassiers,' he said, 'gentlemen volunteers without command. Provide their own horses and arms, though I reckon Sir Arthur made a big outlay for them.' He laughed. 'They're nicknamed the Lobsters, cause of their armour casing.'

They reached Bath early on the third day, welcomed by all, for the chests contained money for desperately needed food and pay.

The Army had reasonable comfort for the time being, quartered in and around Bath, and now at last they had pay. This did not relieve their boredom, waiting for action yet required to stay ready, while Sir William Waller and Sir Arthur Haselrig tried to build up their numbers. The Royalist Army lay a bare twenty miles away at Wells, separated from Bath by a maze of small fields and narrow lanes, impossible for cavalry tactics.

'Where on earth do you suppose we can find Attfield?' Tom said to Hal.

'I'll go round the stables and look for paddy boys we know,' Hal said.

'That could take a long time,' Tom said. 'We'd best find somewhere to sleep.' He secured a poor room in an inferior inn with a yard which could barely contain his cart and horses. Every bed in the town, decent or otherwise, was taken several times over, and more troops were trickling in all the time.

Before Hal's search had yielded any success, they spotted Ralph himself, riding into the town among a couple of hundred troopers who were herding a long string of prisoners.

'So many horses!' Hal exclaimed, for besides the prisoners' mounts there were almost as many led horses. The troopers dismounted in the open space in front of the Abbey and Tom and Hal wriggled forward through the throng. At last they were within reach of Ralph. He turned momentarily, paused, and then sprang towards them with arms wide.

'Hal! You've come!' and then 'Are you staying?'

Hal nodded dumbly. Ralph turned to Tom. 'And are you?'

'I hadn't thought to,' Tom said.

'If we have more successes like today we'll have much loot to carry.'

'What happened?' Hal asked.

'We spent all night wandering about,' Ralph said. 'At dawn we found where the enemy was quartered.' He turned to a boy. 'Hold my horse and wait.' He went on, 'We stormed into the village and threw grenades into the houses – you should have seen them scuttle out, like rabbits from a ferret.' He laughed. 'Sixty cases of pistols we've captured, and over a hundred horses.'

People and horses were milling about all round them, the captured officers separated out to be presented to Sir William, the other prisoners secured. Ralph turned to the boy holding his horse. 'Are you one of the paddies?'

'No Sir. Penny for holding your horse, Sir.'

'If I had a penny,' Ralph said.

'You will have,' Tom said. 'I'm here because I brought in the pay you're owed.'

Jim Hosier was assembling his troop to return to their quarters. Ralph sprang back into his saddle. 'Follow on after us,' he told Tom and Hal.

The troop was quartered in a farm some way out of the town and there they were met by Norman, he who had bullied Hal early on in the Tanyard, now apparently chief among the paddy boys. The troopers were weary from lack of sleep and eager to hand over their equally weary horses.

'Hal will see to my horse, Norman,' Ralph said before he disappeared indoors.

'Hal,' Norman said, hands on hips. 'Seen you before somewhere.'

'Farnham,' Hal muttered, holding Ralph's horse's rein. 'Where are we stabling?'

'Trooper Attfield's boy, eh?' Norman said . 'Good thing you've come. Knowing horses. Hope you're tough.'

Tom asked about the other boys. Some had left, some were sick.

'Alan?' Hal asked. He of the torn breeches.

'Dead,' Norman said. 'Don't remember where. One of the weaklings. He's not the only one.'

'If you're staying Hal,' Tom said, ' you'd better come back with me and collect your bundle.'

They said Goodbye at the miserable inn. Tom felt a tug at his heart, surprised to find he cared about Hal, fearful for his future.

The officer commanding the escort troops had given Tom a warrant for pay, and he had hoped to be quickly in pocket. Already the money he had was dwindling alarmingly, with the inn to be paid and himself and the horses to be fed. But the process was long. The warrant needed a counter signature and then Tom must join a crowd of men waiting for payment. Several times he approached the pay desk with its papers, quills and inks, bags of coins and alert guards, only to abandon the wait.

So he spent several days exploring the City, the Roman baths with their disgusting water, and the hills, steep behind the houses, from which he glimpsed the guards posted all around.

He began to be hungry.

Food was coming in for the soldiers now that funds had arrived to buy it. Sometimes if he sat with one of the many groups perched in the streets, a bite or two might come his way.

Three happenings focused his mind the third day. Visiting the pay clerks' rooms he found that the flood of claimants had receded and he hardly had to wait his turn to present his warrant – and be paid.

The second event was when he tried to buy some food. He realised that Bath itself was running short, and the prices were exorbitant.

And finally, the flea bites from sleeping in the inn became intolerable. He decided to drive the cart to the farmhouse where Ralph and Hal were billeted. He might be taken on as carter, and there even the horse trough held cleaner water than Bath provided, where he could wash himself and his shirt.

Guards challenged him several times along the road, and again as he approached the farm. What was his business? 'You need a carter?'

Clearly they did, the more so when he said he was not afraid to carry ammunition. He stripped in the warm afternoon sun and scrubbed every bit of himself and his shirt by the horse trough, chasing fleas out of his breeches, cracking them between thumb and fingernail. He was glad too that his horses could graze for a while.

And then at last it was time for some food and a scratchy bed in a hay barn, and in the morning a move to the open space where the powder barrels were stacked, to learn his duties from the Commissary of Munitions, to gauge the weight his cart could carry in this hilly terrain, and to await orders.

The escapade that Ralph had recounted had raised morale and Tom could sense an eagerness for action. so that when scouts reported the Royalist Army on the move they were ready, early on the Sunday morning, to obey the order to gather in Bath. It took a while for the four or five thousand men to assemble, so it was late morning when they were sent up Claverton Down, a couple of miles east of the City.

Each troop kept together under its commanders, headed by a boy officer carrying the ensign, a six foot square flag. The wagons brought up the rear, a taxing struggle for the horses. Once atop the Down they stood, drawn up in battle order, waiting.

And waiting.

What must they be feeling, Tom wondered. Drawn up close together in their troops and then just waiting, with only their thoughts. The culmination of training, yet the dread prospect of going out to kill or be killed now viewed in cold blood. Fear, dread, boredom, stiff limbs, and longing for some action, to get going and hammer the foe.

For Tom, although behind them all with the wagons, and little more at that stage than a spectator, the atmosphere was tangible.

From their position they looked down on the river Avon, where Sir William Waller had had a bridge constructed beside the ford. On the near side a redoubt, a fortification of earth and timber, sheltered cannons.

And still the many on the Down stood waiting, iron helmets hot under the July sun, the horses restive, waiting throughout the day.

Once night fell at least they could sit or lie down, propped up against one another, the cavalry troopers close to their horses, and eat some hard biscuit and eke out what water they had. Tom lay under the cart, his horses tethered nearby.

Next day the Army stood to again, and now the Royalist Army was in sight, moving along the opposite bank of the river, moving towards Bath. One of Waller's regiments had spent the night hidden on high ground beyond the river, and now they attacked the advancing columns with musket, sword and dagger, a hot dispute in which men died and cannon were captured

It continued all morning until Waller's men were forced to pull back across the makeshift bridge. There they defended the redoubt, aided by some reinforcements. Once more the main Army played no part, continuing to stand in battle order. Two days standing, waiting, hot and thirsty.

As darkness fell the defence of the redoubt became hopeless, its defenders withdrew up the Down and the trumpet sounded a return to Bath. In the darkness they stumbled along, limbs stiff and weary, grateful that at least the way was downhill. It was midnight before all were inside the city.

No sooner had they found water and somewhere to rest than they were roused again and re-formed.

'March! And keep quiet!'

This time they followed the old Roman road up Lansdown, the other side of Bath. It was even steeper than Claverton Down. Wearily they struggled up the massive dark hill, repeatedly commanded to be quiet. They shuffled into ranks along the top, flanked by cannons. Tom and the other wagons parked behind them, on the reverse slope.

Darkness was just beginning to thin when sounds came from the valley below them. Moving under the steep hill and unaware that anyone was on the top, Royalist cannon and baggage wagons were noisily approaching with their advance guard.

'Fire!' the trumpet sounded, and Waller's cannon cracked into action. Below, frightened cart horses bucked and plunged, their teamsters desperately striving to turn their loads out of range. Seeing them, the front ranks on the edge of the hill above laughed at the spectacle, the laughter rippling back through their fellows behind, releasing tension.

After that they watched the rest of the Royalist Army gradually assemble on a lower hill across the valley from Lansdown.

Nothing happened.

All morning nothing happened. The two Armies simply stood watching each other, until in the afternoon the Royalist commander, Sir Ralph Hopton, ordered a phased withdrawal from his hill towards a village two miles distant.

Instantly a large party of Waller's dragoons and cavalry cantered down into the valley to attack their rear. But the valley was a maze of narrow lanes and a thousand of the Royalist musketeers were lurking all along them. Musket shot peppered the attackers from every hedge. It was useless. Quickly they pulled back and up to the hilltop position, and watched the retreat from afar. At least they had enjoyed some action.

A welcome respite.

'Let's go seek some water,' a fellow carter said to Tom.

Along the Down a spring sourced a stream, and they dipped their leather buckets in, carrying them back between them, careful not to slop it although footholds on the cropped grass of the Down were hard to find.

Thirsty men thronged them, desperate to replenish their water bottles. The two of them had to defend their haul, the horses being their first concern. Unhitched and hobbled, the horses browsed the short dry grass. Men chewed on hard biscuit from their snapsacks and fell asleep in their ranks.

At first light early next morning the Army moved again, moved up to the highest point of Lansdown where the escarpment was a precipice clad in beech and ash woods. Parties were detailed to axe branches from the trees, while others built the branches and stones into a defensive breast-work. Tom, for something to do, helped collect stones. Away up the valley they could see the Royalist Army reassembling on their hill a mile and a half distant.

The valley and lower hills were a patchwork of hedged fields, and throughout the afternoon every one of them was disputed by dragoons from either side. The infantry on Lansdown simply watched, hearing the crack of musket and seeing the flash of fire, craning to see when a dying sergeant major was carried up the road.

A troop of Haselrig's 'Lobsters' trotted down to support the Parliamentary dragoons. Gradually they beat back their opponents to a large cornfield below where the rest of the Royalist Army stood. Hopton's trumpeters sounded retreat.

Instantly Waller unleashed a troop of two hundred horse. Tom glimpsed Ralph among them, cantering down the road and then accelerating into a fast gallop, leaping hedges, charging the retreating army. Dragoons followed, firing support from every hedgerow.

The enemy horses panicked, pounding through their own infantry which they were meant to be protecting. Waller's cavalry quickly compacted their formation and charged two rearguard bodies of cavalry which scattered in all directions.

Their charge was halted by a wall of pikes. Royalist cavalry wheeled and charged. Their dragoons turned back from the retreat to attack Waller's dragoons in the hedgerows. Then their field guns opened fire, shots whistling indiscriminately, forcing the intrepid Parliamentary riders back towards Lansdown.

From then on it was confusion. Cavalry charged and counter-charged, dismounted dragoons and musketeers dodged among the hedges, each man for himself. Horses ran rider-less. Horseless men fled. Through the pall of gun smoke Tom saw Hal pelting downhill into the thick of it. Good God! What could he possibly achieve?

Suddenly the Down itself was under attack, infantry pouring up the road and others, even pikemen, attempting the slopes at either side. They met strong opposition but still they came on, scrabbling through the trees and up and up. Soldier after soldier came to Tom's cart, to hastily replenish gunpowder for bandoleer, pistol and cannon.

A slight breather, while the enemy climbers were in dead ground, out of sight from the top. Then their pikemen breasted the lip of the hill and all hell let loose. Case shot flew, muskets blazed from behind the branches and stones of the breastwork. The Lobsters charged three times, their shouts mingling with shrieks from pike-impaled horses. Other cavalry charged and still the Royalists came on through the hail of shot.

The storm cloud of gunfire smoke was so thick that the afternoon became night, the sulphurous smell overpowering. Men thronged the roadway, dead and wounded being carried down, others running away, and through it all came Hal leading four horses. Calmly he led them past the wagons to the makeshift horse lines and secured them there. Enemy horses, unscathed, rider-less and captured.

The breastwork became untenable. Waller ordered the infantry a hundred yards back into a huge sheepfold surrounded by strong stone walls. He had breaches knocked through in places to allow the cavalry in and out, breaches guarded by pikemen and cannon. His musketeers went on firing well past sunset, ceasing only when it was truly dark. Enemy were close by, perched on ledges, crouched in hollows on the roof-like slope, hidden in the trees.

Behind the sheepfold walls, orders went quietly round the Army. Horses pulled the cannon to where the wagons stood by the road. All along the sheepfold wall pikemen thrust their pikes into the soil, while musketeers hung their lighted match over it, leaving the impression that the defence was still in place.

Then troop by troop, company by company, the Army silently withdrew, the last of the musketeers raining shot as a parting volley.

In the dark they picked their way back into Bath and slept where they dropped in the streets. Tom found water for his horses, tethering them beside the cart in which he fell asleep among the almost empty barrels of gunpowder. Four days seemed to have spanned a lifetime.

No one was eager to move the next morning. Gradually groups assembled and set out for their billets. Tom went to the place where he had collected those barrels of gunpowder before the battle, and a guard directed him to a barn in a closely guarded paved courtyard where what little that was left was being stored. A sergeant ran out at his approach.

'Stop!' he cried, rushing to hold the horses.

'I've brought some empty barrels.' Tom said, 'or nearly empty.'

'Your iron tyres,' the sergeant said, 'on the cobbles. Can't risk a spark. Though Lord knows there's little enough powder left.'

Even as he spoke they heard a massive explosion. It sounded to come from beyond Lansdown, from where the Royalist Army had based.

'God be praised!' the sergeant said. 'That sounds like the last of the enemy's powder supply.'

Such was the general jubilation that Tom felt himself almost one of them, eager to hear details of the explosion. He waited, his horses still hitched to the cart, standing in the shade with drooping heads.

News was not long in coming. Some prisoners held in an ammunition wagon had been given burning match to light their tobacco. A spark from the match had ignited the powder, blowing up the whole cart and killing the prisoners.

'Eight barrels of powder!' their messenger said, 'and they already short. And there's more. Sir Ralph Hopton was close by and is badly burnt. They say his horse is like singed leather.'

'With their commander wounded and their powder gone, we'll be more than a match for them,' the sergeant said. But Tom wondered about Sir Ralph. Surely when the family had first met Ralph Attfield he had recalled Sir Ralph Hopton and Sir William Waller being fellow officers and close friends. And now they were enemies fighting to the death. War was strange indeed.

The jubilation grew when soon afterwards a convoy of wagons arrived from Bristol laden with barrels of gunpowder for Waller's Army. Seeing them, Tom suddenly said 'You'll have no need of me.'

He felt sickened by the news he had heard, appalled for those prisoners, unsure whether he had more sympathy for Hopton or for his horse. He looked at Blaze and Star, not war horses nor just a means of transport, for these two had a place in his heart. More than for himself, he wanted them out of danger.

He would like to have secured a load to pay for his journey home, yet he could not imagine how to find one. Again he spent the night in the cart, next to the horse trough. The streets were foul with so many horses as well as men relieving themselves promiscuously. He was grateful to have the cart to raise him above the muck. Moreover he needed to guard it from ruffians who roamed the streets.

Although he had no memory of the way that he and the escort had entered the City, he felt disinclined to entrust himself to any guide who might offer to lead him. So he set off from Bath in the first likely direction he came across, over the bridge and roughly north-east. He made a few miles that day, stopping at a farm where folk were prepared to receive him and had provision.

'You from Bath?' the goodwife said. 'General Waller? Sounds as if you're on the winning side. We needs to keep in with you.'

'I'm not really part of the Army,' Tom said.

Continuing along the road the next day he was overtaken by Parliamentary cavalry. No one seemed interested in his empty cart, though some of the infantry following on, laughingly called for a lift. They were all in high spirits.

Ahead lay Chippenham. Troops were everywhere. Seeing skirmishes in the fields either side of the road Tom concluded that many of those he could see must be Royalist. He decided to go into the town. With evening Royalist troops were pouring inside, such a press that he could scarcely move the cart. The gates were closed behind the last of them, behind him. Tom was at a loss to know where to park, where to sleep.

As he was wondering, an officer came by and peered at the cart.

'My good man,' he said, 'you ought to know that the baggage train is set up the other side of the town.'

'I'm not part of the baggage train, Sir,' Tom said.

'Are you for King or Parliament?'

'Not either, Sir. I'm just wanting to get home to Surrey.'

'Surrey! So you're not averse to long distances.'

'No Sir,' Tom said, 'And I'd be glad of a load.'

'Ah.' The officer looked him up and down. 'You may be just what we're seeking. Come with me.' He called to one of the troopers hanging about in the street. 'Hold this man's horses. He'll be back directly.'

He led Tom into the servants' quarters of what was clearly one of the best houses in the town. Cooks were attempting to conjure up a meal amid a throng of armed men filling the passageways. Tom made himself as inconspicuous as he could, until the officer returned.

'Right my man,' he said. 'My Lord Hertford has a deal of loot which needs to be carried to safety. You will load it onto your cart in the morning and take it to Oxford. You will be provided with an escort.'

Hardly able to believe his luck, Tom managed to thank him, and then boldly added 'Would you be pleased to pay me something in advance?'

The officer again looked him up and down, and finally said 'I will enquire of the Marquess.'

Secure overnight in the stable yard, it was not until the chests and bundles were loaded into the cart in the morning and he emerged with the escort of a dozen horsemen, some coins newly in his pocket, that Tom realised the degree of activity going on outside. Weary troops were re-grouping to go and face Waller's Army outside the town, and he was glad to be departing in the opposite direction.

For much of the day they rode in silence. Maybe the escorting troopers were glad to be temporarily away from the fighting, though they never relaxed their watch on the surrounding countryside, wary of ambush. The sunshine was thundery hot.

They took three days to reach Oxford, spending the nights where they could, the troopers pillaging as they went. The last day was through steady rain and flooded roads. They unloaded the chests and dripping bundles at Lord Hertford's lodgings, modest and cramped compared with the house he had commandeered in Chippenham. The troopers set off to return to their Army, and thankfully Tom sought stabling and a bed.

Walking in the crowded streets the next day he met Harry Vernon and it was he who, a day later, told him that Waller's Army had been utterly defeated on Roundway Down.

'Runaway Down we shall call it. Even Haselrig's Lobsters with their armour shells ran away. It was a rout! Hundreds killed. The King's Army captured all the cannon and baggage.'

'Hal!' Tom was horrified. 'Back with the baggage. Oh Hal!'

Spreakley

It rained too in Farnham. The river Wey ran high, almost lapping the lowest of the tanning pits, and the air felt suddenly cool. Abigail was standing at the house door looking at the sky to see if there might be a break in the clouds for her to go to Culver Hall without getting wet, when her father called her from the fleshing shed and asked her to come up to his office.

Such an unusual request made her wonder what she had done amiss. He shut the door behind them and gestured her to a stool. His ledgers lay open on the table, and sitting there he traced a line with his finger.

`How do your pupils progress?' he asked abruptly.

Abigail was so surprised she did not answer at once. `They... their progress is uneven. The younger applies herself more readily that the elder.' Why should he want to know? He had never shown any interest before, once he had said she might teach them. He was silent again.

Then he said `You have them to occupy your time and give you a small income. There is time enough for marriage. However.' He looked up now. `Nathan Armstrong has asked me for your hand in marriage. I have not yet given him a reply. He is a fine young man with good prospects, and some inheritance due eventually from his father. The best beamsman I know. I believe he would make a good husband. He is very eager for you. But he rightly wanted to ask me before approaching you.'

Abigail gave an abrupt and scornful laugh. `Did he indeed! Well he approached me months ago. He didn't see fit to tell you that.'

`No, he did not. And did you accept him?'

`Father! I thought you must have noticed how he follows me with his eyes and how I try to avoid him. It's been going on for months.'

`So you don't care for him?'

`I do not.' She paused. `I dislike the way he looks. I dislike his opinions. I dislike his self-seeking. And Easter Sunday was the worst.'

Her father watched her.

'Oh, it was right at the end. He secured the final dance with me, and became so amorous I was thankful that Susan and her brother interrupted and rescued me. I have told him and told him. I don't care for him at all.'

Jacob smiled, just a little. `My dear daughter,' he said, and stopped. Eventually he cleared his throat and said `Perhaps I notice too little. The work occupies my mind.'

He paused. Abigail dared not interrupt this unusual confidence.

`I rely on your mother for discernment. And there are reasons for striving to prosper the tanning.'

He was silent again and Abigail let it ride, watching him marshalling his thoughts.

`Marriage is important Abigail,' he said. `When Nathan asked me for you I thought he presented a straightforward marriage prospect with no complications. I would like that for you.'

Abigail was both stirred and puzzled. `Complications?'

`To have to strive to marry, to prove yourself to be good enough.'

She was still puzzled. Then she said, `Did you have to, Father?'

`Your grandmother whom you never knew considered a tanner beneath a yeoman farmer.'

`You with your own tannery and this splendid house!' Abigail exclaimed.

`Well,' he said, as if excusing his mother-in-law, `I was young to have inherited it, with much to learn.' Then it was as if he shook himself. `But we are here to talk about you and your marriage. Am I to tell Nathan that you refuse him?'

'Yes Father, please do,' she said. 'And oh!' she stood up and put a hand on his shoulder, `Thank you for all you have said. You have given me more than you may imagine,' and she kissed his forehead. He put a hand over hers and she stood still for a precious moment.

The church clock struck eleven. She sprang back.

`I should be at Culver Hall already. But Father I do thank you.' She ran down the stairs. The rain had abated and she ran past dripping eaves all the way to Culver Hall.

No servant but Mistress Vernon herself met her at the door. `Thank God you've come,' she said, almost pulling her indoors. `When eleven struck I feared you would not. Come in quickly.'

`Whatever is the matter?'

`The Bicknell children next door in Timber Hall,. Eliza and the other little one, have appalling throats and fever. The physician says it is highly infectious, and I am afraid for my girls.' She paced from side to side, clutching her fingers.

`I have been wondering... you have told the girls about your cousins, at Spreakley isn't it, and they imagine it to be paradise. I'm sure you'll tell me it isn't paradise, just a farm, but Abigail it's out of the town away from this sickness, and I have been hoping and praying that you could take Rose and Lettice to stay there until the sickness is past.'

`I certainly could if they will let me.' What a gift, weeks without seeing Nathan at every meal!

`I have paper and ink here.' Mistress Vernon thrust her towards a table. `Write them a note and I will tell Sam to ride out with it directly. The maid can pack up clothes for the children without delay. They will say "Yes" won't they Abigail. I feel there is no time to lose. As soon as Sam returns - if they agree - he can drive you there in the coach.'

Abigail wrote a little and then looked up at the anxious mother. `The road is so steep and sandy, don't you think the coach might get stuck?'

`But the children must be carried there.'

`Tomorrow is market day. I could ask my cousin to bring the farm cart and we could travel in that.'

Mistress Vernon shook her head. `I want no delay, not the least delay. I'm sure Sam can manage the coach.'

So Abigail finished her note to that effect and saw Sam ride out of the stable yard with it.

`I've never been in the coach,' Lettice said, jumping up and down with excitement.

`Come to that,' Abigail said, `I've never been in a coach either.'

Both girls looked at her incredulously. Then Lettice began bouncing again. `So it's a great adventure for all of us.'

`If,' Abigail warned, `they will have us.'

It was a good hour before Sam returned, during which time Abigail nipped home for a spare shift. Sam handed her a note.

My dear Sister. John says we must receive you here, a great honour et cetera et cetera, but we have been in such a case because I cannot bear to have my little John exposed to possible infection. Now John has arranged for me and the child to lodge with his cousin, a small house but adequate for now. We will expect you this afternoon. Your loving sister Hannah."

She showed it to Mistress Vernon. `So now you may set off,' she said. 'Take a little refreshment, and this money for your keep, and then make no delay.'

As Abigail had predicted, Sam struggled to keep the coach going on the sandy road. The morning's downpour had scoured out great runnels in the hilly parts, depositing swathes of sand in the dips. Seeing the pair of carriage horses struggling, Abigail welcomed the chance to leave the bumpy coach and walk up the hills, and the girls followed her eagerly.

`It's very wild here' Rose said.

`It's an adventure' Lettice said.

`But look. Hardly any fields and all this heather and skinny cows and horrid little cotts.'

`Spreakley is different' Abigail said. `It's by the river and everything is green.'

The rare sight of a coach brought people to their doors to stare and sometimes to wave. Hearing their approach the Spreakley farm workers came into the yard to greet them. Madge bustled out.

Sam handed down the baggage while the children gazed at their new surroundings, the brick and ironstone farm buildings, the cobbled yard, the house with its great window.

John greeted them even as he bundled his wife and son into the farm cart and sent them on their way. Abigail watched him organising his men. He was certainly in charge of the farm now, she thought.

Lettice was running from door to door of the farm buildings.

`Come and look Abigail! Oh look in here, aren't they sweet!'

She beckoned them over to the half door where she had pulled herself up to see over the top. `Little pigs! How many Abigail? I can count eight but they keep running about.'

Rose followed and peered into the shed. `What a smell!'

`But Rose aren't they sweet. Look at their curly tails. And the mother pig just lying there letting them suckle.'

At that the big sow heaved herself to her feet scattering piglets and came snorting and snuffling to the door.

`Lift me up Abigail - please - so I can tickle her. Her nose is wet and wuffly. No, pig! I'm not feeding you. She's all rough and hairy, like a brush. How the piglets do squeal.'

Madge came looking for them and showed them the room they were to share.

‘Spreakley is simpler than Culver Hall,’ Abigail told the children, ‘and they are very kind to have us. Now come and meet my grandfather. He is more blind than your father, so he'll want to take your hands.'

There he was, as ever, in his corner by the fire though the day was warm. The children hung back while she told him about them, kneeling beside him with her hands on his lap.

He held out his hands and reluctantly first Lettice and then Rose took one each. Grandfather smiled. `You are welcome here children. I am growing accustomed to small hands, though my great grandson's hands are even smaller than yours. Make yourselves at home children. Do what Abigail tells you, and come and talk to me sometimes.’

`We saw piglets' Lettice said very quietly.

`What was that? You saw what?'

`Piglets.'

`You'll have to speak up.'

Lettice leant closer to him and said loudly `We saw piglets with their mother.'

`You did? How many piglets were there?'

`I think there were eight, but they ran about so, it was hard to count.'

`You keep an eye on them and tell me how they grow.'

They settled into a routine. In the mornings the girls learnt their letters, sitting in the window of the farm kitchen where Grandfather Harding sat. In the afternoons they explored outside. They watched the great mill wheel slowly turning, and peered into the floury mill. They walked through the meadows by the river.

Hearing about their expeditions gave John an idea. `They're draining the Great Pond,' he said. ` They do it every few years and harvest the fish. It's a big event. You might like to walk there and have a look. '

On the next fine day Abigail asked for a kerchief of bread and cheese for a whole day out.

The track wound along the north side of the pond, green fields on one side towards Frensham village, purple heath on the other and beyond and beyond. At the furthest end of the pond, men and several carts were clustered.

Standing on the low dam they could see that the grey bottom of much of the big pond was already exposed, and below them in the remaining shallow water were shoals and shoals of fish. Nearby men were manipulating nets on long handles, scooping fish out of the water into stone keep tanks sunk into the ground between the pond and the inn road. When a cart pulled up next to the keep tanks the next netfuls were thrown into it, the great fish gasping and floundering wildly.

`Oh the poor things!' Lettice cried. `Will they die?'

`They will, out of water,' Abigail said. `Some fishermen knock them out so they die quickly, but I guess there are too many to do that.'

`They have to be dead to be eaten,' Rose said without emotion. `You know they kill the chickens we eat, Letty.'

`That's enough!' the carter called to the netsmen, `if I'm to get them to market before it closes.'

The next cart drew up and the carter exclaimed.

`Abi!'

`Tom!' She leapt forward into his arms. `Oh Tom, where have you been? We've been so worried, you away such a long time. When did you get home?'

`A week or so ago. I got this order to collect fish and called at the farm on the way here, and John told me you were here.'

`Is he your lover?' Rose asked in ringing tones. Bystanders laughed.

`He's my brother Tom,' Abigail said. `Tom, what news? Where have you been?'

`I went to Bath as you know, in the thick of the Army, and then eventually to Oxford, and I've a letter for you from Joan.'

`Joan! Wonderful! How is she? Is she well?'

`As far as I could tell. She is great with child. Oxford is crammed with people. They have very little space where they live.'

`And news from home?'

Tom paused, his expression grave, looking at the children. `Very sad I'm afraid.' He squatted down so as to be at their level and went straight to the point. `You know that your little friend Eliza and her baby brother were very sick?'

The children nodded, all attention.

`The little boy has died, and Eliza is not expected to live.'

`You mean, Eliza is dying?' Rose cried out.

`She is dying. I'm told she can hardly breathe, and nothing the physicians have done has answered.'

`Oh no!' Rose cried out again. `She's my friend. She can't die!'

Tom tried the stock answer. `The Lord gives and the Lord takes away.'

`The Lord is unfair. How dare he take my friend. Oh Eliza!' Rose turned and buried her face in Abigail's skirts.

Sad though Abigail was for the child, and try as she did to comfort her with her touch, she had a more urgent concern. `What of Hal?'

Tom stood up again. `There were two battles. I saw one, and Hal was safe through that. The second I didn't see, I was carrying a load to Oxford.' He paused, and went on more slowly. `I met Harry Vernon in Oxford. He told me there'd been another battle, a Royalist victory. A great slaughter. A rout, a defeat, Waller's whole Army scattered. He was jubilant of course.'

`And what about Hal?'

`Abi, I don't know. Harry said the Royalists captured all the baggage, and Hal would have been with that. I've no news of either him or Ralph.'

`Ralph!'

`Yes, I left Hal with him, and I saw him in action. Maybe he's back in Bath. I just don't know.'

`Who are Ralph and Hal?' a little voice beside her asked. Abigail looked down at Lettice, hardly seeing her. Slowly she realised that she must answer. Who were Ralph and Hal?

`People as dear to me as Eliza is to Rose,' she said. `and both with the Army.'

Men netting the fish called out to Tom that they needed to load his cart.

`Come!' Abigail said to the children. `We had better eat however little we're inclined for food.'

They found a bench outside the inn and nibbled desultorily at their provisions.

`What happens when someone dies?' Lettice asked.

Abigail thought of her uncle John, that empty shell, and tried not to think of Hal's mother, bleeding to death.

`Their spirit leaves their body,' she said.

`Where does it go?'

`It goes to heaven, if they love God.'

`We can't see heaven,' Rose said. `Where is it? Can you see a spirit? Could I see Eliza if I went to heaven?'

`It is said there are many mansions there, all prepared for us.'

`They call our house a mansion,' Lettice said. `P'raps Eliza's gone to a house like ours.'

`I wish I could go too' Rose said.

I wish I could follow the Army, Abigail thought, and find Hal and Ralph wherever they are. But perhaps they too are dead.

Over the next days they grieved, each in her own way, isolated in that no one at Spreakley was more than slightly acquainted with the causes of their grief.

Rose cried openly and frequently, her love for Eliza softening her and warming Abigail towards her. Lettice seemed almost untouched. She spoke of Eliza freely as one who had been a good playmate and now was gone. She verged on tears only when the little brother was mentioned, much perhaps as she would have done at the death of one of the piglets.

Abigail spoke of her grief to no one, indeed how could she? She had no claim on Ralph except her unspoken love for him, and who would understand how much Hal meant to her, he whom she looked on as a brother yet who was constantly just out of reach. And then she did not know if they were dead. She was in limbo, perpetually anxious, unable to mourn as she would have done their death, yet acutely conscious of loss.

By the end of July Hannah decided that since after three weeks the Vernon girls were still in full health, they were unlikely to succumb to the fatal throat infection and she could safely return home.

At first she found fault with everything, and viewed the girls with brisk suspicion. Rose however, needing someone to fill the hole left by Eliza, devoted herself to little John. His response and her evident good sense went a long way to settling Hannah and calming her. She became more open to her husband who was demonstrably glad to have her home again, and soon had her in his arms and bed. Abigail observed the transition with interest.

Grandfather observed things too, despite poor hearing and dim sight. One morning as lessons concluded he called Rose to him.

`Sad little girl,' he said, `you are reading well. Would you read to me?'

`I don't know if I could,' Rose said.

`Reach down the big Bible Abigail. Back then folk were just like us, and there's a passage I'd like you to hear.'

Abigail placed the big worn book on a stool and made Rose sit on another close by.

`The second book of Samuel,' the old man said. `David's lament in the first chapter.'

Abigail knelt beside her pupil holding a fold of paper under each line to help her keep her place, and she began to read.

`"How are the mighty fallen! Tell it not in Gath, publish it not in the streets of..."'

`Ashkelon,' Abigail prompted.

`"Lest the daughters of the Pil, Phil..."'

`Philistines,' Abigail said.

`These are difficult words,' Rose protested.

`Go on a little,' Grandfather said. `Start where it says, "Saul and Jonathan, beloved and lovely!"'

`"Saul and Jonathan, beloved and lovely! In life and in death they were not divided, they were swifter than eagles, they were stronger than lions..."' Rose hardly hesitated now, for the old man had it by heart and murmured it with her.

`"How are the mighty fallen in the midst of battle! Jonathan lies slain upon thy high places. I am distressed for you my brother Jonathan; very pleasant have you been to me; your love for me was wonderful, passing the love of women. How are the mighty fallen and the weapons of war perished!".'

`Thank you,' the old man said.

'Is that all?' Rose asked. It seemed that for her it had been just a series of words. To Abigail the words were blurred, and tears were dropping onto her hands, onto the page.

`Go outside now and play with Letty,' she said to Rose. She closed the Bible.

`How did you know, Grandfather?"

`I don't know what I know, child.'

`How that lament would speak to me.'

`It just seemed to be what the Lord wanted read. Tell me child, what distresses you?'

`It's not Eliza, though I'm sorry about her.' Abigail sniffed, seeking control. `I expect I'm foolish, it's someone I know only a little, but, but he was possibly killed in battle, and there's Hal too, a little orphan boy who lives in our house and he was in the battle too, and I don't know what has become of them, whether they're alive or dead, and I love them both so much.'

Her grandfather reached out his gnarled hand and touched her lightly as she fought the tears.

`You were bright and cheerful when you first came, and I have wondered why you had changed.'

`It was an adventure with the children then. And I was glad to be away from a journeyman who wants to marry me.'

`And you would rather marry this soldier. Do I know him?'

`Cousin John does. I danced with him at Hannah's wedding. In fact I was beside you when he invited me. Do you remember? He called me "chicken plucking maiden" because of the first time he saw me. I think it was all he knew of me.'

Grandfather chuckled. `Yes, I do remember. And you fear he is dead and you will never marry him.'

`I doubt he has any such idea. He's fond of Hal....'

`As David was fond of Jonathan, and both had wives.'

Abigail gave him a long look. Then she straightened her back.

`Probably it would be best if I forgot all about him and married the odious Nathan.'

`You don't have to marry either,' her grandfather said gently. `I've heard you with those little girls and marked their progress. You could set up a dame school, and be quite independent of any man.'

`Do you think I could?' Abigail looked at him in wonder. Then she laughed. `The trouble is, I go on wanting Ralph.'

`Bear it in mind. Have several strings to your bow.'

With the little Harding family back together Abigail felt it was time to go home, and a note from Mistress Vernon indicated that she thought so too. The diphtheria epidemic had played itself out, it was safe for them to return and she was longing for her children.

This time there was no coach. They rode to town in the farm cart among the sacks and the caged pullets which Lettice thought the greatest fun. Rose was almost her old fastidious self.

Carter Ricky took them straight to Culver Hall. Mistress Vernon came running down the staircase clutching a wrap round her.

`Oh my darlings!' embracing both at once. `Oh! how glad I am to see you! Let me look at you. Have you grown? They both,' turning to Abigail, `look blooming, in fact quite little peasant girls with their tanned faces.'

The children crowded her, absorbing all her attention. Then she turned again to Abigail. `How can I thank you? But Abigail, you've heard the sad news from next door?'

`My brother brought it, and the children know.'

Since it was next door, she felt obliged to visit the Bicknells straight away. Elizabeth answered her knock looking pale and weary. They faced each other silently for a moment. Then Abigail said `I'm so sorry.'

She need not have worried over what to say. Elizabeth sat her down and a flood of words began. Soon she was rehearsing the whole sad tale, going over every distressing detail of her children's fever and virtual choking to death. Reluctant though she was to hear it, Abigail vaguely realised that the telling was necessary for Elizabeth and allowed it to flow on.

Eventually Elizabeth said `So the Vernon girls have escaped it.'

`They are grieved,' Abigail said. `Rose specially. She must have loved Eliza dearly.'

Mistress Bicknell wiped her eyes, the catharsis exhausted for the time being.

`Tom brought me a letter from Joan,' Abigail said

`I had one too!' Elizabeth brightened. `It didn't say much.' She fumbled in her pocket and spread it out, a crumpled scrap of paper. `Victories for the King, and she anxious for her babe to be delivered. It can't be long now. I wish I could have her here with me, or I go to her, but I fear it is out of the question. I am needed here, and nothing will persuade her to leave young Harry.' A thought struck her. `She might be glad to have you go to her.'

Abigail smiled. `I've only just returned from weeks away.'

Back past the market, where Susan hailed her. `Abigail! Such a long time! Come and tell me all the news.'

She felt she had little to tell, but Susan bubbled over with town trivia. Then Robert Bicknell saw them and came across to greet her. Again she offered condolences.

`A sad time for our family,' he said gruffly. `All change here too,' looking around the wide street. `We Bailiffs are virtually ousted by the new Governor of the Castle. Taken over the town it seems, and the revenues.' He shrugged. `A Colonel Samuel Jones. He's raising a regiment, dressing them in green coats. His Lieutenant Colonel goes all over Surrey recruiting, drilling them hard too. War supplies pouring into the Castle, and he's fortifying that.'

`At least that gives work to the likes of digger Martin,' Abigail said. She had never heard the normally equable Bicknell with this note of bitterness in his voice. `I hear the King's armies have had some victories.'

Robert scratched his beard. `To tell you the truth, it is of little moment to me which side wins, if only we can have peace. And I can tell you, most folk do their best to keep in favour with both sides; like Master Vernon, paying his dues to one and lending his horses to the other.'

So even Master Bicknell was becoming a gossip, thought Abigail, going home with her bundle of clothes, welcomed but treated as if she had not been away which somehow reassured her. Except for Nathan.

An excited letter came from James. *The Yellow Auxiliaries in which I have the distinction of serving as Sergeant have been warned for duty,* which was followed by news that Sir William Waller's army was crowding into Windsor, where the Earl of Essex's army, having driven the Royalists from Newbury, was also quartered.

Carey was still spinning and knitting in every spare moment.

`You must have quite a store of stockings' Abigail commented.

`Oh,' Carey sounded almost shy. `Mistress arranged to sell them to the garrison. We take them up whenever we have a dozen pairs or so.'

`My mother and you?'

`Susan's knitting too. You know, Susan Woolgar.' Carey suddenly became expansive. `The Mistress gave me fleece to start with, and then my Great Aunt was so pleased with me she gave me yarn she had put by. Now we buy fleece out of our earnings.'

`You've quite a business going!'

`Mistress is content so long as I don't neglect my household work.'

One wet afternoon Abigail picked up her Latin books, trying to refresh her memory. *Passer deliciae meae puellae...* The sparrow held in the poet's beloved's lap, and Nathan knew the poem. Was that what he wanted of her, to be fondled in his lap? Involuntarily she shuddered. Surely though her refusal through her father had settled all that. She turned to another passage as if turning her back on him.

So when he walked into the house he took her by surprise. He was wet from working in the rain. His dark hair was laid close over his head and he left damp footmarks on the flagstone floor. All the same when he saw her he came straight over. Hands on hips he looked down at her.

`What have you to say for yourself?' he blurted out.

Abigail looked up, startled. `Me? Nothing!'

`Nothing. You just say nothing. You ran away.'

`Ran?'

`After your father spoke with you.'

`What, ran to Spreakley? Nathan, you know I was caring for the Vernon girls.'

`Your gentry pupils. So urgent.'

`So urgent. Mistress Vernon pressed me to go at once. Anyway there was nothing to say. I gave my father my answer.'

`I've tried all ways.' Nathan's tone changed. `Every approach. I'd thought a spirited girl like you would prefer to be courted, not bargained for like a chattel.'

`That was what you call courting was it.'

`I tried to protect you..'

`When there was no threat.'

`What, gunfire and drunken youths!'

Abigail said nothing.

`And on Easter day...'

That roused her. `Courting! You were violent!'

`I thought a kiss, an embrace, might win you.'

`Under duress. Hardly.'

`But that time in the church, you invited both.'

Abigail was silent. He had accused her once of making use of him. She was not about to admit that on that occasion she had indeed used him. And only just in time had she woken up to what she was doing.

`Admit it. You leant right into my arms.'

`I....it was a mistake. You took me by surprise. It had no meaning.'

`You expect a man to realise that? Since you would not be courted I did the proper thing. Perhaps I should have done that right at the start. I asked your father. He was all in favour of the match, but it seems you countered it, and he has refused my offer."

Abigail nodded.

`And straight away you were off to Spreakley so there was no chance to talk about it.'

`Is that what we're doing, talking about it? All I have heard is a string of accusations.'

She looked down at the book in her lap. Suddenly he was on her level, kneeling in front of her.

`I want you for my wife. I'll have my own tannery – might even have this one. What more can you want?'

Abigail looked steadily at him. `I have made it plain over and over again that I do not wish to marry you. And that is final.'

Nathan jumped to his feet. `You'll remain an old maid.'

'Come come, I'm not yet twenty!'

'A dried up scholar.'

Abigail pressed her lips together.

`Or are you waiting for Attfield. A vain hope. He's probably dead, and even if he isn't he never took any interest in you.'

Oxford

`I've never been on a horse.' Even in the dim lantern light in Culver Hall stable she could see Sam's astonishment.

`They're carriage horses, docile-like' he said.

Abigail eyed them, imagining what it was going to be like perched precariously up on the saddle. There could be no going back though. Mistress Bicknell had rushed down to the Tanyard, almost incoherent with the news that Sam was taking horses to Oxford and Abigail could go too, bearing provisions and gifts for Joan.

Sam put a hand under her left foot and heaved her up onto the saddle so that she sat sideways. The horse under her shifted its position.

`I'll never stay on!' she gasped.

Sam mounted a second horse and was arranging the leading rein of a third, which carried packs hanging either side of its saddle. He looked at her thoughtfully.

`Would you object to riding astride?' he asked

`Like you are? I'd feel much more secure.'

`Swing your right leg over then, and make sure you sit on your kirtle. Feet in the stirrups.' He came alongside her to adjust the length of the leathers. `Now hold the reins lightly, and the pommel if you wish. I have the leading rein.'

They passed through miles of rough heathland. Then they were into kinder country, fields under the plough, arable land where cattle cropped the last of the year's growth of grass.

Every few miles a village marked their progress, villages where people waved and stopped in their work to stare. Gradually she learnt to rise to the trot.

`In case we meet any Parliamentary soldiers,' Sam told her, `I have a safe conduct pass from Colonel Jones at the Castle. You are my daughter and we are visiting your sister.'

`I'm glad to know who I am,' Abigail laughed.

`I also have Master Vernon's agreement to loan two horses to the King. I offer that one should we encounter the King's troops.'

Her legs were tired and her seat sore as they approached Reading.

`Master said it's a Parliamentary garrison here. Let's hope it still is.'

They were challenged well before they reached the town, challenged by a dozen armed men on horseback who surrounded them. The leader asked their business. Abigail felt her stomach tighten with fear. Such tales she had heard!

`Passing through, just passing through,' Sam said.

`What's in your saddle-bags?'

Sam turned to the horse he was leading, as if surprised. `Why, clothes for a baby. Look if you wish.'

He untied the fastening. One of the troopers brought his horse flank to flank with the pack horse and pulled out the white garment that lay on the top.

`A surplice! A surplice!' he cried. `Malignant dogs!' Knives flashed.

Sam reached over and caught hold of an edge of the garment so that it unfolded. `For a midget priest?'

Immediate laughter. The little lace-trimmed dress was self-evidently for a baby. The trooper plunged his hand down inside the bag. Quickly Sam turned to the commanding officer. `Would you care to see our safe conduct pass?'

The officer scrutinised it. `Colonel Jones at Farnham. On you go!'

Starting off again Abigail discovered she had been holding her breath. She let it out in relief, but now after the pause her body protested more than ever. `How much further Sam?'

`We can stop at the next inn if you wish. We're well on the way now.'

When she slithered down from the horse she could hardly stand. Her legs felt as if they could never again go back to their normal angles, and the skin of her thighs and knees was sore. Sam, occupied with bedding the horses, appeared to think nothing of her discomfort but when he came carrying the packs and saw her hobble into the inn, he said `You need some horse embrocation. It'll sting, but it can ease your muscles.'

Next morning, embrocation notwithstanding, she was so stiff and sore that she doubted she would ever be able to get out of bed. She eased her feet painfully onto the floor, dreading a repeat of the day before. Slowly she dressed and found her way down to the inn parlour. Sam grinned at her.

`You'll be right enough once we start.'

They were now in the wide green Thames valley with its rich farms and water meadows, with cottages and hamlets at frequent intervals. Sentries challenged them outside Wallingford which Sam knew was garrisoned by the King's troops. He was determined not to allow them to commandeer the horses before they reached their destination.

`My Lord Vernon has ordered me to deliver horses to His Majesty, as you will see from this paper,' he said. The sentry squinted at it, then calling another to him prodded his finger at the word `Vernon'.

`It's what he said.'

`And the moll? Delivering her too?' they mocked.

Sam wagged his head and they passed on, grateful for illiteracy.

Oxford was thronged. Sam saw fit first to deliver Abigail and the baggage, and enquiries led them to a house tight between others in Long Wall Street. The smell that assailed them as the door was opened witnessed to a large number of unwashed bodies. Children pressed around the woman, eyes inspecting the strangers from dirty smeary faces.

`I've nowhere for horses,' the woman said.

`No, no,' Abigail assured her, trying to make her aching legs hold her up straight. `It's just me. Sam here kindly brought me, to see Mistress Vernon and help her.'

`Don't know what'll help her. It's a sickly babe.' The woman peered out. `Three horses for one wench?'

Sam ignored her. `I'll deliver the two and then ride back,' he said to Abigail. `Send word if you cannot find how to return.'

She took the saddle-bags from him, reluctant to see him go. Then she asked the woman to take her to the Vernons' quarters. They mounted narrow creaking stairs which led to two rooms, one either side of a little square landing.

`Someone to see you,' the woman said loudly. From the room on the left came a baby's whimper.

`Abigail!' Joan was lying in an unkempt bed nursing a tiny baby. Abigail was quickly beside her. `Oh Abi! How marvellous! Can you stay? How long can you stay? Oh Abi!' and she buried her face in Abigail's shoulder.

On her lap the baby's head dropped back, disengaging her nipple, and it lay for a moment before crying again. Joan looked down at it without expression. Then she pushed the nipple back between its lips.

`This is all I do,' she said. `Hours and hours of trying to get her to suckle.'

`What's her name?'

`Eliza, out of respect for my little sister. Hermann baptised her. She was so small and weak, and not much better now.'

A glazed look came into the baby's eyes which reminded Abigail of Elizabeth suckling her babies. `Do you think it might be wind?'

Joan tried to wind her, over her shoulder, on her knee. `You try.'

Abigail was as inexpert as she, and no wind came up. Eliza's head wobbled. She was asleep.

`She'll wake and cry in no time at all and the wretched business starts all over again.'

Abigail looked round the room which the bed almost filled. There was little else. A litter of clothes over a chair, more on some hooks, a basin of used water no one had emptied, a stained chamber pot.

`My poor friend' she said.

`I managed up to a month or so ago. After the sickness eased I used to walk in the City and meet delightful people, and Harry took me about more. He was proud that I was to have his child.'

`Where is he now?'

`Oh, busy with newsbooks and such. We need a servant. I can't abide the woman downstairs. The landlady was kind and fairly clean, but now she's let in this other family and she's hardly ever here. The food is bad. I hope Harry brings something from the baker tonight, but it will scarcely be enough for you as well.'

`I've brought a few victuals from your mother.' Abigail was about to unpack the panniers when she thought better of it. `I'll empty the slops and tidy up a bit and then we'll see what she's sent.' Folding some of the clothes she found a comb and handed it to Joan. `And I'll bring some water to freshen your face.'

The street was the only place to empty the slops. Someone directed her to the communal pump where the water looked little cleaner than the slops had been. She went carefully up the stairs again, careful both because of the water she was carrying and because every step reminded her of the hours she had endured on horseback.

`I never thought it would be so difficult,' Joan said. `Mother and Mistress Gary rear babies all in the day's work if you see what I mean.'

`Maybe it's harder with the first' Abigail said.

She straightened the bed. Together they spread out on the coverlet the contents of the panniers. Joan exclaimed at some of her mother's familiar goodies, and even laughed over the story of the presumed surplice. They shared some bread and slices of ham, interrupted by Eliza demanding another feed. `Stow the food away Abi, else the rats will get it.'

`Shall you get up for a while?' Abigail asked. She looked for a clean shift for her, but found only soiled linen. `I'll lend you the spare shift I brought,' she said and helped her to wash and change. She tidied her hair and unearthed an almost clean cap. Joan smiled at last. `That's better.'

The second room, across the landing, was no bigger, taken up mostly by a table and a couple of benches. In a corner the empty grate reminded them that they were cold. However, a request to the woman downstairs yielded a retort but no fuel. `Perhaps when Harry returns he can arrange some,' Joan said.

When he did return it was to say, after a formal greeting to Abigail, `Hermann Shepheard has invited me to dine with him in Hall.'

Joan looked at him with soulful eyes. `Again? And how am I to dine?'

`The woman will cook for you presumably.'

`She can't cook what you do not purchase.'

Harry said nothing, turning away from the sight of his wife suckling Eliza.

Abigail said hurriedly `We have what I've brought. And perhaps tomorrow I can go to the market and buy a few things.'

Joan nodded. `That will do for the time being.'

Abigail slept on the table wrapped in a cloak, a sleep disturbed by Harry's late return, periodic baby crying, and sometimes the scampering of rats. She woke stiff in a different way and lay wishing for the feathers of her bed at home, wondering how soon Harry would be dressed and out of the bedroom.

The October sunshine poured in through the little window and she could bear it no more. She dressed and slipped downstairs and out into the street. After the chill of the evening before, the day was warming quickly with a crisp tang to the air. Across the High Street down by the river women were already busy scrubbing garments, sending flurries of mud into the polluted water as they trod about. She supposed that would be where laundering had to be done.

Streams of people were moving up the High Street, some laden with baskets, some on carts, so she followed, sensing a market nearby. Early though it was, that too was thronged. She bought a bundle of kindling and half a dozen faggots of wood, and a rush basket to carry them in. She smelt fresh bread and bought a loaf still warm, and some butter. Mistrustful of their being any cooking pots at the lodging she bought a small pan. Then back to the baker who had meat bubbling over a portable charcoal stove.

On her second trip up the stairs Harry came out onto the landing, elegant as ever though his eyes were grey-rimmed. `Whatever have you there?' he asked.

`Food and fuel' Abigail said. `I'll warm the meat when I've kindled the fire, and then we can breakfast.'

Harry stretched. `We ate well last night - and drank too well I expect. I can't say I'm hungry.'

`And Joan?'

`She's asleep at present.' He went down the stairs two at a time and out to the privy.

Abigail found that knives and spoons and platters and tankards were on a shelf. When Harry came slowly back up the stairs she asked him what they should drink.

`I send one of the children to the inn with a jug' he said. `Their ale is tolerable.'

`So please could you? I'm very thirsty and I'm sure Joan will be.'

He took his time. After all, Abigail thought, this is his home. But there seemed to be so little provision.

The fire was bright and the meat simmering by the time the baby cried again. Abigail opened the bedroom door a crack.

`Come and eat while you feed her' she said.

It was hardly a convivial meal. Joan, bleary-eyed, balanced baby, spoon and bread, Harry crumbled bread and ate a little while Abigail, her appetite unabated, wondered at the incongruity of it all. Later she washed dishes in cloudy water and gathered soiled linen to wash that too.

`A washerwoman sometimes comes' Joan said lamely.

The crowd of riverside washers changed all the time, sometimes cheerful and bantering, sometimes disputing little areas of muddy river bank. Abigail hitched up her skirt and decided to take off shoes and stockings and paddle into the river where the flow was clearer, though horrible debris kept floating past. The water struck cold to hands and feet as she scrubbed at the wet cloth, un-practised because at home a woman came to do it.

However much she scrubbed and rinsed, the linen still looked grey. She wrung out each item and bundled them in a sheet, tying the corners together, and went barefoot back towards the house, her shoes in one hand and the dripping bundle over her shoulder.

Now that the day was advanced the nobility and gentry were about, greeting one another in ever re-coalescing groups, their elegant clothes the worse for wear. Their presence made Abigail self-conscious. Here was she, a tradesman's daughter, friend of gentry, acting as any servant or camp follower would do. She was glad to regain the house and be shown where to hang things to dry.

Several weeks passed in this way, trying to return Joan's life to something like normality, though her days and nights continued to be a constant round of trying to feed the baby. Sometimes she became desperate with the crying and even shook Eliza whose head flopped to and fro, and then Joan herself cried. Comforting her partially eased Abigail's own grief.

Harry came in one afternoon bearing an unfamiliar news sheet. `See here!' he said. `Your old friend Sir George Wither has turned from pamphleteer to newsman, though in truth this is more pamphlet than news.'

'Old friend?' Abigail said, remembering her embarrassment at the verse he had recited, 'If she be not so to me, What care I how kind she be', and its repercussions.

Mercurius Rusticus, or A Country Messenger, October 26 1643' Harry read. Not for nothing was Sir George known in Farnham for his scurrilous wit. The pamphlet was one long mockery of the King and his court. It reported his loss at Newbury a month before. 'He lost Lords,' Harry read, 'and a great officer &c, but that is a loss the least worth notice of all the rest, for they are toys, which if he please he can make of the veryest rascals in the Army.'

Harry looked up from his reading. `The trouble is, there is a grain of truth in what he writes. The King is all too ready to create new nobles. He ordered the granting of so many honorary degrees and doctorates that the University begged him to stop, saying he was degrading academia.'

He went on reading as Wither decried the lavish entertainments such as the Queen loved, now reduced owing to diminished facilities in Oxford, and...

'Harry,' Joan said. `Harry, look at baby.'

He turned impatiently towards the scrap lying perfectly still on Joan's lap. `Well?'

'Harry, look at her.'

He looked intently then, and suddenly he was down beside her on his knees, his ear to the child's chest. He looked into Joan's face. `She's not breathing.'

'Harry, I think she has died.'

Abigail held her breath, feeling she should not be witnessing these two staring together at the body of their tiny infant. For a long moment no one moved.

A stray curling strand of Joan's hair had fallen forward. Harry lifted it and eased it back behind her ear, his long fingers gentle, touching her tenderly.

'She has given you nothing but grief,' he said.

Joan looked up into his eyes. `She wasn't the son you wanted.'

With the little burial over Abigail was sure the time had come for her to go home. She was superfluous to them as they re-discovered each other, besides which she had been away long enough. Told of her wish Harry leapt into action and had soon identified a carter going in the right direction who assured him he could connect up with others to transport her back, and it was arranged.

`Thank you dear friend,' Joan said, her arms clasping Abigail in farewell. `Don't think I haven't noticed all you have done for me. I'm truly grateful.'

Wither's news sheet was read in the Tanyard as well, acquaintance with his person adding a certain spice to it. But however much his mocking of Royalists might amuse, threats were real, putting the townsfolk on edge with apprehension. Only a week earlier Royalist soldiers had set fire to Wokingham, and when three days later troops of cavalry appeared in the Park, threatening Farnham Castle, they were terrified that Farnham was about to suffer the same fate. It seemed a miracle when the troops withdrew, back to their base barely ten miles away at Alton.

Only hours after Abigail reached home, Waller's whole Army arrived. In the dark of the last night of October they poured into the Park and through the town and were herded, six or seven thousand of them, into any shelter that could be found. This time foot soldiers crammed into the Tannery loft and overflowed into the louvered barn among the drying hides.

Come dawn, Phoebe boiled up a big cauldron of pease pottage and another of oat porridge, and kept them simmering at the side of the fire ready for when any had the energy to eat.

About noon she and Abigail were tending the fire when they heard the dogs bark and then unaccountably stop. Phoebe looked through the window. 'It's James!' she cried and a moment later he was indoors, grinning at them self-consciously. `James!' Questions flew.

'I'm with the London Auxiliaries,' James said. 'I'm a Sergeant in charge of ordnance.' He would not be able any longer to hide this from his father.

'We're over-run with soldiers,' Phoebe said. 'They appeared over-night, and have slept ever since, or so it seems.'

`They'll sleep all day,' James said. `My Regiment is in the Rectory and some in the church.' He gave a small laugh. 'I thought we'd never get here! They don't take kindly to long marches.'

They had set out in high spirits, these part-time soldiers recruited from servants and apprentices, and managed to march to Kensington the first day. Next day they got no further than Hammersmith.

`I reckon the quarters there must have been too comfortable. Two days we rested there. The officers couldn't get the men to move on - or maybe the officers were wanting to rest.'

After that they managed another four miles to Brentford. `The towns-folk remembered how the King's army sacked their town, so they made us welcome - so welcome we stayed four days.' He laughed.

Abigail was counting on her fingers. `That's two days marching, two days rest, another march, four more rest days - you're over a week already.'

`It showed up the weaklings,' James said. 'They deserted. After that we actually managed fourteen miles, to Windsor, where we met up with the other London regiments. Another four days' rest, and then Sir William Waller's regiments and their guns arrived.

He changed things at once. No more loitering. He set us off in earnest to reach Farnham. That's what has exhausted the men, all the way over that waste of sand and heather with only an hour's stop at Bagshot. We got to Farnham well after midnight, one or two in the morning I'd say.'

`We know!' his mother said. 'They came here demanding beds.'

`I don't suppose you know if Hal is with the Army?' Abigail said.

`Hal? What, the bastard brat?'

Abigail nodded, stifling protest. `With the cavalry.'

`In several thousand men, is it likely! At any rate, we're infantry.'

When Jacob came in, after a moment's shock he quickly assessed the situation; for James to have appeared without warning in the middle of the night, he must be with the Auxiliaries who had flooded in, and protest about the iniquities of war was pointless. He turned the talk to tanning.

`We found a new knack for stretching the tanned hides,' James said. `I'll have to show you once the fighting is over.'

`Trade's good,' Jacob said. `Big demand from the saddlers for good leather. When the troops are here, so many cattle are slaughtered we've plenty of hides direct from the shambles, no need to pay fellmongers or middlemen.'

`If only we could speed up the tanning process.'

`There's some have tried,' Jacob said. `You know that. Hot water and ash. Well, it's no good. The leather's not waterproof and it won't last.'

`Old Trussler, wasn't it. And your father caught him at it.'

Jacob nodded. `He'd try it again with half a chance, the son that is.'

The next day was All Saints' Day, November wet and cold, and Waller ordered a muster in the Park. Two days later the whole Army, in a great long column, guns and all, set out westwards along the Wey valley towards Alton, slipping in the mud as the weather closed in. By evening, snow was blizzarding.

The snow turned to slush and then froze. Intense cold and dense fog beset the Army as they trudged over the bleak countryside, first one way, then another, until they arrived at the well defended Royalist bastion of Basing House. The siege was doomed from the start.

Abigail slithered to Culver Hall where lessons had been resumed, with number reckoning added to the curriculum. `The girls need to know how to keep household accounts,' their mother said.

`Those poor soldiers!' Phoebe said.

Basing

A week or so later the Commissary General received orders to send food from Farnham to the Army which by then was besieging Basing House, and he recruited Tom to carry it, in convoy with Abe Trussler and Matt Woolgar. Loaded up they set out up onto the chalk and clay of the Hampshire hills. The conditions were atrocious, wind and wet wet rain. The three needed each other whenever wheels stuck, and they made slow progress.

'We'll not make it tonight' Abe said as the clouds and rain darkened the day in mid-afternoon. `There's an inn in Long Sutton, stabling and somewhere for the carts.'

`I'm not slithering on in the dark,' Matt agreed. `The army can go hungry a bit longer.'

The inn keeper welcomed them. `Not much custom in weather like this. Will you pay for a fire?'

They bought a faggot each, knowing that these would no more than warm them and make little impression on their clothes. They hung their smocks around the fire and watched them steam while the fire lasted, then went gratefully to bed, three to a bed this time and Tom made sure that Abe lay in the middle. He snored loudly, substantial barrier between himself and Matthew.

They were still well short of Basing, plodding through yet more rain, when the first troops met them, cavalry on rain-soaked horses picking their way through the mud.

`Whoa!' Matthew in front halted his team.

The troopers filed past silently. Behind them came others.

`Hey there! What's happening?' Abe shouted to anyone who would listen.

An officer pulled up. `The Army is retiring back to Farnham."

`God's truth!' Abe said. `All this trouble for nothing.' He called to Tom and Matthew ahead of him. `Carry on. We can turn at the top of the rise where five lanes meet.'

Matthew manoeuvred round and back into the narrow road, followed closely by Tom. Streams of troopers poured by as wet and bedraggled as the first. Their pace was greater than that of the carts, and the more of them that passed the worse the going became, the track pocked and puddled by innumerable hooves.

After the horsemen came the infantry, a straggle of tired cold men making whatever way they could through pot-holes and ruts. They came in groups strung out following their ensigns, six foot square flags carried by boy officers who staggered under their weight. Sometimes a protesting murmur arose but mostly they were too preoccupied to speak.

Until a young officer on his horse stopped by Tom's cart. `What's in those barrels?'

`I couldn't say.'

`Where do they come from?'

`We just loaded them up at the Castle.'

`Men!' The officer halted his company. `Food!'

Instantly they swarmed onto Tom's cart, tugging open the barrels.

`Peas!' said one in disgust, `dried peas!'

'Try another!'

Peas, flour, oats, spilt out as they jostled each other. They came to one filled with the standard hard biscuits and tipped them out for all to grab as they fell.

Ahead, Matt's cart was being invaded too as more and more foot soldiers piled up behind They found salt fish and threw stiff pieces to one another, some even chewing it. Dried peas poured out of overturned barrels. The carters stood by helpless while the officers, hungry as their men, made little effort to control them.

Suddenly cries behind them warned of an approaching horseman. He was swiping the soldiers out of his way with the flat of his sword, hastening to discover the cause of the blockage. Soldiers shrank back, tumbling into the ditch, crowded against hedged banks, the looting mob falling in heaps in the narrow space.

\`Sir!' The young officer was still there on his horse in a vaguely supervisory capacity. \`Sir, the food was destined for us at Basing.'

\`Not to be looted,' his superior said, still shouting.

Men picked themselves up, muddier than ever.

\`Down off those carts, I say!' the order came. With obvious reluctance they obeyed, though in truth by now there was little left for them to forage. Dry goods carpeted the track way, biscuit scraps and fish puddinged into the chalky clay. The column began to move again, spacing out, re-establishing gaps between companies. Tom and Matt tried to restore some sort of order to the carts, retrieving barrel lids and piecing together those broken by trampling feet.

From up on his cart Matt looked back to Tom. \`Armies!' he said, and then stopped, mouth open. \`Hey Tom! Where's Abe?'

Tom looked behind them, at the ever continuing column, and scratched his head.

'Lord knows,' he said. \`The blighter.'

\`You followed me when we turned. D'you suppose he's still back there?'

\`If he is I'm not going looking for him.' Tom threw some broken lid pieces into the cart. \`What are they going to say at the Castle when we bring all this back empty?'

'Exigencies of war?' Matt said.

`I want to be paid for the cartage' Tom said. He still had fodder to buy for his horses, and that night in the inn had left little money in his pocket.

Another line of infantry under a big yellow ensign staggered towards them led by a lean young man. He came level with the cart as Tom lifted more debris from the ruts, and their eyes met.

He stopped. `Tom! Is it you?'

It was a moment before Tom recognised his brother. Inner turmoil occupied another moment. James' forlorn and dirty look kindled a spark of compassion, conflicting with the devastation the soldiers had wrought. His eyes narrowed.

`You and your damned army,' he said. `Look what you've done.'

James' mouth set hard and he walked on without answering.

Matthew went to his lead horse and with a mighty heave his cart began to move. Blaze and Star took longer, straining into their head collars as Tom threw wood scraps from barrel lids under the wheels to give them grip over the slippery mud. Far behind them they could see the baggage train, the guns and the wagons of wounded.

When at last they reached the Castle Matthew had his arguments well rehearsed. Soldiers had been fed he said, albeit not at Basing, and they were returning what was over. Cartage was due to them.

Seeing him in action with the Commissary General's men, Tom felt too tired to bother and left the altercation to him. Besides, his attention was caught by others following behind. Riding one horse and leading two he thought he saw Hal, only to lose sight of him again in the melée.

And then he saw Abe, going confidently forward, his cart full and unscathed. Abe saw him too and looked away, but this time Tom could be bothered. Leaving his team beside Matt's he went right up to him, his eyes blazing. He could hardly speak.

Abe was saying `They had no need of supplies at Basing so I've returned them all. Will you check them?'

Tom watched, his anger rising. Apart from mud, Abe's load was exactly as it had been when they started out. He watched as it was checked, and Abe was paid, and told where to deliver it back into store. He was about to move off when Tom exploded.

`You swine!' he said. `You deserted us!'

Abe looked him up and down. `Not so successful this time eh? Don't know your way around so well, eh? Bye-roads and such?' and with a sneer he turned his back and whipped his horses towards the store. Tom went back to Matt, seething.

`Not much pay....' Matt began.

`Abe Trussler!' Tom said. `Took another road! He's lost nothing!'

`Never thought of that' Matt said. `I know the road he took, too, one of those at Five Roads Meet where we turned round. Here's your token payment. I'll off-load and go home.'

`Get this cart out of the way' someone ordered. Unwillingly Tom obeyed. And then he thought of Hal. He must just locate the horse lines in the hope of finding Hal.

Troopers were rubbing down their mounts and there he spotted him, carrying buckets of water for washing their legs while others brought water and hay for feed. Hal looked thin and tired and clearly his first call was attending to the horses. Water slopped from the buckets onto his already sodden shoes. Tom intercepted him on his way back to the well.

`Hal.'

Hal looked at him wearily, his face expressionless.

'Hal it's me, Tom. We didn't know if you were alive or dead.'

Hal stood still, saying nothing.

`And Mr Attfield?' Tom went on.

`He was alive this morning' Hal said.

Abigail watched the infantrymen returning to their billet at the Tanyard with growing consternation. In the twelve November days since they set out from Farnham they had endured a blizzard of snow, nights of sharp frost, fog, and now cold rain. Rumour had it that for some of those nights they had slept in the open fields. Many were limping and their shoes were falling apart. Those who had slipped up on the road looked as if they had been rolled in clay. A sorry, defeated company, they stumbled past the tanning pits and upstairs to the loft where Phoebe, warned of their return by the billeting officer, had made Daniel spread straw all over the floor.

A cauldron of beef and root vegetables simmered beside the fire, and Mary with Carey had been making bread all afternoon. Having deposited their gear, a few of the men came downstairs again and dared the cold to wash themselves in the yard.

As they limped in again barefoot Abigail exclaimed `Oh your poor feet!' Rubbed and sore, toes bulged red with chilblains. `Sit down here while I fetch my mother. Not too near the fire though with those chilblains!' and she smiled at them. They were young, apprentices and servants dressed in their own clothes which had suffered as grievously as they themselves had done.

`Are you all in as bad a state?' Phoebe asked when she came to them.

They didn't know, but a young man they called Alfred volunteered to go upstairs and ask for any who had foot complaints.

They came down then, a long string of them, and Phoebe told Abigail to fill a basin with water to wash their feet.

Out of the still room she brought jars of the ointment she made every summer, pounding the kidneywort which grew plentifully in walls, pounding and pounding it with grease and then boiling and pounding more leaves into it, a process which spread over more than a week.

`This will ease and heal your chilblains' she said, `and I just hope I have enough for you all. Take the towel Abigail and make sure their feet are dry before I apply the ointment.'

Abigail recoiled. Could they not wash and dry their own feet? She wanted to keep her distance from their overpowering smell, not just their feet but their breeches and their stale unwashed bodies. She did not want to touch those feet.

Were the apostles' feet in this parlous state when Jesus washed them? Surely not, yet the thought of the service he had rendered hardened her resolution. With an effort she obeyed and found that she could after all endure it. Phoebe knelt down and gently rubbed ointment onto foot after foot.

`He'll let us home after this won't he?' a small man, barely more than a boy, asked.

`More walking,' a plump soldier commented.

`But we'd be back in London.'

`We cried "Home! Home!" back at Basing but they didn't let us go.'

`Maybe that's why we've come back this far.'

`We were defeated, that's what, and run out of food.'

`That General Waller, he don't know what it's like to be infantry. Treats us like we could go on for ever, night and day.'

`All right for him, on a horse.'

`Comfortable lodging too.'

`I'll fight no more,' and others assented to that.

They brought their dilapidated shoes downstairs and tipped them on their sides in a line where warmth from the fire could circulate around them. And then they fell upon the food and ate till they began to drop asleep at the table.

Tom came in midway through the meal and looked at the assembled company in disgust. `More food! You had enough already from my cart.' Their sergeant, a husky fellow in his twenties, objected, his accent thickly German.

`Your cart? Ve had no food off no cart.'

`Swarmed all over and spilt the supplies for Basing.'

'T'wasn"t us. Ve got no food.'

`Tom,' Phoebe said. `Whatever happened to you, there were thousands of soldiers by all accounts. You look almost as travel-worn as they. Come and sit down and eat and be refreshed.'

`I'm not sleeping with this rabble' Tom said.

The sergeant pulled his shoulders back, expanding his chest. `Ve are not rabble. Ve are honourable London auxiliaries.'

Tom turned to his mother. `Where do you propose I sleep?'

`Anabel and Carey are coming in with me. The sergeant and so on will have their room, and you with your father,' Phoebe said patiently.

`And us?' Nathan said from where the Tanyard employees were seated together. `Are we on the straw?'

`The Master says you may share with him and Tom. And Peter too. You apprentices must shift for yourselves. The loft with the soldiers, or in a corner down here.'

Thus began four uncomfortable weeks, the store of vegetables running out with more than half the winter yet to come, the militiamen grumbling, chafing for home, unpaid, unwilling for their daily drills. Their chilblains healed but their shoes did not. Some fell sick and could not leave their straw beds. Others stayed to tend them.

The cavalry was mostly quartered in outlying villages, providing a defensive screen around the town. They were not given long to recover their strength, for Royalist outposts as near as Odiham and Long Sutton posed a constant threat.

Abigail was glad she was expected at Culver Hall though she felt a pang of guilt leaving the other women at home with the extra burden of work.

‘We have officers staying in the house,' Lettice said proudly. `They're beautiful.'

`Our cook doesn't think so,' Rose said.

`They are nice to us,' Lettice went on undeterred, `and Mother says they are good company. Father just grunts when she says that.'

`Well, calculate how much it costs to feed a larger household,' Abigail said. `I haven't counted how many my mother is catering for but it must be at least forty.'

`Forty!' Lettice was wide-eyed. `How many cows to feed forty?'

`Let's start with pounds of beef,' Abigail said.

She was late returning home that afternoon because the girls had sewing to complete as a surprise for half-sister Matilda's birthday. Soldiers were in the streets and she hurried through, trying to be inconspicuous. They still looked weary and their lack of pay was so far keeping them from the ale houses. She reached the Tanyard gratefully, to find Tom just returned from a job, talking in the yard with James.

`You can't blame the whole army for the misdemeanours of some,' James was saying.

`It cost me dearly,' Tom said.

`War does cost dearly,' James said and he looked dejected.

`What are you wanting here anyway?' Tom said.

`Am I not allowed to visit my own family?'

Tom turned away and in doing so caught sight of Abigail.

`Oh Abi,' he said, `Ralph Attfield was enquiring for you.'

`Ralph Attfield! He's alive then?'

`Didn't I tell you? Hal told me, and then I ran into him today.'

Ralph and Hal both alive! She could have hugged Tom had he not been so cross. As it was she spoke amicably to James and they went indoors together.

It was all she could do to listen while he told her, and then her parents and others as they filtered in, about the siege of Basing House.

At first he made it sound very valiant and exciting but gradually as he talked himself out, the misery of it became evident, the cold and the hunger and the disappointment, the deaths and the reverses.

In a pause Jacob said `Haven't I always said that war achieves nothing but suffering?'

James gave him a long look. `And what is it trying to achieve?'

Ralph and Hal are alive, Abigail's heart was singing, and Ralph was asking for me, for me. And then she began to be afraid, afraid of knowing him better and perhaps not liking what she found, afraid of betraying herself. Just afraid.

Friday came and went, her duties at Culver Hall almost unendurable for fear he might have come to the Tanyard while she was absent. There were no lessons that Saturday and the day seemed long as she did domestic tasks alongside Carey and Mary.

It was late afternoon when he came. Mary had gone home to Francis, and Carey was knitting at remarkable speed. Abigail had done no knitting for months but now she started to spin. Then outside she heard the voice she had thought never to hear again, as rich as ever with the odd crackle in it and the Hampshire burr, heard him greeting people in the yard before he opened the door saying `May I come in?'

And there he was, as personable as ever, his brown eyes and full mouth smiling.

She stood up to greet him, leaving the spinning wheel turning by its own momentum, winding down. Carey stood up too, pushing her ball of wool into her apron pocket.

`I must tell my parents you are here,' Abigail said.

`Your father saw me come and told me to go along in. I suppose I should greet your mother.'

`She's busy in the still room Sir,' Carey said. `Should I fetch her?'

`Later, later. I actually wanted to speak with Abigail.'

`Take a light with you into the bake room' Abigail said, her stomach churning as she watched the girl pick a rush out of the tray by the hearth and slowly light it at the fire.

They stood while Carey left them, and stayed awkwardly silent until Ralph said `May I sit down?'

Abigail dived for a stool. `I'm so sorry, of course.'

She drew up another for herself and they sat either side of the fireplace. Another silent pause.

`We scouted to Midhurst today. Turned into a raid. Just what was needed, cloth for coats. That'll keep the tailors busy.'

`Where have you been since Runaway Down?'

`Come, that's Royalist talk.'

`I'm sorry,' Abigail said again. `I was with Joan Bicknell in Oxford - she had a baby who died - and that's what they called it, Harry Vernon and such.'

`Well, it's true I'm afraid. We were routed.'

`And since then, where have you been?'

Ralph gave a short humourless laugh. `If I told you that I'd be giving you a lesson in geography.'

`I thought perhaps you'd been killed.'

`I didn't write asking for stockings did I,' and he smiled.

`And Hal, I feared for him.'

`Ah, Hal.' With the toe of his boot Ralph pushed a log further into the fire. `It's about Hal I wanted to talk with you.'

For Hal, Abigail thought, grateful for a subject they could share.

`I'm puzzled,' Ralph went on, `and I thought you might be able to help me, seeing you probably know him best.'

`I wonder if anyone knows him,' Abigail said.

`It was when we were besieging Basing House. I happened to go to check my horse. The barn we'd commandeered as stabling was pretty dark and crowded and I had just a small lantern. I found my horse, and there was Hal, his head against the horse's side, crying his eyes out.'

`But Hal never cries!'

`I tell you he was weeping, shuddering tears.'

`Did he see you?'

`Because of the lantern, and he knew I'd seen him. There was terror in his eyes. Was he afraid of me?'

'Do you beat him ever?'

`Beat him Abigail! I never beat him, there's no cause. He's exceptional with horses, always there when he's needed. I value him. And the Paddy boys do too.'

`I'm sorry,' Abigail said. `Father used to beat him though I never saw cause for it. And I've only once known him to weep, apart from when I first stumbled on him, just a little in a hymn when he was first with us.'

`I didn't know what to do. He turned his face away so I left him. Then I thought perhaps the Paddies might provide a clue, so I went to where they had meat on sticks over a little camp fire, and asked if anyone had seen Hal. They know he attends to my horse so it was a natural question. Young Norman was quite indignant. They'd come by a couple of rabbits which he'd skinned and he handed them to Hal to joint. He said Hal took one look at them and fled. I don't know what to make of it.'

`We don't usually eat rabbit here' Abigail said.

`Poor man's meat, I don't suppose you do. In the Army we'll eat anything, we get so short of food.'

`Surely Hal's seen a skinned rabbit before.'

`He's seen bloodshed that's for sure, and horses screaming in fear and pain not to mention men wounded and dying. He's no coward.'

`There has to be some reason somewhere' Abigail said.

They sat silently for a while in the firelight as dusk gathered. Then he looked up and smiled at her.

`I've had no stockings for months.'

`I've had no address to send any.'

`Didn't I tell you the sutler would bring them?'

`For all I knew you were dead with no need of stockings.'

`I haven't written, have I. Foolish, for I enjoy your letters.'

He left, hastening to his troop's quarters at Pepperharrow before darkness thickened, with the promise of a soon return.

Many of the soldiers quartered at the Tanyard went along to morning service in the church next day, though none appeared from the Castle.

`Strange' Phoebe said. `Sir William Waller is said to be a devout man."

`Call of fighting before call of God,' Jacob said gruffly.

Reverend Duncombe had evidently prepared his sermon with the Army in mind, for he preached from the Book of Joshua, `Be strong and of good courage, be not afraid, neither be dismayed; for the Lord your God is with you wherever you go.'

`The Lord God is with you and his eye sees both the good and the evil men do' he began. He expounded how reverses befell the Israelites when they sinned and disobeyed him. He cried to them to repent so that they might go forth, fight, and win.

Abigail sensed a mixed reaction among his hearers. All that the Auxiliaries wanted was to go home with some pay in their pockets. Some of the soldiers fell to praying, while others were calculating their chances with the women and girls. The youth Alfred made a bee line for Carey just ahead of others heading in her direction. The German sergeant approached Abigail.

`Fine church you have here, hein?'

`You certainly fill it this morning.'

"Vish you with me to walk back?'

`I...I have to give a message to someone,' she lied, catching sight of Elizabeth Bicknell and Betty Gary indulging in their regular gossip. She need not have troubled for no sooner had she spoken than a trumpeter came into the church commanding silence and ordering all soldiers present to muster immediately in the Park. She came up with the gossips as Betty said `Well really! On the Sabbath!'

Abigail enquired of Joan.

`We know no more than you told us,' Elizabeth said. `That poor babe, so soon dead. It's sadder when they live for a few weeks (let alone years like my two dear children) than if they're born dead.'

'At least it didn't carry the mother with it' Betty, said.

Phoebe joined them and Abigail walked home with her.

They picked their way over the cobbles, grateful that for once it was not raining.

'I hate to hear Mistress Gary call Joan's little Eliza "it",' Abigail said. 'I know she was just a little scrap, but she was still a she with a name.'

`Maybe that is how Betty copes with loss. Not that she's lost many, but no one is immune.'

`All of us survived, didn't we.'

Phoebe greeted a neighbour before she replied. `We did lose one, when you were too little to know.'

Abigail looked sharply at her mother. There must be many things, she thought, that I don't know about my parents. She knew however from Phoebe's expression that she did not intend to elaborate.

`I saw Eliza die, lying on Joan's lap,' she said, `and then I helped prepare that tiny body for burial.'

`I'm glad you did that for Joan.'

`I'd been through it all with her, except I suppose her relation to Harry. He made me so cross. I used to admire him, his good looks and his intellect and everything, but he wasn't kind to Joan.'

'He may have felt pushed aside when she was preoccupied with the baby.'

`Joan certainly was preoccupied, trying to get Eliza to feed day and night. Yet somehow her heart wasn't in it.' She stopped, not daring the disloyalty of telling how Eliza's death had seemed like a relief to the young parents. Instead she said `Joan still dotes on Harry.'

They came to the junction with Abbey Street and a new thought struck her. `Hal's mother, what had happened to her?'

`Why, she died in childbirth' Phoebe said, as if stating the obvious.

`I didn't know' Abigail said. `I just saw the woman and blood and then you made me take Hal away. I didn't see a baby.'

`It was on the table. I suppose Hal had put it there, poor distracted child.'

`We never talked about it. Nothing was explained, not even to Hal.'

`Many things in life we just want to put behind us, and get on with our daily business.'

From behind the castle came the boom of cannon firing. Her mind on immediate concerns Abigail said `Once I thought Hal wanted to tell me about it, but I lacked courage to help him.'

`You've been good to Hal.'

`I love him like a brother' she said, and was startled by the look Phoebe gave her.

Did you hear yesterday's fight?' Francis said, twisting off the last nail in Blaze's new shoe as Tom stood holding the horse's bridle in the forge in the Borough. He reached for a coarse file to neaten the hoof.

`We heard cannon fire.' Tom spoke gently as if to Blaze, stroking his neck. `And the crowd quartered at the Tanyard had to leg it quick.'

`Royalists up the top on the heath,' Francis said. `Banged away at each other, and the cavalry had some fun. Our lot drove them back in the end.' He ran his hand down Blaze's hindquarters and leg to lift the other foot.

`You're only just in time. These shoes are worn to a sliver' and he started to claw the nails out of the shoe. It clattered onto the ground.

'I hoped they'd last the week since I ordered the new ones' Tom said, watching him pare the hoof with a sharp knife.

Francis held out his hand for the shoe he had made to measure and his apprentice boy reached it over to him and then pumped the bellows so that the fire glowed on its bench.

With long tongs Francis held the shoe in the fire until it was red hot when he laid it against the hoof. Tom liked the smell of singed hoof and hair.

The burnt imprint showed the adaptations needed and Francis quickly hammered the shoe into shape. Then with a punch that the boy had been heating he hammered in nail holes, and plunged the shoe into a bucket of water. A new smell of wetted iron and a sizzling sound. He put a clutch of nails between his lips and hammered them home one by one.

`I'm running out of iron' he said. `A lot must have gone up to the Castle.'

`Where d'you go for iron?'

`Shottermill, not far. D'you fancy fetching a load? There's that many horses with the cavalry, I'm making shoes into the night some days.'

`Bit risky isn't it? Malignants and such?'

A trooper waiting with his own horse interrupted. `We've horse quartered all around to the south, you'd be safe enough.'

`I was in the forest and they said Royalists ambushed a foraging party there. They were after deer.'

The trooper laughed. `We keep on raiding each other and skirmishing. Just luck which side you fall in with.'

Francis straightened his back and stood with his great hands on his hips. `Can you imagine a party of horsemen carrying off a load of iron?' and turned his attention to the trooper's horse.

Back at the Tanyard broken footwear had been discarded with the arrival of a convoy of supplies and the issue of new shoes, stiff and not yet shaped to the wearers' feet.

`Soak them' the sergeant said, `and then walk in them.'

Footwear was not the only benefit. They had also been paid. At last they were free to go into the taverns with money in their pockets and go they did, as soon as opportunity arose. Young Alfred stayed in.

`Don't you want to go too?' Carey asked him, her knitting needles clacking after she had cleared the meal and swept up and tidied the hearth.

`They need the money at home' he said shyly, and sat the evening watching her.

'Susan collects the stockings on market day,' she explained, `to make bundles to sell to the troops.'

Tom's way to the Sussex iron works might be considered safe, but Susan had to run the gauntlet of raiding parties on her way to the town from her home. Royalist horse came constantly out of Odiham and Long Sutton, looking to skirmish with their enemy but also as much in need of stockings as they. She usually managed to disguise them among Matthew's load.

The following market day Abigail met her with him after she had made her delivery to the Castle.

`I'll always be glad you taught me to knit' Susan said. `We've a real industry going, 'cos you can pick it up at any time.'

`I should teach the Vernon girls to knit, though they're mostly occupied with sewing.'

`Abigail the teacher,' Matthew said. `You should have a school.'

'Take no notice of him,' Susan said. `Come and look at gee-gaws. There's little else to buy.'

Indeed there was not. Hens were moulting and off lay so eggs were scarce. Pyramids of onions seemed smaller and meaner than usual, and buyers were stocking up on leeks and parsnips in case frost cemented them into the soil. Abigail thought of the Martin family and called at their cott on her way home.

She need not have worried. Goodwife Martin greeted her at the door wiping her hands on a rag.

`God bless you, I'm well provided for today,' she said, motioning her indoors out of the cold. Abigail's eyes took a few moments to adjust to the dim light from the single window, and then she saw that the Martin household now boasted a table and three stools, and a shelf on the wall with a few pots and platters on it. The woman could not wait to tell her of their good fortune.

`My man is employed at the Castle as you may know, digging forty - how do you say it? - fortific - those things, trenches you know, and mounds what they need for fighting. And now at last he's been paid again. And that's not all. Some o' them went foraging as they call it in the forest, and look what they let us have! Went with nets and ferrets they did.'

She gestured to the table and now Abigail saw three rabbits laid out on it, gutted and ready to skin. `I'd just started when you knocked' she said, taking up the knife she had been using. With deft strokes she slit the skin insides the legs and rolled the pelt whole off the carcass, cutting it free as she went.

There the carcass lay, a complete rabbit without its fur. And suddenly Abigail gasped. It looked so horribly like a naked baby.

`My grandma taught me how to cure rabbit skin,' Goodwife Martin rattled on, applying herself to the next. `In the end I should have a nice rabbit rug, if my good fortune continues. And it's many a long day since we've had so much meat. My good man may bring a few friends to share it, and the child will enjoy it too.'

A second rabbit lost its skin. `Are your vegetables too wet down there by the river? My leeks are fat again, and I've got carrots in a clamp, if only those military don't steal it - or forage as they say.' She gave a little laugh, and dealt with the third rabbit. `Now you see I shall salt the skins, and then scrape them very gently, and...'

If you'll excuse me,' Abigail said, `I need to hurry home. My mother will be glad to hear you are all well.'

Alton

`Never have I had such unpredictable guests!' Phoebe ladled stew out of the enormous pot she had cooked, ladled it out just for her normal household. The soldiers had been gone all day and not returned

'Guests!' Jacob retorted.

`Anyone in our house is surely a guest, however they come,' Phoebe said. `I'll just add to the stew pot for them tomorrow.'

Jacob watched her. `You're more generous than I,' he said, and their eyes exchanged a private smile.

`Their Commissary General is keeping us well provisioned now,' Phoebe said.

`They've been drawn up in the Park all day,' Thomas said. `I asked our Sergeant when I passed. The King's at Basing hoping to take Farnham Castle.'

`Do they just stand there?' Abigail asked.

`They do. They keep on being ordered "Stand straight in your lines!" poor devils. No chance even to relieve themselves. They're still there now in the dark.'

`Their poor feet' Abigail said, remembering the chilblains.

They remained in formation until dawn, when the majority were dismissed back to their billets. No one, least of all they, knew what would happen from one day to the next. Townsfolk trembled as they heard of looting nearby, wondering if Farnham would be ravaged next.

Thick mist enveloped the land as 27 November dawned. Abigail and Carey milked the kept-in cows of what little milk they had, working by lantern light. As they returned to the house a cavalry-man cantered up to the gate, hitched his horse to the gatepost, vaulted into the yard and ran past them shouting `All troops to muster!' He had his hand on the door latch.

`I'll take you up,' Abigail said, the lantern lighting their way up the dim stairs. `What's happening?'

`Enemy's coming, thousands of them. Castle threatened,' as he bounded after her. He shouted into the loft, made sure the Sergeant knew his orders, and ran back out to his horse.

The men were in no great hurry to obey, anticipating another long day and maybe a night as well standing under the Castle battlements exposed to every wind that blew. What if it was just another false alarm? They straggled down into the hall, buckling on equipment, pulling on their woollen hats. The Sergeant posted sentries at all three doors to ensure no one strayed. At last, after arguing loudly with a few who claimed they were too sick to leave their beds, he lined them up and marched them off. Everything was still shrouded in mist.

Later Jacob sought out Othen. `Let the boys off for an hour or two,' he said. `They'll not want to miss a battle.'

`They'll thank 'e Sir, and work the better for it.'

`What if they take Farnham?' Abigail gasped, remembering horrific tales of towns destroyed.

Towards noon as the mist began to clear Tom walked up with Nathan and Peter. It was an impressive sight. High up on the heath beyond the Park to the north Lord Hopton (as he now was) had his whole army arrayed, eight thousand of them; blocks of musketeers, bristling lines of pikes, and at the flanks innumerable mounted cavalry and dragoons, a formidable army.

At the foot of the hill Sir William's cavalry was in place, but the infantry was still trickling in from their scattered quarters. One observer reckoned those present totalled barely a quarter of Hopton's army. Waller lined them up close under the Castle walls, so close that the cannon mounted above them could safely fire over their heads. Out in the park gunners were grouped around demi-culverins, the lighter and more movable cannons, placed to threaten an enemy advance. The two old friends, erstwhile campaigning companions Hopton and Waller, faced each other in combat array, woefully unequal as to numbers though Waller had the advantage of position.

`Will there be a real battle?' Peter said.

`Looks like that's what they're waiting for up on the hill,' Tom said.

`They'd be picked off like gnats,' Nathan said, `and this lot down here have the Castle to protect them.'

For hours the armies stood to, only a mile apart, Sir William refusing to be drawn out of his defensive position into a pitched battle. Then at last in late afternoon a big Royalist `forlorn hope' of about a thousand musketeers and some horse, slowly advanced down the hill.

Immediately the demi-culverins fired. Men and horses fell, like corn under a reaping hook. Gunfire echoed around them. Gunners reloaded, fired, swabbed and reloaded, picking them out. Cohesive Royalist ranks fragmented into scattering groups.

Soon from the hilltop a trumpet sounded retreat. Columns formed and wheeled away one by one, out of sight over the ridge towards Crondall and Odiham, an orderly withdrawal.

Not so the exposed and broken forlorn hope. They turned in confusion, now a reluctant rearguard, their cavalry like sheepdogs vainly herding together the musketeers.

Waller unleashed his cavalry, fast, which raced upon them, yelling war cries and slashing down with their swords. Men screamed and tried to run. Pistol shots pursued them, felled them. They stumbled on up to the heath, beset on every side by slaughtering sword and pistol, on on and out of sight.

The onlookers cheered, thirsting for blood, urging the cavalry on. `Kill! Kill!' `Another!' as they saw men fall. Peter was carried along by the corporate enthusiasm.

Nathan turned away. `I hope I never see another battle.'

`That wasn't a battle' Thomas said. `You should have been at Lansdown.'

`I'm glad I wasn't' Nathan said, and set off back to the Tanyard.

It was not a battle as far as the Auxiliaries were concerned either. They had not fired a shot. All had stood cold and rigid as they had done only days before, against the Castle walls. Whilst cavalry and dragoons continued to harry the enemy in bloody skirmishes all evening and into the night, they were dismissed and returned complaining to their quarters.

`We're used like cattle' one of them said. `Cavalry see some action but all we do is stand and wait.'

`Wc saw action at Basing.'

`And froze to death in open fields.'

At least now, as weeks of hard frost began, they had some pay and pockets to put it in. Their spirits revived a little though still their chief thought was for home. The army scouts reported that Hopton's army was dispersing into Hampshire, so why stay?

Farnham breathed a sort of corporate sigh of relief, a sense of permission to carry on with normal life despite the continued presence of Sir William Waller's army.

Shivering in the chill of the big Tanyard hall Mary said `Our little cottage is so warm and cosy.'

`I'd love to see it,' Abigail said, and so they arranged that she would call round to the cottage beside the forge an hour or so after Mary finished work at the Tanyard.

Few people were about in the unremitting frost. Minding her footing on the icy cobbles of the Borough Abigail safely reached Mary's door. Warmth greeted her, the little room glowing from the fire, and Mary glowing with it.

`We've just the two rooms' she said, opening the door into the second. Abigail peeped in diffidently. The room was almost all bed. Mary caught her expression. `We have to vault into it, but at least it's warm' and Abigail imagined her warmth and comfort, bedding with the warm and comforting blacksmith.

`He's not going with the army no more,' Mary said, `there's that much work here. And when the baby comes we'll move back to Godalming, so he says.'

She poured hot water onto a mixture of herbs `to warm you up' and they wrapped their hands around the heated tankards and sipped the comforting liquid, chatting of nothing in particular. Sounds of comings and goings and of hammer on anvil and iron formed a background to their companionship.

`Your Thomas should be here by now' Mary said. `He only went to Shottermill for a load of iron for Francis.'

It was almost dark when Francis opened the door and came into the room, and not only he. Behind him came Thomas and a group of cavalrymen led by Jim Hosier, crowding in, and last of all came Ralph.

`Come in, come in, and close the door against the cold!' Francis said. Ralph squeezed past the door and closed it behind him and they all eased a little into the resulting space. `Can you warm some ale, wife, for these men?'

Mary was already on her feet, filling a pan from a cask in the corner and putting it on the fire dogs.

`Well,' Francis said, turning to the men, `that was a lucky encounter.'

`Bit of a rescue. Who said, (Tom dug Francis in the ribs) that cavalry couldn't carry off a cartload of iron?'

`Didn't think of forced escort, did I,' Francis laughed.

`It didn't quite come to a skirmish,' Jim said, `but it damn near did.'

`So you had a Parliamentary escort all the way home?'

`One of our better day's work' Ralph said.

`I haven't tankards enough for all of you.' Mary reached a ladle off a hook. `Can you bring your own horns for me to fill?'

They elbowed their way around to her, and in the process Ralph arrived near Abigail. He bent down and said quietly `Any clues to our mystery?'

`Yes!'

`We can't talk here. Wrap your shawl round you and come outside.'

They squeezed through the doorway. Holding his ale in one hand Ralph put the other on her shoulder to steer her into the forge, still warm from the day's work. `Tell me.'

`I saw someone skin rabbits,' Abigail began.

Ralph waited, and then said `And?'

Abigail shook her head. `I'll have to tell you from the beginning. How Hal came to live with us. About five years ago - he was a little scrap, half starved.' She looked up at him. `Oh dear, I'm not telling this well am I.'

`Just tell me what happened, and how it's connected with rabbits.'

And so she told him, from the beginning, with all sorts of irrelevant details as she re-lived that autumn day with the horror of seeing the woman, and Hal's terrified crying. `I didn't understand it then, I just wanted to help. And no one talked about it afterwards, not to anyone. Now my mother has told me that the woman died in childbirth, and that Hal must have picked up the dead baby and put it on the table.'

Ralph nodded, silently.

`And then I saw those skinned rabbits, and Ralph they looked so like a baby, a dead baby. I could hardly bear it,' and tears came into her eyes.

Ralph stood for a moment or two, pondering. Then he put his arm round her shoulders and drew her gently to him. `How you do love the lad,' he said. And then, `You've never called me Ralph before.'

They stood for a while, he just gently holding her, not pulling her close, not moving. She could feel tension in her muscles, in her jaw, wanting this to go on for ever and afraid of making a wrong move.

Then he dropped his arm and said `Thank you. I'll hope for an opening to talk with Hal. That boil needs to be lanced.' He turned towards the cottage. `We'd better creep back in before we are missed.'

Mary looked quizzically at her across the room, but Ralph came in as if alone and his fellows took little notice.

It was a week later that she saw him again, and what a day that was!

Everyone was well asleep on the Tuesday night, a cold clear night with a sky full of stars, when they woke abruptly to a trumpet sounding right outside the windows. Abigail shot upright in the bed she shared with Carey and her mother, the covers pulling away from Carey's shoulders as she moved. The girl pulled them back tucking them under her chin. But even she stirred at the rattle of feet running down the bare board stairs.

`What's happening?' she said blearily. Abigail was out of bed and peering through the window pane.

`They're mustering outside. Whatever time is it?'

She watched as they formed up and marched away out of the yard, leaving the night eerily still. `Oh, I'm cold' she said wriggling back under the bed covers.

At the far side of the bed Phoebe stirred, awake but saying nothing. Carey did not contribute much warmth. Later, she did not know how much later and she knew she had dozed on and off, a renewed clatter of footsteps woke her fully. They were up and down the narrow stairs, a crescendo of voices, colliding and cursing.

`What is happening?' came Jacob's peremptory voice, and a muffled reply from the sergeant. There was such audible activity in the bakeroom that Abigail whispered across the recumbent Carey `They're taking food Mother, don't you want to stop them?'

`I suppose they need it for some reason, and it's too cold to go and find out. They'll be on God's business if their commander is to be believed.'

It was not long before the scurrying subsided, the outside door banged several times and Abigail heard the soldiers assembling in the yard. `To honour and success!' the Sergeant said in ringing tones, and then their footsteps receded into the lane. She was still awake when the church clock struck midnight. So it really was the middle of the night.

In contrast the next day was blankly normal except for the intense frost.

`They've taken all the bread there was,' Phoebe said, `and cheese too. What about the ale - are the barrels empty?' She went into the still room and when she turned one barrel tap just a dribble came out. Rocking another she could tell how little was left in it. `Helped themselves well and truly - but where have they gone?'

`It can't be the park like the other day,' Tom said. `We'd have heard the gunfire.'

`Did they tell you, Father?' Abigail asked.

`Muttered something about a general muster,' Jacob said. `Going off to redeem their honour, where or how I didn't stop to ask. I doubt they know.'

Day had given way to another clear and freezing night when they poured back, stumbling wearily but jubilantly triumphant.

`We licked them! We licked the lot of them!'

`Where, where? What happened?' Peter was almost dancing round them.

`Alton, ten miles yonder.'

`Sir W'm offered us to redeem our honour, and by God we did!'

`You walked there in the middle of the night?' Abigail asked.

A group of them all tried to speak at once.

`Surprise attack...'

`Over the downs...'

`All trees. Scouts knew the way...'

`The night was that clear...'

`Surprised their outposts we did. Took 'em prisoner.'

`Hard fighting I can tell you.' The speaker's head bulged with a massive bruise. `Musket butt' he said, touching it gingerly.

`Zey ended up all in ze church.' The Sergeant took control of the narrative, `and ve fighting back and forth in ze yard, and zey shooting at us from ze windows, and ve throwing in ze mortars, and ven ve burst through ze doors...'

`Horses!' another exclaimed. `Barricaded with dead horses! We've left the prisoners pulling them out.'

`Once their Colonel was killed they threw down their arms and cried for quarter. We took hundreds prisoner.'

`Poor devils are digging a pit to bury their dead, digging a pit with the ground frost hard.'

`Were many killed?' Abigail asked.

`Near three score' the Sergeant said, `and less than a dozen of ours.' He caught sight of Carey. `Young Alfred's dead.'

Carey gasped, her hands to her mouth. `Oh his poor mother! Can you send his pay to her? He was saving it for her. Oh poor lad!'

The Sergeant nodded. At least he would try.

`Now Sir W'm can't prevent us going home,' they said and many murmured `Aye'. Weariness began to overcome their elation as they dragged themselves up to the loft.

Ralph, as tired as his horse, ambled into Farnham at the pace of the exhausted prisoners through another brilliantly clear night, yet days and nights were blurred in his mind. Was it only last night that they had set out, the cavalry riding in from outlying villages to link up with the infantry around midnight? A Night Owl expedition again, and the auxiliaries were in such a mutinous mood that it had to succeed.

He knew the route they were taking, he had scouted all over those downs. Pity they hadn't made all the enemy scouts prisoners, for one or two had escaped down to Alton and raised the alarm.

The scene inside the church replayed behind his eyes over and over during the ride to Farnham. Before they surrendered it was kill or be killed, the enemy firing from the church windows, Waller's troops returning fire so that there was no escape from the church. No entry either until they surrendered.

It was the carnage that replayed, the ghastly carnage. Piles of dead horses blocked the door, and beyond them the dead and dying men lay among the exhausted living. As victors they had made the prisoners clear away the corpses and the pile of horses, and dig graves for the dead men, hacking into the frozen ground to achieve even a shallow grave, dropping their comrades into it, covering them with a sprinkling of earth. Death, mutilation, grief.

Another tune played into his consciousness. The excitement of the stealthy approach in the dark. The thrill of the surprise attack. This is what bonded men together, redolent of boyhood games. As a soldier he must hold onto the comradeship, the positive side of war, the hoped-for outcome.

Dragoons stood guard in the churchyard while the prisoners, seven hundred of them tied in pairs by the wrist with musket match, were fed through the church door and herded up to the altar end of the wide church. Their way was lit by dim lanterns which cast strange shadows among the pillars, producing scarcely more illumination than the moonlight filtering through the tall windows.

Then at last the horsemen clattered in, leading their mounts to the west end under the tower. All over the church men subsided onto the cold stone floor. A guard was set up, yet it seemed hardly necessary, no one had strength left to do anything but try to sleep.

Ralph propped his back against a pillar and dozed on and off. The night dragged on, marked by the church clock chimes. And then, before dawn, a strange calm descended. Ralph looked about him and saw Duncomb the lecturer, moving among the clumps of prisoners. Clearly this was not an attempt at preaching to this literally captive audience. He seemed to be imparting a kind of benediction.

Dawn light crept into the aisles. Here and there men were weeping, and it seemed that Duncomb was praying with them. This was no Presbyterian or Independent doctrine such as it was said they were fighting over. It was something much more real, almost supernatural.

With the coming of dawn, officers began picking their way among the men, separating those who opted to sign the Covenant and join the Parliamentary Army and marching them off in batches to the Castle. The Quartermaster organised a ration of dry biscuits and even some water for those who remained, and still Duncomb moved from group to group and still the calm was unbroken.

For the townsfolk it was another market day, with cattle's legs splaying on the ice of their pens, and sheep huddled together, and stall holders blowing on chapped fingers and stamping their feet.

`The church is full of prisoners,' Betty Gary said. `They'll never sort them out in time for the lecture!'

Nor did they. Jacob pushed in through the door to find the officers gathering the men who had refused to sign the covenant and would remain as prisoners. Across the nave the Reverend Duncomb was talking quietly with twos and threes.

Standing looking at the scene Abigail sensed the unexpected calm, an atmosphere she could not identify. Perhaps it was just that these men were exhausted and defeated, frightened too, all energy and resistance drained out of them, and yet the quiet was positive, almost tangible.

The door opened behind her to admit a relief guard party. Jacob turned to go saying `There'll be no lecture today' when among the guard being relieved he caught sight of James, dirty and worn. Jacob caught his eye. James spoke with his commander and then fell into step beside his father and they walked away down the path, talking earnestly. The rest of the household followed on behind, back to work.

Work however was not wholehearted, a sort of disjointed mood descending over everyone. The tan pits were almost frozen, no one could safely stir or move the hides hung in them. Othen was sick at home and Nathan organised some tidying up. Jacob stood talking to his son in the yard, and then they went together up to his office. The women went into the house.

And then the day began to fill with people. Coming down into the yard Jacob called to Nathan to gather all the workers into the Tanyard house. He stood with James beside him in front of the hearth as they came in and sat on the benches. Once they were settled he spoke formally.

`As you know, Othen is sick and may not be fit to work again. At all events, my son James is going to take his place as tannery overseer. Armstrong will continue as head beamsman, and the rest of you know your places.'

In the pause which followed James was constrained to elaborate. `I've just been in a great battle' he said. `Not one of those set pieces you hear about, but a fight for a town, and I can tell you the Generals had it all worked out. And we were victors.' He paused.

`Notwithstanding, I want no more of fighting. Our auxiliary regiments are about to return to London, and I'll go with them and then get a discharge. There are better ways than war of bringing about reform, and better kinds of reform. We want reform towards real equality.'

His old passion took hold and he went on, 'Whether you're servant, apprentice or master or even my Lord General, each and every one of you is a man, a he, who should be fairly rewarded for his work and be free to choose which way he should take.

`There should be justice for all. War or no war, the rich are remaining rich, Lords and gentry keep their privileges and they keep the poor poor. If there is to be justice in our land there must be a levelling, and I shall work for this wherever I am. And,' his voice lost its urgent tone as he remembered the actual reason his father had called the tanners together, `I shall be glad to work here in the Tannery where I belong.'

Eyes had widened as the assembled company listened, militia men joining in out of curiosity, all intent on James' words. One of the soldiers broke the silence.

`Is that what we're fighting for, equality?'

`'T'is honour,' another said.

`And what do we gain from it, but sore feet and torn clothes?'

`Whatever' James interrupted, `we won, we've achieved honour, and now we're done. We can go home.'

More and more infantry filtered in, the Sergeant among them. `We're escorting ze prisoners to London,' he said. `Four hundred of 'em. Ze rest have joined Sir Villiam.'

`Anyone at home?' A call came through the doorway.

`Don't be funny Matthew,' they heard Susan's voice. `Looks like a major assembly.'

Abigail greeted her with an embrace.

`Matt is carting wounded prisoners to London. Could I stay with you while he's away?'

`Certainly,' Phoebe said. `Somewhere we'll find a place for you,' and Abigail wondered at her willingness to cram yet one more into her big bed.

Nathan was muttering to Peter, shooting glances at James and looking disgruntled.

`Ve need ale, Mistress' the Sergeant said. `Parched ve are' and he scratched his chest, but the barrels were empty. Abigail and Carey filled jugs with water, and brought them back into the Hall and there, standing just inside the door, were Ralph and Hal.

Phoebe went over to them immediately. `Hal! How good to see you! How you've grown! And Mr Attfield, welcome. Come in and refresh yourselves.'

They came almost shyly, Ralph's hand on Hal's back encouraging him forward. He sought Abigail with his eyes, and when she brought tankards to them he looked down at Hal and back at her, and smiled. As soon as she had supplied everyone she returned to them.

`Were you in the battle too?' she asked Hal.

`No,' Hal said. Ralph waited for him to go on, and when he did not he said `We moved by night - you've heard have you that Sir William is known as the Night Owl? We had the new patented guns. They're leather, so light that a pack horse can carry them. They were all the cannon we had, and no baggage train. So Hal missed a long battle and a victory.'

`And many dead horses so I've heard,' Abigail said.

`Dead horses!' James standing nearby exclaimed. `D'you know what that rogue Trussler was at? Skinning horses fast as he could go. There'll be stolen hides for sale tomorrow, you mark my words.'

The way Ralph looked at Hal, Abigail felt he was longing for him to talk, to say anything, just to make contact with those who had been his family for over four years. But Hal was as silent as usual. Ralph put a protective arm round his shoulders and said quietly to her over his head `You were right. The dam has been breached . Just a trickle, but a start.'

Later Matthew, standing beside Susan as she talked with Nathan, watched him leave with Hal. `Ha!' he said, in Abigail's hearing, `you can see he's that boy's lover!'

The following day the Tanyard house finally emptied of troops, and Phoebe took command of a rush of activity. She made them bundle all the straw from the loft into sacking, carry it carefully down the stairs, and burn it in the garden. Carey swept the floor while Daniel under instruction mixed up buckets of lime wash. Then together they brushed it into walls and floor, climbed up and pushed it into every crevice and across the beams, soaked the place with it.

`We may have to do it again' Phoebe said, `and down stairs too if the lice have migrated. Thank God the men have gone!'

Abigail still had an old rag tied round her head and her ample mother's worn-out shift over her clothes, her face splashed with lime wash and her hands red and raw, when Ralph, all alone, suddenly walked in. He laughed when he saw her. `You look wonderful!'

She looked down at herself and shook her head.

`Oh yes, and I love that spot of white on the tip of your nose! Have you a moment to spare for me?'

`Let me take off this filthy old rag' she said, struggling out of the splashed garment which was dampening her own clothes underneath it. She untied the kerchief on her head and her hair tumbled down, loosened from its plait.

`I'll admit that's better,' Ralph said. `I haven't long. We move off tomorrow. Can we sit for a while?'

Once settled he started to speak slowly and thoughtfully. `That night in the church,' he said. `Have you heard about it? Extraordinary. Your lecturer. He had a captive audience, literally captive, but he didn't lecture them, just a few short words.'

'What sort of words?' Abigail asked.

'I don't remember exactly. None of the "Go in and fight", more about inner peace if you fall in with Jesus. After he finished speaking one or two men called out to him and he squatted down and spoke with them. And then others called him to them. Somehow there was a presence.'

‘I felt it too,’ Abigail said, ‘even in the morning. Father led us in, thinking there might be a lecture, and despite all those men and the activity and everything the atmosphere was different from normal, a sort of calm.'

‘It went on all night,’ Ralph said, On and off, like waves. From time to time a man would struggle to his feet and go over to the lecturer, or someone else would call him to where he sat. Even some of us, there as guards, were touched, as if by God.’

He sat silent for a while. Then he said `I hope it might somehow open the way to talk with Hal, though I scarcely know how to begin. If we're right about a kind of boil, I've done no more than poultice it.' He paused again. `I can easily spend time with him since he cares for my horses.'

Matthew's words echoed in Abigail's mind. She pressed her lips together, trying to shut them out, wanting not to believe what he had said. Ralph looked across at her.

`Abigail please write to me while I am away. I guess there is more campaigning to do while this weather lasts, and then we'll be in winter quarters I know not where, and then more fighting unless some settlement is reached. It does me good to hear about normal life.' He sounded sad.

`Are you weary of war?' she asked.

`Oh yes. Except when there is action. That carries you along, you're in it. Defeating the enemy is all that matters. You're caught up in it. All the training takes hold. Exciting.' He looked at her apologetically. `I suppose I've become battle hardened.'

He stood up to go then and she stood too. `I like seeing your hair like that,' he said, and touching it he put an arm round her shoulders. The gesture was much the same as he had made in Francis' forge, yet this time all she could think of was the similar way he had put a protective arm round Hal, and the look he had given the boy, and Matthew's retort. She longed to slide between both his arms, but if Matthew were right she could not bear to come close to him. She pulled away and with a wan little smile bade him farewell. He hesitated a moment, looking baffled, and then said a formal goodbye and left. Abigail subsided onto a stool, and cried.

A letter from him made no difference to her sad confusion.

We are at Arundel, besieging the Castle. Not much sleep, for short bursts of musket and cannon fire are ordered night and day. We slept our first night under the great trees in the park, very cold. Now we are comfortably quartered in the town. Food is plentiful, though not for the besieged. They are short of water too, for Sir Wm ordered the pond to be drained to lower the water level in their well. That gave us a feast of carp from the muddy bottom. I lodge with a harness maker and try my hand at his trade to pass the time. I shall be glad to hear from you. Ralph Attfield.

She did not reply at once, not until remembering the wistfulness of his request for letters became insistent in her mind. Writing was a sort of duty. 'Frost continues hard, work is at a standstill, ice borders the river, Othen remains sick at home' - daily trivia was all she could think to write about.

Before the frost gave way to snow blizzards and the roads became impassable a brief note came from him.

Arundel has surrendered. I am made Corporal of Horse. My troop and three others are escorting prisoners to London, a city I saw last when I joined the regiment there. It seems a long time ago. Ralph Attfield.

She launched a slightly less brief reply into the unknown, relying on the sutler to discover its proper destination. It was already January.

Meanwhile Othen took pneumonia and despite Phoebe's ministrations and his wife's care he was clearly dying. James came as soon as the snow cleared, ready to take up his position and quickly in control.

And then Joan came.

School

Abigail had finished the day's lessons, Rose and Lettice had gone to their mother's parlour to show her their work, when a servant girl came in, bobbed a curtsy and told her a lady had called to see her. Puzzled, Abigail stacked the last of the books and went into the hallway. There stood Joan, her old green hooded cloak almost smothering her, she looked so thin and weary.

`I wanted to see you just as soon as I could,' she said into Abigail's embrace. `I reached home last evening.'

`Home? Timber Hall? Are you alone?"

Joan nodded.

`But why have you come?' Abigail held her away from her, looking into her sad face.

`Harry has died - Oh Abigail, a terrible death, of typhoid that has killed many many people in Oxford. I can't tell you what he suffered, though it was quickly over. I suppose I should be grateful for that.'

They walked arm in arm to the Bicknell home.

`My poor Joan. And you suffered too.'

`That was so terrible, seeing his agony and being able to do nothing, nothing at all about it. Just be there and watch. We were so close, we loved each other so much, and this separated us. I couldn't enter into it with him. And suddenly he was dead.'

That was the first occasion of many over those winter weeks when Joan wept and Abigail wept with her, her own unhappiness somehow freeing her into empathy with her friend. She watched her listlessness as the weeks passed, visiting her frequently after Culver Hall lessons. Elizabeth tried vainly to cheer her.

`Why don't I invite that nice Colonel Jones from the garrison for a meal? He could bring one or two of his officers with him, and you could come too Abigail and make a merry party.'

`I've no particular wish to make their acquaintance,' Joan said.

`You always had so many young men eager for your attention, and you still have your pretty looks, and your little allowance from your father-in-law, a desirable widow you are Joan dear.'

`Mother!'

To Abigail Joan said `I cannot consider marriage. No one could replace my Harry.' Then a new thought struck her. `But you, Abi, what marriage prospects do you have?'

Her relief that Joan's attention was beginning to move away from herself did not impel her towards their old confidences. She shook her head. `I shall go on teaching.'

We are in winter quarters near Petersfield. Only seventeen miles yet in this weather far from Farnham. R.A. He never mentioned Hal, and Abigail did not dare to ask after him. Better to blank him out of her mind if she were to write at all.

It was mid-February when she found Joan sewing as of old, patching her brother Billie's breeches. She looked up, needle poised, a small sparkle back in her eyes.

`Abi,' she said. `I've been thinking, about you saying you would just go on teaching. Couldn't we start a little school? A dame school?' She almost giggled. `Two old dames!'

Without thinking Abigail blurted out `What, you teach!'

`No, not me. You would teach and I would support you and collect the fees and mother the children. I have sufficient money to pay rent on a room to start out. You surely wouldn't want to run a school on your own?'

`But I had no idea of running a school!'

`I'm giving you the idea! Better than sitting around waiting to marry, which as you know holds no attraction for me anyway. Who could ever replace my Harry? And do you recall that bequest my uncle made?'

`Actually...' Just now it was a better thought than marriage. `Actually the idea is not entirely new. My grandfather suggested I consider it, oh, months and months ago. And someone else (she was not going to mention Matthew whatever happened) told me I ought to be a teacher."

At first Mistress Vernon was dismayed, for Abigail wanted her school to be for the poorer children, the `six poor men's children' of the bequest, even bastards if the local guardians would allow, and not the genteel establishment suitable for Rose and Lettice. They reached a compromise in the end. She would hold school just three mornings a week, allowing the Vernons the remaining three.

Meanwhile Joan with her father's help found a room to rent in West Street, and in early March they received their first pupils, three eight-year-olds one of whom was the Martins' boy Charlie.

`My Pa got a bash on the head with a musket butt at the Battle of Alton' he announced the first day, `and now he can't see straight.'

`Don't have to see straight to dig ditches,' Dick, registered as Richard but scorning the name, said.

`Your Pa can't see straight to walk down the road,' Charlie said, and was promptly cuffed by Dick. The day had hardly begun.

Gradually Abigail cajoled them into compliance, a totally different matter from the little girls. They did not welcome mothering so Joan took to bringing in sewing, and stitching by the little window when she was not hearing them reading.

Now letters to Ralph became a sort of diary of entertaining school jottings which she happened to send on. He wrote briefly back, for in winter quarters there was little to report and he was essentially a factual kind of writer. Until the letter which came in the middle of March.

Sweet Abigail, I cannot keep silent any longer. Over the time that we were in Farnham, and receiving your letters through the winter, I have come to value you more than I can say. I have felt a constraint between us, yet there was a time when I thought perhaps you could learn to care for me. That is what I long for, that you might return the love I have for you.

I make a poor showing when I am with you. I am not a practised lover. You know I have always been a man of action, occupied with horses and latterly with war, but I feel sure that you could tame me if only you will.

I do beg you to put my mind at rest by sending a favourable reply.

I am as always, Ralph Attfield.

It was Nathan who brought her the letter, the last person she would have wanted to be party to her receiving letters from Ralph. He handed it to her and went back out to the yard, and she broke the seal and read it where she stood, and sat down rather suddenly and read it again. Her heart sang, and then that horrible memory recurred, Matthew's mocking voice.

In the midst of her churning emotions, Nathan came back into the house. He stood looking at her for a long moment, and then came and squatted down beside her. He seemed to be searching for words. At last he said `I know who that letter is from. And I need to clear up some matters with you.'

Abigail flinched, wishing she could flee.

`First of all, I should ask you to forgive me for the remarks I've made in the past about Ralph Attfield. I had no grounds for them. They were a misguided attempt to draw you away from him to me.'

Abigail looked at him in total surprise.

`To go one with, I'd like you to know that half the grounds I had for pressing my suit for you no longer exist. I had hoped to take charge of the tannery, and your brother James is now in that place. I expected an inheritance from my father, and now he has taken another wife and a new lease of life, and what inheritance there is will be shared among many more beneficiaries. I have nothing to offer you.'

`Nathan.' Abigail hesitated. `This isn't a new way of courting me is it?'

`No, I just wanted you to understand. I've begun to see that when I thought I loved you it was quite mixed up.'

`Mixed up with what?'

He swallowed hard, his Adam's apple darting up and down.

`Don't be offended Abigail. You did attract me, but part of my desire for you was as the Master Tanner's daughter. Ambition mixed into it.' He looked dejected.

`You're being very honest,' Abigail said. `What has opened your eyes to all these revelations?'

`Your friend Susan. Nothing she has said. Just the love between us. I wanted you to know that my affections are now fully engaged with her.'

`Oh, I'm glad for both of you,' Abigail said with utter sincerity. She looked down then, and saw Ralph's letter lying between her fingers in her lap. Nathan looked at it too.

`I thought perhaps,' he said, `perhaps knowing this might free you for Ralph.'

`It's not that,' Abigail began, and then to her consternation she began to cry. Even as she cried she feared that he would put his arm round her to comfort her, the last thing she wanted, but to her relief he did not. He just stayed beside her and kept quiet.

When her crying subsided and she tried to wipe her eyes he said `What is it then?'

What an unlikely person, she thought, to hear my most secret fears! Yet perhaps that very unlikeliness might make it easier, for to whom else could she tell them?

`People have implied...' she began, and then taking a deep breath `in fact Matthew said, that Hal is Ralph's lover.'

`Matthew!' Nathan almost spat out his name, swinging back on his heels. `Thomas once told me about Matthew. He sees his own inclinations in other people who have no such thoughts. I can tell you that Susan mistrusts him. Pay no attention to him.'

`But Ralph looks on Hal with such love!'

`I watched him that day, after the Alton battle.'

`He did, didn't he. Such a loving look.'

`I watched him, and I'd say he cares for that lad's welfare. Like a father. But he cares for you too. Abigail, I saw the way he looked at you. Given half a chance he'd have had you in his arms.'

Abigail digested this. Then she said `Nathan, you went about things quite the wrong way with me, but in general I think I have misjudged you.'

Nathan gave a short laugh. `Don't be hard on yourself. I've had a lot to learn.'

`I'd never have wanted to marry you, for all sorts of reasons, and I think I've set too much store on looks. You must admit that looks aren't your strong point. Sorry, but it is so.'

`I've no illusions about that,' Nathan said. `Happily Susan loves me regardless.'

`Ralph is so comely and handsome."

`He might not always be so, nor unblemished in virtue. I suspect that love can be partly an act of will, which I suppose I used to hope you would be prepared to make. Hoping the emotion would follow.'

'Susan didn't have to make an act of will. She's always fancied you.'

Nathan stood up. `Are our several loves now sorted out? Do you know how to reply to Ralph?'

Abigail stood up too, smiling. Then she did what she had thought she would never voluntarily do. She kissed Nathan on his stubbly cheek.

Ralph

Dearest, sweetest, beloved Abigail. I cannot tell you what joy your letter has brought me. The days since I wrote to you have been an agony of suspense, I so much fearing that you could not love me. I am longing to see you and to have an embrace which has been too long delayed - indeed not one but many.

We are to assemble at East Meon ready for Spring campaigning. I never before was concerned about my own survival but now I beg you to pray for my life to be preserved so that I may come to you. I love you.

May I sign myself, your own Ralph.

1 April. We won a great victory at Cheriton securing Alresford on the road to Winchester. We rode on to that City the same night. We move on constantly, and I have little opportunity to write. Tell me again that you love me. Your loving Ralph

8 April. We have covered much of Hampshire. I am wounded in the arm so that I am temporarily unfit to fight. I believe I shall see you very soon. My damaged arm will not prevent me holding you close which I long to do my sweet heart. Your loving Ralph.

When he came it was almost a repeat of February fourteen months before except for the blazing sunshine. April had suddenly abandoned showers for a brief summery spell.

Every tree had its own distinctive colour from the tightly curled brown oak leaves through hawthorn, beech and hazel greens to delicately pale birches and the washed yellow of willows. Leaves were opening out almost perceptibly, with plum trees a shower of white and primroses multiplying below them in the banks.

The vegetable garden needed attention. Phoebe set Carey to weed the ground under the hedgerow and Abigail to dig a bed ready for spinach and radishes while she herself bent to sow rows of peas. They were hot and their hands were earthy.

He hailed them as he strode across the bridge, coat-less and waving his right arm. They stood up, brushing earth from their hands, and waited while he came through the yard and round the house. There he stood, like a bashful little boy uncertain what he should be doing.

'Mister Attfield!' Phoebe exclaimed. `We hear of battles all around. Is it well with you?'

His left hand was tucked into his orange uniform scarf knotted as a narrow sling, but all he said was `Aye Mistress, I am well.'

They went on standing, as if an un-crossable void separated him from Abigail though his eyes barely left her face.

`We are all grubby,' Phoebe said, `but we can wash our hands and refresh you.'

`Pray don't trouble,' Ralph said. `I can see you are in the middle of work. But could you spare Abigail for a little while?'

`Why, certainly.'

Abigail stuck her fork into the ground and immediately followed him round into the yard. `Had I better wash my hands?'

`No, let's just go,' he said. `Your hand will feel good to me however earthy it is. Walk on my right side so I can hold it.'

His own right hand felt as good to her as it had at Hannah's wedding.

`Is the wound painful?' she asked.

`A little. A sword slash. My buff coat is being repaired so I'm grateful the weather is kind.'

`A sword slash!' Abigail shuddered.

`My sweet, that is what we inflict on each other in battle, among other injuries.'

`I'm glad it was no worse.'

They were out now in the lush grass of the water meadow. `Abigail!' He stopped and turned to face her. `Abigail! I've so longed for this moment and now....' He seemed to be drinking her in with his eyes.

He put his fingers under her chin and tilted her face up towards him. `You are even more beautiful than I remembered.'

Slowly and delicately he traced the shape of her temples. He ran a finger along each cheek bone while her whole body thrilled. He touched the tip of her nose `even without that dab of whitewash'. Then he took his hand out from its sling and drew her to him into a wholehearted two-armed embrace, and kissed her gently on the forehead.

Oh! the relief, after the years of dreaming and of fleeing, to yield completely! She turned her head to lay her cheek against his chest.

They stood quite still in this long embrace. Then Ralph took her hand again and said `Let's walk on.' Gradually they began to talk.

`Sometimes I felt that there could be affection between us, and then you'd run away from me,' he said.

`I've been so unsure. At Hannah's wedding I ran because my mother was bleeding and my father ordered me to go to her. I never had the chance to explain.'

`Since then though.`

'Mmm.' This was not the moment for explanations. She squeezed his hand and looked up at him, striding through the grass beside her. He looked down and grinned.

`Chicken plucking maiden! Were you insulted?'

`At least you remembered who I was.'

`I'd been dancing with the flirtatious Bicknell daughter, and seeing you sitting with your grandfather, like the first time I saw you, when you just went on with your plucking, not making yourself noticeable. That was the picture I had of you, with the chicken feathers and the sacks.'

`I loved you from that moment on.' Abigail spoke so quietly that he stopped walking.

`Say that again so I can hear.'

More boldly, `I loved you from that moment on.'

`Dear love, I wish I could say the same. And yet even then I suppose I felt you were different.' He paused, seeking for words. Then he said `I've taken a long time reaching the point of realising how important you are to me. Loving you has, as it were, crept up on me. Now it overwhelms me.'

They had reached the bridge below Weydown Mill and memories of when she had watched the water there and tried to understand her own emotions brought her to a halt. He interpreted it otherwise. He gathered her into his arms again, close, close, and this time he kissed her mouth.

She felt as if she would melt, or fly, as she yielded herself into him.

And even as she surrendered to him her mind thought of Hannah. I understand now, she thought, and how harshly I judged her.

He held her away from him and looked into her eyes in such a way that her insides seemed to dissolve. He kissed her again, passionately, filling her mouth, caressing her in his arms.

When at last he released her they stood, gazing at each other almost in disbelief. Then he took her hand again and started to stroll on along the meadow.

`Do your parents know about our love?'

`I've said nothing to them, though my mother has a way of guessing things. Nathan knows.'

`Nathan!' Ralph sounded shocked.

Abigail explained about him delivering that letter which she still kept in her pocket. `He'd courted me quite roughly and he wanted to apologise and clarify things, thinking to free me for you. That amazed me. I'd misjudged him. And now he and Susan are sweethearts.'

`That's a relief," Ralph said, half serious. `I'll brook no rivals.'

Later he said `I'd like us to be open and straightforward. May I ask your father's consent to my courtship?'

Abigail giggled.

`What's so funny?'

`Those formal terms. I'm glad you didn't write to me like that.'

He put his arm round her waist. `I was in far too much of a hurry to think of courtship. I was in a sweat to know, right away.'

`Maybe a bit of courtship will reveal aspects of my character that will make you want to withdraw.'

`Abigail, don't tease. Whatever I find, I'm going to keep on loving you. I'd marry you tomorrow, but sweet girl I am a soldier, and until this war is over I would rather leave you with your school than as a widow with a child.'

`You've survived this far. Please don't be killed.'

`It happens. This wound has caused me to ponder. I think I always accepted the possibility of dying, but not of being maimed. See, at present I can't control the reins with this one left hand, so my sword hand is not free to use.' He flexed his hand in its sling, exercising the fingers, testing. `Being active outdoors and on horseback is my life.'

In a gesture of compassion Abigail put her own right hand between those fingers. He closed them over hers.

`Your hand hasn't lost its grip' she said. `You'll soon have its strength back again.'

`Yes.' Ralph looked down at his hand, and then at her. `What I was saying was that this wound has made me consider the danger of death, and now having you makes me reluctant for it. And it's not just in battle. More have died of sickness than in battle.'

`Like poor Harry Vernon' Abigail said.

They walked back to the Tanyard in sober mood. `I'll go straight away and speak with your father' Ralph said, `so no one need start guessing.'

Abigail skipped into the school room next morning only just ahead of her pupils. She had left the Tanyard household preparing for a new influx of troops, the task eased by gladness over Ralph's declaration which Jacob had welcomed. Here sunshine poured in at the window and seemed to be pouring out of herself as well.

She lined the boys up for their morning recitation.

`The steadfast love of the Lord never fails,' they chanted, `His mercies never come to an end: they are new every morning. Great is thy faithfulness O Lord, Lamentations three verse twenty-three.'

`Charlie, repeat it.' Unsupported by his class-mates Charlie limped his way through. `Come, you've had ample time to learn it. Now boys, repeat it twice together, and you Charlie get it into your head. "The steadfast love..." And now your tables.'

They enjoyed chanting the multiplication tables which they already knew up to the `nine times', at any rate if they chanted them. When it came to the spot game they were not too sure. Lined up she asked the first boy a question such as `seven times eight'. He had to answer quickly and if he failed, the next in line had his chance and so one down the line, those who failed changing places with the one who knew the right answer.

She had five pupils now, each eager to reach the top of the line and stay there, on their toes to produce the answer without first going through the entire multiplication table in their head.

After that it was reading and writing until she had them standing again to recite Latin declensions and conjugations, the way the words changed with a change of sense.

`Mensa table, mensa Oh! table, mensam table as the object, mensae of a table, mensae to a table, mensa by with or from a table.

`Plural, mensae tables, mensae Oh tables....'

'Ben, the smallest newcomer, giggled at this succession of tables, but his class-mates swept on to recite `Dominus', `Master' in the same manner.

She sat them down to write the words on their slates, until again they stood, this time to decline verbs. `Amo, amas,' they chanted. `Amo I love, amas thou lovest, amat he or she loves, amamus we love, amatis you love, amant they love.'

`And before you go home, repeat today's Bible verse once more. "The steadfast love..."'

`Please Miss!' Ben raised his hand. `Why's it all love, amo and all that, and this....?'

`Because love is the most important thing in the world. Now say it all together, twice.'

Then she clapped her hands and dismissed the class. Joan saw them out of the door and turned to her. `What's happened Abi? You're all shining and you just swept the boys along.'

`I didn't know it showed. Ralph has come back and has asked Father for me, and I'm so happy I could burst.'

`You dark horse!' Joan exclaimed. `When did he declare his love? You never said anything about it!'

`Some weeks ago now, in a letter, but yesterday he was here in person.' She did a little twirl where she stood, and took Joan's hands and twirled her too.

`Well!' Joan recovered her balance. `So the school will be short lived.'

`No. He wants me to carry on with the school rather than risk (her voice dropped as she realised what she was saying) leaving me a widow with a child.'

`Or a widow without a child,' Joan said. They faced each other silently for a moment. Then Joan hugged her friend saying `My sadness mustn't spoil your joy. I'm so happy for you Abi.'

No dancing was arranged for Easter Sunday. With Sir William Waller's troops building up again, men greatly outnumbered women in the town so instead of dancing there was an increased range of sports. Several high jumps stood side by side allowing men and boys to compete simultaneously, with the long jump not far away.

Elizabeth Bicknell had worked hard gathering ale for her refreshment stall, gathering helpers too, Betty, Phoebe, Abigail, Joan and Carey as well as her own servant and the younger Gary children to fetch and carry. Billie Bicknell was engaged in more manly pursuits, showing off his archery skills to Christopher Gary at the butts.

A dense ring of spectators cheered on the wrestlers. James was lining up for a turn at the high jumps, Tom alongside him to see which of them could out-leap the other.

Hal was there too, leggier than ever and jumping higher and higher. Whilst the soldiery presented the adults with much more than the normal degree of competition, the boys had only the addition of some of the Paddy boys

Ralph no longer wore a sling but Abigail had persuaded him not to compete in case of injuring the scarred arm. He stood a little apart, watching the jumping, silently supporting Hal. Jacob, having satisfied himself that there were enough men to supervise and record the jumps, joined him and they stood for a while in silence.

`I hear you were a champion at leaping,' Ralph said, `a skill you've passed on to your sons.'

Jacob grunted.

`Hal's doing well too,' Ralph went on, `with those long legs of his.'

They moved to where they had a better view of the boys, back from the crowd, and stood again silent. Jacob seemed particularly intent on watching them. Then, still with his eyes on the jumps he began to speak, slowly and deliberately.

`There is a man in this town who persists in holding an inherited grudge against me and my family. He and his father always sat lightly to the law, and there was a time when my father had cause to expose malpractice. Both men of that generation are long dead, but the son does not let it go. People say there is a feud, but apart from one occasion when I had him arrested for disorderly conduct, I have done my best to avoid any conflict or irritation. He however has played dirty tricks on Tom....' his voice trailed away, and still he kept his eyes on the leaping boys.

After a while he went on. `This same man is spreading it about that I fathered Hal. Look at the lad now.'

Ralph looked, and out of the corner of his eye at the same moment he saw Tom do a flying leap. Hesitantly he said `He's not unlike Tom.'

`Ralph, I want you to know that it is possible that I did.' Then he said in a different tone, `Have you had many women?'

`None. I may have lacked confidence, but most of all I have wanted to keep myself for her who would be my wife.'

`I'm glad. I was the same. But you will find that once you know her carnally, to be deprived of her will be desperately hard. My attempt to assuage my appetite did little or nothing for me, but it may have begotten that lad.'

Ralph looked at Jacob, whose gaze was fixed on the jumping. He hesitated a while before he said `Why are you telling this to me?'

`You are to have my beloved daughter, my youngest child, and you already take an interest in the lad. You are joining my family. I would prefer you to know from me rather than from any rumour, that we are, I am, not above reproach.'

`But does your family know?'

`No. It was seeing that likeness today which forced it into my mind.'

`Mistress Mannory?'

`I shall speak with my wife. But I find that when I tell her something she usually knows it already.' He took a deep breath. `Acknowledged, it will no longer be fuel for slander.'

`I will keep your counsel,' Ralph said.

Jacob turned full face to him. `You are very good to the lad. I have been harsh with him.'

`Sir, I value him.'

Jacob's tone changed. `Come! Let us go and see what our womenfolk have to offer.'

They had laid out extra trestle tables to cope with the increased custom and all were busy pouring ale, the children running back and forth to the barrels replenishing jugs.

`How's my lady bar maid?' Ralph asked.

`Awash with ale,' Abigail said, `and still they come.'

Christopher Gary loped up with young Billie Bicknell, heading for the table Joan and her mother were manning.

`He hit gold more times than I like to remember,' he said, slapping Billie on the back.

`You didn't do so badly yourself,' Billie said.

`He always did like to play with bow and arrow' Elizabeth said. `I remember when he was little....'

`Mother!' Joan warned.

`I was only going to say he's had years of practice. And did you both do well against the competition?'

`I was worsted by the men' Christopher said, `but your Billie made out well against the boys. So what about some ale for us both Joan?'

She came round the table to them and poured into their beakers. Abigail watched her watching them drink, guessing at the changes she would be noticing in Christopher since she left for Oxford eighteen months ago. Christopher's little beard still made Abigail smile, but he had lost much of the old floppy puppy look. He stayed to chat with Joan.

`Come,' Ralph slipped his hand under Abigail's elbow. `I'm sure they can spare you now. I've not seen you all afternoon.'

`Oh yes off you go!' Elizabeth cried. `Make the most of him while he's here.'

Rain had held off all day but now a steady drizzle began. `Where can we go,' Ralph said `and be alone?'

Abigail thought. `We could go to my school room.'

It was not very inviting. They sat down on a hard bench, the low cloud outside preventing much light from coming through the window. Abigail shivered and Ralph put his arm round her and pulled her close.

She nestled up to him, burying her nose in the folds of his sleeve and he took off his buff coat and draped it over them both. `Now I can feel you better with only a shirt between us.'

Feeling was all she wanted to do for the time being. This was not the thrill of an embrace, but a comforting closeness, a new bonding. He bent a little and kissed the top of her head. Then he eased off her cap and loosened her hair, running his fingers through it so that it fell about her shoulders, stroking it. `I love your hair.'

`I like you playing with it.' She lifted her face to him and he kissed her.

Then he looked round the room. `So this is your school. Shall you go on with it after we are married?'

`Will we live here? I thought you came from Andover.'

`I can live anywhere. I've a little land there but nothing to call me back. Whereas here, there is you.'

`I can go anywhere. Anywhere you like.'

For answer he kissed her again, and suddenly there was a new passion, his mouth was in hers and his hands moving all over her body. At the end he sighed and relaxed with his arms still round her, leaving her strangely unsatisfied. She remembered Hannah again; `It stirs me up something terrible.' And yet she longed for more.

They continued to meet, not always alone, most days in the following three weeks. They talked and talked, learning each other's history, gauging each other's reactions and assumptions.

`A long time ago,' Abigail said once, `when this war had just begun, you said I knew nothing of you. In some ways that's still true.' She wondered how she could ever broach the subject of Hal, to have it aired and tidied away for ever.

`I pray you'll have a lifetime to find out, and that somehow you can keep on loving me.'

Always he kissed her and held her. But when he became passionate she began to be wary, drawing back to protect herself from disappointment.

They were in the school room again one afternoon in May and he had her almost lying along a bench. Suddenly she swung herself round and sat up. He reeled as if she had hit him.

`What is it? Did I hurt you? I'm sorry, the bench is so hard.'

`It is but it's not that. Oh Ralph, I love you so much, but when you become passionate like that you leave me all churned up and for nothing.'

`My poor sweet....'

`I'm afraid....'

Ralph pushed his hair back from his face and drew her gently beside him. `Forgive me. I reach completion but you cannot. Not yet.'

`I wish....'

`Beloved, I'd lie with you now were it not for this war. I'll try to be more restrained. It's just that you stir everything in me.'

She felt ashamed then. `That is hard for you.'

`No more than for you. Maybe this is a part of loving that we need to learn. Restraint for the other's sake.'

`I could become a camp follower.'

`No my darling. Guard yourself for me for when I am free to be wholly yours.'

Guarding and waiting. In a way it began then. In the middle of May it began in earnest.

Sir William Waller having been travelling round raising new troops and presenting his needs to Parliament, arrived in Farnham and mustered his Army in the Park. Ralph's arm was healed, he was able to ride as he always had, and suddenly his attention seemed to be entirely on his duties, his troop and the next move.

Do I no longer matter? Abigail cried to herself. He came briefly two days after the muster, just before in unseasonably cold weather, the Army set out northwards. He dismounted in the yard, hitching his horse by the gate, and hugged her quickly with the smallest of kisses.

`Remember I love you,' and he was gone.

There were letters at irregular intervals. Once in her own letter she hinted at her sense of being supplanted by the Army.

My beloved, I did not mean to hurt you,' he wrote in reply. *'I suppose my holding back was a sort of defence. I had to go, and I needed to ease myself away. Not rejecting you, how could I when I love you so dearly. But I had to armour myself and my own spirit for what lay ahead. Forgive me if I have hurt you but I can do no other.*

I had a task to do, responsibility for our men, a duty to my superiors, to which I needed to give my full attention.

I love you no less passionately. Riding over long distances as we do, your face is often before my eyes, and your letters I treasure.

Hal is well as far as I know. I've had no further occasion to talk with him as we had hoped. Guard yourself my dearest heart.

I am your devoted husband-to-be, Ralph.

But from the end of June there were no more letters.

Abigail was about to close the school for the summer. She had dismissed the boys and went round the room gathering slates and scraps of chalk, tidying up. Joan in her seat by the window shook out the jerkin she had been sewing.

`How's that from a scrap of fabric?'

`Very elegant. Who is it for?'

`For Billie. He grows so fast these days. Garys let me have the end from a bolt of cloth, and it cut out perfectly.' She folded it into her sewing bag. `Any news from Ralph?'

`Not for a while,' Abigail said. `The mail is uncertain.' She swept the floor, quelling the anxiety she was beginning to feel.

One day Peter brought home the latest news sheet. `The Royalists have been defeated at a place called Marston Moor,' he reported. `But wait a minute. Here it talks of a Parliamentary defeat. At Cropredy wherever that may be. Oh, it's different armies. Waller's Army had the defeat. Not so much of the "William the Conqueror" by the sound of it.'

Abigail did not want to read about it. Ralph would write soon with all she needed to know.

He did not.

July was wet and the early harvest poor. August began very hot and every hand was at work gathering the later grain. And still there was no word from Ralph.

Abigail was so afraid that she dared not speak about her fear. She kept it tight within herself. If her family noticed the change in her they did not see fit to say anything.

Joan sought her out one of those hot days and they strolled along between the river and the foot of Vernons' gardens.

`Haven't they made the gardens lovely,' she said. `My father-in-law can scarcely see them now his eyesight is so poor, but they give great pleasure to his family.'

`I enjoy them through the window,' Abigail said, `and the girls are always eager to be there among the flowers.'

They sat down in the shade of a tree.

`Thinking of the Vernons,' Joan said, `give me your opinion. Would I be disloyal to Harry if I were to marry again?'

`I thought you said no one could replace him.'

`Oh it wouldn't be the same. Harry and I adored each other as you know. I don't suppose I'd ever love anyone else in quite that way. But I could do with a husband. And I dare say love would grow in time.'

`Have you someone in mind?'

Joan smiled. `I could have Christopher Gary if I put myself to it.'

`You never used to like him.'

`I didn't dislike him. He just didn't appeal to me, and then his mother was so determined that we were destined for each other. But he's a good match, and he's improved over the last few years. What do you think?'

Abigail pulled a piece of grass and sucked its juices, gazing across the meadow towards the Mill where Ralph and she had first embraced. `I can't imagine marrying someone on that basis.'

`You are where I was two years ago, starry-eyed with love.'

`Joan.' Abigail pulled more grass, a handful of it. `I don't know what has happened to him. He was in a battle, a defeat.'

In mid-August Waller's much diminished Army straggled into Farnham. Abigail allowed herself a small flutter of hope, but he was not among them. Nor, it seemed, was Hal.

`Do they not inform people of casualties?' Joan asked.

`I don't know. But I have no claim to be informed. I am not his wife. We are not Hal's family.'

This was even worse than her unknowing after the Battle of Lansdown, worse because now she and Ralph belonged together, worse because of her expectation that soon, soon, they would be one. She had never felt so empty, so deserted.

Whatever he has done, whatever he has been, she told herself, I want him more than anything, anyone, I've ever wanted in my life. Yet as each day passed her yearning appeared less likely to be fulfilled.

She thought about the deaths she had witnessed; Hal's mother, and little Eliza lying like an abandoned rag doll; and most telling, way back at Spreakley, seeing her dead Uncle, his body just an empty shell, the person gone.

Oh God! is that dear body I've held so close now no more than an empty shell?

Cropredy

Ralph opened his eyes in a quiet calm. He was lying on his back. The ceiling low above his head was of boards, running away from him across a dim room. Whitewash reflected light from a tiny window, old whitewash that peeled in places and allowed the wood-grain to show through.

His eyes followed the line of a board, slowly tracing the grain through the whitewash, pausing at a knotty place. They travelled on towards the far wall around the window, across in the shadows and back up the next board. It seemed important, in a listless way, to be thorough, to weave his way back and forth, to travel every plank. The boards became dim in the room's corner. He raised his head to peer after them and suddenly gasped with a pain that sliced through his left cheek and neck. He lay back, his eyes swimming.

As the pain subsided he tried to touch his cheek with his hand, but it was not skin nor beard that he touched. The side of his head had become bulbous and rough. Linen rough. Linen texture. His fingers felt further up his head, down to his chin. Rags all around his face.

Bandages!

Somewhere he could remember being angry and terrified in one, falling and being trapped, blows, and numbed nerves releasing blinding pain in face and leg, and passing out. Now he tried to move his legs under the heavy cover, and gave up exhausted.

Twilight began to seep into the room. The room became indistinct, the window a square of gauzy light until it too turned almost black. Over to his right the remains of a fire was a glowing cluster of orange caves among the embered faggots. It shed no light beyond itself, but his eyes rested on it as a centre of comfort. He rested.

A yellow slit appeared in the wall opposite the fire. It expanded to become the flame of a rush light in an iron stand held by a sturdy hand. It flickered on the heavy lined and double-chinned face of a woman, who crossed the room and threw a faggot on the fire. Then she turned towards the bed. Her turning seemed to him like a ritual that he had witnessed repeatedly, yet the memory eluded him, a half-remembered dream.

The hand holding the light was on a level with his eyes. A wide hand with earth-darkened cracks around strong nails chipped by outdoor work. The rush flame lit up her sagging chin from below, highlighting scattered bristles. Then she raised the light to illuminate her face, a face that suddenly came alive, and a smile creased her mouth showing startlingly few teeth.

`Praise God!' she whispered, `The fever's past!' She laid her free hand on his forehead, another movement that had the familiarity of ritual, except that unexpectedly her hand did not feel cool.

`Yes,' she said, smiling into his eyes, `Your brow is as it should be.'

She had a broad, gentle accent, reassuring. `Lie still now. I'll stir the fire, and warm some gruel.'

She adjusted the embers around the faggot she had added, and left the room. Suddenly the bundle caught alight with a dancing flame. As the flame danced, shadows jerked on the ceiling, irregular, unsettling. A blur was there and not there. His eyes were troubled by it. The flickering blur took him back into the disturbingly real yet unreal nightmare world that had inhabited his head, on and on as if it had no beginning and no end, and he cried out.

The woman was back at once. She carried a small iron pan which she balanced in the fire embers. Then she sat down on a stool beside the bed.

`There's nowt to fear, dearie,' she said. `You were wounded in the battle, a right terrible state you were in, and the ague has been on you these many days. But that's past, praise God!'

`My face....' he muttered, and the movement renewed the pain.

`It's damaged, but it's healing. Same with your leg. We've a long road ahead before you're whole again.'

She went back to the hearth and fetched the pot, holding it in a bunched cloth. `Try and take some gruel,' she said, settling herself on the stool again and bringing a spoon out of some pocket in her clothing. `Just ope your mouth a little.'

The gruel, trickling past his dry lips into a mouth that tasted musty, was warm and delicious. He eagerly savoured each spoonful she offered him, moving it around with his tongue before he swallowed it.

Then he had had enough. He closed his lips and tried to shake his head but the pain was there.

`You've done well,' the woman said, setting the spoon in the pot.

A sudden fear struck him. `Where's Hal?'

`Hal, bless 'im, he's champion. Off with the carter today, to earn himself half a groat. I reckon he'll be home betimes. You've a right lad there.' She smiled again and stood up.. `Now rest. You've a might of strength to recover.'

She threw another faggot on the fire and went out of the room.

The fire flickered but now the flicker did not trouble him. He lay watching the light come and go on the boards over his head, aware now that if he kept still the continuing level of pain did not spurt into agony.

So Hal was here too. But where was `here' and who was this dame caring for him, so concerned for him. And where was his horse, his faithful friend who had carried him - he remembered now - all over the Midlands in unrelenting rain...and this last place...something bridge... Cropredy? She would tell him by and bye. For now he was too tired to trouble. He slept again.

When he woke later the fire was burnt through, invisible. Moonlight shafted through the little window catching two humped shapes on the floor, one large, the other a thin twist of blanket. He stared at their outline for a long while, scarcely curious, and then it came to him; the woman and Hal! This meant, he slowly realised, that he must be sleeping in her bed

For days and nights he drifted in and out of sleep punctuated by bird-like quantities of food and painful changing of the dressings on his face. Hal helped the old dame alter his posture on the bed or prop him up in a half sitting position. He was distressingly weak and his words were slurred as he thanked them. Often Hal sat on a stool nearby watching him.

`What's her name?' Ralph managed to ask.

`Mother Metcalf. She saved your life.'

The woman heard him from the doorway and turned back into the room.

`Nay, Hal saved your life.'

Later, when he was less easily tired, they told him the story. A musket ball passing between the protective iron hoops of his helmet had gouged along his left cheek bone, tearing away some of his ear before it ricocheted off the iron ear flap and dropped. He could remember the impact. He could remember that he felt no pain and simply went on fighting.

And then a cannon ball at close range killed his horse which toppled over onto its side taking him with it. He lay trapped under the weight of the horse, unable to move. He had felt blows as the battle moved forward and back around him. Blood ran into his mouth and the pain began. His right leg was broken.

`Hal found you,' the old woman said. `He searched and searched, and had them bring you to the village.'

`And villagers told me of Mother Metcalf and the bone-setter.'

`No Army surgeon?' Ralph asked.

'No real victory' Hal said. `The King's Army just moved off after a day. We lost more men than he did and most of our cannon.'

Ralph knew now that his leg was bandaged and strapped to several wooden splints which felt heavily immobilising. He could not imagine the state of his face. `Only a wound' he said. `Why am I so weak?'

`You bled. And then the ague, the fever.'

`Mother Metcalf knows all about herbs' Hal said. `Many a time we feared you would die, but her herbs and her nursing saved you.'

'Are you being paid for all this?'

'Not yet' she said, `but the officer came and checked who you were, so in the end they'll pay something.'

One afternoon she came and perched at the bedside.

'A small conventicle do meet here from time to time,' she said. `We're not in the danger we used to be as dissenters, but still they prefer to meet indoors. So folk will be coming in here. You've no need to take notice of 'em. You just keep resting.'

They came in twos and threes, labouring men and women, tradesmen and craftsmen, and sat themselves on the floor leaning their backs against the walls. A middle aged man took a stool near the bed.

`You bin wounded in the battle I hear,' he said. `Praise the Lord the armies have moved away.'

`Armies keep moving,' Ralph murmured.

`And the Army of the Lord is moving too. Each time we meet, more folk come.' He looked round the room. `Now that carpenter over there' (he dropped his voice) `he's walked a tidy way. Seen him before Bedford way I have.'

Ralph pushed against the splints in an attempt to sit up, and the man helped him. His head pained him less now and he chafed at his continued weakness.

`Him over yonder,' the man went on as if there had been no interruption, `he's been faithful all through the troubles and the persecutions, back before I ever come.' He turned a searching look on Ralph. `Do you know the Lord?' but before Ralph could consider a reply a man of a different class came into the room. `Ah! here be our scholar, nipped out from Oxford. Hard being a dissenter in Oxford.' He raised his hand in a determined greeting and the scholar came over and shook it.

`Silas, you managed to come.'

`Yes Sir, I'd not willingly miss a conventicle. And here's this poor brother wounded in the battle.'

The scholar shook Ralph's hand before taking the stool that had evidently been kept for him. Mother Metcalf came in then (`She has a prodigious memory' Silas said) and they all fell silent.

She looked round the now crowded room. `What is it to be today?'

A murmured discussion ensued until the scholar said `We've not heard a gospel lately.'

She started straight away, and without pause recited the whole of the gospel according to St Mark. Ralph found himself caught up in the narrative, the story moving urgently from episode to episode. She recited well, even dramatically, and after the concluding words there was a long silence.

Then he became aware that many were praying under their breath, lips moving but nothing audible, until one spoke out in a torrent of praise. Others followed, bit by bit, and then they all spoke together in words he could not make out, speaking that turned into a sustained singing until it died away in chorus. There was another long silence.

At last Mother Metcalf broke it. `I don't yet have it by heart, but I'd like to read a little to you from the Song of Solomon.' She propped a heavy Bible on the foot of the bed.

So where has this love of yours gone, fair one? Where on earth can he be? Can we help you look for him?.. Dear friend and lover, you're as beautiful as Tirzah, city of delights, lovely as Jerusalem, city of dreams, the ravishing visions of my ecstasy. Your beauty is too much for me - I'm in over my head.

Your hair flows and shimmers like a flock of goats in the distance streaming down a hillside in the sunshine. Your smile is generous and full - expressive and strong and clean. There's no one like her on earth, never has been, never will be. She's a woman beyond compare. My dove is perfection....

Tears were running down Ralph's face which he could not stop. He felt Silas put a hand on his shoulder but all he could do was weep.

Gradually he realised through his distress that the whole room was centring on him. He felt embarrassed yet strangely upheld by the way they remained in their places, all praying in that quiet internal way. After a while he turned to Silas and said `I need to write a letter.'

It was the scholar who gave him paper torn from his notebook and a pencil, saying `Perhaps I can send it on its way for you.' He tried to write, but his hand was still too feeble to hold the pencil and his emotions so fraught that he could not think what to write.

`Later, later,' he said.

Several days passed and still he had not written. He tried exercising his hands to improve their grasp and control, hesitating to write in what appeared as an old man's wavering scrawl. If his letters looked unlike anything he had written before, he dreaded to imagine what Abigail might think, whether her love would sustain the change in him.

He did not realise that Hal had been observing him until the lad said `I could write a letter for you.'

`Can you write?'

`Abigail taught me. Tell me what to write and how to spell the words, and I'll do it for you.'

`The letter should be from you. Just write what has happened.'

`To Abigail?'

Ralph smiled though the movement hurt his cheek. `You know it's to Abigail.'

Laboriously, with much licking of the pencil and questions of spelling, he wrote the barest of facts.

`Tell her where we are,' Ralph said.

`Where are we?' They had to ask Mother Metcalf.

`Cropredy, five miles north of Banbury in the County of Oxfordshire.'

She took charge of its dispatch.

The bandages were hot around his head and in the August heat he longed to shave off this unfamiliar beard. His hand no longer shook holding a spoon to eat the simple meals Mother Metcalf provided. He moved about a little with the crutch she had contrived for him, his broken leg still unfit to bear weight.

Weary of being caged indoors, he managed one afternoon to hobble across the floor and through the open doorway. It led into a lean-to store place and, out in the sunshine beyond, the old woman was sitting on a bench with Hal cross-legged on the ground beside her, both intent on some work they held in their hands. On seeing him Hal leapt up and helped him onto the bench.

`Stupid to be so feeble' he said. The others smiled at him, registering his progress.

`What are you making?' he asked, once he had recovered from his exertions.

`Harness,' Mother Metcalf said. `Hal be learning the craft. 'T'were my husband's trade, and I carry it on.'

`I tried my hand at harness making down at Arundel,' Ralph said. He looked down at his hands, white and thin, and remembered Abigail testing his grip that other time and assuring him he would recover it. The hope, and she, seemed equally remote.

Mother Metcalf noticed. `The needles are chiselled to cut through the leather, and sometimes I make holes to guide the stitches."

`No horse and a broken leg. Perhaps I'd better learn.'

Hal looked up smiling. `Still to do with horses.'

After that they worked daily, sitting outside. The bandages came off allowing the sunshine to do its healing work. Ralph felt his cheek, a raw hollow which had dislodged teeth, with no beard growing on the scar tissue and a ragged ear behind. His mouth felt pulled towards the left side. Mother Metcalf shaved off his beard for him.

`Hal tells me he and his mam used to sit like this outside their cott.'

`She span,' Hal said, `all the time.'

`Do you remember much about her?' Ralph said.

`Just when she died, and they took me away.'

`No chance to say goodbye?' the old woman said. Hal nodded. `We've talked about it,' she said to Ralph, `because no one had before. And the dead baby and Hal not understanding.'

Ralph squinted into the light to thread a needle. `You gained Abigail,' he said and when Hal looked puzzled he added `She loves you like a sister. Did you not know?'

Stabbing his needle into his work Hal muttered, `I thought she loved you.'

Mother Metcalf laughed. `You can love more than one person at the same time. Different sorts of love too. No letter for you yet then?'

There never was a letter.

`Tom!' Abigail's voice came out of the dusk as Tom led his horses into the meadow for the night.

`What on earth are you doing out here?'

`Walking.'

`Odd time of day to be walking.'

`Tom, I've had a letter, a note, from Hal.'

`He's alive then! Always thought he'd survive. What about Ralph?'

Dumbly she handed the battered scrap of paper to him. He was just able in the fading light to make out the pencilled words.

Cpl of Horse Attfield got a musket ball in his face and his leg is broke. We lie at Cropredy 5 mile from Banbury. Your servant Hal.

`In his face Tom.'

When James had casually handed her the letter, collected from the Bush Inn, she had fled to the meadow to unseal it alone. And then she had walked and walked, anguishing over the image of Ralph wounded and disfigured, lame and seemingly unable to write.

She visualised each part of him; the firm jaw and full mouth and smiling eyes. Suppose he were unrecognisable. And those strong padded hands that had explored her body and she loved to hold. And those shapely legs in their long boots, striding to meet her, swinging him up onto a horse.

Face, hands, legs. Are these all that I loved?

Surely he could have written, however feebly. Perhaps in these long months of absence his love for her had failed. Perhaps after all Hal mattered to him most.

`What are you going to do?' Tom took her arm to go back through the buildings.

She shook her head, clutching the note. `I don't know.'

Somehow she managed the morning's school. Somehow the boys picked up her subdued mood and behaved quietly, Joan taking more than her usual share with reading and writing. As they closed she said `You've heard, haven't you.'

`He's been wounded, maimed.'

`Where?'

`In the face. And leg.'

`But where is he?'

`Near some place called Banbury.'

`I've been there! It's not far from Oxford, King's country.'

`Oh.' Didn't that make it worse?

`Surely you'll go to him.'

Abigail did not reply at once. Then she said `D'you know, I hadn't thought of that. He always came to me. And however would I get there.'

`I could care for school while you're away.'

Abigail smiled. `I really believe you could now.'

`I'd get Christopher to come in sometimes to keep up the Latin.'

Abigail and Carey were sharing a bedroom again, now that billeting was at an end. That evening the girl could scarcely wait for them both to be in that private place to tell her news.

`Did you know,' she burst out, `that Nathan and Susan are to be married?'

`I knew that was their intention.'

`Well.' Carey gave a great pause for emphasise. `Well. My great-aunt is so pleased with me and with the knitting business, and she's taken such a liking to Susan, that we're all to live with her, Nathan and Susan and I'm to be their maidservant.'

`Well!' Abigail could not but repeat.

`And Mary and Francis are moving back to Godalming, so the Mistress will be having to start with all new servants, poor woman.'

`Maybe I can help her' Abigail said absently, and then unaccountably she gave Carey a hug.

Mistress Vernon surprised her. It had not occurred to her that people such as she would be concerned for her and Ralph.

`My dear, you must go to him. Surely Sam could guide you, he knows the way to Oxford, and we could spare him for a few days. Only, we could not spare a horse for you.'

`I could!' Tom said when he heard. `You must take Star. He's stout enough to carry you both back here if need be.'

`And,' Mary said, `after we've moved you could rent our rooms while Mister Attfield regains his strength.'

They were all organising her, propelling her in a direction she did not know whether she wanted to go. Their assumptions were impossible to resist, and she found herself willy nilly setting off with Sam on that route they had travelled before in such different circumstances.

Mistress Vernon's generosity extended only to three days absence for Sam, so that having in Oxford enquired directions to Cropredy and put Abigail on the road, he returned home. Star, despite being used to a cart, was a not un-pleasant mount and her confidence had grown as her aching muscles had eased.

In Banbury she checked the way from an elderly roadman. He waved his stone cutter's axe in the direction she was already going.

`Carry on Missee, and at the crossways turn right through Great Bourton. Cropredy's in the valley.'

She was tired now, and more anxious with every yard Star took her. From Great Bourton she could see Cropredy down below, with a church on a slight rise surrounded by houses of golden stone and humbler ones of wood. She was relieved to find a shop there. She hitched Star to one of the rings set into the wall and walked stiffly inside.

`Could you direct me please?' she said. `I'm looking for a soldier who was wounded and I think he lodges somewhere here.'

`Wounded in the face and leg?' the comfortable woman replied. Abigail nodded. `Only one left now. Mother Metcalf's. You his sweetheart? He'll be right glad to see you.'

`And where is Mother Metcalf's?'

`I don't rightly know if she'll be home today, she does go about and some of her fields are t'other side of river, so with harvest and ploughing...'

`Where does she live?'

`Up beyond t' church.' And she called to her husband to tell Abigail which way and how many cottages to pass before she reached Metcalf's.

Too weary to re-mount, she led Star up the street.

She saw Ralph while still some way off. He was sitting alone on a bench outside the cottage, his head bent over something in his hands, his right leg stretched out awkwardly in front of him. She stood still then, holding Star's rein, just looking at him.

She stood for what seemed a long time, taking in all she could of this man, watching his concentrated efforts. His brown hair was falling forward around his face. He's still Ralph, she thought, and walked closer.

The sound of hooves roused him. He looked up and for a moment they both froze. Then seizing his crutch he staggered to her, almost stumbling in his haste, almost falling into the arms she found she was holding out for him.

`Abigail!'

He kissed her and his mouth felt strange. Then he stood back, leaning on the crutch, and drank her in with his eyes.

`I never dreamt you'd come.' Whatever else had changed, his deep crackling voice was the same.

`Hal's note reached me last week.'

`He wrote it weeks ago.'

She pulled it out of her pocket, a crumpled scrap. `A miracle it arrived at all.'

Star, the rein dropped, moved to graze by the roadside and caught Ralph's eye. `Where's Tom?'

`At home. I rode here.'

This merited another embrace, but he was toppling and led her back to the bench. She sat on his right side so that the damaged side of his face was partly hidden. Not yet, she told herself.

`We must see to the horse' he said.

Abigail laughed. `Oh Ralph, you're still the same!'

`What, caring for horses?'

She nodded. `Hal's note, and all that long time hearing nothing, I was afraid you'd have changed and maybe didn't love me any more.'

`I feared too when you didn't write.'

`Ralph...' The moment seemed right but the words were hard to find. `One thing has troubled me. About Hal.'

`He's gone to town with some harnesses that were ordered. He'll be back before dark.'

`It's not that. I'll be glad to see him of course. It's just...' she swallowed. `It's just that Matthew said you were his lover, and although I didn't really believe it, it has haunted me.'

`My darling Abigail!' Ralph put his arm round her and pulled her close. `My poor dear heart. That never entered my head. I won't deny I love the lad. I respect him too. Like a son. Never any other way.'

She turned her face to him and he kissed her.

`On the subject of Hal,' he said then, `there's something I think you should know if you don't already. Your father told me that he may have begotten Hal.'

Abigail gaped at him. `My father? And a whore?'

`I think I understand the circumstances, just one visit of which he's ashamed and chose to confess to me. It seems someone is already spreading that rumour.'

`Abe Trussler.' Abigail said, remembering his words years back at Judith's cottage.

`Strange. He wanted me to know that he's not above reproach.'

She took a while to digest this. Little incidents from the past fell into place, and somehow a new respect for her father emerged. Taking Hal into his household had been costly for him.

Then a new thought struck her. `Do you think, Ralph, that we could adopt Hal as our son?' Even as she said it she realised she already knew, knew once more, that she and Ralph would be one.

Ralph squeezed her hand, staring at his splinted leg. He did not answer her directly.

`Hal wrote to you because I was too weak. Not just the wounds, I was fevered with the ague, and losing blood. I'm still enfeebled.' He looked at her. 'I don't know when I shall be able to give you a child.'

She thought of his former passion. Maybe this would be a slower, gentler way of becoming accustomed to each other.

`I can wait, and I love you just the same. I just suddenly thought, Hal is so much a part of both our lives.'

They unsaddled Star and tethered him in a field behind the cottage. They took ham and pies out of the pannier Phoebe had packed and laid them out on the table in the lean-to. Taking his weight on the crutch quickly tired Ralph and they were back sitting on the bench in the evening light when Mother Metcalf returned.

`So this is Abigail,' she said without being told. `Excuse an old woman begrimed from the fields,' but Abigail jumped up and shook her earthy hand. `You've taken your time coming,' she went on, looking her up and down. Then she smiled her toothless smile. `He needs you to share that big bed he's in.'

She exclaimed with delight at the provisions Abigail had brought and showed her where to find plates and beakers. They heard Ralph greet Hal's return and the murmur of their talk together. Hal's eyes were bright when they came in to eat.

`You'll stay, won't you, till Ralph mends,' Mother Metcalf said to Abigail.

`I would, but Tom will be needing his horse.'

Hal said at once `I'll ride him back.'

`And,' Ralph told Abigail when they were alone, `he'll best hear from Tanner Mannory himself about his fathering. I'll send a letter with him.'

She lay shyly in the bed by his side, away from the cumbersome splints, but next to his damaged face. `Come,' Mother Metcalf had said to Hal. `We'll sleep in the store and leave them be.' Ralph lay on his back, holding her hand.

Cautiously she ran her fingers along his arm where the sword slash had healed into a narrow ridge.

`Hal and I,' he said `have been learning harness making from Mother Metcalf. I believe we could live by the trade in time. I have some money stashed with Bicknell to keep us till then.'

`Not horse dealing?'

`That took me away all over the country, and I want to be with you.'

`And I with you.' She enclosed his hand between both of hers.

`We could live here,' he said `and work with Mother Metcalf. I'd like to understand more of the dissenters who meet here.'

`I'd be sad to abandon my little school.'

`There'll be time to decide by and bye.'

Now was the time to decide another matter. Reluctantly she reached out to touch his face. Her fingers explored the torn ear, and then crept along the scarred hollow in his cheek to the tautened muscle by his mouth. Exploration turned into caress. There was nothing to fear. She laid her own cheek on his, and he held her to him.

Keep therefore a true woman's eye
And love me still but know not why.
So hast thou the same reason still
To dote upon me ever.

Author's Note

The framework of this story is as far as possible the story of the Civil War in Farnham and elsewhere during the early 1640s. All the public personalities are verifiable in the historical records.

Of the townsfolk, Robert Bicknell living in Timber Hall grew hops and Michael Gary was a wool draper, and each held office as Bailiff. The wife of each was called Elizabeth. Duncomb was the lecturer who became Rector, Clapham the disgraced Rector and Shepheard his curate. Dr Harding of Spreakley was one of the "School" who translated the Prophets in the Old Testament. The Vernons lived in Culver House, and Henry Vernon's memorial in St Andrew's church tells of his blindness and his kindliness.

A Mannory was a tanner though little is known of his family. There were many tanners living in Red Lion Lane where the Tanyard can still be seen, now separated from the river Wey by the mass of the Maltings. The church tower in that era was square topped, the pinnacles added only later.

Joan Bicknell did in fact marry Christopher Gary, and her brother Billie later became a preacher. Subsequent Attfields were saddlers and harness makers based in West Street.

Imagination has provided how these people related both to one another and to those who are fiction. It is to be hoped that they all blend together seamlessly, and that none of their descendents is offended.